SAVAGE SUNSET

NOX SPACEY

THE WHUMPY PRINTING PRESS

Cover Illustration by Robin

Cover Typography by Nicole Alessi

First edition 2024

— • —

Dedication

To Kane and Jim

CONTENTS

— • —

Content Warnings

This story contains dark content, including torture and sexual assault.

Below is a list of content warnings by chapter.

Prologue: Kidnapping

1. Knife violence, blood, broken bones, nonconsensual bondage/restraint, gag/muzzle

2. Nonconsensual bondage/restraint/being trapped, gag/muzzle, heavy emotional distress, mentions of mass human rights violations

3. Nonconsensual bondage/restraint/being trapped, gag/muzzle

4. Nonconsensual bondage/restraint/being trapped, gag/muzzle, broken bones/broken nose

5. Nonconsensual bondage/restraint/being trapped, gag/muzzle, "it" as a dehumanizing pronoun, transphobia, violence against a transmasculine character, forced nudity/stripping, sexual assault

6. Nonconsensual bondage/restraint/being trapped, gag/muzzle, heavy emotional distress, references to torture, burns, violence against a transmasculine character

7. Knife violence, misgendering, drowning

8. Nonconsensual bondage/restraint/being trapped, gag/muzzle, aftermath of torture, cuts, burns, nonsexual nudity, heavy emotional distress, suicidal ideation/euthanasia discussion

9. References to torture

10. Nonconsensual bondage/restraint/being trapped, gag/muzzle, aftermath of torture, starvation, nonsexual nudity, heavy emotional distress, mind control, violence against a female character

11. Nonconsensual bondage/restraint/being trapped, gag/muzzle, aftermath of torture, starvation, nonsexual nudity, heavy emotional distress, mind control, violence against a female character, lots of blood, unsanitary/vomit, brief eye injury

12. Aftermath of blood loss

13. Aftermath of torture, starvation, heavy emotional distress

14. Nonconsensual bondage/restraint/being trapped, gag/muzzle, aftermath of torture, starvation, heavy emotional distress, mentions of off-screen rape, cuts/broken glass, burns

15. Nonconsensual bondage/restraint/being trapped, gag/muzzle, aftermath of torture, starvation, heavy emotional distress

16. Nonconsensual bondage/restraint/being trapped, gag/muzzle, aftermath of torture, starvation, heavy emotional distress

17. Aftermath of torture, starvation, heavy emotional distress

18. Aftermath of torture, broken bones, heavy emotional distress, nonconsensual bondage/restraint/being trapped, gag/muzzle, suicidal ideation,

homophobic slurs (reclaimed usage), teeth pulling (off-screen)

19. Aftermath of torture, starvation, heavy emotional distress, mind control, violence against a female character

20. None

21. Discussion of disordered eating/self-harm/cutting/homophobic parents

22. Weight discussion, mentions of rape and torture (off-screen)

23. Heavy emotional distress

24. Nonconsensual bondage/restraint/being trapped, gag/muzzle, character death

25. Blood, corpse, knife violence, casual misogyny, prejudiced vampire

26. References to character death

27. Guilt, references to abusive spouse

28. Tension

29. Mind control, misgendering

30. None

PROLOGUE

"He didn't invite me to the dance. Can you believe it? Our last high school dance, and he didn't even invite me. The last prom of my *life*. And he didn't even *invite me*." Lex groaned.

Ari looked from Lex down to the ground, putting her hands in her pockets. Ari was privately wrestling with some very complicated emotions, because she didn't have a prom date at all and was considering not going. "He didn't ask you because you're dating Dustin. Dustin would've busted his nose if he caught him asking you to senior prom."

Lex stepped down from the crumbling cement curb she'd been balancing on, letting out a sigh that shot a cloud of vapor into the cold night air. "Yeah, but I don't want to date *Dustin*. I want to date *Nathan*."

Ari didn't say anything, pushing her hands deeper into her pockets to keep them warm.

Lex stopped walking. "What? You're pouting."

"I'm not pouting."

"You have something to say?"

"Break up with him if you don't want to date him."

"It's not that simple."

"How on earth could it possibly be more complicated than that?"

"Well, it's like, it's like – Dustin took me to the drive-in to see a movie I really wanted."

"And?"

"And, well … " Lex trailed off and started walking again. "And I don't know."

Ari followed, wanting to hold Lex's hand but not taking action. "We should hurry home," she said instead. "Before it gets any darker out."

Lex scoffed. "You're not worried about vampires, are you?"

Ari said nothing.

"You *are*. Are you scared?"

"Just being cautious."

"Come on, they don't come *this* far in. Right?"

" …Usually."

"We don't even have vampire hunters here."

"That's why I'm worried."

The truck Ari had used to drive them out came into sight in the parking lot. "Not because your dad is going to be mad at you for bringing his truck back late?" Lex teased.

"…Whatever."

A pair of red eyes flashed in the darkness ahead of them, accompanied by the sound of footsteps going *inhumanly* fast.

Lex looked spooked.

"You were saying?" Ari sniped.

"Let's – let's just get in the truck," Lex said. She hustled over.

A blur darted into the parking lot and snatched her up. Her scream faded into the distance alarmingly quickly as her kidnapper zoomed away.

Barely able to register what had just happened, Ari cursed and cursed and cursed, got into her father's truck, started the engine, and slammed the gas to follow.

1

The neighbors complained.

Not that there *were* that many neighbors, all the way out here in bumfuck nowhere. They were almost too far south to even *worry* about vampires, almost too far out for the vampire hunters to even bother. They were so far from vampire territory that Lex had initially thought she was being pranked when someone asked her to come all the way out *here*.

He only comes out at night, the neighbor had complained. *And when he does come out during the day, he's always dressed head to toe in black, not a square inch of skin showing.*

And Lex had said, *Well, which is it? Does he not come out during the day, or does he come out during the day and cover all his skin?* To which the neighbor had snapped that she was scared and wanted to be taken seriously.

It's not a crime to be goth, Lex had informed the neighbor, much to said neighbor's irritation.

Then she'd gotten another call. There weren't many neighbors, but the ones there were were fucking *nosy*. They never saw him bringing in groceries, they said. He had a car, but he never drove it. He stayed up all night and slept during the day. They'd never seen his face because he never showed *any* of his skin.

Except, reportedly, one neighbor had snuck up to peek into the window at midnight and caught a glimpse of pallid skin. And then burning red eyes, as he'd apparently heard them with his preternatural hearing and swung his head towards them.

Any of these things by themselves could be dismissed. But all together, from multiple people, they couldn't be ignored. Lex had no idea what a vampire could *possibly* be doing all the way down here – and apparently camping out in a house, living there like a person, not maiming anybody. Not following the usual MO of vampires on human territory, which was kidnapping someone and then hightailing it back over the border out of reach of humans.

From beside her in the car, Ari sighed and tapped her balled-up fist on the steering wheel. "Sooo ... one more time ... We need to decide before we get there. Are we knocking on the door or not?"

"If he *is* a vampire, he'll hear us approaching the house," said Lex. "We should try talking first. From the reports, it sounds like he's unsociable, but not violent."

"But – " said Ari. "I mean, but – if *he* is a vampire, he'll hear us coming, and I doubt he'll be very keen *to* talk to us. In case you forgot, we're vampire hunters."

Lex sighed. "I don't know. Well, it's the middle of the day, maybe he'll be asleep. Or not home."

They continued to argue right up until the point where they got to the reported address, but they had to work as a team, so they had to agree on a plan. Eventually, Ari gave in and agreed to just go knock on the door first.

"But I'm still bringing my gear," said Ari, belt jangling as she strapped said gear on.

"Of course," said Lex. She was carrying more lightly, but she was afraid that if this vampire somehow *was* willing to resolve things nonviolently, it would scare him off if she was too heavily armed. But ... walking in without *anything* would be stupid. No one ever really *managed* to resolve things nonviolently with a vampire. It just didn't happen.

That didn't mean she wouldn't try, though. She was an optimist. At the very least she wanted to know what was up with this vampire's strange behavior. Still. She had her gun, and her wooden stakes, and her silver-core handcuffs on her belt.

Ari holstered her own gun. "All right then, let's give it a try."

4

Up to the door. The blinds were all drawn. Everything was quiet. Out of the corner of her eye, one of the nosy neighbors was visible at the property line, peeking over the fence.

Lex knocked. Nothing

"Hello?" said Ari. "Is anyone home?"

No response.

"He left a few hours ago," the neighbor shouted distantly.

Lex sighed and grimaced, giving the neighbor a wave. "Okay, thank you."

Ari tapped her gun. "This is ... just such *weird* behavior for a vampire. What could he possibly be *doing* if he's a vampire?"

Lex didn't know how vampires behaved in their own homes, miles and miles away in their own territory. But when they were *here,* their purpose was usually to kidnap someone and then go back home immediately to use their victim as a perpetual source of blood. Vampires were a looming threat to humanity, but one concentrated geographically – and they usually stayed where they were comfortable, up in the weak light of the north. Vampires gave birth instead of spawning from corpses like archaic misconceptions, so they could effectively be shunted off to their own corner of the world. Humanity had basically drawn a big line around vampire territory and said "enter at your own risk" – and as such, encounters with the creatures were exceedingly rare unless you were unlucky.

So for a vampire to just ... cross the border into the territory of vampire hunters, make its way allll the way down here, and apparently not even show any interest in biting the human neighbors ... It was puzzling.

This person, who may or not be a very weird vampire, had apparently been living here for weeks, doing ... something. Something the neighbors couldn't see, but which worried them immensely.

"Dunno," said Lex. "That's why I wanted to ask first." Maybe he would just reveal himself to not be a vampire, laugh at the misunderstanding, and send them on their way. Maybe it *would* be a vampire and they could kill it for the bounty. They needed the money.

"Well," said Ari, cracking her knuckles. "Are we breaking in or what? He's not home."

Lex averted her eyes nervously. "I guess that would give us some clues. And we could always just get out before he gets home."

Lex hemmed and hmmed about how to break into the house – this was not something her career of vampire hunting had ever required her to do. Ari, on the other hand, simply strode over to the back of the house with startling confidence and broke a window, glass tinkling under her flashlight.

Glass crunched under their boots as they delicately maneuvered into the house, knocking loose shards of glass out to avoid cutting themselves. It would definitely alert him that someone had broken in, but not until he'd seen the back of the house, which was hidden from the front door.

The window led them into a pantry. Which was completely barren except for some empty jars ... and a few baskets of some orangeish mushrooms.

"What are *these*?" Ari said, crinkling her nose.

"Dunno," said Lex. "But I'd say that's one mark in the 'not a vampire' column."

Ari's admittedly quite limited imagination couldn't conjure up any use a vampire would have for mushrooms, so she bobbed her head in agreement.

They pushed the door open and came into the kitchen, walking quietly in the dimness of midday streaming through the curtains. The kitchen had none of the usual trappings of food preparation – no knives, no silverware, but it did have a few empty glasses in the sink, residual dredges of fluid left at the bottom.

Ari opened the fridge, and her eyes boggled out of her head. "Um ... Lex."

Lex peered over to see and a wave of disgust hit her stomach. The fridge was full of blood. Gallons of it, glass bottles of varying sizes crowding the shelves in the otherwise sterile and bare fridge. There were even a few jugs in the door, as though he'd just run out and bought a half gallon of milk.

"I'd say this is a big one in the 'is a vampire' column."

Lex nodded, face white.

Ari silently closed the door. "Fuck. *Fuck.* To get that much, he's either bled a few people absolutely dry, or bled a lot of people. A *lot* of people, very frequently."

"We have to check the house," said Lex, aghast. There hadn't been reports of people screaming, or any sightings of other people at all, but it was inconceivable that any vampire could have harvested this much blood without having human captives nearby and convenient.

Ari nodded, thinking the exact same thing.

But as their boots passed the threshold into the living room, they heard the keys in the front door jingling. "We can get the jump on him," said Ari, and Lex nodded.

With the practiced ease of two people who'd worked in tandem together for years, in perfect sync, Lex stepped backwards into the coat closet behind her, while Ari crept down the stairs into the basement. They positioned themselves so they could still make eye contact, ready to go on a hair trigger.

The front door opened. Lex heard the stomp of boots and heavy breathing. The front door closed.

The footsteps moved closer. He came into the room, and now she could see why the neighbors were complaining.

Despite it being a hot, sunny day, he was dressed head to toe in thick black leathers, complete with gloves and a scarf wrapped around his neck, not that he needed it with the billowing cloak completing the ensemble. The hood was up, and as he pulled it down, she could see he was wearing a mask ... a black mask, with a beak and frosted lenses, darkened like sunglasses ... and through them, she could see the distinct gleam of red eyes. He was not extraordinarily tall for a vampire – in fact, Ari was much taller than he was. Despite that, he had a terrifying, commanding presence. It wasn't a crime to be goth, but she shivered knowing what kind of creature would hide itself like that, and what it was capable of.

Definitely a vampire. So they had to treat him like a vampire. All thoughts of talking went out the window immediately.

He panted into the confines of his mask, fogging up the lenses. He walked past Ari's hiding spot, then past Lex's. They were both surprised that he didn't smell them – vampires had an extraordinary sense of smell, so they'd both been preparing to strike when he noticed them. It must be the mask. They quickly recalculated.

He strode towards the kitchen and pulled his mask up off his face. His skin was pale – vampires came in a range of skin tones just as humans did, but theirs extended into a distinctly non-human range of corpse-like colors, and this particular vampire was well into that range, with almost translucent skin showing blackened, lifeless veins under the surface. He still panted, streaked with sweat. He ran one leather-gloved hand through his hair, which was a silvery white color, slicking it back with his own sweat. He licked his lips dryly, giving them a flash of his fangs.

Ari's eyes flickered from him to the kitchen. Lex knew what she was thinking. *He's probably going for the fridge. That's when we get him, when he's distracted.*

Lex nodded.

The vampire's gloves came off next and he slapped them down onto the coffee table, exposing his talon-like fingers. He strode into the kitchen, continuing to shed layers of his wrappings, throwing them on the floor or over nearby furniture. He opened the fridge and leaned over.

Lex and Ari both emerged from their hiding spots, taking up positions on either side of the kitchen door. The vampire closed the fridge and emerged holding a glass of blood, which he lifted to his lips, teeth clinking on the rim of the glass as he drank. He didn't seem to notice them, distracted by the smell of the blood he was drinking. Perfect.

Despite vampires' enormous physical strength, the greatest threat they posed was actually their voice: vampires had the power of persuasion, the ability to command humans to do their bidding with a word.

Therefore, while Ari readied her gun, Lex readied a bit gag. It was made of a silver core with steel coating, and if she could get it into his mouth, it would be game over for him – without persuasion, they could overpower him if they were careful.

They could also just blow his head off with a gun and then stake him, but they could take him alive this way.

They leapt. Lex pulled the bit over his head, yanking it back and slamming it into his mouth when he opened it to yelp in surprise. At the same time, Ari came up and used her considerable bulk to immobilize him, bear-hugging him and slamming him into the ground.

Lex quickly pulled the bit tight and fastened it. She could tell by the angry noises – noises, not words – coming from their prey that it had worked.

The vampire reared up, standing and slamming Ari into the wall, audibly cracking bones, drawing a pained gasp out of her. Lex jammed her silver knife into his abdomen, under the ribs. He let out a muffled scream, one hand clawing at the bit in his mouth in an uncoordinated way, torn between trying to fight the two hunters and using both hands to remove it.

The pain from the knife clearly got to him, because it gave Ari the opportunity to get back on him. He cried out wordlessly again as Ari pressed him into the ground, sinking the silver knife further in, prompting an audible sizzling from the silver on his flesh.

"The cuffs!" Ari yelled. "Get the cuffs!"

The cuffs, not the stake. Ari wanted him alive too. Lex was already in the process of fastening the silver-core handcuffs onto him.

The vampire writhed, movements pained and weakened by the silver burning into his core, but Lex grabbed his wrists and forced them behind his back. She snapped the cuffs shut.

"I have ankle cuffs on my belt," said Ari.

Lex took them, but when she leaned over to cuff his ankles, he lashed out and slammed his heel into her nose. Her head exploded with pain as her nose crunched under the blow. "*Fuck!*" she screamed, clutching her broken nose as blood erupted out.

"Son of a bitch!" said Ari, and she grabbed him by the back of the shirt and yanked him up. He let out more muffled growls, flailing his legs as she lifted him into the air. "Stop struggling!"

She slammed him into the wall, prompting yet another pained whine as the silver knife jolted deeper in. She pressed her body against his, pinning his legs to the wall with her own. Even restrained, wounded, and much smaller than her, it still took considerable effort to immobilize him. "Lex!"

Still clutching her nose with one hand, Lex came over and shakily fastened the ankle cuffs on, adding her blood to the spatters of the vampire's blood accumulating at his feet.

He writhed but could make no progress. Panting, Lex got out the final piece of restraint: a muzzle, which went over the bit and kept it in place, forcing his mouth shut completely.

There. They'd done it. He was in handcuffs, ankle cuffs, and a muzzle, all of them made of silver and therefore impossible to break. Ari pulled away, wheezing, and pushed him onto the floor. He landed with a *thunk* and a whimper. "Fuck," said Ari, cradling her ribs. "He got me good." Her eyes flickered up to Lex.

She came over and tenderly cradled Lex's bloody face. "Are you okay?"

Lex swallowed the blood pooling in her throat. Ari produced a paper towel. "Here. Just take it easy. We'll see the medic when we get back to base."

Lex groaned. "Shit," she hissed through clenched teeth. She looked over at the vampire. He had rolled over and was worming around on the ground desperately, pulling at the cuffs.

Ari came over, kneeling down. "Hold still."

He let out a rumbling growl, but it quickly died into a pathetic sob when she grabbed the handle of the silver knife. "I said *hold still.*"

She pulled the knife out, releasing a spatter of blood. The vampire let out a final pained sound, but sagged against the floor in relief.

Lex still held her hands to her nose to stop the bleeding. "All right. I didn't think this far ahead. Now what do we *do* with him?"

Lex was now preoccupied with her broken nose, but she still wanted to know what the fuck this vampire was doing here. The easiest way would be to ask him, but ... they couldn't do that, because if they removed the muzzle, he would just use persuasion on them.

Ari was clearly thinking the same thing. She hesitated. Eventually, she said, "Let's put him in the coffin, then search the house."

There was a contraption in their van affectionately dubbed "the coffin," put together by one of the hunters back at their base who kept repeatedly asking everyone who would listen to bring back a live vampire for him. His name was Nick, and he loved to do experiments to learn more about vampires and invent new weapons and new ways to kill them, so it was easy to imagine what he wanted one for ... It was very difficult to capture one live, though, so the coffin had been unused so far.

The device itself was simple enough: it was a box about seven feet long, bars made of silver coated with steel, with silver chains inside, basically a cage just large enough to contain a person. It was made to lock a vampire inside and render them completely immobile, hence the nickname. Lex hadn't really thought she would actually use it, but they did need to secure him while they searched the house. It didn't look like this vampire was going anywhere the way it was now, but ...

"Are we going to take him back to base? To Nick?"

Ari grimaced. "I mean ... what *else* are we going to do with him?"

From the floor, the vampire lowered his head and whined.

"Oh, shut up," Ari snapped. "You tried to kill us. Don't expect us to feel bad for you."

The vampire was silent, but a fearful tremor racked his body.

"Let's do it, then." Lex came over and grabbed the crook of his elbow in one hand, keeping the other on her nose. Ari knelt and hefted him by the other arm.

With a defeated look on his face, the vampire let himself be dragged towards the front door. When Ari actually opened it, though, he let out a growl and locked his knees, pushing against the doorframe.

"Fuck *off*," said Ari, pushing him impatiently. "You're *going* outside to the van."

She shoved him so hard he fell over and out onto the porch. He flipped to his side and started to crawl away as best as he could.

Lex took note of the sun: the porch was mostly shaded, but he was desperately trying to put some distance between himself and the line where the sunlight cut into the porch.

"He's scared of the sun," said Lex.

The vampire's head thunked onto the porch, his hair falling to cover his face, his body racking with silent sobs.

"Yeah, and I'm sure all his human victims were scared of getting all their blood drained out of them," said Ari gruffly. "I'm not coddling a monster. Let's *go*."

The vampire looked up at Lex with desperation and shook his head rapidly. Whatever he was trying to communicate was lost in a tidal wave of panic on his face as Ari grabbed his ankle and started to drag him. He writhed, letting out more muffled pleas.

Lex sighed. "Hey, if we throw your cloak over you so you don't get burned, will you stop fucking struggling? We just want to get this over with so we can get first aid."

The vampire's squirming stopped. He caught his breath, then nodded.

Lex walked back into the house and grabbed the cloak from where he'd thrown it over a chair. She came back out and tossed it over him, arranging it over all the exposed skin on his face and hands.

"Softie," Ari said. "You grab his ankles."

Ari moved to the front and wrapped her arms around his chest from under his armpits. Lex went to the other side and grabbed his ankles. They carried him down the front stairs like that, like they were moving a piece of furniture.

Lex dropped her end of their load and pulled the van door open. Ari hefted him up and dropped him on the van floor. He rolled over, moaning, tangled up in his cloak.

Lex clambered into the back of the van where the coffin lay waiting. She used the silver key to unlock the padlock keeping it all shut, then opened the bars making up the lid. It creaked open. "Okay. Just lay him in there."

Ari pulled the cloak off his head. And *oh,* when those red eyes locked on the coffin, Lex had never seen that level of panic and anger. Ari got up into the van to pull him over, but he lashed out with his legs again, crunching his boots into her shin.

"Fuck!" Lex shouted. "Goddamn it!" She rushed over, but the vampire had managed to get upright, using the wall as leverage. The van shuddered and briefly rolled up onto two tires as he slammed into her, denting the metal of the wall, knocking the breath out of her. She felt something in her skeleton snap. "Fuck!" Lex yelled again, unsheathing her knife and once again plunging it into whatever part of his body she could reach, tearing it down and leaving a ragged hole in his flesh.

The wounds smoked as the silver-lined blade tore through him, and he screamed as loud as he could with his mouth forced closed, jaw grinding on the bit. Lex gave him a vicious shove, and he tumbled over.

Ari hobbled to her feet, steadying herself on the wall. "Fucker. Goddamn. Just – just get in there." Chest aching, Lex grabbed him roughly by the back of his shirt and shoved him into the coffin. He *still* fought wildly not to be put into it, lashing out as much as he could while restrained, catching her a few times with his claws and tearing holes in her clothes and skin.

She managed to get his torso aligned as intended into the coffin, and she quickly stretched the chains over his body, pulling them tight. As he thrashed and wailed, she moved to his feet and secured them to the bottom.

There. He was in it. As soon as she shut the lid and re-did the lock, sealing him inside, it was like he turned into a completely different creature instantly. Tears welled in his eyes, rolling down his cheeks, and he sniffled pathetically. He let his body go limp. *Fucking finally.*

"You good?" said Lex, offering Ari her hand.

13

Ari tried to put weight on her foot, then immediately lifted it up again, wincing. "No."

Lex sighed, helping her down and out of the van.

"Maybe we should call someone else in to search the house," said Ari.

"Let me do it," said Lex. "You stay here."

"We can't split up."

"He's been secured." At this pause in the conversation, the wordless wailing from inside the van could be heard in the silence. "Your leg looks pretty fucked, but if there's people trapped inside, we can't leave them there."

Ari hesitated, then nodded. "Okay. But just do it quickly. Come right back out."

2

— • —

It felt wrong going into the house alone – vampire hunters always worked in pairs, because the creatures were so dangerous that going up against one alone was practically a death sentence. Not only that, but Lex and Ari were rarely ever apart. They'd been fast friends ever since they were young, and then more than friends later. Ari had been Lex's rock through some of the darkest moments of her life, through the tragic events that led to her becoming a vampire hunter in the first place. They never wanted to separate.

It would definitely be counterproductive to make Ari walk on that leg, though. Lex watched as her partner opened the passenger side door in the van and sat with her leg stretched out. Ari made an irritated motion for her to get a move on.

So Lex walked back up onto the porch alone, hand gripping her knife. She was fairly certain the only vampire around was currently locked in the van, but that didn't stop her from being afraid of there being more. She had to find any captives that were inside, and maybe she could find some clues as to what was going on here.

Back into the kitchen. The half-full bottle of blood lay spilled on the floor, cracked in the scramble of their fight. Lex's boot crunched over the glass. The pool of blood on the floor was upsetting. There was just ... so *much* of it.

She opened the fridge and looked in again. Just as before, gallons and gallons of blood. She took a few jugs and started to dump them down the sink, then halfway through, thought better of it and closed them again. The metallic scent hung heavy in the air.

She walked back into the dining room, checked the closet where she'd hidden. There were some clothes hanging up, but that was it.

Then the basement. She was … nervous about what she'd find there. But as she came down the stairs and flicked the light on, there weren't any half-dead humans chained up as she'd feared.

There *did* appear to be a workstation of some sort, with laboratory glassware scattered about. Another basket of mushrooms. A container of some white powder. Metal shavings. A mortar and pestle, with orange sludge sitting in the bottom of it. She came over and tentatively sniffed the things, but could make no sense of what they could be for. There was a stack of handwritten notes sitting on top of a notebook, which she picked up to try and read. The handwriting was atrocious. She put it back.

She went back upstairs. The living room was bare except for a few stacks of books.

Up to the second floor. There were even fewer furnishings up here. In the first bedroom, thick blackout curtains had been stapled to the wall to cover the window completely. Besides that, there was a cheap-looking cabinet with clothes folded inside and an unglamorous mattress sitting on the bare floor. She found a wallet next to the bed and flipped it open.

There was a photo ID inside. She thought this was ridiculous. Vampires' entire society depended on the vicious kidnapping and murder of sentient human beings without an ounce of regret. And they still did shit like *have wallets* and *photo IDs*. It just felt wrong. It felt too normal and human. She imagined the vampire going to some version of the DMV in the middle of the night. Taking a number and waiting behind a line of other vampires to go talk to another vampire that would have him fill out vampire paperwork. Monsters that drained the life out of others shouldn't be doing *paperwork*. Why are you filling out *paperwork* when there's a whole section of your society performing mass human rights violations? Their society depended on the fucking ghoulishness of human blood farms, but God forbid there were any vampires out there with fake IDs. Ridiculous.

At any rate, the photo ID did tell her that the vampire's name was *Valen Kithrara*, which of course didn't mean anything at all to her because she wasn't familiar with vampire families. Few hunters bothered to learn such details. They weren't of much use. The people who *did* want to learn about vampires, like Nick, were mostly interested in learning how to hurt them more efficiently, not their social lives.

She sighed and opened the wallet all the way. Her eyes boggled to see that there was a few hundred dollars inside. *Don't mind if I do.* She clicked her tongue and put the wallet in her pocket.

There was a second bedroom, which was completely empty. The bathroom, which had a damp towel on the floor and – bizarrely – some needles in the sink, clearly used. She couldn't imagine what they were for. Vampires were unaffected by drugs.

She retraced her steps through the hallway and found a door leading to the attic, which she climbed into with some effort. It was little more than a crawlspace. Absolutely empty.

She came back downstairs, baffled. The only things of any note had been the things in the basement. She should grab some of them, then have the other hunters come take another look to make sure she hadn't missed anything.

Where had all that blood *come* from? She'd expected to find human captives, and a lot of them. Had he brought the blood with him from somewhere else? Was it animal blood? Vampires couldn't just drink animal blood, that much everyone knew, otherwise it wouldn't be necessary for them to do the things that caused them to have such poor relations with human society. They *had* to drink human blood, and they'd seen him drinking the stuff in the fridge, so where had it come from?

She went back down to the basement, finding a box and moving some of the things into it, containers and glassware and the notebooks. She stared at the mortar and pestle very hard. The residue inside was the same color as the mushrooms. He'd been grinding them up for something, right? What was he trying to *do*? She stared at the workbench, very deep in thought, gears in her brain grinding to try and draw a conclusion.

She made sure she had as many clues as she could carry in the box, then went back upstairs. She set the box on the counter and opened the fridge again.

She brought one of the bottles to her nose, smelling it, brow creasing. It certainly *smelled* like blood to her. Vampire hunters had all smelled their fair share of blood, both human and vampire blood. The color and smell were certainly closer to human blood than vampire blood. She cautiously lifted the bottle to her lips and took a sip, then spit it out immediately because of how foul it tasted.

It was metallic, familiar from all the times she'd had blood in her mouth from getting the shit kicked out of her. What had she expected? It was blood. She probably didn't have a refined enough sense of taste or smell to get any useful information out of sampling blood this way. She sealed the bottle and put it in her box of clues.

She came outside. Ari looked relieved to see her walk out in one piece. "What'd you find?"

Lex came over and set the box on the ground next to Ari. "There was some sort of workstation. I gathered this stuff up from it."

"Nobody else inside?"

"Not a soul ... unless I missed them somehow."

Ari huffed. "There's *got* to be."

"You'd think."

Ari hobbled around the van to the back, throwing the doors open. The vampire locked inside flinched, facing away from the harsh sunlight she'd just let into the van.

"Hey, you," said Ari.

"His name is Valen," said Lexi. "I found his wallet."

Ari rolled her eyes. "Fine. Valen."

He turned his head back towards her.

"Don't give me that look. Stop being a baby. We're not even hurting you. The muzzle is padded, the cuffs aren't bare silver. We could be being a lot meaner."

"We did stab him," Lex said, then fell silent as Ari glared daggers at her.

"My point is," said Ari, trying to be intimidating as she stepped up into the van, but she stumbled and ended up having to do an undignified hop because of her leg. She recovered, dragging herself over to the coffin. "My point is, if you want us to *continue* not being mean, maybe you can help us out."

His huge, watery eyes locked directly on her. She leaned over. "Where did all that blood come from? There weren't any people in the house."

Valen furrowed his brow.

"How do you want him to answer?" Lex piped up.

Ari once again glared at her. She frowned, then turned back. "They aren't in the house?"

He shook his head.

"Are they nearby somewhere? Outside?"

He shook his head.

"Do you have captives at home?"

He shook his head. The tears started rolling down his cheeks again, down onto the muzzle, terror clearly growing as he sensed Ari's mounting frustration.

Ari sneered. "Then where the hell did it come from? Is it animal blood?"

He nodded desperately.

"So you're some special vampire that can drink animal blood instead of human blood?"

He squeezed his eyes shut, taking a shuddering breath, grinding his jaw on the bit in his mouth.

"Erm, babe," said Lex, clambering up beside her. "I'm not sure if this is really going to go anywhere. Listen, do you think that maybe ... I don't know, do you think he *made* it somehow?"

He nodded wildly, pulling his arms as though trying to gesture.

"Well, which is it, then?" Ari snapped. "Is it animal blood or did you make it somehow?"

He kept nodding.

Ari groaned. "Okay, this is pointless. We're not gonna get any real answers out of him until we can find some way he can communicate without using persuasion."

"No, no, listen, the stuff in the basement, it looked like ... Well, I don't know, I'm suspicious it might be that one."

"Why would any vampire come all the way out here, set up camp in the middle of human territory, to *make fake blood*? Like, why would any vampire make fake blood at all, let alone come all the way out here to do it?"

Lex deflated. "Well, I – I don't know. I'm just guessing. There's – there's some notes, but I can't really read the handwriting."

"Well, let's just hand it all over to Nick and see what he can make of it. And maybe someone there will have an idea of how to safely talk to him. We can get some pen and paper, maybe."

Ari stepped out of the van, cussing up a storm once again about her leg, limping. Lex turned back to look at their captured prey one more time.

She didn't want to feel bad for him. She really didn't. All available evidence pointed to him probably being a mass murderer. He'd thoroughly thrashed both of them even while tied up. He was a monster by any definition.

But he was giving her *puppy dog eyes*. She'd never seen that before. It was so much easier to be mean to a vampire when they did what they usually did, which was *act* like a proper monster. He just looked so miserable and scared. Despite her best efforts to remember that was probably how his victims felt when he showed them no mercy, she did end up feeling bad for him. Her brain scrambled to try and concoct explanations for how maybe he wasn't actually bad, because she didn't *want* him to be, but how likely were they? Making fake blood? Did she really believe that?

But ...

She leaned over the coffin once again, his puffy, pleading eyes snapping up to her. "Hey," she said. "It's gonna be all right. Okay? We're just trying to keep everyone safe."

He broke eye contact.

"Hey, Mother Teresa." Ari was clearly also feeling guilty, because Lex knew Ari reacted to feeling guilty by getting grumpier. "When you're done, let's get moving."

3

— • —

"Christ alive," said Ari, stretching her stiff legs out. "Babe, you have *got* to start speeding or we're never going to get there before the earth falls into the sun." She opened the door of the newly parked van and pivoted to sit sidesaddle, giving herself as much room as possible.

"Sure, Ari, let's get pulled over for speeding with a vampire locked in the back of the car. That'll go over real great." Lex circled the van, tousling Ari's hair and almost regretting it when her hand scraped against the gel-stiffened spikes Ari had fashioned her mop into. "I'll be right back."

They'd spent more of this day *driving* than actually hunting vampires. Not really an effective use of their time, but oh well. Lex was anxious to get back to the hunters' base of operations – maybe there, they could start figuring out some answers.

She walked around the rest stop aimlessly for a few minutes before ordering something from Burger King and bringing it back out.

She took a moment to peer into the back of the van and made eye contact with their captive for the briefest moment before he deferentially averted his gaze. She found herself feeling bad once again. Her heart was softer than Ari's – she didn't like to see suffering, even if it was from a monster. But they couldn't be expected to just let him loose. For all they knew, he was a horrible killer … like most vampires. They had no reason to believe otherwise.

But still. She felt bad, seeing him so scared and sad. Maybe they could figure something out.

She came around and into the driver's seat again. She tossed the bag onto Ari's lap, putting the drinks into the cupholders. "Holding down the fort okay?"

"Yep," said Ari. "Ugh, did you get me diet, at least?"

"If you don't want it, I'll drink it," said Lex, starting the car. "It's lemonade. It's good."

Ari picked at the drinks. "Don't suppose we've got anything red for our friend back there."

"Hardy-har. Check if anyone's coming from the outbound, I can't see the road with that truck parked there."

Ari helped navigate as they swung back onto the interstate. "How's your leg?" said Lex.

"I mean. Still busted as fuck. The nose?"

"I mean. Still broken. Do we have any ice packs left?"

"Nope. Just water packs."

Lex sighed. If Ari's judgment based on the road atlas was anything to go by, it was still an hour drive. She didn't want to stop at the hospital with their prisoner in the back, but *God* did it hurt.

Ari's hand gently rubbed her arm. "We'll be there soon enough. I know you're tough."

They held their hands together on the stick shift, occasionally giving each other small kisses and letting the other bitch about whatever was on their mind.

There was a sound. At first Lex thought it was coming from Ari, but she glanced over and saw Ari sitting there completely silent. In fact, Ari's head was tilted in confusion, as though she heard it too.

"Oh hell," Ari muttered when the sound increased in volume and it became obvious their captive in the back was wordlessly crying, sad whimpers choking out.

Ari twisted and leaned back. "Hey."

"Be nice," Lex whispered. "There's no reason to be mean."

"That's what I'm trying to do," Ari muttered under her breath, then raised her voice again: "Look at me."

Lex couldn't see, but apparently the vampire had complied. Ari continued, "Are you in pain?" Silence for a moment. "Hey. You're making sounds that sound like you're being hurt somehow. Is there bare silver touching you?"

Further silence.

"Just nod your head if it is. I'll come fix it. No sense in torturing you."

"He's probably just scared," Lex said.

Ari stared back hard at the vampire. She turned back around and crossed her arms. "Whatever it takes to make him shut up."

Oh no, be careful, Ari, you almost cared about someone. Then everyone might know you're not actually a heartless bitch.

Lex put a soft hand on top of Ari's. Ari grumpily held her hand, seemingly determined to be sour no matter what.

They passed the rest of the trip with nothing but the car radio. Normally what Lex would do in this situation would be to endlessly pester the person in the car she didn't know anything about with personal questions, but ...

They were able to make it back to the base of operations before sunset, which was always a relief. Lex felt comforted at the sight of it – it was an impressive three-story house that had been repurposed by the group. The most noticeable aspect of it was the silver-coated bars covering the windows, something a lot of people might find foreboding, but this close to the border, even many private homes had them.

They pulled into the driveway, nosing up as close to the house as they could. Lex turned the van off, the engine dying into silence, and they both just sat there for a minute, slumping against their seats, injuries throbbing.

"I keep saying we should get a carphone in this thing," said Lex. "It would be so convenient. We could just call whoever was inside to come help us."

"We are not getting a *carphone*," Ari said. "Those things are expensive as hell." Ari nudged Lex with her foot. "Go on, I'll watch Nosferatu. It was fine when you visited the burger monarch."

Lex rolled her eyes. "Fiiiine."

The van dipped as she got out, slamming the door behind her. Ari watched her walk off, and in the newly fallen silence, strangulated keening from the back filled the cabin.

Ari sighed, leaning against the window. "I know, buddy, me too."

4

"Fuck!!"

The exclamation came accompanied by an unsettling crunching as the medic set Lex's broken nose back into place. She let out a groan, scrabbling for the offered painkillers as Gabriel snapped his gloves off and went to wash his hands. "That should do ya."

"Uhh – that's it?" said Lex.

"Yep. You're lucky that vamp didn't kill ya. Most of 'em are strong enough to just crush your nose right up into your brain."

He's also lucky he didn't kill me, Lex thought. *Because if he had, Ari wouldn't have been as nice as she was to him.* She still held the bloody tissue to her nose. "I'll be sure to thank him, then," she said wryly.

Gabriel slipped a full bottle of Tylenol out of the drawer. "No hunting for a few weeks, okay?"

"Won't be able to till Ari's leg is fixed, anyway."

"Sure. Just take it easy. Take painkillers when you feel like you need them, but not more than eight every twenty-four hours. Oh, and try to make yourself look a little less tasty, if what I heard about our newest guest is to be believed."

Gabriel had already heard that they'd brought a vampire home. Of course he would have, everyone would be abuzz about it. No one had managed it before. They were *very* hard to handle live.

"Well, if what you say is true, apparently he has such delicate, gentle kicks that I don't need to worry," said Lex, tossing the bloodied tissue into the bin.

"Thanks for the Tylenol. And the excuse to sit on my ass for a few weeks." It would probably be a little difficult to squeak by on their savings for a while, since they would have to go without winning any bounties until they could hunt again, but they could probably manage ... especially since the prize for bringing home a live catch had been pretty generous. And it would be nice to have some time to just focus on recovering.

"Sure," said Gabriel. "Oh, and ... if I were you, I would steer clear of the director for a bit. He's not gonna be happy about this."

***

Lex saw the other hunters gathered around the coffin when she came back out. They parted slightly to let her through, and she couldn't help feeling a little upset when she saw the vampire had blood on his face that definitely hadn't been there when she'd left.

This was what she was afraid of. There was no reason to hurt him when he was already all trussed up. Some hunters could be vindictive as hell, though. It was needless cruelty. Still ... she didn't want to be the one sticking her neck out to tell off her colleagues for their treatment of a vampire, of all things. She shook her head. "Where's Nick?"

"He's on the phone with the director," said Jerome.

"Oh boy," said Ari. "I bet he's just *thrilled* with this new development."

"I thought he gave Nick the okay to do this?" said Bailey, puzzled. "He authorized Nick to put a bounty on bringing a live vampire back."

The other hunters laughed.

"Yeah," said Jerome wryly. "To get him to shut up. He didn't think anyone would actually *do* it."

27

"The director was bluffing," said Ari. "Because vampires are so damn *hard* to catch live, he thought none of us could do it. He doesn't *actually* want a vampire in the building."

Lex came over and put a foot up on the coffin, like she was posing with a hunting trophy. "Hah! That'll show *him*. And he's contractually obligated to pay out the bounty."

One of the other hunters experimentally copied Lex, putting a hand on the coffin, and the vampire inside went ballistic, slamming his skull up and narrowly missing crushing a finger on the offending hand.

The hunter jerked his hand away, grimacing. "Yeesh ... Well, Nick can have him."

"Speaking of," said Ari, and Nick appeared in the doorway.

His eyes sparkled. "You *did* it. Thank you! Thank you!"

He sounded like a kid at Christmas. Lex had always been a little bit creeped out by Nick. In fact, most of the hunters weren't thrilled with Nick on a day-to-day basis.

Nick seemed ... like he wasn't quite all there. They all knew why, of course – Nick had been imprisoned by vampires for an alarmingly long time before he'd gotten away. And anyone who spent too long over there eventually turned into a mindless husk as their brain melted from being under the thrall of vampire persuasion for so long.

Nick had apparently been ... part of the way there when he'd gotten out. Part of his behavior was because of trauma, but part of it was because his brain had been supernaturally tampered with ...

... and some of it was also just the sheer bitterness and hatred stemming from what he'd gone through. Looking at him now, at how excited he was to be presented with a vampire gift-wrapped, Lex felt unease crawling up her spine.

"Come on, Ari," said Lex, tugging at Ari's hand. "You have to get your leg seen to."

"Wait, ladies, I have to give you the bounty for your hard work!" He clapped his hands together. "And, everyone, after some ... heated discussion ... with the director, he has simply given me the guideline that, for safety, we can only open the coffin when at least two people are present. So, who wants to be the lucky volunteer and help me take this specimen downstairs?"

"I will," Lex volunteered instantly, and then felt embarrassed about the speed at which she'd done so.

"I see how it is," said Ari. "Rather spend time playing with Nick in the basement than helping your poor, hurt girlfriend to the nurse."

Lex blushed. "We can – we can do that together and then go help Nick right afterwards."

Nick looked around. "Well, I don't hear any other volunteers, so ... " He beamed. "I'll wait right here for you to get back!"

5

The coffin thumped as it slid down the stairs, banging into the wall at the bottom. There was silence for a moment before the captive inside let out a miserable whine.

"Oops," said Nick.

"All right, Nicky, how about you slow down a bit," said Ari, who obviously shared Lex's thought that he had definitely let it slip down the stairs on purpose. With her leg newly encased in a medical boot, she came down the stairs one step at a time with Lex supporting her elbow.

"Of course," Nick said sweetly. "Sorry."

Nick bounced down the stairs and pulled the coffin into the basement. Lex had never actually been down here before – the director had given it to Nick to work in, and Lex usually avoided him when she could. It had a concrete floor with a drain in the center, a variety of chains mounted in various places around the room – ghoulish, Lex thought. He'd really been preparing for this.

There was also the metalworking equipment – Nick was the one who made the silver weapons and gadgets for everyone, so he had the necessary furnace, tongs, and hunks of silver in various states of being melted.

Lex set her cardboard box of clues collected from the house onto the workbench. "Okay, before we do anything else, I wanted to get your thoughts on all this stuff."

"Hmm?" said Nick. "What is that?"

"Stuff we collected from his house. He had a *lot* of blood in the fridge, but we didn't find any signs of violence or any human captives."

Nick tilted his head. "Oh?" He came over to the box.

Lex handed him the notebooks. "I can't really read his handwriting, but maybe you can."

Nick flipped through the pages, pausing to look at the diagrams of chemicals. "Oh? Interesting."

Lex started unpacking the box. "And this is some of the blood that was in the fridge, and these mushrooms, and some of the stuff he was using – "

"What exactly," Nick interrupted, "are you expecting me to do with these?"

Lex's hands faltered. "Well, I – it seemed really weird. He was deep in human territory for *something*. This is really irregular behavior for a vampire, and we were trying to figure out what he was doing."

"Is there some way we can ask him?" said Ari. "That would just be fastest. I was thinking, like, if we could get a pencil and paper – "

"No!" said Nick. "Absolutely not! Vampires can use persuasion through *any* mode of communication! Even writing! It kicks in as soon as the victim understands the message imbued in what the vampire was communicating. So long as there's a shared language, it'll work. Some can even do it with nothing but eye contact!"

Lex glanced over at Valen and saw his huge, pleading eyes and thought this *must* be bullshit – he was *clearly* communicating *Please let me out.*

"O-okay, then," said Lex, rattled. "Well, can you make anything out of the stuff in here, then?"

Nick picked up the bottle of blood, holding it up to the light and swirling it around. "Looks like blood to me."

" ... Right, but is there, I don't know, some tests you could do on it?"

"To ... ?"

"To see if it's actually blood?"

"What else would it be?"

"I don't know!"

Valen writhed inside the coffin, letting out frustrated, muffled screams.

"The mushrooms are the weirdest part to me," said Ari. "I can't *imagine* what he was doing with them."

"I don't know if this is a fruitful avenue of investigation," said Nick. "When I asked you to bring me back a vampire, I wanted it to do experiments on, not ... whatever this is."

"Can't you at least *try* a little bit?" said Lex. "There's something unusual going on here."

Nick sighed and put down the bottle. "All right. If you really want to know." He tapped his chin. "Well, a large volume of blood, with no human victims in sight ... The simplest explanation would be it was harvested elsewhere and brought with him. Having access to this much blood this fast, I would guess that this vampire is affiliated with the blood harvesting facilities, and was granted this large portion to feed him as he came deep into human territory to do something."

The coffin rattled as Valen thrashed as much as he could.

"Er ... " said Ari, rubbing her neck. "I guess that makes sense, but what would he come in this far *for*? It doesn't seem like it was to collect human victims, and that's pretty much the only reason vampires come in."

Nick picked up one of the mushrooms, examining it closely. He then immediately went and washed his hands in the basin sink, then grabbed a book off the pile next to his workbench. It was a field guide – he flipped through it until he found a page with the mushroom in question.

"Here it is – ah, this is illuminating. This mushroom species only grows in warm climates, which means it couldn't grow in vampire territory. Hence he must have come here to collect it."

"But what could he use it *for*?" Lex asked for the millionth time.

Nick held the book out. "Well, this mushroom species apparently produces a potent tranquilizing poison. If we assume this vampire is affiliated with the blood farms, then we can guess that maybe he's here on a sponsored trip to research more effective ways to hunt down humans. His notes support that – there's a lot of drawings of chemical compounds, and notes on combining things in different ratios. Maybe it was to develop a tranquilizer that would be easier to use than hunting down humans manually."

That got a reaction from the coffin. More banging, desperate growling. Lex's face faded into disappointment. "Oh ... "

Ari took Lex's hand. "Come on, Lex, we kind of knew he must be here for something no good."

"Right, but ... I dunno, I guess I thought maybe ... "

Nick snapped the book shut. "Well, I will let you know if I discover anything else, but I think for now this is the most likely explanation."

Lex knew she was being foolish. It *was* the most likely explanation. She *knew* this vampire was probably a monster, and here because he meant ill. But she *wanted* him to be good. She *wanted* there to be some other explanation.

Ari clearly saw the dark cloud hanging over her, because she rubbed Lex's hand. "Hey, just to settle the matter, if you want, we can go call Patrick and ask him if he knows anything. We have the vampire's full name."

Patrick was a contact the hunters had who was more familiar with the inner workings of vampire society than the average hunter. He knew the names of some of the more prominent families, and occasionally particularly important individual vampires.

That was worth a shot. Maybe if Patrick happened to recognize his name, he could tell them about him ... after all, such a strange trip into human territory would probably only be performed by a notable vampire.

Lex nodded. "That sounds nice."

"I'll go give him a call." Ari started the painstaking process of limping back up the stairs.

"Do you want me to – "

"I don't need help!" Ari snapped.

Lex smiled wryly. "Okay."

Nick watched her go with amusement. Then he turned back to the coffin. "Well, now we can, perhaps, get on with it."

Lex watched as Valen shivered. "Okay ... Well, I guess I count as a second person here, so it's not against the rules to open the coffin." Maybe she would feel a little better when they let him out of the coffin. She felt guilty that he'd been in there for so long. "What exactly are you going to do?"

"Well, I need to document everything, so we should start with photographing its condition when it arrived." He gestured to the chunky camera on the workbench.

"O-okay," said Lex. "Um, what are you going to do – to – that will affect his *condition*?"

"Well, the first thing I wanted to try out was to establish the optimum percentage of silver for an alloy to still be effective for vampire hunting. We've been using pure silver, and we go through a *lot* of it. If, say, fifty percent silver is just as effective, we could be much more efficient."

"Okay?"

The chains in the coffin rattled as Valen shuddered. Nick came over and tugged at the coffin. "May I have the keys, please?"

Lex removed the key from her pocket and handed it to Nick. He clicked the lock open.

Valen started to thrash as soon as the lid to the coffin was open. Of course, there were still multiple layers of restraints keeping him immobile. Nick just watched the performance with an amused smile. "Go ahead, get it all out of your system."

Valen fell back, limp, chest heaving.

Nick went over to his tool bench and withdrew something: a long pole with a clasp on the end. Lex realized with some bemusement it was an animal control pole, the kind that people would use to handle a particularly violent dog.

He came back over and slipped the noose around Valen's neck, cinching it tight as Valen's enraged wiggling started back up again. "Feisty, aren't you? Lex, will you please undo the restraints?"

34

Lex came over and unclipped the chains wrapped around his chest. After a moment's pause, she removed the bare silver metal chains entirely and put them in her pocket. Then she moved to his feet. Having learned her lesson, she kept her face out of kicking range and leaned over comically far to release the chain keeping his cuffed ankles secured to the bar, then scooted backwards quickly.

Nick lifted the pole. Lex *almost* wanted to say this was excessive, but Valen had managed to break her nose *and* Ari's leg while he had his hands cuffed behind his back *and* his ankles shackled together, so she wasn't eager to volunteer to handle him manually and not with a five-foot-long pole between them.

Still, she felt a twinge of pity as the wire dug into his neck. He squirmed, choking, as he tried to find a way to balance supporting his weight with his bound limbs as he was stood up.

"Now, Lex," said Nick, when he had the vampire upright, "we're going to use those chains in the center of the room, if you'll please attach them to its arms when I get it over there."

He was talking about the shackles hanging from a chain in the ceiling. Okay, that seemed harmless enough. At worst it would strain his arms a little bit. It was hardly worse than the way he'd already been restrained.

Valen hissed like a snake as Nick dragged him over to the center of the room, trying and failing to walk with his ankles shackled. He shivered with rage as he fell to his knees under the chain in the ceiling.

Lex came over and started to hook the new chain to his wrists.

"No, no, in the front, if you please, so we can have his arms above his head."

Lex froze. "Er, how do you want me to do that?"

"Unshackle the wrists and move them to the front."

Lex looked into Valen's enraged eyes, his nostrils flaring. "Er ... " said Lex. "I don't think I can do that without him being able to claw me."

"You're the one who managed to capture him in the first place. I'm sure you can figure something out."

Lex grimaced. "Okay ... Um ... " Valen froze as she reached a hand out towards his face. "Shh," she said. "It's all right."

She put a gentle palm on his cheek. "Listen ... I know that this ... isn't fun for you. But I think you know fighting back isn't going to do anything, yeah?"

His gaze softened and he broke eye contact, lip wobbling.

"It's gonna be all right," she said, and unlocked the shackles behind his back. "Easy, now, shh, shh." She moved his hands to his front and locked them again. "There, you're okay. It's gonna be okay."

"Brilliant!" said Nick.

She shot him a venomous glare, which he ignored. She reached up and pulled the chain from the ceiling, clamping them onto the vampire's wrists. "There we go," she said. "See, it's not so bad."

He hung his head miserably. Nick walked over to where the chain was secured to the floor before being fed over a bar in the ceiling, and pulled it taut. Valen jerked in surprise as his hands zoomed upwards, stretching his arms so that he was forced up onto the balls of his feet.

"There," said Nick, walking forward. "Now, we can – "

As soon as Nick was close enough, Valen wrapped his shackled hands in the chains above him and pulled himself up, using them to swing himself like a pendulum and kick Nick square in the chest with both feet.

Nick stumbled back, shock plastered on his face, coughing. Lex caught Valen's feet before they could land back on the ground, and he growled and twisted ineffectually in the air, trying to wrestle his feet back out of her grasp.

"All right," said Lex, "what did we just talk about?" She really couldn't blame him, all things considered – she was surprised that talking him down had worked the first time.

Doing it quickly, and leaning partially away out of fear of the dreaded face-smashing boots, Lex brought his feet down and secured the shackles to the mount on the floor that limited their range of movement.

Valen stood there shaking with some mixture of fear and anger, hands secured above his head, feet stuck to the floor, forced up with his heels off the ground.

Nick staggered to his feet, the wind completely knocked out of him. Lex couldn't help feeling a little smug. Valen's face mirrored hers in that regard.

"Ah, yes," he said, clearing his throat. "This is why – why it's important to – to have two people to handle it, I suppose."

"Right ... "

He stalked forward with a *tsk tsk* sound. "You've already been damaged." He got out a handkerchief and wiped the blood off Valen's forehead. "Now, now, we'll have time for that later. Right now ... "

He removed an enormous pair of scissors from his workbench. Valen suddenly looked like he was regretting struggling so much.

Nick moved behind Valen. "Stay still," he hissed as Valen squirmed. "It'll only be worse if you struggle."

Valen fell still. Lex watched with increasing discomfort as Nick slid the scissors up the back of his shirt, cutting the fabric away. "Is this – is that really necessary?"

Nick's hands worked to peel off the fabric, cutting the sleeves next. "What did you think I meant by photograph his condition? I can't very well do that when he's all covered up."

Lex felt really stupid. What had she expected? Had she really thought Nick would just be *nice* to him? Why did she offer all those reassurances that it was going to be okay, when she knew they weren't true?

Nick pulled the shredded clothes off Valen's torso, casting them to the floor. "Hm?" he said with a raised eyebrow when, instead of a bare chest as they'd both expected, there was another layer of fabric, tight against his chest.

Lex cocked her head. "Uh?"

Valen sobbed as Nick brought the scissors up again, snipping the remaining clothing off with three short bursts, letting it fall to the ground.

There was a stunned silence. He had breasts. They weren't very big, but they were definitely there. "Well, well, well!" said Nick. "It seems this vampire you've brought me is actually a *vampiress*."

"I ... " said Lex. "I didn't know vampires could be transgender." His short stature and soft, boyish face suddenly made a lot of sense. But it was like seeing he had a photo ID card. It felt too human. Too bizarrely out of place to care about gender, but not people's very lives and safety.

Nick scoffed. "Don't be absurd. I'm sure vampires have no use for such nonsense."

Lex couldn't help being a little offended at that, before she realized she didn't really have any rebuttal or right to a moral high ground. She was just standing there watching Nick strip him.

Him? Surely this vampire was a *him*, right?

She pulled his wallet back out of her pocket, sliding the photo ID out to look at it again. She hadn't noticed before, but – the sex marker on it said *F.*

But clearly there'd been significant effort to present male instead. He had body hair – just wisps of it, but very clearly masculine peach fuzz trailing down his belly and under his pants. He'd been taking testosterone, by the look of him. Again, that felt absurd.

Her eyes snapped back up his face, the thin tufts of facial hair there, and then unfocused to see his terrified expression, the trembling in the androgynous features she'd been inspecting so closely. *I'm sure he has other things on his mind right now. I'm sure he would prefer to be safe and misgendered, than gendered correctly and held hostage.*

Nick came forward and started to unbutton Valen's pants. The vampire let out a pitiful whine, trying to lean away.

"Come *on*," said Lex. "You can't be serious. What could you possibly need *that* for?"

"I already told you," Nick snapped. "I need a nude photograph for comparisons later. I'm positive vampires have no concept of nudity being shameful, so stow your antiquated sensibilities."

It echoed Lex's own thoughts about it being absurd how vampires would share human sensibilities in some things, but not in other, larger ones – but the flush of humiliation on his face, cheeks tinged dark red, was undeniable.

It only deepened, more of the black, lifeless blood rushing to his face, when Nick pulled his pants down, revealing he was wearing a pair of blue boxer briefs. He pulled those down too, revealing an unshaved pubic mound, more silvery, delicate hair. Indignant tears rolled down Valen's face as Nick pulled both the pants and underwear all the way down around his shackled ankles.

Lex grimaced, averting her eyes from the scene. She wasn't sure what she was feeling, whether she thought this was okay or not. It felt like it wasn't, but in her heart she knew this creature was a monster who'd likely hurt many other people much worse than this. Even if he felt pain, even if he felt the same shame and embarrassment humans did ... surely he'd never given his victims any consideration for those things, so why should *he* get them now that the shoe was on the other foot?

Nick started snapping photos, kneeling at points, circling around to get all angles. Valen remained strung up, quivering, exposed, following him with watery eyes.

Despite herself, Lex eventually found herself looking. He was ... attractive. It was a wholly inappropriate time to be thinking about such things, but seeing him stripped and laid bare in front of her, she felt ... urges. Which she would never act on, of course – that would be heinous, when he was in such a vulnerable position. But he looked like the kind of person who, under other circumstances, would be great to have some fun with. There was no harm in just looking, surely.

There was thumping on the stairs as Ari came back down. She paused for a moment as Nick kept clicking away on his camera. "The fuck?" she said gruffly. "I interrupt your boudoir photography session?"

Nick waved a hand dismissively, not even looking at her. "It's strictly for research purposes."

Ari huffed, continuing her labored journey down the stairs. "Well, when you're done *researching*, I managed to get ahold of Patrick."

Lex perked up. "Oh? Okay! What did you find out?"

Ari's face was stormy as her medical boot hit the cement floor. "Yeah, nothing about this guy in particular, but he recognized the family name Kithrara. They're the ones who own and operate the blood farms."

"Oh." So then it was true ... as much as she hadn't wanted to believe it, it would be foolish to continue to deny it after that final nail in the coffin.

Horrible memories flashed through Lex's mind, talons grabbing her, multiple pairs of cruel arms around her, the sound of *laughter* as she thrashed and screamed and cried. A voice telling her how juicy she looked, how delicious her blood smelled, how they couldn't wait to get her home.

This vampire she'd been so worried about was the same kind that had taken her to the blood farms all those years ago, when she'd narrowly avoided the worst fate possible. The experience that'd made her become a vampire hunter because it was so terrible, she couldn't sleep at night knowing she wasn't doing everything in her power to keep that fate from happening to as many people as possible.

Any softness and kindness she'd been giving him rotted in her mouth instantly. His tears and shaking and pleading – they were all just him not being able to take what he doled out. He was a bully. He was the *worst* kind of vampire, the worst kind of *person* in the world. His full-time job was kidnapping people for torture and slaughter, and he probably had the blood of hundreds if not thousands of people on his hands.

Lex knew that there must be vampires who weren't bad people, but this wasn't one of them.

"Do whatever you want to him, then," she said, her voice flat and emotionless. "I don't care." She wanted to care, it didn't seem right *not* to care, but she couldn't bring herself to. She wouldn't have cared even if he was a human. Although she would never want to be the one to carry it out with her own hands, she wanted him to suffer, to realize the horrors of what he'd done. To be taught a lesson.

"There you have it, then," said Nick. "Asked and answered." In stark contrast, he seemed absolutely *delighted* by this news. "No need to trouble your conscience over it." Nick's face peeled into an upsetting smile. "Thank you, Lex and Ari, for your service."

Ari glared at Nick as she hovered over Lex protectively, as though trying to shield her from the cruel reality they'd just discovered, to try and pick up the pieces of her optimism, her desire to see the good in people. "Right … Just hurry up and finish what you're doing so we can leave."

Lex came over to the cardboard box of things she'd taken from the house, a haunted look in her eyes. She uncorked the bottle of blood and poured it down the sink.

6

—⦁—

Lex felt so fucking *guilty* for telling him everything was going to be okay.

She didn't know why she'd done it. It'd seemed to make him feel better in the moment, but after that initial comfort, surely it must have made him feel infinitely worse. They'd both known it was a lie.

Nick needed someone there to supervise while the coffin was open, and who better to do that than two hunters who were injured and off-duty to recover, but still needed a paycheck?

So they were up bright and early the next day to head to the base. Ari couldn't drive because her foot was in a boot, which she was perpetually pissed off about. She always seemed to find some aspect of Lex's driving to criticize.

She hefted herself into the chair at Nick's desk, sitting down sourly. "All right. Go on ahead and do your grim work."

Lex leaned against the wall, guilt radiating through her. Valen was lying still in the coffin, fixing her with a hard glare. Lex had just sort of assumed the coffin was a temporary method of confinement, and felt a bit sick at the revelation that it was obviously now meant to be more or less permanent. It looked like the vampire was only going to be taken out when it was needed for *experiments* – whatever those would entail.

Given that sometimes Nick called it "weapons testing," she tried not to think about it too hard.

Valen growled as Nick passed by and bumped the coffin with his leg. "Thank you. Now that we're all here, I can open the coffin and start my experiments. Lex?"

Lex started as she realized he wanted *her* to open the coffin again. "Uh. Okay." She knelt and unlocked the coffin. Valen bared his teeth and growled at her, thrashing. He was much more agitated than yesterday, nostrils flaring. *Stop looking at me like that. You earned this. It's not* my *fault.*

Nick used the same pole he'd used yesterday to lift Valen out of the coffin, choking him in the process. Lex helped support his weight so it'd hurt less, then helped him move to the center of the room.

He tried to headbutt her when she attached the shackles to the ceiling again. Nick grabbed him from behind and managed to attach the chains. Valen let out a frustrated growl, trying to kick as Nick did the same for his feet.

"Come on," Lex scolded.

Valen hissed, clinking his teeth on the bit in his mouth and chuffing angrily. Nick finally managed to secure him – and then the first thing he did was pull Valen's pants down, leaving him completely exposed and vulnerable. Surely he was doing that to make Lex and Ari uncomfortable, right? Ari scowled at him. He loved to piss her off.

Valen's body trembled, his posture more scared than defiant now, but he let out an even more desperate growl.

"Yes, you're so big and scary." Nick walked to the lab bench and opened a drawer. "I'm doing an experiment I've been wanting to do for a long time now. I have some rods of varying percentages of silver alloy. I've got to test at what point silver starts to lose its effects when it's diluted with other metals."

"You're going to burn him," Ari translated flatly.

Nick glanced at her.

"This is basically torture."

"We all agreed he deserved it, didn't we?"

Ari looked away. Lex was trying not to stare at his nude form once again. Except, now that she was ...

"He already has a burn mark," she noted. A bright red line was burned into the back of his thighs.

"It must be from when you captured him."

Valen let out a muffled howl and thrashed once more. Ari narrowed her eyes.

"I also have some silver from pawn shops. Once we know how the different alloys burn, we can compare to see if they're real silver or not."

Valen hung his head, tears brimming in his eyes. Lex turned away, unable to bear looking at him anymore.

"First, the one hundred percent silver rod." Nick drew near with the rod.

Valen squeezed his eyes shut, and when he pressed the rod to Valen's stomach, the vampire let out a muffled scream and the tears spilled out. The metal sizzled like it was a red-hot pan.

Valen went limp and panted as soon as Nick pulled the rod away. He rolled the rod back into the lineup of rods, which Valen eyed with despair.

Lex sat down on the desk facing Ari, away from Valen. She couldn't bear the look on his face. "Hi," she said.

Ari turned her scowl towards Lex. "Hi."

Another scream from behind Lex, more sizzling, the smell of meat cooking. "So ... you come here often?"

The muscles in Ari's jaw twitched. "More often than I'd like."

Lex fiddled with a pencil on Nick's desk, then resorted to doodling to try and distract herself. Ari never looked away, watching Nick hatefully.

"Finally. This one is pure iron. For a negative control."

Lex turned around. Valen had a ladder-like run of burns down his chest, down to his knees. Nick touched the iron rod to his shin. Valen didn't react to this one except to shiver and sniffle, still crying freely. His eyes were glazed over and far away.

There, that hadn't taken so long. That wasn't so bad, right? Sure, it was ... a bit fucked up to do that to anyone, even a vampire, but this vampire had surely done worse. And it was useful information to have, for sure.

Nick opened another drawer and set it on the table. The old jewelry and silver trinkets inside clattered with the motion.

Oh, right. The pawned silver. Lex felt like she was going to be sick.

"I have to go to the bathroom," she said, and bolted up the stairs.

She leaned against the front door, breathing heavily with her hands over her mouth. Muffled screams and more sizzling came from downstairs. Ari gave some sardonic comment.

Lex stayed there until she heard the coffin lock shut and Ari's boot clomping up the stairs. Her face was red. Lex made eye contact with her.

"What?" Ari snapped.

"That felt ... not good."

Ari scowled and opened the front door, apparently deciding their shift was over already. "Yeah, not just for you, I bet."

***

"Nick, are you really sure there isn't some other way to test this? This ... don't feel right."

Jerome had been the one who'd spoken, but it was currently Bailey who was looking down the rifle sight at the vampire chained to the tree across the yard. In the crosshairs, he could see the vampire's terrified face, tears streaming down its cheeks through the muzzle and dripping off its chin.

"Would *you* like to test this out mid-combat, Jerome?" was Nick's answer. "With a real live vampire that will kill you or worse if it doesn't work?"

Jerome shuffled his feet awkwardly. "Well, no, but – "

"Then I suggest you keep quiet and let me run the experiments. Bailey, you may fire when ready."

Bailey's hands were clammy on the rifle stock. The vampire was sobbing so loudly it could be heard even across the distance.

He got up. "I can't do it." He walked over to Jerome, head hanging. "It don't feel right."

45

Nick rolled his eyes and picked up the rifle, bracing it against his shoulder. "Fine, then."

"It's all right, man," Jerome said softly to Bailey, taking his hand.

"I know he deserves it, but it feels bad," Bailey said. He couldn't look down-range at the victim chained to the tree, desperately clawing at the silver chains keeping him immobilized, trying to call out for help. "Like, I know it's for the greater good, but it still feels bad."

"That means you have a heart, man."

There was a *pop* as the rifle fired a dart, which landed squarely in the vampire's shoulder.

Valen's entire body went rigid and he *screamed*, an unearthly shrieking that seemed to vibrate the ground even muffled as it was by the muzzle.

"You two needn't trouble yourself about it," Nick said casually, writing something down in his notebook. "Vampires don't feel pain the same way we do. They have no need for it, since their healing factor means their body is less vulnerable to damage, and pain is just the body's signals to the brain to avert damage."

Well, there was certainly no way to avoid the damage being done to him. He tugged wildly at the chains on his arms and legs, raking his claws into the tree, teeth cracking with the force of him biting the bit from clenching his jaw. Foam dripped out of his mouth and down his chin, eyes wheeling around wildly, a cacophony of growls and pleading, desperate sounds falling from his mouth.

Nick leaned the rifle on the ground, checking his watch. "So, by my estimation, this one will take three hours to wear off. We'll have to wait until nightfall to cart it back to the lab anyway, but we have to test different distances, so I think we can spend the week repeating this until we establish the effective range."

"This is fucked, man," Bailey said.

"Bailey," Nick said tersely. "This will have a longer range than crossbows, and also the ability to incapacitate non-lethally. Doesn't that sound like an incredibly effective tool to – "

"F-fuck you," Jerome said. "Man. I'm not hanging around watching this anymore." He turned around and started to walk off.

Nick sneered at his back. "That stupid – "

"You are *not*," Bailey interrupted hotly, recognizing the tone, "about to call him a slur."

Nick stood there in stormy silence.

"What the fuck ever," Bailey said, waving to Nick dismissively as he turned to follow. "Count me out."

That left Nick standing there with the rifle, while Valen squirmed and moaned in the background. "Technically, this is breaking the rules," he called after them.

Neither of them responded.

Nick shrugged and turned back to face the tree, where his victim was still twitching, eyes bloodshot. "I guess it's just us for now, then."

***

Lex and Ari got roped into supervising Nick while the coffin was open quite a lot at the start, because they were both injured and therefore couldn't hunt and therefore were spending a lot of time sitting around the compound doing nothing in particular.

Lex was fine with this at first. She'd decided he deserved it, after all. But her stony facade broke after the first day or two. He was terrified and in pain and clearly asking for help without words.

Please stop looking at me like that. You earned this.

After what must have been a grand total of six or seven times babysitting Nick as he experimented on his vampire captive, Lex quit mid-session, staunchly refusing to ever come back.

He was a mass murderer. He was a monster in any sense of the word.

47

So why did she feel *guilty?* Every time Ari caught her crying thinking about his situation, Ari reminded her this was a vampire, and a bad one, a pitiless creature who put no value on human life, and that his captivity here was preventing him from hurting anyone else.

The *captivity* was not what made Lex feel guilty. If they had just been keeping him *captive*, Lex would have felt A-OK about that. No, it was the sounds she heard every time she passed the basement, the pitiful muffled screams and Nick's soft yet merciless voice. The rattling of chains and the sobbing she heard *every time*, because you had to pass the basement to enter and exit the building. Occasionally there would be the smell of something burning.

She tried not to think about it too much. *Just ignore it. You know he deserves it. This is an emotional reaction, not a logical one. He's a monster that's in the shape of a human to hunt more efficiently, he's like a parrot, he's mimicking the sounds that evoke the urge to help in humans.*

But she couldn't just *ignore* it when Nick started showing up to their weekly all-hands meetings to report the results of his experiments. He brought photos, which he proudly reported he developed himself in the dark room. He arranged them in a notebook alongside his notes and the results, like a ghoulish scrapbook.

The first week, he showed them all a photo of the gradient of burns from his first experiment. Nick proudly reported that he'd discovered that a weapon with a coating that was sixty percent silver and forty percent steel yielded results that weren't significantly different from a weapon that was one hundred percent silver, and since silver was getting harder and harder to find, this could save the hunters quite a lot of money. The steel also made the weapons more durable and more effective in combat.

The second week, he reported that he'd tried a variety of sedatives, poisons, and anesthetics and found that none of them were successful, as he'd suspected. He did, however, develop a type of dart that delivered a shot of silver colloid into the bloodstream, which was as close as he'd gotten to a poison and which caused seizures when administered.

The third week, he reported he'd developed a device that could replicate the effects of sunlight, which could be effective in a situation where silver bullets weren't available. Nick pointedly did not show any pictures that time. Lex later found out that was because the pictures were so incredibly graphic that even Nick knew they wouldn't be well-received; the charred flesh was so melted and burned away that bone was visible at certain points.

It went on and on like this. The experiments started to get gradually less justifiable.

I've found out vampires hold up better under extreme cold than extreme heat. It was seven minutes till loss of consciousness in flames, but three hours in an ice bath. This could be useful for choosing where to stage fights and for incorporating fire into hunting.

I've found out a vampire can hold its breath for fourteen minutes before its body begins to shut down. This could be useful if we were somehow able to trap one underwater long enough as an alternative method of subduing them.

I've found out a vampire can have forty percent of its brain removed and still remain conscious. A non-silvered weapon to the head can potentially be effective if it removes more than this.

I've found out that starving a vampire slows its healing capacity by two percent for every day it's gone without feeding, at least for open wounds. I'm still testing if this is true for broken bones.

According to my calculations, a vampire's strength is lost at a rate of about one point five percent for every day gone without feeding, judging by ability to lift objects with the pectoral muscles. Walking speed and balance are lost at three percent per day without feeding.

I've discovered that a silver bullet in the lung will immobilize as much as three elsewhere in the torso, and that bullet wounds can close up without removing the bullet.

After a week where he showed a picture that included what was *clearly* flayed skin, as well as whip marks, and was interrogated about when and why the marks had been left, Nick stopped bringing pictures.

Ari was stoic about it, but Lex knew her well enough to know how her discomfort manifested: she ruthlessly criticized every new development Nick brought to the table.

And how's that supposed to help us?

That's all you found out? Were you just sitting around with your thumb up your ass the whole week?

Big whoop, the world is saved! Three percent per day. We've got them on the run now, boys!

Nick claimed vampires didn't feel pain the same way humans did. That since they were sturdier, they didn't have any use for such a sensitive nervous system; it would only hamper their supernatural physical prowess.

Nobody was buying it. Nobody was thrilled with what Nick was doing, even though it did occasionally provide some very useful information, and even though the director – who, notably, was rarely at the actual physical location to hear the screaming – ended up being pretty pleased by it, since it led to improvements in the way they hunted vampires.

There was a reason for it, but it was still torture. And vampires didn't die easily, not at all, so there was no way for this vampire to escape it – not even by dying. It made the situation even more gruesome, knowing this vampire would be forced to endure whatever abuse was heaped onto it without concern of accidentally killing it.

Despite the fact that most of the hunters at their base had been hurt by vampires in very personal ways and hated the creatures, few of them thought *torturing* one was okay. Even the ones who found satisfaction in killing vampires did so because it meant taking out threats and serving justice. Some could call this justice ... but most wouldn't. Anyone who heard about what was happening and laughed or said *Good, that thing deserves it* immediately fell silent upon seeing the photographs and hearing the sickening sounds.

But … none of them wanted to be the one to pull the trigger on saying it needed to be stopped. Nobody wanted to be the one defending a cannibalistic serial killer. Nobody wanted the others to see them saying *This monster deserves kindness despite the earth-shattering abuse it's propagated*, but more than that, nobody wanted to carry the emotional burden of *extending* said kindness to said monster. Being a conscientious objector was easy. It was easy to walk past quickly and keep telling yourself *He deserves it he deserves it he deserves it*. Being an active participant in helping someone who'd hurt you and your family so badly was quite another matter.

Most of them were like Lex and had either been attacked, almost snatched away or taken and escaped, or had loved ones disappear. It was … hard to extend sympathy to someone who did that, even if not to them personally.

But still. The pool of humans willing to watch Nick do what he was doing shrank. About half a dozen told Nick they would from here on out refuse his requests to open the coffin the day after Lex had done so. Nick started having trouble getting enough coverage to satisfy the "two people present when the coffin is open" rule.

Lex saw Valen less and less – she avoided it on purpose – but every time she did see him, he looked worse. Eventually she refused to go down in the basement at all, and rejected Nick's requests to help bring the coffin upstairs.

She walked past the basement quickly these days. Everyone did. They tried to ignore the sounds and go about their business. They still had vampires to hunt. People to save. Most of them weren't there that often, or for that long, and the discomfort hearing it was only temporary.

Except for Lex. The guilt settled in her stomach permanently.

7

— ⋅ —

Their first hunt back on duty was a vampire working for the blood farms, rather than an individual feeding itself. They could tell because it was snatching up multiple humans instead of just one for itself. That meant it probably had a vehicle somewhere, because although a vampire could easily run at the speed of a car or carry multiple humans, it would be clumsy and cumbersome to do that for catching whole batches of humans at once, even with persuasion.

Lex and Ari were good hunters because they hunted smarter, not harder. It was why they'd been the ones to collect the live capture bounty.

They found the van within ten minutes of the alert going out about a vampire being spotted. It was a rusty, dented thing with a logo on the side – a drop of blood and a smiling, be-fanged mouth. It wasn't the first time either of them had seen the logo, not by a long shot – their own trusty van had once had it – but it never failed to give them shivers.

They pulled their own van up reasonably close to the target and waited. The vampire showed itself soon enough – and it didn't smell them because they were sitting in a gasoline-powered vehicle, and they knew from experience the scent of the lead and the exhaust masked the smell of human blood well enough. It hadn't spotted them yet either.

It had a human slung over its shoulder – the human wasn't struggling, probably because they were under persuasion. The vampire set the human down and opened the door of the van.

Ari timed the opening of her own door so that it happened at the same time, to mask the sound. Lex crawled over and slithered out of the driver's side door as well.

"Get in," the vampire told its victim gruffly. The human complied, stepping up into the van. The vampire followed, starting the process of securing them inside the van so it could go gather more victims. There was no telling how many were already inside the van.

Ari unholstered her revolver and crept towards the van. The vampire could be heard telling someone to be quiet.

Ari knelt and sighted down the barrel. Lex stepped behind a nearby tree and got ready to run.

Ari let out a sharp whistle, and when the vampire jerked its head to see what the noise had been, Ari put a shot in its throat. The sound was like a starting gun to Lex, who sprinted over, stake in one hand, silver knife in the other.

The vampire staggered out of the van, blood welling from its throat. It looked more angry than scared – but it couldn't speak, which was the most effective way to hamstring it. It glared at Ari and crouched down, clearly getting ready to pounce – when Lex arrived, slamming her knife into its chest. It let out a gasp and a savage growl.

Ari put the second shot right through its eye. Its brain exploded out the back of its head, and the creature collapsed, not dead but certainly not able to continue fighting.

Lex plunged the wooden stake into the chest of the creature, ending its life for good.

Ari stood and walked over, peering around cautiously in case there was a second one. There usually wasn't – vampires bought into the macho bullshit of not needing help even harder than humans did – but it never hurt to keep your guard up.

Ari stood out front, keeping watch as Lex ducked in and started freeing the captives. There were four of them, wide-eyed, scared, tearstained things, all of them gagged to silence them. They were tied with rope, which was simple enough to cut.

"Thank you," the first one said shakily. "Thank you. Oh my God. I thought I was done for. Holy shit."

Lex untied the gag on the second one, who gasped in relief. "You're safe now, don't worry."

Ari glanced over her shoulder at the victims. "Free van if any of you want it. Got a few bullet-holes, but seems fine otherwise. You'll have to get the logo scrubbed off. And install seat belts, I guess, since vampires don't use them."

***

Lex drove the van full of victims straight back to the hunter's compound, where they could call their families, be safe for the rest of the night, and shower the vampire hunters with the typical far-too-generous bullshit praise they usually got when they rescued someone. Ari ignored it all, as though she resented being praised.

Nick was there, on the premises as soon as he was technically allowed to be. He wasn't allowed in the building unless there was one other hunter there, since he didn't have a hunting partner and no one was allowed to be in the building alone.

He probably *did* come into the building alone, but that wasn't anyone else's problem as long as he didn't get caught doing it.

"Lex, Ari!" he said. "How was your hunt?"

"Fine," Ari said gruffly.

"I don't suppose you'd be willing to supervise me while – "

"No. Go away."

"You wouldn't have to do anything! Just kick your feet up and watch! It's just that the rules – "

"Wait until Cyril is here," Ari snapped. "Since he likes sucking your dick so much."

Nick frowned at her, then went downstairs. They heard the sound of the downstairs faucet running, then water sloshing everywhere.

The last of the vampire victims was still in the base, sitting on the couch they used for a breakroom. Her eyes were wide. "What is that?"

"He's got a vampire in the basement," Ari told her. "Doing experiments on it."

"Oh."

Cyril and Isaiah came into the base, having just arrived from the hunt. "I hear Nick in the basement," Isaiah said.

"Fuck yeah," Cyril said. "You wanna join today?"

Isaiah gave a dismissive wave. "Eh. Not in the mood today. Have fun, though." Cyril was the only one who still wanted to go down, ever.

Cyril dashed down into the basement. Isaiah went upstairs to use the shower.

The woman sitting on the couch twiddled her thumbs. There came sounds from downstairs, chains rattling and water sloshing and muffled, pleading sounds.

"Can I go watch?" she said suddenly.

Ari blinked at her. "I don't give a fuck. But it might make you throw up."

She scampered down into the basement.

Ari sat down on the couch. Scowled. Crossed her arms. Closed her eyes. Scowled. Scowled. Scowled.

Growled with irritation and got up, clomping down the stairs and into the basement.

The woman was hovering in the corner of the room, watching Nick work with wide, fascinated eyes. Cyril had his boots up on Nick's desk, leaning back and enjoying the show.

Nick had the basin sink filled up with water. And he had Valen gripped by a handful of hair, shoved face first into it, feet up off the floor.

"The fuck are you doing?" Ari said.

Nick looked up from the stopwatch he had in one hand. "I'm establishing how long a vampire can go without breathing before passing out. There's many basic details about vampires that we just don't know. Their physical limitations are completely uncharacterized."

"I bet someone in the world knows," Lex said bluntly. "There's places in the world where vampires and humans talk to each other. Some people have vampire pen pals."

Nick rolled his eyes. "Anecdotal evidence. And the integrity of foreign research is questionable, especially if vampires have any control over it."

Valen's feet started to faintly kick.

"Still awake, huh?" Nick murmured. "It's been ten minutes. Remarkable."

"Ten minutes!" said Nick's guest. She had sparkles in her eyes. "This is so cool!"

"It's not *cool*," Lex snapped. "It's a necessary evil."

"Well, I don't think it's so evil," the horrible woman Lex now regretted saving said. "I think it's justified to put a vampire through the wringer for a change. Show them how it feels to be on the other side of it for once. You know? And it doesn't even kill them, right? A vampire can survive without air for who knows how long. Freaky, right?"

"Freaky, sure. It's freaky that you want to watch. Go back upstairs."

"But you just *told* me I could come down," she protested.

"This ain't a fucking peepshow!" Ari growled. "This is serious! Get out! Go back upstairs and wait for your ride!"

The woman mounted the stairs. "Crazy dyke bitch," she muttered as she passed Ari.

"Are you done?" Cyril said. "The fuck you having a tantrum for?"

Ari crossed her arms, looking away guiltily.

"Fuck off, Cyril," Lex said.

Nick ignored their sniping at each other, watching the stopwatch.

He pulled Valen's head out of the tub, revealing that he'd gone entirely limp, wet hair plastered on his face.

"Not as long as I expected," Nick said. "But I guess we'll need more replicates."

Valen came to life, chest shuddering, coughing violently. Water spilled from his mouth around the muzzle as he hacked miserably to try and get it all out.

Nick let Valen fall wetly onto the floor, where the vampire collapsed onto his side, still heaving in great, gulping breaths. Nick clicked his pen and started to write. "Subject went eleven point five minutes without air before she – "

"He." Lex said it before she could think about it.

Nick paused. "What?"

"The vampire is a *he*."

Nick glanced over at Valen. Topless, body hair mostly gone. His face had gotten a lot softer, his facial hair disappeared. Whatever testosterone treatment he'd been giving himself must have worn off. He looked very female. "Um. No, I don't think so."

"He's transsexual."

Nick gave Lex a patronizing smile. "Okay." He went back to his notes. " – without air before she – "

"Valen is a *he*," Lex insisted.

Valen glared at her.

"Fine," Nick said. "If you won't drop it. Without air before he stopped responding."

Lex looked smug. Valen gave Lex a look like he was trying to set her on fire with his mind. He tugged at his restraints.

"I'd think you know what a woman looks like," Cyril said. "Considering your, um. Y'know. Lifestyle."

"Yeah and I'd imagine you *don't* know what a woman looks like," Ari savaged him, "considering no woman willingly gets within a hundred yards of you."

Cyril scowled. Nick smirked and clicked his pen. "If the two of you would like to help – "

"We don't."

"Well, I have about ten pounds of ice in my car that you could help me carry down. I have some temperature experiments to run after this."

8

— • —

There was only so long you could go ignoring it. The months dragged on, interspersed with blips of discomfort, with valiant attempts to ignore Nick, until –

"Oh, Lex, Ari, while you're here, I was wondering. I don't suppose you'd be able to bring me back another live catch sometime? I'm not sure how much more use I'll be able to get out of this one."

Lex turned back from where she'd tried to hurry past the basement to get out the front door. She looked at Nick, at the top of the stairs, the open door letting out the deranged wailing from downstairs.

"What the fuck is that supposed to mean?" said Ari.

Nick wrung his hands. "Well, it's in a state of starvation, which means it takes much, much longer for injuries to heal. It's not really a pace I can work with to do experiments anymore. And I'm positive the director won't consent to us feeding it."

They'd had plenty of opportunities to repeat their feat in the intervening months. They'd nabbed about one kill per week, but they'd never even discussed trying to take another vampire alive. Not after they'd seen what happened to the first one.

Ari sneered at him. "It's not our fault if you broke your toy. You're not getting another one. Come on, Lex, we've got shit to do."

"Wait!" said Nick. "Hold on, please." He clasped his hands together. "*Please* will you help me today, just this once, I know you said you wouldn't, but *nobody* has been around *all week* to open the coffin with me. I need to clean him off."

Lex wavered. Clean him off? That ... sounded okay, actually. If he was dirty enough that *Nick* agreed he needed to be cleaned, it probably *felt* horrible and washing him would be doing him a favor.

Ari clucked her tongue, clearly thinking the same thing. "Well ... all right, fine. I'll do it. Lex, you don't have to if you don't wanna."

"I'll help."

They followed Nick downstairs. The pathetic warbling sounds got louder as they descended.

God, the creature in the coffin was almost unrecognizable. He was rail fucking thin and covered in a layer of grime ... it looked to be mostly blood, based on where it was, streaks of it below still-open wounds. It looked like his pants had been lost in the intervening months, dressed in only the now equally grimy boxer briefs, and a heavy metal collar around the neck had been added. It was padlocked shut, but there was a handle at the front – an easy way to lift him up out of the coffin, perhaps? He was ... starting to smell. Lex nearly gagged.

"Thank you so much," said Nick with relief. "I really cannot continue anything until he's been cleaned up. It's interfering with measurements. Here, if you would be so kind as to unlock the cage and bring him over here."

He handed the key to Ari, then came over to the basin sink and unrolled a hose from underneath it. "There," he said, and pointed to the drain in the floor. "Just position him right on there, if you please, this won't take very long at all."

Lex's heart sank, guilt coming back. She wasn't sure what she'd expected, but of course Nick would just hose him off. Surely it wouldn't be comfortable. The water would probably be cold. Well ... he would probably feel better once it was over, right?

Ari stared at Nick, the hose in his hand dripping. "All right," she said, and she knelt, unlocking the coffin and creaking the lid open.

The vampire's eyes were unfocused and lifeless. He was already shaking and whimpering. Ari reached down and grabbed the handle on the collar around his neck, lifting him out with ease – it was unsettling how little he appeared to weigh.

It didn't seem to hurt at all, but Valen brought his hands, which were shackled in the front of his body, up in front of him, curling his head away, as though to shield himself from a blow.

Ari clicked her tongue, looking down at the pathetic, trembling, grimy stick of a man in her hand. "All right," she said, and she knelt down, pressing her shoulder into his midsection, draping him over her shoulder. She stood, carrying him like a sack of potatoes and starting to go up the stairs.

"Um," said Nick. "Ari, where are you – "

"I'm taking him to the bathroom," Ari snapped. "Because I can tell it would upset Lex if you did it like that."

Lex nearly bounced in excitement, following Ari. Nick quickly moved to intercept them. "Hold on," he said, blocking the door. "I insist we do it in the basement."

"Nick."

"Y-yes?"

Ari lifted one foot up slightly. "Do you see this foot?"

"Y ... yes?"

"I just got it out of a boot. But I *will* break it off in your ass if I have to. Get out of the way."

Wringing his hands, Nick stepped to the side.

Lex's face was about even with Valen's, in the small of Ari's back. His hair drooped over his face to cover most of it, bobbing silently with each step Ari took, but she could see his desperate, tired eyes looking at her.

This time, she suppressed the instinct to tell him everything was going to be okay.

As they came up onto the first floor, a sudden realization struck Lex, and she dashed over and closed the blinds. The hunters who'd been talking in the living room fell silent with a questioning look.

"Don't worry about it," huffed Ari, pivoting and going up the second set of stairs to the second floor. Valen started whining again, eyes wheeling around, as though the mere stimulation of being in a different environment was overwhelming.

"Shh," said Lex, and then bit her tongue. *Don't. Don't tell him it's okay. He definitely hates you.*

The bathroom door was closed, the sound of water in the sink behind it. Ari pounded on the door. "Yo!"

"Geez, what?" said Bailey's voice from inside it.

"Get out. We need to use the bathroom."

The faucet squeaked off, the sound of towels ruffling. The door opened, showing Bailey's disgruntled face. "Geez, fine." His face twisted when he saw the vampire, and he skittered out of the way.

Lex filed into the bathroom after Ari. She turned around to see Nick following them. "Now – now listen, we should make this quick, because – "

Lex shut the door in his face, then locked it.

Ari had sat Valen down on the toilet and started running the water in the shower. "Go ahead, Lex. Since I can tell you want to."

Lex approached Valen like he was a wary cat. He shrank back. "Shh," she said. "Hey, I'm not going to hurt you. Do you want to take a shower?"

He looked at her foggily.

She took his elbow. "Can you stand up for me?"

He didn't start to move until a second hand on his back gave him a gentle push. His knees trembled as he stood. He caught a glimpse of himself in the mirror above the sink – vampires had reflections in modern mirrors that were backed with aluminum instead of silver – and startled violently, falling over.

"All right, you're okay," said Lex soothingly, helping him lean on the counter. "Just relax."

"You don't have to talk to him like he's a puppy, Lex. He's still a serial killer, he doesn't really deserve what we're doing, so – "

"Wh – " Lex sputtered. "You're the one who brought him upstairs!"

"Only because you made me!"

"Wh-uh – no, I didn't! You did that all on your own."

"The look on your face was enough."

Lex rolled her eyes. "Sure, okay, Ari. You don't care at all. Got it."

"Hmmph." Ari stuck her hand in the stream of water, testing the temperature, then wiped her hand on her shirt. "All right, that should be good."

Lex turned back to Valen. "Do you want to take your underwear off?" she said gently. His chest heaved in and out with panicked breaths. "You don't have to. But I'll clean them for you if you want."

With shaking hands, Valen brought both cuffed hands to his left hip, sliding his underwear down, then repeating it on the right hip until they could drop to his ankles, on top of the ankle cuffs.

"All right, you're doing great," said Lex, and she knelt. "Ari, do you have a handcuff key?"

Ari took out a keyring and handed it to her. She unlocked the manacles around his ankles, then stood, supporting him by the elbow again. "All right."

She helped him step out of the ankle cuffs and underwear, leaving him completely nude except for handcuffs and the muzzle. God, this was horrific, the sheer number of injuries on his body. The newest ones appeared to be the series of cuts at regular intervals going up his arms and legs, along with some fresh burns, but there were a lot of older burns underneath those. Nick hadn't been exaggerating about his rate of healing slowing down. No wonder Nick wanted another one. His body looked a little bit like he'd been put through a woodchipper.

Ari put a hand on Lex's shoulder and whispered in her ear. "Should we just kill him?"

Valen's breath hitched and he flinched repeatedly, leaning away from both of them.

"No!" said Lex.

"Are you saying that because you're thinking of his best interests, or your own?"

She looked at Valen. The pitiful creature just braced himself on the sink, head drooping. "Well ... " said Lex. "I mean, we could ask him."

He raised his head at this, a look of panic on his face as they both looked at him expectantly.

"Do you want us to kill you?" Lex said softly. "We'll make it painless. If you want it ... to just end."

Valen's body hitched in a rapid-fire series of gasping breaths, and then he steeled himself and slowly nodded.

Ari put her hand to her mouth. "Shit. Okay. All right."

Lex grimly took his elbow and turned him around to face Ari. Ari reached into her belt pouch and took out a wooden stake.

"It'll be fast," said Lex. "Then the pain will all be over."

Tears spilled over in Valen's eyes as Ari steadied the stake over his chest, resting the point over his heart. He suddenly flinched away, raising his hands, shaking his head, letting out muffled whimpers, squeezing his eyes shut.

Lex put her other arm around his back to steady him. His skin was cold and she could feel his bones. "Did you ... change your mind?"

He nodded vigorously, quivering.

Ari sighed, slipping the stake back into her belt. "Okay, then. Let's just forget that and wash you off."

Trying to forget his waffling on the matter of mercy killing, she guided him towards the shower. He kept his hands folded up in front of his chest, looking at the water as though it might bite him. Lex wrapped a hand around his wrist and extended his hand into the stream of water. "How's that?"

He didn't respond.

"Too hot? Too cold?"

He shook his head.

"Up you get, then."

Even with Lex helping him keep his balance, he didn't lift his foot high enough to clear the rim of the tub and tripped, falling headfirst into the shower. Lex redoubled her grip, pulling him right-side up as the shower waterfalled over his soggy form.

"How about a bath, then," said Ari behind her.

Lex sighed and pulled the valve to change the flow of water to the bottom faucet, then plugged the tub. "Jesus Christ, Ari, he can barely *stand*." This skeletal creature that couldn't look at them without flinching was a far cry from the dangerous predator they had subdued and gotten their bones broken by.

The only part of that predator that was left was what was in front of them, a starving, bleeding, miserable thing that hadn't been allowed to open its mouth in months and existed only to be battered well past the point at which a less resilient creature would have died, unable to escape starvation and torture even through death.

Nick's voice was at the door. "Is everything quite all right in there?"

"Yeah," said Ari.

"How much longer are you going to be? I have timepoints that, ideally – "

"Don't come in, we're having gay sex."

Lex helped Valen sit back in the tub as the water rose up around his thighs. "There we go," she cooed. "Does that feel good?"

He silently brought his cuffed hands to rest on the bathtub rim.

"Here," said Lex, laying the bar of soap next to them. "You can do it yourself, if you want."

He looked at the bar of soap like he couldn't remember what it was. His hands weakly fumbled with it, and it slipped down into the tub.

"Okay, that's okay," said Lex, noting that it looked like he was about to start crying again. "You're doing great." She retrieved the keyring again and brought his wrists forward.

"Be careful," said Ari in a warning tone as Lex unlocked his wrists.

"Come on," said Lex, "he's clearly not in any state to do much of anything."

She set the handcuffs on the sink, then twisted back towards Valen. He was bringing his hands shakily up towards the muzzle.

"No," said Lex softly. "I'm sorry, that has to stay on."

He let out a pitiful whine like a dog, face scrunching up.

Lex gently grabbed his wrists and lowered his hands down into the soap and water. "I'm sorry. That has to stay on. I'm sorry." She twisted to look at Ari, voice tinged with desperation. "Are you sure we can't take the muzzle off?"

Ari sighed and sat on the toilet. "Lex, you know he could just open his mouth and tell us to kill each other, and we'd have to do it."

"He ... he might not. He might not want to do that."

"If he didn't before, he certainly does *now*."

Lex looked at his hopeless expression, staring down into the bathwater, which had already turned reddish brown.

"Okay," said Lex, getting up. "All right, let's clean you up, then."

There was a detachable showerhead, so Lex removed it and snaked it down over his head, unplugging the drain and letting the water wash over him for a few minutes, the murky residue swirling down the drain. He made vague motions to rub the bar of soap over himself like he wasn't sure he was allowed to do it.

"There you go," said Lex. She plugged the tub again, now that most of the gunk was gone and the water wouldn't instantly get completely dirty. "You're already looking a little bit better."

She let the tub fill up and walked over to the sink, picking his underwear up off the floor. She tried not to look too hard at what exactly it was soiled with as she set it in the sink and let the water run over it, adding some soap. Not the best way to wash clothes, but it would do.

Out of the corner of her eye, she saw Valen's hands move towards his face again. "No," said Ari flatly. "Don't try it."

The hands slowly lowered back into the water.

Ari reached over and turned the water off once the tub was full, plunging them into the warm, comfortable silence of a steamy bathroom. Lex let him soak in there for a while and wrung out his underwear, which was much cleaner despite the lackluster wash. She got a damp cloth and wiped the manacles too, which were crusty with dried blood and some sort of grimy ash and who knows what else.

She came back over to the bathtub and knelt. "Do you want me to help rub the soap on your back and stuff?"

He nodded slowly.

She lathered some suds onto her hands. Despite the gentleness in her touch, he flinched when her palms landed on the bony vertebrae creating ridges on his skin.

"There we go," she cooed. "It feels nice, right?" He didn't respond. She lifted the metal collar on his neck to wipe underneath it, running a finger around. His skin was warmer now, after soaking for a bit. She got the shampoo bottle off the floor. "Close your eyes for me."

He did so, shaking with anticipation now that he could not see. She squeezed some shampoo out onto the top of his head, which startled him. His white hair was stained nearly pink from the blood in some places. She worked it into a lather on his scalp. He went limp, face melting into relaxation. A clump of hair came out in her hand, and she grimaced and wiped it on the wall. He didn't seem to notice.

"All right, I'm going to touch your face, don't be surprised by it. Just keep your hands down there." She rubbed some soap on her hands and slid a finger around the muzzle. The metal parts of the device were padded with leather where it touched him, so it wouldn't burn him, but there were still inflamed, angry patches of skin where it'd been chafing from months of continuous wear.

Lex loosened the strap on the muzzle. Just one notch. It was barely enough to make a difference, but he sighed with relief and teared up. She got one finger down between the muzzle and the skin, rubbing the irritated flesh. She could feel his jaw working at the bit under her hands. "Sorry," she said. "I'm sorry we can't take it off. You know you have to keep it on."

He sagged.

"All right, let's rinse you off." Lex stood and retrieved the showerhead again, setting it to a gentle stream. He closed his eyes and leaned into it, water streaming down his back.

The faucet squeaked as she turned it off. She looked down at him. He still looked pretty fucking gnarly with all his injuries, open cuts layered over old bruises and half-healed wounds, not to mention him being very visibly in a state of starvation that humans couldn't even reach and still be alive and moving around. But he was *clean*, and no matter how miniscule the comfort had been, it must have been the first he'd received in months, and he clearly appreciated it.

"Okay," said Lex. "You did so good. Now, let's just get you dried off, and then we'll go back downstairs, okay?"

He burst into sobs instantly, leaning into Lex's knees, wet hands twisting in the fabric of her pants as he desperately clung to her.

"Oh," said Lex. "Oh, shhh, shhh, it's okay, it'll be okay ... "

"Alex," Ari snapped, and both Valen and Lex looked at her sharply. "Don't."

"What?"

Ari sighed in irritation and came over, squatting next to Valen. He still pressed into Lex, loathe to let go of her.

She locked eyes with him. He let out a tiny whimper of fear.

"Hey," said Ari. "It's *not* okay. I know it's not okay. I know it's not all right for you right now. It's actually pretty fucked up right now. But me and Lex are going to see if we can make things a little better, okay?"

His grip on Lex tightened.

"All you have to do is hang in there just a bit longer. Can you do that for me?"

He nodded morosely, even as he continued to white-knuckle Lex's thighs.

Ari smiled. "Great." She tossed a towel on top of his head. "Dry yourself off, then."

Lex helped him sit up on the lip of the tub and lent a hand to towel him off. Ari found a blow-dryer under the sink, and Lex used it to dry off his hair and the skin under the muzzle and the collar.

"All right," said Ari, holding both pairs of cuffs. "Sorry, but it's time these go back on. We can't hide in the bathroom forever."

Face drooping sadly, Valen held his wrists out. Ari fastened them, then knelt and did the same for his ankles.

"Do you want me to carry you back down, or can you walk yourself?"

He didn't move, didn't meet her gaze.

"I'll take that as a vote for carrying." She leaned him onto her shoulder again, picking him up and steadying him with a hand across the back of the legs.

Nick wasn't there when they came out, surprisingly. That gave them a moment of reprieve as they walked back down the stairs.

"Everything all right?" Bailey said warily as they emerged onto the first floor.

"Just peachy," said Ari, knocking the basement door open with her foot. "Just right as rain."

Nick was downstairs at the furnace, handling something with gloves and tongs. "Ah, there you are, thank you so much, just what I needed ... While you're here, while we have him out, I could, perhaps, just very quickly get data from this timepoint – "

He pulled a stone cup of glowing molten silver out of the furnace, holding it at a distance. "I'm testing the effects of silver on wound healing, you see – "

The cuts up his arms and legs, the fact that some of them had burn marks and some didn't – to compare them. Nick wanted to fucking pour *molten silver* into the open wounds.

Lex looked over at Ari, who was standing there with a horrified expression on her face, to see that Valen was squirming on her shoulder, twisting and writhing as though he could run away.

The coffin lid was still open behind Ari, and she turned around and dumped him inside of it, not even fastening the restraints to keep him secured to the sides before closing it and locking it.

"Ariana, I need – I need him outside of it to – "

"Sure thing." Ari held the key to the coffin out like she was going to hand it to him, then yanked her hand back and put it in her own pocket. "But, you know, I just remembered there's somewhere I gotta be real fast, so maybe I'll come back later and help you with that."

Ari pushed Lex up the stairs, then when they were at the top, she turned and made eye contact with Nick before shutting the basement door.

"Sick fuck," she muttered.

Lex followed her as she stomped into the kitchen. "Ari – what are you – what were you thinking we would do to help him?"

Ari ran a hand through her hair, letting out a breath. "Ummm ... Well, okay, I know a good place to start." She walked over to the corded phone hanging from the wall and picked it up.

"And for the record," she insisted, holding one finger up. "I'm only doing this because *you're* clearly upset by it. *I* don't care at all."

Lex suppressed a smile.

Ari turned and ran her finger over the important phone numbers posted next to the phone, then dialed, waiting. Then: "Yeah, Jenny? Hey, what's up. Is Director Griswald in his office today?"

9

_— · —_

It was easy enough to get past the secretary – they hadn't made an appointment to talk to the director like they were supposed to, but Jenny had told them he was free at three and she would pencil them in on short notice. The fact that Lex was pretty and batted her eyelashes at Jenny probably helped.

Jenny walked down the hallway and approached the door with a plaque that said:

Dir. Dalton Griswald
Department Director
Dept. of Nocturnal Security

"Your three o'clock is here," Jenny said, cracking the door open, then she opened it wide and gestured them inside. Director Griswald sat behind his desk, important-looking paperwork spread all over it in front of him.

Lex's eyes swept up and down him. She barely ever saw him, and was struck afresh by how intimidating he looked each time. He was a solid, tall man with a serious expression, accentuated by the scarring on the side of his neck: two telltale puncture wounds sitting in a web of white scar tissue, indicating they had been reopened many times.

"Yo, Director G," said Ari, plopping down into a chair and setting her boots up on his desk. "We gotta talk about something."

The director looked a bit peeved, but said nothing. Lex took the second chair more primly, crossing her hands on her lap. "We've met before, right? We interviewed with you when we were recruited."

The director's face broke into a smile. "Oh yes! Alexis and Ariana, I remember you now! Nick told me you were the ones who brought him the live capture. Excellent work, very good."

"Yeah," said Ari gruffly, "that's what we wanted to talk to you about, actually." She leaned forward and rifled through the candy dish on the director's desk, taking out a lollipop and sticking it in her mouth, chewing on it. "Shit's fucked, DG. It ain't right."

" ... What do you mean?"

"Nick is torturing him," said Lex. "It's inhumane. It's not moral to do that to a living being. We wanted to talk with you about putting a stop to it."

"We treat animals better than that," said Ari.

The director tented his hands and leaned forward. "Vampires are not animals, Ariana."

" ... I'm aware."

"Vampires are neither animals nor humans. They're dangerous creatures capable of rational thought, but not morals. They know what they're doing is wrong, but they choose to do it anyway, and they don't feel bad about it. So forgive me if I'm not sympathetic to one's plight."

"It's not about sympathy," said Ari. "Trust me, I'm not sympathetic either. I wouldn't be here unless Lex made me come. It's just basic morality. It's just not right to do that to any living creature, no matter how evil it is."

The director folded his hands. "You've never seen the blood farms, have you?"

"I was almost sent there," said Lex angrily. "I was *right* outside the blood farms, about to be delivered, before I was rescued."

"But you were *outside.*"

Lex still had nightmares about it. The cruel laughter of the vampires delivering her. The plume of black smoke from the smokestack of the building out the barred window of the truck.

"Yes," she said icily. "I was outside."

"You weren't *in* one. Everyone who's been kept in vampire territory for a significant amount of time can testify that their cruelty is breathtaking. If you'd been kept there for longer than a few hours, you would probably change your tune."

"Lex just said   *no matter how evil it is,*" said Ari. "What are you saying?"

"I'm saying it's idealistic, but unrealistic, to have such lofty ideas like that. This is an extreme situation, so extreme measures are warranted. That creature was here to steal humans. The depravity needed to condemn masses of people to such a fate by your own hand without remorse ... This vampire has forfeited whatever version of humanity applies to it."

"I'm not sure if you understand how bad it is," said Lex. "There are pictures – "

"I've seen the pictures."

"You've ... seen the pictures."

"And it doesn't bother you?" Ari snapped, aggravated.

"Of course it bothers me. I'm not a sadist. I'll admit, at first I was resistant to the idea too. But I think, in this situation, it's a case of the ends justifies the means. The results speak for themselves."

Lex felt guilty. She'd noticed that Nick *had* been improving the weapons and gadgets he'd been designing for the organization. They had better knives, more silver bullets, and things like tranquilizer darts. Nick's work was paying off, despite that ... some of it was probably less than necessary.

He shuffled the paperwork on his desk. "In the intervening months, the vampire hunters have killed an additional thirteen vampires beyond expectations from before Nick's innovation started, and saved an additional twenty-six human lives. That's just in our county. For this period of time, we would have expected four or five pairs of hunters to be killed in the line of duty, and that number in the past few months has been one."

"One?"

"One pair of hunters killed. Nick's findings are making vampire hunting more effective and safer for us. Now, I don't take the thought of human experimentation – er, vampire experimentation, I mean – lightly. But I would gladly trade the life of one vampire – and the life of one of the *worst* kinds of vampire that exists – for a few dozen innocent human lives. Wouldn't you?"

Ari was stone-faced. He looked at her. "Ariana?"

Ari sneered and leaned in, rolling the lollipop from one side of her mouth to the other with her tongue. "Only my mother calls me Ariana."

"Well, I apologize. But the point still stands."

"Surely there must be some *other* way to do those experiments."

"I doubt it. Having a live test subject right there can't really be replaced in terms of special weapons development."

"But," said Lex weakly, unable to mount a defense. "It's – it's so cruel. I don't think anything justifies that. I-I know it makes sense to try to save more people, but – but, I – "

"I understand what you're saying. I really do," said the director. "And I think it's very noble of you to raise the complaint. But I authorized Nick to carry out those experiments, and I'm not going to tell him to stop. In fact ... "

His hand slid into his desk and brought out a checkbook. " ... Nick told me to keep up his pace of work, he would need a second live capture. I'd be willing to increase the bounty for a repeat of your feat. I know you find it distasteful, so I'd make it worth your while."

Ari narrowed her eyes. "How much?"

"Twenty thousand."

Her eyebrows flew up. That was ... quite a number. They could pay off the house with that.

"Half up front. If you agree, you walk out with a check today."

"No," said Lex, while the candy in Ari's mouth crunched. Lex looked over at her. She had a stormy look on her face. Lex could tell she was considering it. "We can't."

Ari pinched the lollipop stick between her fingers like it was a cigarette and stubbed it on the desk. "We will discuss it and get back to you later."

"I-I won't," said Lex. She stood. "I won't be part of an organization that does such things. I – I'll resign on the spot if you don't – "

"Lex," snapped Ari. "Stop."

"You can't – can't expect me to go along with – "

"I'm not expecting you to *anything* besides talk about it *later*. We're obviously not gonna change the director's mind on this, and quitting won't fix anything." Ari stood, reaching out to the candy dish and taking a handful of suckers, sticking them in her pocket. "We'll be in touch."

Lex was on the verge of tears as Ari took her arm and dragged her out. Ari closed the door to the office behind her and waved to Jenny on the way out.

Only when they were out in the parking lot did Lex wrench her hand out of Ari's grasp. "How could you!" she cried. "Ari, you can't sell your soul like that! Kidnapping people to bring them back for horrible torture is what *they* do! That's why we fight them!"

Ari made tight, aggravated gestures, voice strained and impatient. "I *know*, that's why I thought we should get out of the office without making a *scene*, because if we make a big *stink* about how much we disapprove, then it's gonna raise *suspicion* for when we *later* go do some shady shit the director doesn't *want* us to, if you catch my drift."

" ... Oh?"

Ari smiled wickedly, unlocking the doors to the van. "I mean, I just kind of assumed we would be sneaking back in later tonight, when everyone else was gone. Since you're forcing my hand and all."

10

— • —

"I can't believe you're making me do this."

"For the millionth time, this was your own idea."

"Yeah, well, it's not my fault you needed someone to step in and tell you how to get from point A to point B. *You* were just going to quit and walk away. And then down the road when you were pissing and moaning about how guilty you felt leaving him there, it'd be my fault."

"Ari, it's okay to just admit you care."

Ari's hands tightened on the steering wheel. "That thing is a monster that deserves what it gets."

"Yeah, that's why it's so noble to want to help it."

Lex could tell Ari viewed her own feelings of compassion as weakness. As though she had to be as emotionless and cold as the creatures they fought.

"Twenty thousand," Ari growled. "That stupid vampire better be grateful. Twenty thousand. I've never been offered that much money for anything. I've never *had* that much money. I'm an idiot for doing this."

"An idiot with a conscience."

"I'm positive that thing is just going to try and kill us anyway."

"Maybe he's learned his lesson."

"A serial killer does not *learn their lesson*, Lex, it's a fundamental problem with the way they view the world and other people. I'm not even sure if a vampire *can* think the same way as a person."

Lex tapped her fingers. "Well ... I guess we'll see. He was pretty docile earlier. What, ah ... what are you thinking we'll do, exactly?"

Ari sat in stormy silence.

"Babe?"

"I don't know," she admitted grumpily. "I haven't figured it out yet, okay? We gotta do *something* though."

Lex bit her lip. "Right ... it's not like we can just let him go."

"And he doesn't want to die – "

"And we can't take the muzzle off – "

"And it's probably not safe to take him out of the house – " Ari sighed. "Okay, so what's our goal here? Ideally, we want to stop Nick from torturing him. Which is going to be a problem, because he's here *specifically* to be tortured by Nick, because apparently there's no *humane* way to carry out the experiments. What options does that leave us?"

"We could just steal him."

"What, take him back to our house?"

"I guess?"

"That wouldn't solve the problem of him being fucking starving, though. We can't feed him as long as he can't open his mouth, which is something we need for *our* own safety. No persuasion from him. Absolutely not. *Especially* now that he has *plenty* of reason to hate all of us, if he didn't already."

"We could get a cup of blood and use a straw. It might fit through."

Ari groaned. "I guess, but then what? We just have a vampire in our house for the rest of our lives using us as a Capri Sun? Keeping him locked in the basement out of sight because we can't let the hunters know we have him? That hardly seems better than just killing him."

"He might prefer that. We could ask him."

Ari banged her hand on the steering wheel. "I fucking hate this. I hate that it's on *us* to figure out how to comfort this monster."

Lex looked over and saw tears in Ari's eyes. Her thoughts were clear. *If we don't, nobody will.*

And was that okay? If nobody did? It was gradually sinking in for Lex that she wasn't okay with that, and clearly Ari wasn't either, despite both of them instinctually feeling that a creature like the one locked in the basement didn't deserve their help – and that it was probably stupidly dangerous to try and help, anyway.

She'd felt morally superior for walking out, but walking out had been the easy thing to do. It'd just spared her from having to watch. Out of sight, out of mind. It'd helped her, but hadn't changed the situation at all. It made her feel cowardly and weak now that she realized the depths of torture she'd condemned this creature to for the past few months. Not having the stomach to look the violence in the eye didn't make her *better.*

All he'd needed to move him to grateful tears had been a warm bath and loosening the muzzle one notch. Maybe he'd changed. Maybe he'd realized the harm he'd done. Maybe he would just be grateful enough to Lex and Ari for saving him that he would listen to them. Everyone deserved a chance. Surely torturing him more wouldn't do anything – either he'd learned to see the value of human life, or he hadn't.

And even if he hadn't changed at all, no one deserved this, not even a monster. He was still a living creature. Besides ... he was barely a threat anymore. He couldn't even stand on his own in the shower. And it's not like they were going to let him go free to hurt other people. Just ... try to improve the situation somewhat.

But ... how?

"I kind of wish we'd just killed him," said Lex glumly.

Ari grimaced. "Yeah ... "

They both sighed, watching the car eat up the road in front of them.

Ari pulled down the visor to block the light as they headed straight into the setting sun. "Well, maybe we'll fucking figure something out."

***

They were still arguing by the time they got there. They normally didn't argue this much; the guilt and stress they'd managed to suppress until now were getting to them.

They fell silent as they pulled their van in front of the hunter's compound, next to a white sedan they both recognized.

"What is ... what is Nick doing here?" said Lex. It wasn't unusual for vampire hunters to be active at night, obviously, but Nick was the *one* vampire hunter in this compound that didn't have a partner and therefore was not allowed to go into the field or be in the compound alone. Which he would be, since his was the only other vehicle there.

Ari stormily shut the car off, kicking her door open. "I have a hunch."

The front door opened as Ari got to the porch. Nick tried to hurry out the door, but Ari blocked it with an arm. "Hey, Nick."

"Oh, ah, hello," said Nick.

"What are you doing here?"

Nick held up a notebook. "I was, ah, doing some late-night work at home and realized I forgot my notes. So I just came to get them. In and out – "

"Because you know it's not allowed for anyone to be in the compound alone. Always at least two people together. That's the rule when anywhere on vampire business. Too dangerous to be alone. Especially now that there's a live vampire inside the place."

Nick sweated a bit. "Ah, I understand, but I really was just coming in quickly to – "

Ari leaned in, sneering. "I *know* you weren't here to try and get in some private time with your little toy in the basement, because *that* would be against the *rules*, and fucked up, and if that were the case, there would be consequences from the director, I'm sure, so you *wouldn't* do that."

Nick forced his face into a tight smile. "Well, Ariana, if you *recall*, I don't have the key to the coffin. *You* have the key to the coffin. So if *anyone* was going to open the coffin in secret, it would be *you*. I'm sure the *director* wouldn't be happy about *that*."

Ari's eyes and demeanor were that of a demented hyena in the face of a wounded lion. "Well, Lex and I aren't breaking any *rules*. Only one of us is breaking the rules, and it ain't *us*."

"Ariana – "

"Call me Ariana again," said Ari, slamming her hand on the doorframe so hard the windowpanes rattled, "and I'll kick you in the balls so hard your grandchildren will feel it."

Nick held his notebook up like a shield, frozen.

"Go. Home."

When Ari removed her arm, Nick scuttled away into his car. Nick's headlights came on and swung away as he backed out. Lex slunk up behind Ari. "Was that really necessary?"

Ari huffed. "No, but it made me feel better."

Lex turned the lights back on as she stepped into the base. "Okay, um ... "

Ari closed the door and locked it. "Yeah?"

"We still haven't decided what to do."

This had never happened before. Usually together they were able to come up with *something*, or if they disagreed, they just talked about it until one of them caved.

Ari clucked her tongue. "Well ... maybe something will come to us."

Lex pushed the basement door open and flicked that light on as well. The ghastly, battered creature in the coffin was lying facedown, but on the cue of the light, he rolled over, whining pitifully and sticking his hands through the bars of the lid as far as he could, until the chain on the cuffs caught against the bar.

"All right," said Lex, coming down the stairs. "Don't worry, we're going to help you."

When she reached the bottom of the stairs, she took one of the bony hands offered through the cage. It was shockingly cold, but she kept it in her own.

Ari huffed, coming down behind her. "All right, listen, Dracula. I'm not Lex. I'm not gonna bullshit you about how it's all gonna be okay, but we know this is fucked up and we're here and we're trying to figure out how to fix it."

The relief on his face was palpable.

"I'm sorry," said Lex. "I'm sorry we let this happen. This wasn't at all what we were imagining when we brought you here."

Ari knelt and unlocked the coffin. He seemed to not want to let go of Lex's hand, even as Ari tilted the lid of the cage open. "All right, come on, buddy," she said.

Valen looked at her with panic, both hands still reaching through the top, grabbing Lex. It was like a cat crying to be let out in front of a door that was already open.

Ari sighed and stuck her hand in towards him. "How about you take my hand? Can you do that?"

He shakily let go of Lex and grabbed onto her, like a man afraid he would drown if not holding onto someone for too long.

"All right, easy now, just relax." Ari's cooing was nowhere near as comforting as Lex's, much more gruff and rough, but Lex knew from experience that tone combined with strong hands holding you could do a lot. She hefted Valen up, moving him into a sitting position, then gently lifting him up under the armpits to get him to stand.

Lex supported him by the elbow and helped him step out of the coffin. He quivered, a walking skeleton in their hands, shuffling with his ankles chained together and his wrists bound in front of him.

"God," said Lex, once again taking in the emaciated, ravaged state of his body. "I still can't believe this. I can't believe *any* creature could go through all this and not die."

Valen flinched, trembling redoubling, eyes wheeling around the room.

"We're not going to hurt you," Lex soothed. "Just relax."

Ari pulled a chair out from Nick's desk and turned it around. "Here, go ahead and sit down."

Valen's bones creaked as he did so, awkwardly, as though he couldn't remember how to use a chair.

"Hmph," said Ari. "The fucking furnace is still warm. Just getting his notebook, my ass. I'm not leaving him alone where Nick can get to him again." She leaned forwards and put her chin on her hand. "Okay, listen, Dracula, I'm kind of at a loss here. You know we can't just let you go, and you know we can't just take the muzzle off, even if you promise nicely that you won't use persuasion. We talked to the director, and he said he's not going to make Nick stop. You already said you don't want us to kill you, and we can't just take you to our house, but we can't just leave you here either. So." She spread her hands. "You gotta work with us here."

The vampire fidgeted.

Lex sighed. "Hey, Ari, we both agree that thing Nick said about not letting him write was bullshit, right? Like, that was definitely something he made up so Valen couldn't communicate with us?"

Ari gave a disgusted sigh. "Yeah. For sure. He either made that up, or exaggerated it. I never seen any vampire use persuasion through writing." She hadn't seen many vampires write at all, since her only interactions with them were in deadly combat, but that was besides the point. The only kinds of persuasion she'd ever seen were eye contact and spoken speech ... and clearly this one couldn't do eye contact.

"Yeah ... another excuse. I'm not buying it anymore."

Ari tore a piece of paper out of the notebook in front of her. "Here, get a pencil out of that cup, would you?"

Lex retrieved a pencil from the cup of writing utensils, handing it to Ari.

Ari took his wrists and unlocked the handcuffs, the chain tinkling as she set them off to the side. She slid the piece of paper and the pencil over in front of him.

"Here," she said, setting his bony hands down in front of the writing supplies. "It's been so long, I imagine you have a lot to say."

He looked absolutely petrified, like they'd just threatened to shoot him, hands trembling but otherwise making no motion.

Lex slid the pencil into his hand, folding her hands gently over his clammy, emaciated fingers. "It's okay. Just go ahead and write something. Any ideas you have for us, maybe? What we can do to help?"

He fumbled, the pencil clattering out of his hand and rolling across the desk. He whimpered pitifully, groping for it, unable to muster up the dexterity to snatch it back up.

"It's okay," said Lex, sliding it back towards him. "Take your time."

Tears rolled down his cheeks.

"It's okay," said Lex. "I promise it's okay. Here." She held the pencil steady for him until he was able to notch it between his fingers, then lowered his hand down until the tip was on the paper.

Ari suddenly got antsy and stood. "Just in case," she said, pointedly looking away. "Just in case it *wasn't* bullshit, just in case writing persuasion *is* a thing, I'm going to stand over here and not read what he writes."

Lex nodded. "Okay." She turned back towards Valen, whose shaky hand was working hard to produce a series of illegible squiggles. "Why don't you start writing out the alphabet," she said. "To warm yourself up. It's been a long time, and you're out of practice." *And your hands have probably been beaten to shit and had all their bones broken, but let's not talk about that.*

He let out a frustrated whine, scratching the pencil on the paper. The alphabet started to appear in a shaky, uncoordinated font.

"There we go," said Lex, putting a hand on his back. "You're doing great. When you're ready, try to write something for us."

He took a deep breath and tried to steady his shaking hands. He started writing.

"What have you got for us?" said Lex. "Any ideas?"

She watched the painstaking process as the letters came out.

A

T

T

A

"Attack?" said Lex. *Attack who? Nick? Nick, probably.* Surely he knew they couldn't do that?

C

K

"Who?" said Lex.

"Jesus, let him finish," said Ari, still standing in the corner facing away.

Valen seemed progressively more upset as he wrote, lip wobbling as the pencil continued.

A

R

Fuck. Fuck. *He's writing* Attack Ari. *That's what he's writing, he's writing –*

That was the point at which the persuasion kicked in, the exact moment it registered that he was giving her a command, as soon as she comprehended what he was telling her to do. *Attack Ari.*

Persuasion was one of the most unpleasant feelings Lex had ever had the misfortune to occasionally be subjected to, and she felt panic lance through her as the hypnotic haze fell over her mind. Her willful sensations dulled, her own thoughts and wants shoved to the side, as though someone had just pushed her out of the driver's seat.

Her limbs moved in a dreamlike way – part of her knew she should be upset, that this was wrong, wrong, wrong, that she should be fighting through it. She felt barely there, like she was looking through a frosted glass window into the situation instead of her own eyes.

She knew she had to attack Ari. She didn't understand why, but she had to.

Out of all the damn stupid things Nick hadn't been exaggerating or lying about, this one had to be *true.*

"What's he saying?" said Ari, and then she whirled around at the sound of Lex unsheathing her hunting knife. "Shit!"

The smaller woman moved at her with mechanical efficiency, no emotion in the lunging. Ari hollered in shock, narrowly avoiding the knife, which left a gash up her arm. "Lex! Fuck! *Fuck!*"

Lex could see out of the corner of her eye that the vampire had raised both hands to the muzzle, fumbling to remove it.

We're done. We fucked up. I'm sorry, Ari. I love you. We're dead. We're fucking dead.

"Stop!" said Ari, locking Lex's attacking hand in a pin. She twisted her hand to strip the knife from Lex, tossing it to the ground, then struggling to pin her to the wall without hurting her as Lex started to kick and elbow. "Fuck! Lex!"

"Be still!"

The voice was hoarse from months of disuse, scratchy like dry bones being pulled through cobwebs. Both women froze in place, a look of panic plastered on their faces. They knew the power dynamics of the situation had just shifted dramatically, and not in their favor.

We're either going to die right here or spend the rest of our lives as vampire thralls, because we cared too much. Holy shit.

"Turn and face me."

They did, like puppets.

Why did I think he might be any different from the ones who almost got me to the blood farms? Why did I think he might be able to change?

Valen was still sitting, the muzzle unbuckled and lying on the table. He had a red patch of skin around the lower half of his face where it'd rubbed him raw, in the shape of the muzzle. His eyes were wild from beneath his stringy hair, set above his hollowed-out cheeks and gaunt features devoid of any fat or muscle. His chest heaved, the skin sliding upsettingly over visible ribs.

With a weakened hand, he tossed the muzzle away from himself. "D-destroy this."

Lex wasn't sure how her hijacked brain made the decision, but she found herself compelled to walk over and light the furnace. Simultaneously, Ari walked over and picked the muzzle up, smoothly walking over and chucking it in. They both watched it in the flames, the leather peeling and curling away from the metal, which started to deform and melt.

"You will – you will remove the manacles from my ankles."

Ari knelt and unlocked them obediently.

"You will – will – you will destr-destroy this as well." He groped forward and gripped one of Nick's notebooks from the table, the one with all the photographs of him in various states of torture, with grim captions lovingly transcribed under them all. Despite the horrors of the book, Lex found herself sick at the loss of such a huge amount of work.

Into the fire it went, flames racing up the paper cover, photographs shrinking in the heat.

Valen had managed to stand, one hand supporting himself on the chair. He pointed a gnarled hand at a device on the shelf, one with a light bulb. "Destroy this."

Ari walked over and smashed the bulb, throwing the thing onto the floor and breaking it into pieces.

The vampire's eyes were glowing, mad with newly seized power, frantically scrambling for every hated object he could get his hands on.

"Destroy this." Several lengths of chain from the ceiling and around the room.

"Destroy this." A spool of what looked like silvered thread with a silver needle.

"Destroy this." Lengths of sharpened iron that looked like railroad spikes, rusty with dried blood.

"Destroy this." The handcuffs, the wrist cuffs, every device conceivable to hold him immobile.

"Destroy this." A saw with silver teeth.

"Destroy this." Pliers, belts, scissors, knives, a variety of metal implements neither of them could even name.

The furnace filled quickly. They were starting to run out of room. Valen licked his dry lips, shaking growing. "You will – you will remove this."

He curled his hands around the metal collar padlocked around his neck, now the only thing gracing his naked form besides his tattered underwear.

The command short-circuited in Lex's head, and the thought snapped shut as soon as she opened it. Persuasion couldn't make you do things you couldn't normally do, and she didn't know where the key for that was and did not know how to remove it.

Valen's face sank in desperation. He repeated the command to Ari, who similarly looked at him blankly.

He let out a sobbing curse. "F-fine! Des-destroy ... " He looked at the coffin, but stopped the command halfway through.

Lex waited to see the result of his thought process with some fear. *What are you going to do with the coffin?*

"You." He pointed at Ari. "Go – go, you will go lie down in there. And you, you will lock her in there."

No! Shit, shit, shit, shit ... Panic rose inside Lex as Ari set the key on the table, then clambered into the coffin like it was the most natural thing in the world, lying neatly inside. *I don't want to do this, I don't want to do this.* Tears welled in her eyes as she took the key and knelt, closing the lid and locking it. Their eyes met through the bars, knowing they were in deep shit, and they both shared one thought specifically:

If Ari was to be locked in the coffin to keep her here ... what was his plan for *Lex?*

"You will help me up the stairs."

Lex tearfully walked away from Ari and supported the vampire by the elbow, just as she'd done before, this time without gentleness, without emotion, without anything except mechanical obedience.

They went up the stairs one at a time. As much as Lex hated Nick, maybe, *maybe* if he hadn't listened and was still hanging around, they could still be saved.

Maybe they could avert the disaster that was unfolding, and she wouldn't be found dead and her drained body thrown into a ditch somewhere in the morning.

Lex's heart sank. They hadn't given him any reason to be merciful when the shoe was on the other foot. None of them had. After months of heartless torture, it would be a miracle if he didn't just slay every human he could get his hands on as fast as he could.

He ground his teeth as they made their way up the stairs at an agonizing pace. Lex wanted to cast her eyes back to look at Ari one last time, in case it was the last time they would see each other, but she was under some spell that made it hard to do so, like swimming upstream against a current.

They reached the top of the stairs. Valen doubled over, clinging to her, wheezing, out of breath. Lex tried to suppress her horror, her terror at how close his ravenous fangs were to her vulnerable flesh.

"You will – you will take me outside." His voice was growing fainter, raspier, as though this much sudden use was taking a toll on it.

Lex went through the motion of opening the door, letting in a wave of fresh, cool night air and the sounds of the crickets outside. Nick's car was no longer parked out front. *Nick, for God's sake, the one time I actually want you to be a nuisance and stick around. I've never actually wanted to see you before this.*

"You will o-open the door to your van." His voice warbled, with obviously increasing difficulty with each word. "And – help me – inside – and then – drive me – to – the place where – you found me."

He leaned over, on the verge of collapse, chest heaving. Lex supported him and walked up to her van, opening the door and helping him step up into the cab.

She walked around, hauling herself up and settling into the driver's seat.

Maybe she'd be lucky and the van would break down. Maybe it wouldn't start. Maybe there wouldn't be enough gas to get them the whole way there ... But no, Ari was too much of a car person for that to happen. Lex fought tears again as the car turned over and then started, and the dashboard indicators were all clear, the gas tank full.

She was going to drive this car all the way out into the middle of nowhere with a hungry, pissed off vampire in the passenger seat. She had no choice.

She was, ironically, and unbeknownst to her, thinking the same thing Valen had been thinking when they'd taken him.

I'm going to die, or something worse, because I tried to be kind.

11

Ari was only lying in the coffin for about ten minutes before she heard footsteps upstairs. She craned her neck to see Nick at the top of the stairs, a stupid grin plastered on his face. "Well, well, I bet now you're happy that I didn't listen when you tried to chase me off."

"I'm never happy to see your ugly mug," Ari said.

Nick came down the stairs. "You could at least try being nice to me instead of being an ugly bitch all the time."

"Just let me out. The key is on the table."

"The vampire left the key, how thoughtful." He picked up the key. "Maybe I will, if you apologize to me."

"For what?"

"For threatening me."

"I'm not doing that."

"Don't you want to save your girlfriend?"

"I will, as soon as you let me out."

Nick frowned. This wasn't how it was supposed to work. Nick had the power; that meant Ari was supposed to grovel, the way his vampire toy did. He'd never met anyone so utterly impervious to bullying.

Ari stared at him with hard eyes. He relented and came over, unlocking the coffin. She sprung out of it, getting up and immediately starting to rifle through Nick's supplies.

"I see you destroyed all my hard work," said Nick, seeing the pile of molten goo in the furnace.

"Yeah, I'm sure there's some stuff left, though." She made a face as she dug in a box and stumbled upon a whip.

"Ah," said Nick. "Well, maybe we can scrounge up some supplies ... If we want to do some real vampire hunting, though, we can simply forge some of our weapons again."

"Hm?"

He smiled. "We won't have time for anything complicated, though, like padding or steel coatings. Just simple silver."

***

The ride there was long and awkward.

Lex was tense the whole time, fully expecting him at any moment to have her pull over so he could feed. He was obviously starving, and when she saw the flash of fangs in his mouth, there was also drool pooling in the corner, like a well-trained dog sitting at attention in front of a juicy steak. Maybe he just didn't want to affect her ability to drive, since he was clearly in no state to do it himself.

They went deeper and deeper into the night, away from salvation. Lex tried to cry, but it felt like her emotions had been locked behind bars.

As long as Ari was out there, she had a shot, had hope. Ari would move heaven and earth to get her back. Ari would walk through the fires of hell to save her. Ari would gnaw through the metal cage to get out if that's what it took. She was willing, and more importantly, she would figure out a way and not just sit there crying and feeling overwhelmed like Lex might.

Ari had already done it once before. Teenage Ari had simply driven her father's pickup truck straight into vampire territory to retrieve her, against all odds, and came out successful, somehow. Adult Ari could handle this. Adult Ari would crash through the door soon with fire in her eyes.

It was the only thing that was keeping Lex from having a total breakdown. She was suddenly eighteen again, snatched up by vampires and taken lightyears away from her home in the middle of the night, crying and begging for them not to hurt her, which had only earned her scornful laughter.

Of course we're going to hurt you, girl, that's what you're here for.

She looked at the vampire in the passenger seat out of the corner of her eye, tense panic pooling in her stomach, building. She knew exactly what he was going to do to her once he had her where he wanted her, in his lair, in safety.

He licked his dry lips, eyes bouncing to her and back. And then:

"For the record," he croaked, "I never killed anyone."

Sure, maybe not directly. But he was with the blood farms, here to snatch up helpless people like her, to cause years of nightmares and anxiety in the case of someone like Lex, who was the *best* case scenario. He'd personally ferried hundreds or maybe even thousands of people to their untimely ends.

Of which Lex was the latest in line. Her hands shook on the steering wheel. The persuasion made it an uphill battle to do anything he hadn't commanded her to do. She wanted to cry, but it was stuck inside of her.

The irony of the sudden reversal of their situations wasn't lost on her.

His bony hand suddenly reached out and turned on the radio. The squeal of the emergency broadcast system came out. There was a V alert on the radio, which meant someone had called in and reported a vampire had been spotted somewhere in the county.

Had Ari already gotten out and sounded the alarm? Normally this would be accompanied by chatter from the CB radio with details to coordinate movements in the field, but it was turned off right now and he showed no inclination to turn it on, if he even realized it was there.

He said nothing and, with shaking hands, turned the radio back off. Time crawled by in silence, but eventually the sun started to come up. They were still on the road, not to his safety yet. Maybe this could be her salvation.

He let out a terrified moan and crawled over the seat into the cargo space in the back of the van. Lex glanced in the rearview mirror, but caught no sight of him. He must have been taking cover away from the windows.

Finally, when they were truly out in the middle of nowhere, Lex found her hands pulling the van into the driveway of the house they'd pulled Valen out of. The one car out front – presumably Valen's car, since it didn't appear to have moved an inch since her first visit – was missing its tires, up on four cinder blocks. The front passenger seat window was also smashed in.

The vampire behind her scrabbled to get upright, to peek out. Lex caught a glimpse of him in the rearview before a stray patch of sunlight reflected onto his face.

Lex nearly jumped out of her skin at the sound he made. It was an earth-shattering, preternatural screech no human would ever be able to make. He immediately dropped down out of sight once again.

Her ears were still ringing a few moments later, but she heard faint whimpering, followed by the next round of persuasion: "You will – you will go – go inside – into the house and – and you will – go into – the closet – and find – and bring to me my cloak – and boots – and – enough to cover myself."

Here we go. Dread built up inside her again. As soon as he managed to get her inside the house, it was coming. The thing she'd had nightmares about for years.

Her feet moved mechanically to get her up onto the porch. The front door wasn't locked. The lights were all off – the electricity must have been shut off long ago when no one had been paying the bills. The broken kitchen window had been boarded up – by who? A neighbor?

She checked the first floor closet and found a cloak and boots, but nothing else. She went upstairs and found pants and shirts. She did not find that getting further away from him would let her somehow break the persuasion.

She bundled up her finds and brought them outside, walking harmlessly through the sunlight and throwing the van doors open. The vampire scrambled backwards in terror as though she weren't literally his slave at the moment.

She clambered into the cargo space and dropped the clothes next to him, waiting for the next command. She stood perfectly still like a coat rack as Valen shakily stood, pulling his pants on painfully slowly, one hand on her for balance. He stepped into the boots, kneeling to try and tie them and failing miserably. He did not make Lex do it. His torso disappeared last, a t-shirt swallowing his breasts, followed by the cloak coming over his whole body and being cinched tight. "You will – you will escort me into the house."

She helped keep him upright as they crossed the lawn. She could feel him shivering with fear.

Why are you scared? Why are you scared? I'm the one who's about to be drained of my blood.

Every step towards the house increased her anxiety. This was it, she had managed to escape being a vampire's snack all those years ago, only to fall back into it now. If he didn't kill her, it would probably only be because he wanted to keep her as a thrall for the rest of her life.

She was having flashbacks, trudging through the muck to get her brain not to freeze in the way it had when she'd been narrowly rescued from the blood farms. But this was so much worse. Being taken hostage by a vampire keeping her as a personal source of endless blood would be so, so much worse.

They came into the shelter of the house. Safety for him, a death knell for her. She expected him to fall on her and start tearing into her throat then and there.

He shut the door. "Close all the blinds."

They were mostly already shut, but she walked around and pulled the blinds, drew the curtains. Her feet padded from shag carpet to tile as she finished up in the kitchen, finding herself compelled to draw the shade over the broken, boarded-up window despite the lack of sun.

He hovered in the dining room, lurking, looking like he was making a decision. *Where to bite me? Where to dump my body when he's done?*

He walked unsurely into the kitchen, ignoring Lex and going straight for the fridge.

The fridge. The fridge that had been full of blood when they'd been here last. Besides the fact that the electricity was off, and the fridge surely hadn't preserved it in the intervening months ... What was so special about that blood that he would rather have it, old and spoiled, than feed from Lex?

He leaned forward to stick his head in the fridge, then jerked back at the smell. Lex nearly gagged when it hit her nose as well. She couldn't see into the fridge. She was thankful for that.

His face dropped into despair. *Why aren't you feeding from me? What are you waiting for?*

"F-follow me," he stammered. "Help me – help me down the stairs."

Ah, downstairs, into the murder basement. Of course he would rather do it down there.

She supported him as he wheezed and chugged down the stairs, clearly grinding against the limit of his physical endurance in this weakened state. Lex saw a blur of motion in the dimness, and he gave a shriek, stumbling backwards into her arms.

Based on the pattering feet, it'd been a rodent of some kind. Of course. The house was abandoned.

Lex couldn't see very well, but the basement was mostly as she remembered: a laboratory bench of some kind, glass bottles and bins everywhere. She could see their outlines in the dim light.

He let go of her, staggering over and nearly falling, catching himself but knocking over some of the glassware and shattering it.

Was he going to clear it off and have her lie down on it to feed from her?

But no, he didn't clear it off. He started tinkering with the supplies there, lighting a flame and then extinguishing it, desperately scrabbling for bottles that turned out to be empty, letting things fall to the floor in despair when they turned out to be insufficient.

He clung to the workbench and leaned over, head down, crying pitifully.

This was the point at which she realized. Realized what he was doing.

The frantic, hungry quality of his motions. The fact that half the glassware was still crusted with red. The output nozzle positioned so perfectly above a glass jar, identical to the ones in the fridge.

He was trying to make something to eat. This setup that had so baffled them, it was for *synthesizing blood.*

The blood in the fridge wasn't actually blood. There had never been any human captives because he'd made the blood from scratch. Some of Lex's off-the-wall guesses about him had been *correct.* She'd *never* heard of such a thing, never would have thought she would have been right. He wasn't biting her because *he didn't want to.* He was looking for some other way to feed his starving body, and was despairing because it wasn't working.

He'd been telling the whole truth about never having killed anyone. His family name was that of the blood farm owners, but he himself ... ?

Who are you, Valen Kithrara?

It seemed absurd, impossible, but what other explanation was there? She could think of nothing else that so neatly encapsulated all the evidence she'd seen so far. And she probably wouldn't have believed it, if she hadn't pieced it together herself.

Had they somehow managed to find the one vampire out of the whole population who was inclined to be nonviolent?

Her stomach dropped out from under her. Had they somehow managed to find that one vampire and ... *given him to Nick?*

Her overwhelming terror gave out under the weight of the *guilt.* She'd been trying so hard to make herself believe he'd deserved it, and he *hadn't even deserved it.*

She'd managed to find one vampire who was actually trying to be a good person, and just utterly crushed that out of him. She'd forked him over straight into months of brutal torture.

Yet he *still didn't want to feed on her.* That was the kind of person she'd so completely torn apart, someone who would look the person responsible for his torment in the eye and still try to find a way to help himself that didn't involve hurting her.

She'd held something so incredibly rare and valuable in her hands, oblivious, and had destroyed it. Could she still save that side of him? Could she appeal to it to save herself?

He got up, knocking more things off the counter, and snarled at Lex, tearful face twisted up. "You will help me up the stairs."

What is he going to do now? The looming panic about being fed upon was still there, but now there was crashing terror about the possibility that he wanted revenge and weighty guilt about what a rare thing she might have thrown away.

She supported him up the stairs, now reading into every little motion of his, every wheezing breath and shaking step.

She helped him back up, trailing off as he staggered back into the kitchen, ripping the door of the fridge open again. She was behind him this time, and saw the bottles of rotten, congealed blood, with mats of mold floating in them.

She stood catatonic and watched him, unable to decide what to do, unable to think of any way to solve this huge nightmare the both of them were in. Not knowing what she could say even if she wanted to fight through the fog to say it. Still processing the implications of what she was seeing: a vampire desperately looking for an alternative to feeding on a human, as though it were unthinkable.

He knocked bottles out of the fridge, shoving them to the side, heedless of how they cracked and rolled away. He took out one that looked like it didn't have any mold, holding it up to the light and looking at it like a man drowning.

Don't … Please don't drink that. He tilted his head back and upended the bottle into his mouth, clumsily spilling half the thing on himself, the thick, rotting fluid dripping down his neck and onto his clothes. He immediately gagged, spitting it back up, throwing the bottle to the ground.

He sat there on his hands and knees among the glass and dark, lifeless liquid around him, heaving with desperation, a vampire painted with blood and still starving. Water everywhere, and not a drop to drink.

Why don't you want to feed from me? Why do you care this much?

As if he'd heard her thoughts, he slowly raised his head, looking at her with fresh, hungry, appraising eyes. She caught a sob in her throat. *Please. Please don't hurt me.*

He scrambled to his feet, his face and arms and torso absolutely drenched with blood, a terrifying, ghostly image, a skeleton approaching her with vicious intent. "Kn-kneel down."

Lex did so. *Please don't, please, please don't hurt me.* There was something inside of him that wanted to be good, that didn't want to be cruel, she knew it now. Was it too late for that? Or had that already been completely crushed out of him?

I know I made this monster, but please. You're just doing this because you're starved and terrified. You aren't too far gone. It's not too late. She tried to open her mouth to say something, but nothing came out.

Lex whimpered and averted her eyes as he came closer and knelt down. This close, the stench of the rotten not-blood was overwhelming. He fell onto her, pushing bloody handprints into her clothes, smearing rotten liquid on her thighs with his own.

He lowered his head into the crook of her neck. A disgusting, slick hand came up and took a handful of hair, tilting her head, opening her neck. She could feel his breath and his too-cold lips. It was surprisingly tender.

His body trembled with sobs, and she felt a gentle kiss on her neck. Just one, a shocking, miserable action, an act of yearning for gentleness when none could be found.

She slowly brought her hands up behind him, onto his back, hovering there as though she wanted to return the embrace, to hug him. Maybe she should say something.

Please just stay here. Just stay right here. Just cry right there, and when Ari gets here, I'll explain everything to her. You don't have to say anything if you don't want to, but you can. We'll be gentle with you, we'll help you. I see you now. I see –

Her eyes widened as she felt the softness disappear, the sharp bite on her neck, the two points sinking in and releasing blood. She felt the warm, wet drip down her neck.

She felt his tongue lapping at her broken skin, his breaths getting heavier and more intense. She tried weakly to pull away, but his grip had suddenly become iron-tight, hand in her hair keeping her bent that way, other hand on her shoulder, her legs pinned underneath his legs.

No, no, this can't be happening. I'm not food, I'm a person, you know that, you see it, please, please –

She cried out at the pain when he bit down *a second time*, making a bigger wound, opening the firehose of blood even more, slurping it like a drowning man.

She heard the sound of his throat swallowing right in her ear, again and again and again. He wasn't stopping. Blood dripped down her shoulder, soaking her shirt. He'd released so much of it that he couldn't even drink it all, and yet he still ravaged her neck for more. She started to feel lightheaded. Her limbs grew heavier. *He's not going to stop.*

"You're – " she choked out. "You're going to kill me." *Please don't kill me. I don't want to die. Don't make yourself a murderer.*

His tongue dipped into her wound over and over, mechanically, like a cat lapping up water from a bowl. Black started to creep into the edge of her vision.

He released her suddenly, staggering away. She gasped, panting, shaking with panic, clamping her hand over her neck to try and stem the flow of blood, blood running through her fingers immediately. She heard him retching distantly, collapsing onto the floor himself.

Lex cried, expecting each breath to be her last, fighting the urge to pass out.

She was vaguely aware of the vampire moving past her, to the phone on the wall, dialing. She slipped in and out of consciousness, only hearing snatches of the conversation.

"I want to talk to – "

" – come get me."

" – please, please, *please*. Please come rescue me. I'll be – "

"I even – I even have my own – "

"I'll do anything."

" – It doesn't matter now. Just – just please, please."

"The hunters know where I am, they're coming, they're going to find me. *Please*, Priscus, please save me, I'll do anything, *anything*."

In, out, in, out. Her eyes fluttered closed, then open. Vague shapes moved above her, a loud sound, followed by another, activity and people shuffling far away, way up there.

"Give her *back*!" yelled a voice, breaking through her haze. Ari. *Ari!*

"Ari ... " she managed to get out, before her limbs collapsed under her and she passed out one final time.

12

— • —

Lex felt so very cold, but she was getting warmer. She reached out and grabbed blindly at the warmth surrounding her. "Ari?"

"There she is," said Ari's voice, and as her vision resolved, Lex saw the woman herself, kneeling with Lex in her arms, her face breaking in relief. Nick was also leaning over her.

Lex flailed a bit, and Ari soothed her like a started horse. "Woah, girl."

"Where – what – " She stopped as she felt something on her lips. A straw. Ari was holding a juice box to her mouth. "Ehuhuhm?"

"You lost a lot of blood."

Lex's eyes slid half-closed and she let herself be fed juice. But then she suddenly sat bolt upright again. "Wh – wait, where is – where is Vam – Valpire?"

"Hm?" said Ari. "Don't worry about him. He can't hurt you anymore."

"Did you – did you kill him?"

"No," said Nick, while Ari simultaneously answered, "Not yet."

"Don't kill him," Lex cried.

"You shouldn't get all worked up," said Nick, leaning down and reaching a hand out.

"Don't touch her," Ari snapped.

"Geez, I'm just trying to help."

"I think you've helped enough."

Nick frowned and walked off. Grumbling, Ari turned back to the woman lying in her lap. "This guy ... Are you feeling okay?"

"Can you – wait, please," Lex cried, muddled brain scrambling to make her thoughts from before she'd passed out known. "Don't – don't kill him, don't hurt him!"

"Don't worry about him."

"No," Lex cried. "Just – just don't – "

"All right," said Ari. "I won't hurt him. Just calm down."

Lex relaxed, sipping her juice.

"Here," said Ari, handing her Nick's snacks, which she'd taken off of him without asking or saying thank you.

"Cheense cwacker," said Lex. "Mmm."

"Yeah ... I think we need to get you to the hospital ASAP. It looks like you'll need stitches. I managed to stanch the bleeding, and I think you'll be okay if we can get fluids in you, but you definitely need to see a doctor."

"Right." She munched on a cracker. "Thank you. Hey ... "

"Yeah?"

"Are you single? You're really hot."

Ari smiled. "You dork." Her smile faded. "Why was that the first thing you said when you woke up? Are you not scared of him?"

"I ... I am scared of him. But I – I think – I think he was just scared too, and hungry. I think if – I think he never actually wanted to hurt anyone."

"Well, he *did*."

"I think we were wrong, Ari. I don't think he was here to kidnap people. I think he only got violent because he was desperate."

"That doesn't make any of this okay!"

"Well, no, it doesn't make it okay that he did this, but ... it kind of shows his real character, right? When he's not put in dire circumstances?"

Ari tiredly looked over the ocean of blood on the floor. "Okay ... Well, whatever."

"I mean – I mean it. Hey, is he okay?"

"Is *he* okay?"

"Yeah."

Ari stared at Lex. Then: "No, not really."

Tears pooled in Lex's eye. "Ari ... Please don't hurt him."

Ari moaned. "Fine! Okay, fine. Jesus. Only for you."

She took Lex and set her at the table, putting a bottle of water, more juice, another bottle of water, and several more snacks in a pile and shoving them towards her. "I'll take care of him. *You* sit here and start replacing all that blood you lost."

"Okay. Wait!"

Ari had tried to turn away. "What?"

Lex gave a loopy smile. "I love you."

Ari grumbled, rubbing the back of her head and walking away. She went back out to the van and got the first aid supplies, then rifled around through the house for anything that might be useful. She carried them in a pile in her arms towards the basement.

Nick's voice could be heard in a sinister whisper as she got closer. As Ari pushed the door open, she saw him kneeling next to Valen, the vampire's immobilized neck in one hand, craning him so he could whisper in his ear.

She caught the tail end: " ... so I can see you writhe in agony when I sew you back up. And after that – "

Ari stepped purposefully loudly on the top step, letting the wood squeak. Nick dropped the vampire immediately and backed away.

"What the fuck is wrong with you?" said Ari, tossing her supplies to the ground.

"Ari," said Nick. "I was just – I was just – I was making sure he was secure – "

"Come up here."

Nick glared at the vampire before coming up. Ari shooed him through the doorway and then closed it. She pushed him into the dining room, away from the basement.

"You have five minutes to get your shit and get out," said Ari.

Nick nearly choked. "I helped you save Alexis!"

"Yeah, that's why you're getting five minutes instead of zero minutes."

Nick flared his nostrils. "Fine, then. Just help me get that creature into the coffin, and I'll be out of your hair."

Ari extended an arm to block him as he tried to walk back towards the basement. "Leave him here."

"What! What are you going to do?"

"I'm going to kill him, like I said. You said you'd need a new one soon anyway, since this one isn't working for you anymore, so there's no reason you need it back."

Nick's lip twitched. "The director would want me to take him back."

"Well, the director ain't here."

Nick huffed, walking over to the phone on the wall. It was still off the cradle. He picked the handheld unit up, starting to peck at the numbers. "Well, I can call him and see what he has to say about this."

Ari came over and snapped the cradle of the unit off the wall, pulling the phone line out and throwing it to the ground. They locked eyes for a brief moment.

"He. Ain't. Here."

If looks could set people on fire, Ari would be in flames. Nick's face was twisted in hatred. "Fine." The two women watched him walk off, slamming the front door, getting into his car and driving away.

"Oh," said Lex, looking at the broken phone. "That reminds me, I think I heard him talking on the phone, asking someone to come pick him up."

"His vampire buddies, I'd expect." Ari sniffed. "We should get out of here ASAP, then. Definitely by nightfall, but probably before that."

Lex thought briefly that ... maybe they should just let him go, if someone was going to come rescue him. But no, her realizations had been too tentative, not enough to know for sure he wouldn't hurt anyone else if they let him go. It was their job to protect humans from vampires, so anything he did was on their heads.

And she ... was selfish. She wanted to keep him.

Ari sniffed. "Well, why don't you sit there and make a list of everything we need to do before we leave, and I'll go, uh … I'll go check on him."

"Okay," said Lex. "Please don't hurt him, okay?"

"I said I wouldn't, you big whiner."

Lex watched Ari walk off. She kicked her feet idly and sipped juice, thinking about the possibility of a blood juice box. *Oh, right, Ari wanted me to …*

Well, they were going to leave … and Lex had to go to the hospital …

They certainly couldn't leave Valen here, or take him back to the hunter's compound. *I guess the only thing really left to do is take him to* our *house …*

It would be easy enough to convince Nick and the others that they had killed him – Ari had said she was going to do as much. A few of the other hunters knew where they lived, but they knew better than to tell Nick their address.

And they would do … what with him there? Well … they would have enough time with him to hopefully finally figure out an *actual* way to safely talk with him that didn't involve writing … maybe they'd jumped the gun a little bit on trying that out.

We'll help you, Valen, we'll be gentle with you. Just be patient a little longer.

It hit her that this meant he would be what, living at their house for a while? He would be their … guest? Should they take some of his things with them, to make him more comfortable? They should grab his clothes and toiletries at a bare minimum. She was sure that even something as simple as being able to change clothes everyday and brush his teeth would make a huge difference in how safe he felt. Did vampires even brush their teeth?

Her head started to spin. *We're really going to do this. We're going to just take him home like he's a lost puppy.* She would have to convince Ari, and Ari probably wouldn't be happy about it, but they'd already run through all their options earlier, and the one they'd settled on had ended in disaster … clearly they had to try something different.

Ari came back into the room, holding a bare metal muzzle, which had burnt skin and flecks of blood on it. "All right, what – "

"You didn't put that on him, did you?" said Lex, dismayed.

"I already took it off! You don't have to yell at me!"

Lex wanted to cry. If her guesses about him had been correct, he didn't deserve any of this at all, and it just kept getting worse for him. He must be absolutely terrified at the prospect of what was going to happen to him now that he'd attacked Lex. He probably wouldn't expect Lex, of all people, to advocate for him after what he'd done. But it wasn't like humans couldn't be driven to do monstrous things when they were scared and hungry and in pain. It was so, so unfair that when they saw what he did to Lex, everyone would judge him based on the things he'd done at his absolute most desperate, driven there by their monstrous treatment of him, as though that was fundamental to his character. It must be stressful to know everyone else was watching you like a hawk for evidence that you should be denied your basic human rights – well, vampire rights. She tried to imagine herself put in a scenario where people hated her and were physically violent towards her, but if she did the same to them, it was taken as evidence that she deserved it, and therefore didn't deserve food or water or to be free from pain or to just be able to *talk* and *move*. She felt an odd need to shield him from that now.

"Listen, Ari," said Lex. "I think – I can't really think of anything else to do right now other than just take him back to our house. Maybe we can figure something out later, but we've gotta go, right?"

Ari huffed. "Yeah, I was just thinking that. I'm not too happy about the idea of having a vampire in the house, but I'm certainly not letting Nick get at him."

Lex twirled her hair. "So, handsome ... Do you think you could put those muscles of yours to good use?"

A few minutes later, Ari was insistently snapping at Lex not to help her move things.

"You're way too injured to be moving that," Ari growled, blocking Lex from helping her move the dresser into the cargo van.

"I can just get the corner."

"No, you can get nothing."

"But your hand is hurt! Let me help!" Ari's hand had suffered some damage in the fight to reclaim Lex, which Ari refused to take into account as she moved things.

"I do not *need* – " Ari said with a grunt to pull the dresser into the van, " – *help* from somebody who currently has about one teaspoon of blood in their body."

Ari brushed her hands on her pants and surveyed the van. "Okay, we decided not to take the mattress because we have the pull-out couch, we have the dresser, all his clothes, all his shoes and coats from the downstairs closet, some of that ... weird science stuff from the basement. The stuff from the bathroom. Most of his books. Anything else? Not that we can fit much else in here, since Nick left the fucking coffin."

"I think that just about does it," said Lex. "Except for the man himself."

Ari closed one of the back doors. "All right, let's go get him, then, and we can be off."

Despite the amount of stuff they'd removed, the house didn't feel much emptier – it had already been pretty barebones. It had clearly been meant for short-term accommodations.

Lex stood at the top of the stairs and watched Ari go down to retrieve him. He was lying face-up on the ground, tied and gagged. God, he looked fucking *miserable*. The shirt he'd finally managed to get ahold of was soaked with blood and torn up. His bony face was taut with despair as Ari bent down and hauled him up. "All right, let's go, buddy, time to leave."

He started hyperventilating as much as he could through the cloth gag over his mouth, eyes watering.

"Do you want to walk up on your own? I don't think we need to chain your ankles."

His knees shook. He was absolutely petrified.

"Come on," said Lex. "It's gonna be okay. Come on up here." That seemed to make it *worse*. Lex felt guilt crash on her – she'd probably blown her ability to make him feel any better that very first time she'd told him it would be okay right before abandoning him for six months.

Ari's hand on his elbow was half-guiding, half-supporting. He took a few wobbly steps and mounted the stairs.

"You're doing great," said Lex. She tried to make her voice sweet, magnanimous.

He painstakingly climbed the stairs, coming face to face with Lex at the top. He saw the bandages that had been plastered on her neck and dipped his head, sobbing, tears dripping down his cheeks and onto the floor. The one eye that had been hit by the sun earlier was shriveled and blackened, but tears still managed to come out of the destroyed tear ducts.

"It's okay," said Lex. "Don't worry, I'm not mad at you. I understand you were hungry."

He didn't meet her eyes.

Ari continued to guide him, and he cooperated – until they got to the front door and he saw the patch of sunlight on the porch.

He planted one foot on either side of the doorframe and locked his knees, making hysterical noises. "Jesus – Fuck – " said Ari, wrestling with him. "Lex, go get that cloak, will ya?"

Lex strode out into the sunshine, fishing in the van for the thick black cloak she'd previously retrieved for him under duress. She came back over and tossed it on him.

"All right," said Ari, pulling it over him so there was no exposed skin. "There, see, no reason to freak out."

They carried him out and down the stairs to the van, just as they had before. He was much lighter this time, and more vocal about how unhappy the situation made him.

Ari climbed up and pulled him into the van. She dropped the cloak so he could see.

His eyes immediately fell on the coffin, underneath all of his belongings, and he let out a muffled scream, leaning his head into Ari's knees, shoulders shaking with sobs.

"We're not going to put you in there," said Lex. "I promise. You're not going back in there."

Ari squatted, putting a hand on either side to steady him. "Hey, look at me. I'm not bullshitting you, we're gonna help you, okay?"

He looked at her with red-rimmed eyes, disbelief written across his tear-streaked face.

She gently took his hands, pulling them forward onto the cloak. "You can pull this on over yourself if any sunlight starts to get in through the window. Or even if you just feel like it's all a little too much and want to hide. You're allowed to do that, okay?"

He kept his eyes on his lap.

"All right, you got this, buddy. We're going to the hospital first, and then you're coming back to our house." She gave him a final pat on the shoulder, then clambered down and shut and locked the back doors.

"All right, Lex, how about what's *hopefully* gonna be our last road trip for a while?"

13

—•—

Lex was awarded yet more juice for the incredible feat of being the most adorable little teddy bear who needed to get stitched shut to keep all her fluffing stuffing in, she'd claimed. Ari had refrained from commenting, instead taking a pretzel rod from the secretary's desk, munching on it as they walked outside.

Lex was particularly bouncy because the local anesthetic on her neck from getting the stitches hadn't worn off yet. "And we can – we can show him our VHS tapes, don't you think he'd like them? Do you think he'd like *Star Wars*?"

"You're such a geek. No one but you likes that shit."

"Star *Trek* then?"

Ari rolled her eyes. "Well, we can ask him. I doubt he ... Look, I don't think vampires really do that stuff, yeah? Like, they're not ... really people the same way as us? Do they watch TV, even?"

"They must, right? Those people who have vampire pen pals must talk about something, right?"

"The pen pal thing is ridiculous."

"It's true."

"I've got a bridge to sell you."

"Well, we can ask him if he wants to watch TV."

"He's not going to want to watch TV. He's not a human person. They must be different somehow. Right?"

"Maybe," said Lex. " ... I don't know. They have to hurt people just to eat, so they have to think at least a little bit differently from us, right? Most humans wouldn't be able to handle that, I think."

Ari held the pretzel rod between her fingers like a cigar. "Hmmph." She strode across the parking lot.

"Ari, you should have seen how hard he tried," said Lex, bouncing behind her. "He tried *everything* before he finally fed from me. He tried to drink the rotten sludge that was all over the kitchen floor before he finally bit me."

Ari huffed. "Well, I dunno, I still don't really buy this idea you have that he was synthesizing blood. But if ... and that's a big if, but if it's true, then we owe him a hell of an apology. But you're *not* doting on him like he's your fucking hamster," she added quickly, seeing the excitement on Lex's face. "He's still an apex predator. We need to think about things like how to feed him and make sure he doesn't attack anyone before worrying about whether or not he'll like your VHS collection."

"I don't think he's done anything wrong, Ari."

"Don't get carried away," warned Ari. "Even if he wasn't here to kidnap anyone, he's still a vampire. He had to be eating something up till this point, and I doubt it was one hundred percent ethically sourced, vegan blood from perfectly willing volunteers every day for his whole life."

"What do you *want* from him? He was born that way, he can't help that he *has* to drink blood. He can only do the best with what he was given."

"Hmph. Well, I'm not gonna let him go free until I'm one hundred percent sure he's not gonna hurt anyone. It's our job to keep vampires under control, and regardless of what you saw, he still almost killed you. Even if he's not evil, he's still dangerous ... Like any animal that's wounded and starving."

" ... Or at least he *could* be dangerous," said Lex quietly. "If he had the strength to stand on his own."

They'd reached the back of the van. Ari rapped the window lightly with her knuckle. "Hey, we're back. I'm opening the door."

She unlocked the cargo doors and cracked them open. The only sign anyone was in the back among the furniture and boxes was a single booted leg sticking out from under a quivering mound of black cloak, which withdrew further into the cargo area away from the intruding sunlight.

"There he is," said Ari. "Didn't move an inch, just like we asked him to. Thanks for sitting so pretty."

"We're about halfway there," said Lex. "Maybe it'll be dark by the time we get home. Wouldn't that be nice?"

"Everything okay?" said Ari, giving a tentative thumbs-up. "At least, relatively speaking?"

Valen pulled the cloak off himself with shaking hands, eyeing her apprehensively.

"Anything you want us to do before we drive off again?"

He held his wrists up, twisting them to show that the chain had slipped a little off the cloth, so now a few links were grazing his skin, where there was a considerable red mark.

"Oooh, poor little guy, let me fix that," said Lex, coming over and fiddling with the cloth to pull it up and block the contact between the bare silver and his skin.

Ari shot Lex death glares at the way she was talking to him, but made no move to stop her. When she finished, she stepped back and Ari repeated: "All right, all good? We're getting there, but it's still a while to go. Thumbs-up if it's all good."

He gave a shaky thumbs-up.

"All right," said Ari. "See you in a bit." She shut the doors.

They went around front, getting in, buckling their seat belts, and starting the car. Lex turned in her seat to look into the back, to catch a glimpse of him all the way at the rear of the vehicle, the piles of stuff between them. He was sitting limply, leaning into his end table, vacant gaze downcast at the floor, tears pattering onto the bed of the van. He didn't seem to notice her looking at him.

***

They stopped for Burger King, which Ari ate as she drove. Lex started to turn around and offer some of hers to their captive in the back, until remembering partway through why that wouldn't work.

It felt like they were half dead by the time they dragged themselves up in front of their house. Ari pulled the van up, killed the ignition, then they both just sat there for a few moments.

"I'm fucking exhausted," said Ari.

"Me too," whined Lex.

They'd had a full day of regular work, then stopped by the director's office in the evening, followed by going straight back to the hunter's compound to give Valen a pencil that night. *Then* they'd spent the whole night into the morning getting kidnapped and drained of all their blood and throwing together a mad dash to give chase, respectively, and *then* they'd spent that whole day packing a moving van, and then doing *another* road trip. It was starting to get on a full thirty-six hours since they'd slept or even rested. The adrenaline was starting to wear off.

"We'll unload all this junk in the morning," said Ari. "Christ. That should be fine, right?"

"I think so. I'm so tired I can barely think."

They got out of the van and opened the back door. It was, in fact, still light out, so the vampire scrambled backwards away from the sunlight.

"How about it?" said Ari.

He trembled.

"Lex, go make sure the neighbors aren't watching, would ya?"

Their house did have a generous yard setting them apart from the neighbors, along with a tall hedge fence ... They would *probably* have enough privacy, but best to head off problems that could arise from someone seeing them carrying a bound and gagged person into their house. Everyone around them *did* know that they were vampire hunters, so they could probably make up something to explain why he was here, and random humans nearby would definitely be too scared to argue with them, but still best to avoid having everyone see him.

Ari sat down on the edge of the van while Lex scurried away. Ari felt a small tug on her sleeve and turned to see the vampire looking at her with a tearful expression.

"We're at our house," said Ari. "Nick isn't here, and he doesn't know where we live."

That seemed to relax him slightly.

"All right," said Lex, returning. "Ella isn't home, Delores wasn't answering the door so I assume she's asleep, and I told Abraham we're moving some stuff and it sounded like he was preoccupied with something, so I think we'll be okay."

"Great." She gently pulled at the fabric on Valen's lap. "Get your cloak."

Valen pulled the cloak over his head with unsteady hands, crying softly.

"No need to get worked up," said Ari. "All right, come on, buddy."

She leaned him over her shoulder, carrying his limp form like a sack of potatoes.

"You'll like it here," said Lex, shutting the van. "It'll be nice."

They went up the crumbling cement stairs onto the porch, which had ancient white paint peeling from it. Lex was suddenly embarrassed, as though maybe a vampire would judge their abode for being messy and out of date.

Lex unlocked the front door, holding the screen door open while Ari took him inside. She then shut and locked the door, then walked around and drew all the blinds.

Ari stood Valen up in the center of the room, then removed the cloak from over his head. He was still crying, cheeks flushed dark red and snot dribbling down from his nose.

"Oh, shh, shh," said Ari, taking a napkin and wiping his face. "All right. No need for that."

"We're home now," said Lex.

Ari sighed. "Listen, Lex and I are tired as *fuck*, and we're not in any state to be making decisions, especially not ones that affect your wellbeing. So, how does it sound that you just lie down on the couch for a bit while we get some sleep?"

He ground his jaw, not answering.

"Is that okay?" said Lex guiltily. "I know you're, well ... " She looked him up and down. He desperately needed a bath to wash all that blood and gunk off of him, but she currently couldn't think of any way to give him a bath or shower that wouldn't be basically waterboarding him. Last time, the gag had been metal, but this time it was cloth. And they'd need to come up with a plan for a way to take the gag out while minimizing the amount of harm he could do, if for no other reason than just to avoid a repeat of what'd just happened.

"I'll go get the liner for the couch," said Ari.

Lex assisted, getting a clean trash bag from the kitchen and wrapping a pillow in it. Ari came over with a huge plastic sheet and tossed it over the couch.

"There," said Lex. "How does this sound for now?" Her head was swimming with exhaustion. This should be fine, right? It would be comfortable enough, and relatively safe for all three of them.

He was still standing petrified in the middle of the room. Ari gently guided him over to sit on the couch, which now crinkled under his weight.

"Is that comfortable?" said Lex.

He didn't respond.

"Hello?" said Ari, waving a hand in front of his face. His eyes bounced to track the movement. "Yes, no?"

He nodded.

"Okay. Listen, now, okay? You don't need to try and escape. We're not going to hurt you, and tomorrow we're going to figure out a way to feed you."

His eyes brimmed with hopeful tears at that.

"First thing in the morning," said Lex. "We'll figure out some way to let you talk that'll be safe for all of us."

"It'd be a bad idea to try and get out anyway," said Ari. "You know you won't make it on your own outside in this state."

He slowly lowered his head.

"Here, lie down," said Lex, patting the pillow.

Lex helped him swing his legs over, so he was lying down on the couch. Ari took another cloth out and started to loop it around his ankles.

He leaned into the pillow, hiding his face as Ari tied a knot, securing his ankles together. "Just as a precaution," she said. "It'll come off first thing in the morning."

"Okay," said Lex. "Will you be okay if we leave to go to sleep?"

He peeked out from the pillow, tired, haunted eyes looking up at them. He nodded weakly.

"Okay," said Lex. "Good night."

She flipped the light switch on the way out, plunging the room into darkness, broken by the light reflecting off the two red eyes in the direction of the couch.

Lex and Ari collapsed nearly as soon as they got into the bedroom. Lex had already changed out of her bloody clothes earlier and knew she should probably get a shower, but the siren song of the bed was too much for her to resist. She lay down immediately. "Hell."

Ari crawled into bed. "I guess we need to think of some brilliant idea soon, then."

"I'm sure it'll be fine," said Lex, already half asleep.

Ari contemplatively looked out the window at the clouds streaked pink by the sunset, and set her alarm an hour before sunrise.

14

The alarm went off way, way too soon.

Ari smashed it into silence and groaned, rolling over and burying her head in the pillow.

"Ari," said Lex. "We can't sleep in."

Ari raised her head, eyes like death. "Oh. Right."

"I guess we need to think of something." Some way to safely talk to this person who was potentially very, very dangerous and evil, but also potentially very, very innocent.

Ari blinked slowly. "I need some coffee."

They shuffled into the kitchen, talking quietly to try and minimize Valen hearing them. "Okay," said Ari, pouring hot water into the coffee maker and turning it on. "I've got it. He can't make us open locks we can't open, like we don't have the key to. So let's just use a combination lock that you don't know the combination to, and you can talk to him safely while I stand out of earshot."

"Oh, brilliant!" said Lex. She retrieved the milk from the fridge. "He could still, I don't know – he could do other things though, right? Like, he could make us attack each other again."

The coffee machine gargled. "Right," said Ari. "So let's do it outside. If we can't take him back inside because he figured out some way to kill or incapacitate us, then good for him, he gets to burn."

Lex took the pot of coffee off the machine and poured it into her cup, adding milk. "That's a good idea. That should be enough, right? To take the gag out and let him talk, while still keeping us safe? To avoid a repeat of ... that."

Ari poured the scalding hot black coffee from the carafe directly into her mouth. "Hggn."

"I'll go check on him."

Lex padded into the living room. To her relief, the vampire was still on the shrink-wrapped couch, having barely even changed positions. His eyes were half-lidded, heavy, but clearly awake.

"Did you sleep okay?"

His eyes snapped open, then swept up and down her. He looked exhausted, and he tilted his face into the pillow.

"Ari has something we're going to try, okay?" Lex took a sip of her coffee. "I think this'll solve our problem. Just sit tight for a minute, and we'll come get you." She tiptoed back into the kitchen, where Ari had started to demolish a protein bar. "Poor guy. He can't have slept well."

"He's been through a hell of a lot worse than sleeping on a crinkly couch." Ari ducked into the dining room closet, rifling through it. "I think this is where that combination lock is."

She came out a few moments later with a lock, a hammer, and a stake. "Okay, let's do this."

They came back into the living room. Ari gestured for him to sit up, and he pivoted on the couch as best as he could. Ari knelt down and untied the restraint around his ankles. "Okay," she said, tossing it to the side. "Let me see your wrists."

He held them out, and Ari unlocked them, unwinding the silver chain to its full length. He watched her work with some trepidation.

"All right, keep them together just like that," she said, re-wrapping the cloth on his wrists. "Good boy."

His face flushed deep red. He must be embarrassed from Ari talking down to him like that.

She wrapped a portion of the chain back around his wrists, just one turn, and took out the lock and fastened them together, leaving a long length like a leash.

He got a look of dread on his face. Ari kept the lead in her hand. "All right, Lex is going to help you walk. Don't panic."

Even underneath Ari's reassurances, he could be heard whining softly like a scared dog. Lex took his elbow and put a hand on his back, pushing him up. Ari tugged gently at the chain, pulling him forward, hands first, through the living room, into the dining room, through the kitchen, and towards the back door.

He seemed to like that even less. He stopped dead at the threshold to the backyard, eyes searching the sky as though for aerial predators.

It was clear enough what he was thinking. Lex started to second-guess their plan. But they had to do *something* to keep themselves safe, given how wrong it'd gone last time they'd tried something like this.

"Come on," said Ari, tugging at the chain on his wrists.

"It's all right," said Lex, bumping him gently, hoping that maybe this time, reassuring him wouldn't backfire.

He took a few shaky steps forward. Ari opened the door and helped him step down onto the back porch, and then out into the yard.

He walked out into the yard with the resignation and general air of a man being led to the gallows. He stopped when they prompted him to in the center of the yard. They'd have plenty of privacy here, with the hedges closing them in ... but not so much that they would be shielded from the sun when it rose.

Ari withdrew the stake. His face screwed up in apprehension, clearly anticipating it being stabbed through his chest, but Ari knelt and aligned the stake through one of the chain links and pounded it into the grass, securing him to the ground.

"Okay, here's what – Jesus Christ." Ari had started to stand and explain things to him, only to see his entire countenance locked into an expression of absolute unbridled terror, all color drained from his face, eyes glazed over and hands half-extended as if to fend off a blow, nostrils flaring.

"It's okay," said Lex, "we're not going to leave you out here."

"Let me explain it to you," said Ari.

"You're safe," said Lex.

Tears welled up in his eyes, words rolling right over him, entire body shaking.

"Woah, hey, hey," said Ari, and they both got handfuls of him to stop him from falling over.

"Shh," said Lex. "It's okay, it's okay, I promise it's okay."

"This is going to be good," said Ari. "This is a safety precaution, but you're going to get to talk."

A squeak slipped out, and he swallowed, eyes bouncing between the two of them.

"All right, here's how this is going to work," said Ari, crossing her arms. "We're going to take the gag out, and you and Lex are going to talk. Just talk. You *will not* use persuasion."

He nodded vigorously, shaking.

"But you know for our own safety, we can't just ask you nicely not to use persuasion. So we have precautions. *I* am going to stand in the house and watch from the kitchen window." Ari pointed to the lock that was keeping Valen's wrists together and chained to the ground. "I know the combination to that lock, and Lex doesn't. So there's no way you can force her to unlock you. And if you somehow manage to incapacitate her, or get us to kill each other or something, your only reward will be being locked outside when the sun comes up in an hour with no one to bring you inside. Got it?"

Valen shook his head desperately, tears flowing down his cheeks.

Come on, I know this is scary, but you almost killed me. You can't expect us not to take precautions. "You must understand that we have to do something to prevent a repeat of what happened last time," said Lex, with a hand crawling up her neck to the bandages there. "Okay?"

He tried to steady his breathing and nodded.

"Great," said Ari, and she walked all the way across the yard, into the back door, and appeared in the kitchen window.

Lex turned back to Valen, who'd folded his legs neatly under himself, sitting in the grass. Lex leaned over him, gentle hands brushing against the cloth gag. "I want to take this off now. I don't want to keep you restrained unless we have to. I'm not going to hurt you. Do you understand?"

He nodded.

"Do you believe me?"

He nodded.

" ... Are you just saying what you think I want to hear?"

He nodded tearfully.

"Okay. Don't do that. I need to know what you're thinking to make this easier on both of us. Okay? I promise I won't get mad. Now, do you understand?"

He nodded.

"Do you believe me?"

A pause. Then he shook his head.

"Okay. That's okay. Thank you for telling me. I don't know how to convince you, but it's true. I want us to talk. Just talk. I'm going to take the gag out, and we're going to talk. Ari already explained to you. Okay?"

He trembled.

"Are you ready?"

He looked up at her with huge, tearful eyes.

Lex's fingers felt for the knot at the back of his head, the cloth tied with his hair caught in it. She undid it, and the cloth slipped out, and she folded it neatly and put it in her pocket. "There. How's that?"

His lip wobbled. He seemed at a loss.

"Maybe we can start by – "

"Please don't leave me in the sun." He was nearly hysterical, clearly already pushing his hoarse voice to its limits. "Please, please don't leave me out here in the sun – "

Oh God, he hadn't understood correctly, he thought they were *threatening* to leave him in the sun. "Woah, hey, hey, hey," said Lex. "Don't misunderstand.

We're taking you back in before sunrise. The only reason we wouldn't is because we were dead or something. It was just – it's just to make sure you have some incentive to not try to kill us."

"I won't," said Valen, voice cracking uncontrollably. "I won't, I'm sorry, I'm sorry, I'm so sorry I attacked you. I'm so sorry, Lex, I'm sorry, I'm so sorry."

Oh, please don't. She'd been prepared for him to ask the question that had been eating at her: *Why did you leave me there?* But she hadn't been prepared for him to beg so fearfully. It broke her heart.

She put one hand on his chained wrists, on his lap, and used the other to caress his cheek, hoping that would maybe make him feel better. "Shh, it's okay. Like I said, I know you're hungry."

He squeezed his eyes shut, clearly trying not to cry even more.

"I think maybe we got off on the wrong foot. Let me introduce myself. I'm Alexis, but you can call me Lex."

"My – I'm – my name – name is – Valen."

She squeezed his hand. "It's nice to finally meet you." She gestured towards the window. "That's my girlfriend, Ari. She can be kind of scary sometimes, but that's just because she cares, even if she pretends she doesn't."

Valen was clearly very, very afraid of Ari, hunching down as though he could hide from her.

"Now, let me ask you something, Valen. And it's okay to tell me the truth even if it sounds bad. I promise I won't get mad at you." This was the million dollar question, which would determine how guilty she should feel. "Why did you come here, into human territory? What were you doing?"

Please just say you were here to hunt and torture and kill humans, and it was for the best that we stopped you, and that we taught you a lesson and you're a good person now. I don't think I could bear it if you were actually innocent this whole time.

Tears flooded his eyes as he started to stammer. "There's – a mushroom – mushrooms are – more closely related to – than to – plants – and – the – fiber

122

– orange – because it – it – it's similar to – to hemoglobin – " His disused voice cracked and gave out. He hung his head, gasping in huge, panicked breaths.

Well, *that* wasn't what she'd expected. She couldn't make heads or tails of what he was trying to say.

Lex's hand caressed his jaw gently, tilting his chin back up to make eye contact with her. "Take your time."

He visibly tried to steady himself, then broke down immediately once again. "Please don't give me back to Nick. Please, please don't give me back to Nick. Please don't let him have me."

Nick had been the one to do this to him, but Lex had given him to Nick, knowing full well what sort of fate was in store for him. This was her fault, as well as Ari's, even if Nick's hands had been the ones to carry the torture out. She squeezed his hand, resolute. "I won't. You're done with Nick. You're not ever going to see him again if I can help it."

He shuddered, hiccupping. "I was – I was – I was trying to – to ... " He swallowed. "I know you won't believe me, but please, please believe me, I wasn't ever trying to hurt anyone."

It almost didn't matter whether or not she believed him at this point. What difference did the initial reason make? It mattered more for Lex's own conscience and to give Valen the chance to vindicate himself.

"I was here because I was trying to – to make – to make blood substitute."

"Because you were hoping to be able to drink something other than real human blood?"

He nodded.

The pit that had been forming in Lex's stomach fully manifested. Not only had she let such a horrible thing happen to someone on her watch, but it had been to someone who had been fighting upstream against a tidal wave of cruelty, the same one she herself had been trying to stop.

But ... she'd never heard of this. It was generally regarded as impossible for vampires to drink something other than real human blood. "Why?"

"*Why?*" he choked. "Be-because – the blood – the farms – it's – "

He's trying to explain he's horrified by the way other vampires feed, she realized. That was it. He was clearly struggling to explain his thoughts adequately, but combined with what she'd seen and her own guesses, it was enough in her mind. "Because you didn't want to hurt anyone?"

"Yes," he exploded, and he slumped over, weeping violently. "That's all I ever wanted. Please, please, *please* – "

"I believe you," she said. "Hey, look at me."

He did so, eyes wide and desperate. Lex felt so, so bad. She'd doled out the ultimate punishment for someone else's kindness. A *kind* vampire was such a rarity that Lex felt like she'd found a lost painting by Leonardo da Vinci at a garage sale, bought it for five dollars, and taken it home to use as a coaster.

She had to fix this. She *had* to fix this. If there was *any* chance that Valen still wanted to be a good person, she *had* to nurture that instinct in him, to keep it from dying out. She wouldn't be able to live with herself otherwise, knowing that she'd snuffed out something like that.

"I believe you. I'm ... I'm sorry I let this happen. I'm sorry I let Nick do this to you. I'm ... I'm sorry I did this to you. I'm sorry I didn't give you a chance."

"I'm sorry I bit you," he said. "I'm sorry that I bit you."

He was *still* apologizing to *her*. Out of fear, perhaps, but nonetheless. He had every right to be furious at her. He'd been trying to feed his starving body, to save himself from the state *she'd* let him get into. She raised her shoulders, sighing. "I ... kind of deserved it."

"No!" said Valen. "Nobody – nobody deserves that! Everyone d-deserves to feel – to feel safe and in – in control of what's happening to them – to their own body." His voice gave out again, leaving him shaking and coughing.

Holy shit. He still thinks that. He still wants that. We haven't driven that out of him. It's not too late to fix this. She felt her own tears prickling at her eyes, and she gripped him fiercely, resisting the urge to pull him into a hug. "Thank you.

Thank you for holding onto that all this time. Thank you for not letting us beat that out of you."

A flash of emotions contorted his face, bloody saliva dripping from his mouth as he dipped his head, sobbing.

She felt bad again. He'd gone through all this, and now he was trapped outside before sunrise. From his perspective, these safety precautions must have just been unnecessarily terrorizing him even more. She couldn't take it anymore. She curled her hands around his back. "Do you want a hug?"

"Y-yes," he warbled.

She wrapped her arms around his shoulders, drawing him in. It was only when she felt his breath on her neck did she truly realize what she'd just done: pulled his face right into the position he would be in to feed from her.

He could bite her again and kill her, and it would be justified, probably. Her limbs locked up, flooded with new traumatic memories. But she refused to let go. His bony frame shook in her arms, jerking with hitching breaths.

She felt his teeth on her shirt, nibbling it. He clearly *wanted* to bite very, very badly. But he was holding himself back, which was impressive.

And clearly the hug was very deeply appreciated, with the way he leaned into it. But best to disengage, to not push their luck. And ... he still smelled like rotting blood.

"Are you ready to go back inside now?"

He sobbed pitifully as she pulled back from him. "Yes."

"Okay. We'll just have Ari come over here, and we'll get you all taken care of."

The sun rose a while later, onto a stake securing an empty chain to an empty lawn, starting a new day.

15

— • —

Valen's boots clattered on the kitchen floor as Lex helped him step up and back into the kitchen. Ari shut and locked the back door, then walked over to the kitchen window to shut the curtains as the sky started to streak pink with the sunrise.

"Okay," said Ari, giving a tentative thumbs-up. "We're good? We're cool?"

Lex returned her thumbs-up. Valen let out a choked sob but also gave a thumbs-up, the weakest and least convincing thumbs-up in history.

"It's all right," said Lex. "Things are going to get better for you now. We're going to help you. Things are only going to get better. Ari."

She took Valen's wrist and drew him forward. "Let me introduce you to Valen. He was here in human territory because ... he was gathering ... mushrooms?" She glanced at him out of the corner of her eye for any sign that her statement was incorrect. When he gave none, she continued, "That he was using to try and make artificial blood."

"Mushrooms are more closely related to animals than to plants," Valen mumbled, eyes glued to the floor.

"Ah, right ... " said Ari. She rubbed the back of her head. "Well, I ... Well, if that's true ... I mean ... I'm glad you weren't here for anything nefarious." Lex could tell Ari still did not quite believe it, but she could see what was obvious in front of her: this creature was a person, not a monster, despite the fangs and the blood painting him, who just wanted to be safe and who was capable of carrying out a conversation if treated fairly. Ari was protective, but she was also clearly

126

thinking that she didn't want to hurt this poor guy any further, and they might be able to work it out safely.

And when they'd set up Lex and Valen in the backyard, the message from Ari had been clear: *I trust your judgment. If you say he's fine, I'll believe he's fine.*

Lex could see Ari struggling to think up what to say now that they'd actually reached that point, though. Lex herself was struggling to contain a slew of curious questions for her strange new friend, wanting to hear everything about who he was and how he'd gotten to this point, but there would be time for that later.

"I-I'm sorry I locked you in a cage," Valen blurted out.

"Hgn?" Ari gave him a befuddled look. Lex knew what she was thinking: *I would have done the same thing. That was completely reasonable.* "I mean ... " said Ari, averting her eyes. "That was just kind of fair play. Y'know." She cleared her throat. "Well, I – Given what all happened, I would say ... "

Just apologize, Ari, Lex thought, bemused. *It won't kill you. You're still plenty macho.*

"Well, listen, dude, I ... Sorry about ... all that." She looked ashamed. "I owe you one, so – so if there's anything you need, you just let me know."

Lex took a moment to look Valen up and down and take stock of what they actually had in their kitchen.

Okay, they had a vampire. A person. Who wanted to be a good person and who hadn't committed any crimes. Except for biting Lex, which Lex thought wasn't really his fault. It was *their* fault. Okay. So this was sort of their responsibility. He was starved and weakened, very, very scared, in clothes that were several sizes too big for his skeletal frame, beat to shit and back with open wounds all over his body, very tired by the look of it, and covered in dried, tacky blood, down his chin and up to his sunken cheekbones, down his front, half of it months old and rotting. One of his eyes was a charred, shriveled lump nestled among a burn across his face, he had cuts all up and down his limbs, burns in the shape of the muzzle, burns on his wrists, and probably plenty of broken bones they couldn't see.

What would be the best thing to do?

"Let's get you taken care of. What would you like to do first?" said Lex. Being in the enclosed space with him again drove home how bad he truly smelled, so a bath would probably be a good first step, then they could clean his wounds. "We can get you cleaned up – "

"F-feed," he said instantly. "Pl-please allow me to feed. I'm so – so – I'm so hungry, *please*." He shrank back instantly after the outburst, as if afraid of being reprimanded.

Oh, of course. Lex should have guessed that'd be what he wanted first. Luckily, when they'd been at the hospital, they'd convinced the hospital staff to let them have some donated blood from their stock, which they'd stowed in the fridge. All they'd needed to do was prove they were vampire hunters and make up some excuse about how they were trying to set up a trap for a vampire and needed bait, and they'd been given as much as they wanted.

"Eager, huh," said Ari, turning back to the fridge. She emerged with one of the bags of blood. "Well, it's your lucky day, because ... hello?"

Valen was frozen, knees quaking, as though he were deathly afraid asking had been a mistake, eyes glazed over.

"Hello?" said Ari, waving her hand in his face. "Earth to Dracula."

His eyes snapped to her hand, then fell onto the blood.

"Like I was trying to say," said Ari with a grin. "Today's your lucky day, my man, cuz it turns out if you're at a hospital to get stitches, all you need to do is flirt with the nurse a little bit, tell her you're vampire hunters, and fudge the explanation for what you're going to use it for, and they'll just give you some blood."

"G-give it to me!" Valen snapped with sudden savageness, mouth screwing into a snarl. He immediately drew back, hand over his mouth, fearful expression returning.

"Hold on a second," said Ari, drawing it back, and again Lex and Ari were in perfect sync with their thoughts.

Lex put a hand to his back. "Didn't you throw up ... before?" She'd been phasing in and out of consciousness, but she remembered a few things, which she'd recalled to Ari: he'd thrown up, and he'd gotten off a phone call to someone. They'd have to ask about that second part later.

"So, how much of this do you think your stomach can handle?" said Ari. "Decide beforehand, so you don't get carried away."

"For a human who was breaking a fast, we would probably give them crackers or something," said Lex. "Something light, so they don't get sick. You know?"

"Do you want just a little bit, and we can wait a bit to give you more?" said Ari. "Or, maybe, I don't know, we can thin it out with water or something?"

He looked like they'd just asked him to do quadratic equations in his head. His face was frozen in indecision, then: "If ... if you dilute it with water ... M-maybe half of that would be a good start. Thank you."

Ari smiled. "There we go. Let's give it a try."

She turned and put the bag on the sink. Lex fetched her a drinking glass, then came back over to help Valen stand.

Ari lowered the bag into the sink to contain any spills, then cut it open with a pair of scissors.

The second the bag was open, something slammed into both of them from behind, claws and teeth thrashing violently, growling ripping through the air.

"Shit!" said Ari, regaining her balance. "Fuck!"

"Stop!" said Lex. "Valen, stop!"

His face twisted in anger, then dissolved into horror. Ari swept his leg and jammed him into an arm bar against the counter.

"Easy, easy!"

"Woah, woah – "

"Stop, stop – "

"I've got him."

"We've got you."

"I'm sorry!" he sobbed instantly. "I'm sorry! I'm sorry! I – I didn't mean to – I didn't mean to!"

He shifted under Ari's weight, and Ari grabbed a handful of hair, pressing him down into the counter. He writhed, eyes locked on the blood now splashed in the sink, but Ari pulled him back.

"Please," he wept. "Please just let me lick the sink, I'll do anything, I'm sorry, I'm so sorry, please – please have mercy, please just let me – "

"Easy," said Ari's voice, and the legs behind him pressed into him even further, stifling his squirming. "Easy. Take it easy. Breathe. Sit still."

It was the smell. The smell was making it impossible for him to control himself. He was that desperately hungry. Especially with him pinned to the counter right next to the sink. They needed to do something to bring him back down, so they could talk again. They wanted to feed him, but it was dangerous for all of them if he couldn't control himself.

"Lex, turn the water on." If the lingering blood was gone, maybe he could think more clearly.

"No," Valen cried. "Please, please, please just let me – "

Lex started to get concerned at his desperation. Was he going to use persuasion again? He must know that wouldn't end well, right? The sun was up. He couldn't pull a repeat of what he'd done earlier. *Please just trust us.*

Lex turned on the faucet, rinsing the bag and sending the remaining blood down the drain. He tried to chase it, prompting Ari to pin his remaining wrist to the counter.

"This isn't going to work if you can't control yourself," said Ari. "We're trust-ing you to behave in a civilized way."

"I'm sorry," Valen said pathetically. "I – I – I – I didn't mean to, I-I-I'm trying."

"All right. Just stay still. Lex, are you hurt?"

"No, are you?"

"No."

Lex let out a shaky breath, then rubbed his back soothingly. "It's okay. See? You didn't hurt us. We're okay. You're okay."

"I'm – I'm – I'm sorry."

Lex felt her heart breaking again. He clearly wanted so badly to behave himself, but his eyes were wide with such desperate hunger. "It's all right. Don't worry. We're going to help you."

Lex took stock again, with fresh eyes, of what they had in their kitchen. A person. A vampire. A desperate, starving, dangerous wounded animal. Of their own creation. Who would hurt them despite his own best intentions. They had to pull him back up out of the deep pit he'd been thrown into. They *had* to grab his hand and haul him back up out of the muck, they had to put on gloves and armor to stop the panicked kicking and screaming and clawing as they did so, because he was starved and half-feral and had no way to help himself besides lashing out at things he thought would hurt him. He could do nothing *but* lunge desperately, and he had no reason to believe anything would get better unless *he* was the one who made it happen.

They had to help him, and they had to take precautions to make sure all three of them stayed alive while that happened. He needed to be restrained, even if he didn't want it, if he couldn't stop himself from lunging.

"We're going to help you," said Ari. "But we're going to do it in a way that *doesn't* put me and Lex at risk. Understand?"

"Yes, I understand, I understand, sir – m-ma'am."

Ah, there it was, the dreaded *sir-ma'am* that Ari was subjected to so often. She smiled wryly, then leaned over. "Because Lex lost a *lot* of blood, and if she loses more, or reopens her stitches, you could hurt her really badly."

"I – I know, I'm sorry, I d-didn't mean to – "

"We know you're hungry," said Lex, "and we know you're scared, and in pain, and we know people do things they wouldn't otherwise do when they're scared and in pain and hungry."

Valen sobbed.

"But that doesn't change the fact that you can hurt us even if you don't mean to," said Ari. "This might have been too big of a leap. We'll do baby steps."

"Th-thank you," said Valen, body wracked with tremors. "Thank you, ma'am, thank you."

"Lex, go get the muzzle."

"*No!*" Valen cried, and Lex had to fight to keep herself together at his expression, his squirming. "Please, please, no! Please don't put the muzzle back on! Please, please, I'll do anything, *anything*, I'm begging you – "

"Relax," said Ari. "Hey, relax. We're not going to use the bit. You'll still be able to talk. It'll just be a barrier between you and lunging at us again. We know you didn't do it on purpose, but we still need to prevent it from happening again."

"But, Ari," said Lex, dismayed, "the muzzle we have burns him."

"Go get some duct tape too."

Good old Ari. She always knew what to do right away. Lex pattered into the closet, rummaging through it to find the duct tape. She heard Ari and Valen talking softly to each other, his voice trembling and desperate, hers firm.

Lex put the duct tape and muzzle on the counter. "Go get the chain from outside too," said Ari.

Lex nodded. She went out the back door, pulling the stake up from the yard and retrieving the chain.

She came back into the kitchen and started wrapping duct tape around the part of the chain that would be closest to him, then took the muzzle and curled tape over all the parts that would be touching his skin.

"All right," said Ari. "Try not to panic. You're okay. You're safe."

Valen was rigid, sobbing hopelessly. *It's okay, it's okay for real this time. It's just temporary. It's just temporary, sweetheart. It's not like before.*

Ari's hands eased up, returning him to a standing position. "There we go," she cooed. "Nice and easy, now. Turn around, please."

He did so slowly. "All right," said Lex. "You're okay."

"I'm going to attach the chain to this hook," said Ari, gently running her finger along the metal collar still attached to his neck. "We're not going to bind your hands. We're just going to make it harder to bite and lunge, so you can stop yourself before you hurt us. Your hands will be free, and you'll still be able to talk. Then you'll get to eat."

Shit, they didn't have the key for the padlock on the metal collar around his neck. And they couldn't ask Nick for it ... Maybe they could figure out some way to get it off later. But for now ... maybe they'd need to use it.

"Please," said Valen tearfully. "I – I – I – " He choked, breaking off.

"Do you think you can handle that?" said Ari. "It's just as long as you can't keep yourself from lunging when you smell it. Okay? We're leaving your hands free, we're trusting you to work with us here. We know you want to feed without hurting us. Think you can handle that?"

"If you can't, it's okay to say so," said Lex. "We'll think of something else."

"I can handle it," he said. "I can – I can handle it, thank you, thank you for trusting me. I won't bite you, I won't use persuasion." His chest hitched. "Thank you for trusting me."

Lex put her hand on his shoulder. "Thank *you* for trusting *us*."

She'd been half-afraid he wouldn't, that he would just use persuasion again as soon as he could, even after the conversation in the backyard. He didn't have many options with it being daytime outside, not able to make another getaway like before, but he could have certainly tried. She squeezed his shoulder. *Thank you, thank you. Thank you for letting us help you.*

He flinched as Ari clipped a carabiner onto the ring on the collar. Lex handed her the silver chain. "Just stay still," said Ari as she clipped the carabiner through the chain. "There we go. Good boy."

He flushed with humiliation. Maybe Lex should ask Ari to stop doing that.

"Okay, let's go into the living room," said Ari.

Lex helped him walk as Ari led him out. They had him kneel in front of the radiator, where Ari connected the chain to the radiator with the combination lock from earlier. "There," said Ari. "Does that feel okay?"

"Y-yes," said Valen, curling up on the floor. "Th-thank you." He could at any time unclip the carabiner and free himself, of course. That was the point. They had *trust* now, maybe just a little. This was a tool to help all of them get him fed without anyone getting hurt, and he knew it.

"Okay," said Lex, putting a few more loops of tape onto the parts of the muzzle that would touch his skin. "Are you ready for this now?"

"Y-yes ... No! Yes. Yes, I'm ready."

"O-okay," said Lex. "I'm going to put it on now." *If you're actually ready ...*

Lex made sure all the parts that would inhibit his ability to speak had been removed, then approached, prompting Valen's trembling to start up again. She gently slipped it on, then came behind him to do up the buckle.

He freaked out, pawing the muzzle off like a dog, sobbing and throwing it to the ground. He immediately wrung his hands and started apologizing. "I – I'm sorry, I tried not to – it was – it was a reflex – I'm sorry."

"Okay, that's okay," said Lex. She gave him a reassuring touch and reached down to pick it back up. "Here, why don't you take it and put it on when you're ready."

He eyed the proffered device warily.

"You don't have to put it on until you're ready," said Ari. "But we're not going to feed you until you have it on. Okay?"

"O-okay," said Valen. He took the device from her, and she stepped back. They both just watched him, giving him time.

He stared at the inside of the muzzle, clearly trying to control his breathing. He lifted it to his face with trembling hands, holding it there, fumbling with the belt with uncoordinated hands. "Can you – can you please – help me – "

Lex came over before he even finished asking, securing the buckle. "There, is that okay – "

"Let me – " Valen said, panic rising again. "Let me – just-just-ust take it off again."

Lex backed away. Valen struggled to undo the buckle, then eventually got it to snap off. The muzzle fell into his lap.

"All good?" said Ari, with a thumbs-up.

"Y-yes," said Valen. "J-just let me ... just let me put it on and take it off a few times."

He did so, getting gradually better at doing and undoing the buckle. *Take your time, sweetheart. We'll go when you're ready. When you really believe the muzzle will come off when you want it to.*

"O-okay," he said, doing it up for the last time and folding his hands in his lap. "I think I'm ready now. I think I'm ready. P-please."

"All right," said Ari. "You stay here. Me and Lex will bring it to you. Stay *there*, just like that. If you take the chain off, our priority goes from feeding you to restraining you. Got it?"

"Yes," said Valen. "Thank you. Thank you."

Lex and Ari went back into the kitchen, watching him out of the corner of their eyes. Ari took another bag of blood out of the fridge and repeated what she'd done before, setting it in the sink and cutting it open with scissors.

Just the same as before, there was an instantaneous response, him slamming to the full length of the chain, hissing and spitting, eyes dull with base animal intelligence, strangling himself to try and reach them.

Maybe it was just their imagination, but it looked like his fangs had gotten longer and his fingers sharper as he raked the floor.

"J-Jesus," whispered Ari. She poured blood into a drinking glass, then ran some water into it, swirling it to mix.

She stuck a straw into the glass, then turned to assess Valen. He panted, still kneeling on the floor, his cheeks flushed, but he looked a little embarrassed, which meant he had the presence of mind to be embarrassed.

"All right," she said, bringing it in. "Good job, you're doing good. Back up a little bit."

He shuffled backwards. Ari set the glass down on the floor next to his claw marks, within his reach, and then backed up. "All right. Go ahead. All yours. Drink it slowly, so you don't get sick."

Valen crawled forward, extending his hand to take the glass. His unsteady hand knocked it over instead, spilling the blood all over the wood floor. His face fell, looking like he was discovering new hopes he didn't even know could be taken away. "I-I'm sorry."

"It's okay," said Lex.

"We still have the other h – No." This last part came as Valen knelt and tried to lick the blood off the floor, pressing the mesh muzzle into it. After a second, he wet his hands with the diluted liquid and tried to push it through into his mouth. "No, no, don't do that."

"Please – " said Valen as Ari came over and gently took the chain, hauling him back, sliding him across the wooden floor. "Please – just let me – "

"You don't have to eat off the floor," said Lex. "We'll get you a new glass."

"Don't lick the floor," said Ari. "We don't do that here. We're all people. We all get treated like people. People don't make other people eat off the floor."

Part of Lex wanted to let him do it, he seemed to want it so badly. But she knew Ari was right. He'd already been humiliated enough as it was. He didn't need to eat blood off the floor, through a muzzle, on top of all that.

Lex got some towels to wipe the spill up. No use making him look at it if they weren't going to let him at it. Ari went back to the kitchen and ran more water, making another glass.

They'd try as many times as it took to get food into him. It was what he needed and deserved, and it fell to them to make sure he got it. Lex's softhearted compassion and Ari's sense of duty and responsibility made them both arrive at that answer independently.

Ari came back over, and both of them knelt in front of him. "Come here, big guy," said Ari.

He tentatively crawled over, staying at arm's reach, not further.

"Give me your hands," said Ari.

He extended them out. Ari took one and used it to pull him closer, his thighs sliding across the wooden floor. Then she put the glass in his hand, using both of hers to fix both of his onto the glass.

"You got it?"

"Y-yes," he said. "B-but I'm not sure if I have the – hand strength to lift it to my mouth."

Ari smiled gently. "That's what the straw is for."

Valen lowered his head, and Lex poked the straw through the muzzle so he could start sucking the blood up.

The blood moved up the straw and into his mouth, and he shuddered. Tears welled in his eyes, and he let out small, overwhelmed sounds.

"There we go," said Ari, as he continued to obediently sip. She removed one hand and stroked his hair. "Good boy."

He shuddered and flushed.

"I'm not sure if he likes it when you do that," said Lex.

Valen flushed even more deeply, averting his eyes.

"See, he's embarrassed," said Lex.

Ari huffed a laugh. "Lex, that's exactly what you look like when I play with your hair and call *you* a good girl."

It was Lex's turn to blush. *Oh God, really?* Leave it to Ari to embarrass her in front of a vampire.

But he didn't seem to care much. His eyes slid closed, enjoying the feeling of feeding straight from gentle hands touching him.

16

His hands were cold, cold, cold in Ari's own. But she didn't let go. She watched him with the proud approval of someone feeding a stray kitten. It had been a while since she'd felt this way about anyone, the urge to protect and shield. Not since Lex.

His eyes fluttered open, looking morosely at the emptied glass. He released the straw from his mouth, licking blood from his teeth. "Is there – is there more?"

Ari set the glass on the floor. "There's more. But why don't we wait a little bit for your stomach to settle?"

He swallowed. "Yes, that makes sense."

"Are you starting to feel a little better?" said Lex, squeezing his hand.

Valen flushed and looked down. "Y-yes, thank you."

"How about a bath then, huh?"

He seemed to just notice for the first time the utter filth covering himself. He pulled at the hem of his shirt. "O-okay."

"Go ahead and unhook yourself."

Valen removed the muzzle, just as he'd practiced, then unclipped the chain from his collar. God, they'd put a chain and leash on him, like he was a dog. Lex felt kind of bad about that, even though in context it had made perfect sense. To add insult to injury, he was just stuck wearing the metal collar until they could figure something out.

Apparently Ari was thinking the same thing. She crossed her arms. "Hmph. We'll have to figure out some way to get that off you eventually. We don't have the key."

"O-oh," said Valen, visibly disappointed. *We'll figure something out, sweetheart, it's not permanent.*

"Well, we can work on it," said Ari. "Hey, do you want me to carry you up to the bathroom? Our stairs are a bit fucky."

The stairs were easily the worst part of their shitty house, worse even than the paint peeling off the porch. The previous owners had started to remodel them and then just never finished. Lex and Ari kept meaning to set money aside to fix the place up, but ... well, it usually got eaten up by other bills quite fast.

Valen drew in on himself. He looked scared of Ari. "If – if – if you want to. That – that would be – appreciated, ma'am."

"All right, up you go, then." Ari scooped him up, one hand on his back, the other under his thighs. He looked like a deer in the headlights as he slid into her chest, arms curled up.

Ari looked down at him, and he averted his eyes quickly. "Hold on, bat boy." She winked.

This poor guy just couldn't win. He was just constantly being talked down to, as though he hadn't been humiliated enough already. Ari was ... just kind of like that, though.

Ari carried him up the stairs, Lex behind them, just as it'd been that first time. Lex felt less guilty than she had that first time.

"There we are," said Ari, setting him down in front of the bathroom. "Taxi dropping you right off. Have a good time."

"I imagine you'd like some privacy," said Lex.

"We'll get you a towel and stuff, and you can take as long as you want," said Ari.

"Um – " said Valen. "I – I – I might need help getting in and out of the tub. You can – you can stay, if you want. If you want to. Please. You don't have to."

Ari quirked an eyebrow. "Eh?"

"You don't have to."

"Start running the water, Ari," said Lex. "I'll be back with the towel."

Lex walked back down to the hall closet, retrieving a towel and a washcloth. She felt so much better about it now than she had that first time, bathing him out of guilt and pity.

Valen was sitting on the toilet when she came back up, looking down at his lap. "I've got a towel! Bath time, then?"

Ari closed the flow of water. "Do you want us to look away while you undress?"

"I – I think I'll fall down if I have to – I think I need help to – "

He just couldn't win; he couldn't even have the dignity of undressing himself in privacy. "All right, that's okay, I'll help you," said Lex.

He pulled his shirt over his head, then almost lost his balance if not for Ari's hand on his back. He let it fall to the floor, then leaned over and pulled his pants down, again only staying upright because of the two women holding him up. He was just as emaciated as before, and just as injured, but the motions of his hands were less unsure.

"Are you sure you don't want some privacy?" said Lex. Part of her wanted to stay with him despite his indignity, his being so vulnerable.

"I don't mind," he said, voice impassive. It was impossible to tell what he was actually thinking. Had he been like this before, or was he just afraid of saying something that would upset them?

"Okay," said Lex. "As long as it's what you want." Valen pulled his underwear down, then turned to step up into the bathtub and immediately ate shit, tumbling down. Ari hollered and grabbed him, lowering him by the arm into the tub.

He took a minute to settle, sinking down into the water. "It's nice?" said Lex.

"Yes," he said, eyes watering. "Th-thank you."

Lex shrugged. "Well, we kind of had to." What'd happened to him had mostly been their fault, so it seemed like this whole process was the very least they could do for him. Lex produced a folded-up washcloth, sliding it onto the edge of the tub. "Here, the soap's over there. We, ah, don't have one of those nice detachable shower heads, so we'll just have to refresh the water more than once."

Part of Lex wanted to run the washcloth over his body with her own hands, but that was probably too much. He needed to do some things for himself to feel in control, surely. He needed to not be humiliated so much. Face once again unreadable, he took the washcloth and wet it, then rubbed the soap on it.

He started washing the copious blood off his face, then looked down at the water already staining red, apparently startled. "O-oh, I-I-I'm – It must have been ghastly to – to look at me like this the whole time."

Lex was amused by the concept of a vampire being self-conscious about how much blood they'd gotten on themselves while feeding.

Ari cleared her throat. "I'll start getting your stuff out of the van. You'll need some new clothes." She prodded the pile of vile, blood-soaked clothes on the floor. "Um, do you think it's worth trying to save these? Can we just get rid of them?"

Oh God, Lex hadn't even thought about that. The clothes were black, so bloodstains wouldn't show up too badly, but sheesh, how to even start washing those?

To her dismay, Valen perked up and said he could mend the shirt if given proper sewing supplies. Ari grimaced, but reached down and picked up the clothes without complaint. "Right ... I'll go throw this in the wash, then. We brought all the clothes you had in your closet and dresser."

"Th-thank you. I – I'm grateful to – that you thought to b-bring my things."

Ari shut the door behind her, leaving Valen and Lex alone in the bathroom. She leaned over, reigning in the urge to pet his hair. "Do you want me to wash your hair? Since you don't seem to be able to lift your arms above your head."

"Yes, please," he said, barely above a whisper. He wouldn't look at her. *Please look at me. It's all right.*

Lex squeezed some shampoo out and started to lather it onto his head. He gave a few soft sighs, leaning into her touch. *There we go. It feels good, right? We can make you feel good. We didn't hurt you on purpose. We're not bad.* She worked out the knots in his hair and rubbed the spots where blood had soaked onto his scalp.

She wished he would talk more, but of course his voice was strained. She was surprised so far by how soft and formal his voice was. The frantic, violent way he'd spoken earlier must have just been because of circumstances, voice dying down as he landed in safety. Had he always stuttered this much, or was that just nerves too?

He broke the silence after a minute. "Are you sure – is it – " He clamped his mouth shut, letting out a soft whine.

"Go ahead," said Lex. God, it was probably going to take *ages* before he could behave like a normal person again, without the constant fear. She couldn't even imagine the psychological effects what he'd been through would have on a person.

"Are you sure Ari would not object to the way you're touching me?"

Lex almost choked. *What?* Was he ... afraid that Ari would be *jealous?* Why would he ... ?

Did he not think that Lex and Ari washed each other's hair? Did he think it meant something it didn't? She was baffled by the question. She was washing his hair because he *physically couldn't* lift his arms above his head to do it himself.

But then again, he wasn't thinking normally.

"Of course," said Lex, her voice tinged with amusement. "She doesn't care. Why do you think she would?"

Valen shook, sending out tiny ripples in the water, and let out an overwhelmed squeak. *Oh no, did that scare him more?* "I – I'm not sure – I'm sorry."

"It's okay." She started scratching his scalp again. "Have you ... Has no one ever washed your hair for you before? Besides that time I did it at the hunter's compound, I mean."

"N-no, no one has."

That made her sad, imagining a life without the kind of casual intimacy needed to just wash the hair of someone you cared about. "It's nice, isn't it?"

"Y-yes."

"Me and Ari do it for each other all the time."

He let out another strangulated whine. *Geez, I keep messing it up. Maybe best to finish the wash and change the subject before I say something else to scare him.*

Lex poured some water over his head to rinse the shampoo out. "Oh, um ... " she said. "Right, I needed to ask you ... I think, at your house, I heard you ... talking on the phone? I assume that was someone you wanted to come help you right?"

He went rigid. "Oh – oh, yes, yes, I – I'm sorry – I'm sorry, Alexis."

"Don't apologize," she said. "It's okay. I probably would have done the same thing. We just need to talk about it because it means someone is on the way to get you, right?"

He blanched. "I-I-I asked my husband to come rescue me."

"Oh." She fidgeted. Of course. What had she been thinking? He had a life, a family. He wouldn't want to stay with her and Ari forever. He was probably eager to get back to his old life, back to real safety. Should they just let him go? Ari's criteria had been that she wanted to be sure he wouldn't hurt anyone, and that seemed fair ... and his husband was probably kind and gentle, if he was married to Valen. That was probably where he belonged, not here. "Well, should we – should we call him again and make arrangements for him to come get you?"

"No!" Valen blurted out, eyes wide with panic.

Well, *that* wasn't what she'd expected. If she was in his shoes, she'd want nothing more than for Ari to come get her. "Really? But – but you called him. Do you not want ... ?"

His face crinkled, and he looked away. "My husband is – my husband is a horrible man, whom I despise. I would only – I only called him as a last resort, because I was desperate to escape torture. I would count myself lucky if I never saw his face again."

Oh. Oh no. Valen had an abusive spouse. He had an abusive spouse he never wanted to see again, and he'd rather go back to *that* than face the situation Lex had put him in.

Well, luckily for him, his escape attempt had failed, and he wouldn't be going back to that. A fierce sense of protectiveness flared inside Lex. The thought of losing her strange new friend was curiously heartbreaking. "Oh. Well, if that's the case ... does he know where you are? Do we need to hide you?"

Valen's face melted into a touched expression. "I was unable to give him the address before – before – those two arrived, and if he – even if he was able to track the location based on the phone number, or some trick, it would only lead him to – to my house out deep in the country."

"Sheesh, that's a good five hour drive." Lex had driven that road trip more often than she'd liked recently. "Yeah, I don't know if he really has any way to find you then ... right?" The last thing she wanted was to have to come face to face with some vampire who was an asshole even by vampire standards.

"I believe so," said Valen. "At least, I hope so."

The door cracked open, and Ari's disembodied arm came in, laying clothes on the sink. "Clothes," she said succinctly, pointing to them without sticking her head in. "There. Bye."

The arm withdrew, and they both heard the sound of furniture moving downstairs.

"So, if I can ask," said Lex. God, she *really* wanted to talk about it, but maybe that was pushing it, given his state. He probably didn't feel comfortable saying no to anything, but ... "I'm – I'm curious as to why you're married to him if you hate him so much."

Valen let his eyes fall down into the soapy water. "It was my parents' idea. I – I did not have the courage to defy them on the issue until well after we were married and it became obvious to me how truly horrible it was."

"Oh," said Lex. She could relate to that, a little. Ari had always defied her parents without worry, but Lex had always shied around corners to avoid upsetting her own. "Kind of the same thing happened to me. Well, not quite that bad, but my parents tried to set me up with this family friend's son as soon as I told them I was dating Ari. They seemed to think they could convince me not to be queer if they just tried hard enough to find a man I would like better than Ari." The fact that Lex had had childhood crushes and flings with boys probably didn't help disabuse them of that notion, since they seemingly couldn't comprehend the idea of being interested in both men *and* women.

Valen got a look of pity on his face. "They – Mine also seemed to think they could convince me – not to be transsexual – if I married a proper husband and had proper wifely d-duties. They were – were also trying to break me of my – pacifist beliefs, believing them to also be im-improper."

Jesus Christ. Lex tried to imagine if her parents had tried to convince her out of being queer *and* out of wanting to not literally murder people. "I'm so sorry. Oh my God, that's awful. I'm so glad you got away from that."

"As am I." He swallowed, voice sticking in his throat. "I – I still couldn't get him to sign the divorce paperwork I initiated, which is why I – I still have his last name. Any time he – he s-starts to consider just letting me go, h-his parents say that divorce isn't something to – to consider, and that he needs to be a proper husband to make me a proper wife."

Oh God, his last name, that stupid "clue" they'd gotten to link him to the blood farms, which in their minds had been all the evidence they'd needed to confirm Nick's suspicions. It had been linking him to a family he hated and was trying his hardest to escape. "I'm – I'm so sorry, Valen, I feel – I feel so horrible."

"It's not your fault."

"No, I – " Her voice wobbled. "When we looked up your last name we assumed it meant you were an evil person working for the blood farms. I-I-I feel so horrible about what we did to you."

He looked at her tiredly. "It was – Your train of logic was sound ... It was a fair assumption to make, given the circumstances."

Somehow it felt like things would be easier if he were mad at her. Tears slipped down her cheeks. "It doesn't matter, I – I'm so sorry, Valen, I'm so so sorry, I don't know if you can ever forgive me. It's our fault this all happened to you. I'm so, so, so sorry. How can I even begin making it up to you?"

"You are already off to a good start." He smiled weakly, showing those fangs – Lex had always found the flash of fangs scary, for obvious reasons, but now she was delighted by it. He was smiling, really *smiling*, a smile that went to his eyes. "This still feels – not quite real. This is – the rescue I'd been hoping for. I am st-still a little afraid of waking up back in the basement."

"No!" said Lex fiercely, so horrified by the idea. "Absolutely not. I won't let that happen to you. I shouldn't have let it happen in the first place."

"Thank you." He dipped his head. "I think I am quite ready for a water change."

Lex pulled the drain in the tub, watching the muddy brown water be flushed away, then plugged it back up and set the water to warm again. She tried not to stare at his exposed nude form as he sat in the tub waiting for it to fill back up.

"So, if – if I may ask in turn," said Valen. "How did you and Ari – become involved?"

"We were childhood best friends," said Lex. "And we both got tired of boys breaking my heart over and over again." Ari had known she was mostly into women from a young age, but Lex had taken a while longer to realize. But Ari had been there the whole time, through everything. Lex couldn't imagine her life without Ari. That probably made her … a little codependent, but it was how it was.

"That is – that is wonderful." Lex could not help but notice the envy in his voice. She decided not to elaborate further or prompt more conversation on the topic. She still burned with about a million and a half questions, but best not to overwhelm him.

It took one more water change before he was clean to his own satisfaction, at which point Lex helped him stand and towel himself off. Lex felt … better about taking him back downstairs after this bath than the last one. There was no torture to send him back to. Unless being subjected to Ari forcibly arranging your belongings was torture.

Lex offered to bandage his wounds before he got dressed again, which prompted the same deer-in-the-headlights look, but he agreed. She tried to be as gentle as possible. He still trembled under her touch, but he offered no comment.

"There we go," she cooed, securing the last bit of gauze on him. He was practically more gauze than skin at this point. "How's that feel?"

"Better. Thank you."

"Great, want to get dressed, then?"

"Yes, please."

"Geez, good thing Ari brought you a belt too," said Lex as she helped him step into his pants. "You're, like, five sizes too small for your clothes now."

Valen said nothing. Geez, what a stupid comment that had been. Obviously he could see and feel that for himself. It must be embarrassing to have attention drawn to it. Geez, why did she *say* that? "Well – well, we'll get you back up to a healthy weight, don't worry." Oh, smooth. Sure, that would make him feel all better.

He remained silent, but she could see tears pooling in his eyes again. "I promise!" she doubled down. "It'll be okay – please, I promise it'll be okay, please don't be upset."

He still said nothing, putting a hand to his face. *Oh, please, please, I'm trying my best.* "Can I give you another hug?"

"Yes," said Valen instantly.

Her arms came around him. This time she was free to lean fully into it, since there was no blood on his shirt. His skin was still cold, but it'd been warmed significantly by the bath, like cool tile warmed by sunshine.

"Thank you," Valen whispered.

Lex smiled. "Come on, let's go downstairs."

She went down first, in case he fell. Ari's voice could be heard from the kitchen. "Are you *really* sure there isn't anyone else there I can talk to?"

Fuck. That was the voice she used when she was talking to Nick. Lex considered making Valen go into the living room, as far away as possible, but he was already at her back, at the threshold to the kitchen.

Ari was leaned against the ugly kitchen wallpaper, next to the cradle of the phone. "Fine," said Ari. "Whatever. Just tell everyone else we can't go on patrol tonight ... Yeah, and we already didn't do that."

She turned to Lex and made a motion like she was shooting herself in the head, making a face. "I know we're *scheduled*, Nick, I'm telling you we have to be excused for now because Lex lost about seventy-five percent of the blood in her body. You were there."

Valen whimpered behind her. Fuck, he could probably hear Nick's voice from the phone with his enhanced hearing. She turned around and tried to soothe him, but he didn't seem to notice.

"Just as I told you, I killed it," said Ari. "And no, we're not catching you another one, before you ask ... You're lucky I can't kick your balls through the phone lines. Bye, scumbag." Ari slammed the phone into the cradle. "It seems like it's getting harder for Nick to hide what a piece of shit he is. He usually behaves to your face, at least."

"Ari," said Valen weakly. "Thank you for telling him I'm dead. Thank you for – for – for – for – "

"All right," Ari grunted. "No need to cry about it."

Of course we would, sweet boy. Lex wondered what he *thought* they were going to do with him, if he was so overwhelmed by the fact that they would lie to hide that he was still alive. Did he think they would just say *Oh yeah, he's here, but you can't have him, don't come over* or something?

"Come on into the living room," said Ari. "I guess it's doubling as your bedroom for now."

Oh, arranging things nicely, Lex loved doing that. They brought in Valen's dresser, end table, towels, all his clothes, some of his lab equipment and books, and whatever else they'd thought to grab. There really wasn't that much of it, and it *sort* of fit in the living room.

Ari arranged things and kept looking back at him for a thumbs-up or thumbs-down, but he always assured her that it was perfect where it was, even if it was clearly blocking the door or some other way that was obviously not perfect. They helped him put some clothes and shoes in the hall closet, and hung up extra curtains and taped them to the wall to ensure absolutely no sun could get into the room.

Once that was all done, Valen reported that he might be ready to eat more, so they went back into the dining room and had him repeat the exercise of loosely restraining himself. They did this a few more times over the course of the day, and each time he seemed a little less afraid of the muzzle.

Valen was obviously extremely tired, so they eventually offered to just let him go to sleep, which he found agreeable. They pulled the plastic off the couch and removed the cushions, and unfolded it to reveal a mattress stored inside.

He started crying when he saw them setting up the bed.

"Geez," said Ari. "I knew our couch was shitty, but it's not *that* bad."

"I – I – I'm sorry," said Valen. "N-no, I mean no offense. I'm very grateful."

Lex came back into the room with her *second* favorite pair of pajamas, which were blue with yellow duckies on them. (She was wearing her first favorite pair, which were pink with kitties on them.) "Do you want to borrow some pajamas? I noticed you don't have any." *Please say yes. Holy shit, please say yes. This is gonna be adorable.*

"I ... " The tears spilled over. "I – Thank you, yes, thank you, I would like that so much."

Lex helped him, a vampire, an apex predator, step into a pair of ducky pajamas, the too-big set swallowing him, the sleeves too long.

"You like that?" she said, slipping into the same voice she used to talk to sleepy kittens.

He nodded, drawing his hands into himself. It probably didn't entirely make up for still having a metal collar locked on his neck, but he looked a lot cozier.

"Want to lie down, then?"

He sat on the bed and pulled his legs up. Lex pulled the blanket up over him. He rolled over and buried his face in the pillow, shaking.

"Everything all right?" said Ari, giving a thumbs-up.

Valen bit the pillow, face squeezed tight. "Mmm-hmmm," he whined. It was the same motion he'd been making on the gag and the muzzle, biting down and grinding his teeth.

"All right. Well, good night, then," said Ari. "Er, good day." *Nice, Ari.*

They turned off the light and left him alone, going back into the kitchen, lowering their voices. "What do you think?" said Lex.

Ari sighed. "I think he can still hear us, so we should go upstairs."

They did so, fucky stairs squeaking under their feet. They shut the bedroom door. At one point Lex might have been worried about leaving a vampire unsupervised, but it was broad daylight out by now. He had nowhere to go.

"What information did you get out of him?" said Ari.

"He was trying to make artificial blood."

"You believe him?"

Lex nodded.

Ari rubbed the back of her head. "Well, shit. Fuck. All right. I mean, that jives with his whole ... way he is. Most vampires I can think of would be at our throats first opportunity."

A smile ghosted across Lex's lips. "I mean, technically ... "

"Well ... you know what I mean." Ari crossed her arms. "All right ... I guess we need a long-term plan now ... We can keep him here for a while, but I guess we can't keep him prisoner. What do we do when he asks to leave? I'm not letting him go until I'm – "

" – One hundred percent sure he's not going to hurt anyone, yes I know, Ari."

"Hey, I'm a vampire hunter, it's my job to hunt – Well, I suppose the core of my job is really to *control* vampires to make sure they don't hurt anyone, and that just historically has been synonymous with hunting them. This is new to me."

"He's married," said Lex. "The phone call was to his husband."

"Ah. And the husband is a complete scumbag, I assume?"

"Well, it sounds like it. But why would you ... "

"Most men turn into scumbags when their wife cuts her hair short. Besides, all the hot ones end up stuck with scumbags anyway."

Lex put on a fake pout. "You don't think I'm hot?"

"You're hot. I'm the scumbag."

17

— • —

The rest of the day passed uneventfully. They'd called off work, and Lex had the perfect excuse to sit around doing nothing, being injured and all, and Ari also had the perfect excuse, having to take care of Lex and all. They did fuckall, which seemed fine with Valen, who also did fuckall.

Lex checked on Valen before going to bed, but he was still lying there with his eyes closed. "We're going to bed now. Is everything okay? Are you good to keep lying down until morning?"

He'd flinched at her voice, but he kept his back turned, not answering.

He was probably still so overwhelmed. Poor guy. Well ... the sun was setting soon, but he didn't seem to be in any state to try anything, nor did he seem inclined to. They'd had a real conversation earlier. He seemed to understand he wasn't in immediate danger, and didn't need to try and escape, or attack them. It was probably safe enough to just leave him be. "I'll take that as a yes, then. Good night."

She went back to the bedroom, recalling her thoughts to Ari.

"Yeah, that sounds fine," Ari agreed. "The guy's just spent a solid day on the couch and he looks like he'd rather die than get up. I think it should be safe to assume he'll stay put overnight." She flopped down with a huff. "Well, good night."

She was asleep instantly, snoring loudly. Lex eased into bed after her. "Good night, then."

***

Lex woke up the next morning feeling particularly well-rested and full of blood. Ari was sprawled out overtop of her, dead to the world.

Lex was too excited about their curious houseguest to stay in bed much longer, though. She threw the covers back, padding out and down the stairs.

"Good morning," she said, peeking into the living room. "Did you – "

The bed was empty. The borrowed pajamas were tossed to the floor. "Valen?"

She withdrew into the dining room, but there were no signs of him. He wasn't in the kitchen either. Panic growing, she came back upstairs and poked her head in the bathroom. Empty.

"Valen?" she yelled. "Valen, where are you?" She thumped back down the stairs, coming into the living room and crouching to look under the bed. Nothing. "Valen? Valen, please, where are you?"

"The fuck you shouting about?" said Ari's irritated voice distantly.

"Valen's gone," Lex said tearfully. "I can't find him."

There was a distant *Fuck*, followed by Ari's frantic footsteps.

Ari performed the same examination as Lex and came to the same conclusion. They even got out the ladder and checked the attic, pulled the furniture out from the wall, checked the crawl space. Nothing.

"His boots are gone," said Ari, her head in the closet. "So is his cloak."

"The blood from the fridge is gone too," said Lex from the kitchen.

Lex shut the fridge, and Ari shut the closet, and they met in the dining room. "Fuck," said Lex, starting to cry. "Ari, fuck. He's gone."

Ari grimaced and took her arms. "Lex ... I think he wanted to leave. He just took what he needed and left."

"We have to find him," said Lex. "C-come on, before the sun gets any higher."

"Lex ... " said Ari. "I ... I know you're worried for him, and I also would have ... I would have liked it if he'd stayed longer. But ... if you think he didn't do anything wrong, and we both think he won't hurt anyone, then it's not right to keep him prisoner here. He's not a stray cat. If he wanted to leave, that's his decision."

"B-but," said Lex. "What if he doesn't make it? What if he's in danger?"

"He obviously preferred that risk to staying here with us."

"But," said Lex, sniffling, wiping her face. "But – but – but *why*? We were helping him. We – we were *trying* to make it right. It seemed like he wanted to stay."

"I don't know. We might never know. But it might be for the best that we just let him go."

Lex stumbled backwards and sat in the easy chair, crying like a child that had lost their favorite toy. "I – I – I guess so. I guess you're right. I'm sorry. This is stupid. It's stupid to cry."

"It's not stupid." Ari walked over and leaned Lex's face into her chest. "It's sad. It's okay to cry when something is sad."

"Yeah." Lex sniffled. "I wish he'd at least said goodbye, though."

Ari petted her hair. "Yeah … let's do something nice today, okay?"

"Okay."

Ari's clock radio alarm, which was set to go off at eight a.m., sounded faintly upstairs. She sighed. "I'll go turn that off. You go pick out something for breakfast, and I'll cook it for us."

"Okay. Thanks."

Ari disappeared upstairs. A second later, she raced back down, a look of panic on her face. "Fuck! Lex, turn on the CB radio!"

They had a CB radio in the van, which they used when on patrol or hunting, but they also had one at home. They used it less, but it was nice to be able to eavesdrop on the hunter's channel from home. Lex snapped the radio on, and the crackly voices of their fellow hunters came on. "Folks," said Luciano. "You're not gonna believe this, since it's, y'know, fucking eight a.m. and the sun's up, but there's a V alert. Over."

"What?" said Franklyn. "The hell? We just finished patrolling. Where at? Over."

"Luton. Over."

"Me and Jerome are close by there," said Bailey. "I can head over. Over."

"Any details on the call that came in?" said Nick. "Over."

Lex's blood instantly turned to ice. Nick was out there, and he was interested in the V alert, and *Valen* was out there –

"Yeah," said Luciano. "Teacher at an elementary school says a person dressed in black approached children on the playground, and then fled when she confronted them. Says they had red eyes and had covered all their skin. Wearing a mask, even. Couldn't tell if it was a man or a woman. Over."

"No," said Lex, horrified. "No, no, no, that's him. It has to be." She looked at Ari, eyes brimming with tears. "Right?"

"Christ, and they put out a V alert for that?" said Bailey. "Over."

"Two other calls from people who claim persuasion had been used on them *very* close by," said Luciano. "Worth looking into. Over."

"We can go," said Bailey. "That's really close. Shouldn't even take ten minutes. Over."

Ari fumbled with shaking hands to pick up the mic, pressing in the button and saying in a desperate rush, "L-Lex and I can handle this one."

Silence for a moment. "Over."

"It really would make more sense for me and Jerome to go," said Bailey. "It'll take you a lot longer to get there. Not to mention your girl's still hurt, right? You canceled your night patrol and everything. Over."

"R-right," said Ari. "But – but listen, Bailey, this one sounds easy, right? Can you let me have it, as a favor? W-we need the bounty. You know I'm trying to get my girl a new kitchen."

"Ariana – " broke in Nick's voice.

"I didn't say over!" Ari exploded. "I didn't say over! I'm not done!"

Silence on the radio. Ari bumped her head into the wall in defeat. "Over."

"May I remind everyone," said Nick's slimy voice, "that the bounty on a live capture is still in effect. Over."

"Fuck off," said Franklyn. "You're fucking sick. You're not right in the head. Over."

"With all due respect, fuck you," said Bailey. "We're killing it. Over."

"N-no!" said Ari, trying and failing to hide the desperation in her voice. "No, don't kill him. Me and – me and Lex can do another live capture. Please let us take this one, Bailey, please, as a favor to me."

Silence on the radio. "O-over," said Ari.

"This is interesting," said Nick. "Because as I recall, you'd previously said you would never, under any circumstances, bring me another live capture. And yet you're so *eager* for it now."

"Well, I came home and saw the kitchen, and it reminded me – "

"In fact, you found my behavior so abhorrent that you killed my last research specimen to keep me from taking it back. You *did* kill it, didn't you? Over."

Ari laced her fingers behind her head, breathing heavily, nostrils flaring.

"And I think it's interesting that you assume the vampire is a *him*. Given we don't have any other information about it. Over."

Ari yanked the mic back to her mouth. "We have the coffin," said Ari. "We still have it in our van, it would make the most sense to let us do the live capture. Over."

"You're not doing a live capture," Franklyn said heatedly. "Fuck off. Come on. Over."

"I want this one, okay? I need the money. I need the bounty. Over."

"We got this one," said Bailey. "Sorry. I mean, you can come over, but we'll be done by the time you get here. Over."

Ari ground her teeth, huffing, leg bouncing. Then: "Roger that. Over and out."

Ari slammed the mic back onto the radio, pulling her day clothes on as she moved to the door. "Go, Lex! Go, go, go!"

They were out of the house in record time, Ari starting the car and Lex turning on the CB radio in the van. "Lex here, requesting clarification on the location. Over."

"Last seen was at Dalry Street," Nick said sweetly. "And remember that the bounty for a live capture is, as of this morning, ten thousand dollars. Over."

"Fuck, that's forty minutes away," said Lex despairingly.

"Tell them about the kitchen," said Ari. "Pretend to be upset about the kitchen."

Lex clicked the mic back on. "Ari keeps going on about the fucking kitchen needing remodeled," said Lex. "But – but in reality, her mom has unpaid medical bills, she's just too embarrassed to admit that's what she needs the bounty for. Over."

Ari groaned.

"Police have set up a blockade," said Luciano. "Apparently the target isn't moving. Perched on the side of I-76. Over."

"No," cried Lex, imagining him sitting helplessly on the side of the road. Maybe he'd gotten stuck in the sun, or hurt himself and couldn't move. Lex scrambled to pick up the radio. "That's perfect, then, cuz you can just wait for us to get there, since he's – since it's not a threat, not moving around. Please? We really need the money. I know we said we wouldn't do any more live captures, but – but it sounds like Nick really needs one, since we killed his last one. Over." God, if they could just convince the ones who *did* get there first to take him alive, they could figure out a way to rescue him later. But they'd taken *such* a stand against taking live vampires for torture, there was no way to believably walk it back. She was just about ready to throw off the mask and reveal they'd lied about killing him, if it meant they could save him.

God, she *really* didn't want Nick to know he was alive, though, because it'd be obvious they intended to just snatch him back again and someone might make efforts to block that. As much as she didn't want him killed, she wanted him to go back to being tortured with no hope of escape even less.

"Sorry, Lex," said Jerome's voice on the radio. "We're already through the barrier and approaching. Going dark now. Over and out."

"No!" said Lex. "Jerome, wait! Hold on."

"Give it up, Lex," said Luciano. "You can't get every kill just because you want it. Over."

"Yes," said Nick. "It's ... odd how distressing you find this. Over."

Lex slammed the mic back onto the dashboard, sobbing. "Fuck, Ari," she warbled, face in her hand.

Ari nosed the speedometer up to twenty over the speed limit, driving in tense silence, gritting her teeth.

A thrill of fear surged through her as Jerome's voice came back on. "Got it. Target neutralized. They can resolve the V alert now. Over."

"And I don't suppose you were able to secure a live capture?" said Nick. "Over."

"Nope," said Jerome. "On account of fuck you. Over and out."

Knuckles white on the steering wheel, Ari slowed down and pulled over onto the shoulder. Lex kept crying wordlessly. Ari killed the engine, sitting there in stormy silence.

"He – he went through all that," Lex wept. "And – and we couldn't even save him. Ari. Fuck. Ari."

The van dipped with her weight as Ari got out of the van, slamming her door. She paced the length of the van a few times, then started kicking the tires, mouth contorting into unheard obscenities.

18

They finished the drive there just for posterity. They found the area where the confrontation had taken place, the persons of interest long gone, evidenced only by the abandoned sawhorses that had been used to block the road, shoved off to the side. Ari drove slowly past it, then pulled a U-turn and rolled past it again in the other direction.

She pulled the van over to the side and got out, walking around and kicking the nearby innocent shrubs whenever they got too close.

Lex dragged herself out, aimlessly walking around. "What are we looking for?"

"I don't know," Ari muttered. She walked in a straight line, mimicking the drive-by she'd just done. Lex followed, not really searching for anything. Just feeling ... bad.

Ari made a beeline for a shrub at the base of the hill and pulled a bedraggled object from underneath it. It was a satchel, stained and still dripping with red liquid.

"Fuck," said Ari. She inverted it, and out dropped the familiar sight of one of the plastic bags of blood that had been in their fridge, emptied, contents soaking the bag and ground beneath it. Something else also fell out – a book, mercifully spared by being wrapped in a plastic bag.

"We took this from his house," said Lex tearfully, reaching down and picking up the book. "He – All he wanted to bring was the blood and this one book?"

Ari grunted, throwing the bag back down on the floor. "Fucking idiot. Fucking. Fucking moron. Got himself killed. Got him – He kind of deserved it. He was kind of asking for it."

Lex unwrapped the bloody bag and dropped it to the ground, taking the book in both hands. *The Natural History of Viruses.*

All his books had been like that. He was a nerd. They'd managed to accidentally torture and murder a nerd vampire.

"Let's go," Ari huffed, legging it back to the van.

Lex opened the book and saw a note on the title page, written in a fancy, looping handwriting.

To my dearest turtledove,

I hope this will start making you feel more at home. I want you to be comfortable here.

Love,

Priscus

Lex snapped the book closed, hugging it to her chest and crying. He was a person, he'd been a person and there had been those that'd loved him and given him gifts and had pet names for him. And he was gone, turned to ash because of Lex. And Ari too, she supposed, but she could never bring herself to blame something like this on Ari. Only on herself.

"Hey," said Ari nastily. "Let's fucking go."

Lex furrowed her brow, crying harder, and walked back to the van. Lex got in, and they both just sat there for a moment.

"Sorry," said Ari.

Lex said nothing.

"Let's ... let's go do something nice. Let's get brunch."

An hour or two later, and they were in a booth at a diner with a smorgasbord of brunch food in front of them. Ari had already eaten through a decent portion of it. That was what she did when she felt bad. Instead of crying like Lex, she got snippy and ate her feelings.

"Okay," said Ari, setting down a muffin. "We fucked up. But what do we do with our mistakes?"

"We don't let them happen again," said Lex.

"We learn from them. So let's ask ourselves, what went wrong, and how do we prevent it from happening again?"

"I don't know if I want to be a vampire hunter anymore, Ari," said Lex tearfully.

Ari sighed and took a sip of coffee. "Christ. I guess I could be a security guard or something."

"All those vampires we killed were people. They – they had families, and – "

"Now hold on a second," said Ari, slamming her cup on the table. "You can't blame us for that. Most vampires *do* come into human territory to hurt people. Pretty – pretty viciously. They know the risk they're taking to do that. I mean, Christ, there's a huge sign at the border with skulls that says HUMAN TERRITORY – KEEP OUT – VAMPIRES WILL BE KILLED ON SIGHT. We can't try and interview every single one to make sure they're really a bad person."

Lex deflated. "I – I just wish there was some way it didn't have to be this way."

Ari's gaze drilled into her. The waitress came over and refilled her coffee, and Ari didn't even try to flirt with her. As soon as the waitress left, Ari leaned forward and hissed, "And you think I don't?"

Lex put her head on her arms on the table.

"It's easy to just *say* that, Lex. *Everyone* wishes that. You didn't realize until now the vampires we were killing were people? You don't look them in the eye as they die? Because I do. Every time. I know I've killed innocent people by accident. You've been lying to yourself if you don't think you have too."

"Don't talk to me this way," Lex snapped. "It's not okay for you to talk to me this way."

Ari leaned back and crossed her arms. "This was a risk we were taking when we became vampire hunters. It's not avoidable. Just practically, just because of how dangerous vampires can be if we give them a chance. We just had to decide it was worth the risk to save all the innocent people who would be hurt if we *didn't* hunt vampires. Did you not fully understand that? Were you not prepared? We know there are vampires who aren't bad people. We *know* that. But we can't tell that at a glance, and we've already taken as many steps as possible to ensure the only ones we run into are the ones who are here to hurt people. Sometimes someone will end up as the unlucky exception."

"I *know* that," said Lex. "Stop talking to me like a child. I'm not stupid."

"You sure act like it sometimes."

"You always do this. You always take it out on me."

"You act like you're better than me because you don't have the stomach to own up to – "

"Which one of us was it who – "

"You did this when – "

They stopped arguing, breaking off and looking away with red faces as the waitress came back to give them the check.

"Let's not fight," said Ari. "I'm sorry. We're both upset. We shouldn't fight. Let's talk about this more later."

"I'm sorry too," said Lex.

They paid the bill and went home. The ride home was a long, miserable forty-five minutes. They kept the radio on, and the CB radio, but all was quiet.

They came into the house, and Lex started crying again when she saw the remnants of Valen's belongings in the living room.

Ari sighed. "I'll start ... taking this back outside, I guess. Why don't you go lie down?"

"Okay. Thanks. I love you."

"I love you too."

Lex shuffled into the dining room. She stared at the ground, sniffling, and then noticed a blinking light out of the corner of her eye.

The answering machine. Someone had called and left a message.

She pressed play, and the tape spun. "*You've reached the dyke patrol,*" said Ari's voice, the outgoing message. "*We aren't home. Catch ya later.*"

Beep.

"Yo, what's up, dyke patrol," said Bailey's voice from the machine. "This is fagtown here, it's about, uh, eight twenty-five and we're pulled over at a payphone right now. We've got a special little something for you locked in the trunk. Call me back when you get this. We should be home any time after nine a.m."

Lex ripped the phone off the wall and started mashing buttons as Ari came in. "Was that Bailey?" said Ari.

"Yeah," said Lex, heart racing. "Holy shit."

Ari leaned in so both their ears were near the receiver. It rang, and then:

"Yo," said Jerome's voice.

"Jerome," said Lex, tears welling in her eyes again. "It's Lex and Ari. We got your message. Please tell me – "

"Oh yeah," said Jerome. "Girl, listen, you are both *so* bad at lying. Like, I knew Lex was bad at lying, but Jesus, Ari, I've never heard you that nervous before."

"Cut the crap," said Ari. "Get to the point."

"Right," said Jerome, "Well, listen, you never submitted a pair of fangs to prove that you killed Nick's, erm, 'research sample,' so hearing the way you were, uh, panicking to try and get that vamp alive made it preeeeeetty obvious you'd lied and kept it, and something had gone wrong. So we figured we'd just snap it up before anyone else could get to it, and let Nick keep believing it was dead."

"Is he still alive?" said Ari.

"Yeah," said Jerome. "Although I'm sure he's not gonna be happy with us when he wakes up, so if you could get over here – "

"Th-thank you," said Lex tearfully. "Of course, of course we'll come right away. Thank you, thank you so much."

"You owe us one."

"Of course."

"And you'll have to explain to us, er, why you want this one alive so badly."

"Yes. Yes, of course. Thank you so much. We'll come over right now."

"All right, see ya."

"Bye."

Lex hung up the phone, and she and Ari just looked at each other for a minute before taking each other in a tearful hug.

***

Ari drove the van partway up onto the sidewalk and didn't bother fixing her parking job before they both leapt out and ran to the front door.

"Dammit!" said Lex, wading through some obstructive, distinctly out-of-season Halloween decorations blocking part of the porch. "Get out of the way!"

She reached around the enormous fake spider and through the cotton cobwebs to ring the doorbell. Bailey opened the door a second later, leaning against the doorframe with a smarmy grin. "Who's there? I'm not interested in anything you're selling."

"Very funny, shithead," said Ari, all but shoving past him to get into the house. Lex thought they really ought to be more polite, considering Bailey and Jerome were doing them a huge favor, but she was so, so antsy to see –

She rounded into the living room and saw him on the couch next to Jerome. Muzzled, cuffed, chained to the radiator, the whole nine yards. He looked so, so scared, eyes puffy from crying, but *oh*, he was alive. "Valen! Oh my God, oh my God, oh my God, thank you, thank you, thank you, thank you." She sat on the couch and took his hand.

Valen's eyes stayed on Ari, fearful, as though he were expecting her to punish him. But she just leaned him into her chest, putting her arms around him. "There you are. There you are, we've got you."

Holy shit. Ari never did that with anyone besides Lex. She must have been way, *way* more upset than even Lex had guessed.

164

It was only at this point she registered what it was she was looking at on the coffee table in front of her: a pair of canine fangs next to bloody pliers. "Wh – Did you – did you fucking *rip his teeth out*?" She imagined poor Valen, helpless and restrained and in pain as Bailey and Jerome held him down and took pliers to his mouth.

"We need to submit them to prove we killed him," said Jerome. "You know that."

"Nick was probably suspicious when *you* didn't do that," said Bailey.

"We did it while he was asleep," said Jerome.

Lex lowered her hackles a little, then scoffed, "Whatever." She leaned Valen's head to the side to access the buckle keeping the muzzle on. "Shh, shh, it's okay, I've got you."

"Are you sure that's safe?" said Jerome. "Like really sure?"

"Yes," said Ari. She'd had enough of seeing Valen treated this way.

The muzzle came off, a string of bloody saliva stretching out after it, his newly freed mouth gasping and panting. "There we go," Lex cooed, palming his cheek, trying to steady him as his eyes wheeled about in terror. "There we go, there you are, sweetheart."

"I'm – I'm sorry," said Valen, instantly in tears. "I'm – I'm sorry I ran away."

"You don't have to apologize," said Lex. "Can I have the key for the cuffs?"

Jerome produced the key, but then retracted his hand before Lex could grab it. "You have some explaining to do. We nabbed him because you obviously wanted him alive."

"Right," said Lex. "I will, but – can – can we explain it after we – He really doesn't like being tied up."

"As long as you're sure he won't try anything." Jerome handed her the key.

She unlocked the wrist cuffs, dropping them to the ground, then she detached the chain from the collar on his neck. "There, is that better?"

"Th-thank you," he whispered.

Lex stroked the nape of his neck. He hunched in over himself, refusing to make eye contact.

"This is Valen," said Ari. "And he hasn't committed any crimes, so it's not right to punish him."

Bailey and Jerome looked at each other.

"You're ... you're sure?" said Bailey.

"Yes," said Lex. "He was here because he was gathering ingredients to make artificial blood. Valen, do you want to tell them about it?"

Valen trembled, entire body tense. His lip quivered and he dipped his head. "Please kill me," he whimpered.

"Wh-what?" Lex gasped. Oh God. Oh fuck. This was all their fault. They had to fix it. They *had* to. She couldn't live with herself. She *couldn't*. "No, no, we're not going to kill you, sweetheart. Hey, talk to me. What's wrong?"

"It hurts," he said, wobbling. "It hurts, it hurts so bad and it's never going to get better."

"Hey," said Ari, and her hands squeezed his shoulders. "You're feeling really bad right now because of temporary things. Don't make any permanent decisions right now."

Lex's hand squeezed his. "All right, all right. It feels bad physically or emotionally?"

"B-both," he wailed. "Please, please have mercy on me. I – I'm sorry."

"This is weird," said Bailey. "Geez, this is weird."

Lex glared at them. She knew what he meant, of course: it was rare to see a vampire expressing any emotion other than anger, or indignation, or anything outside the range of things they would express in combat. It was rare to talk with one, and listen to them talk about their feelings, and beg for mercy.

"Shut up," Ari snapped, expressing the impatience Lex felt at the commentary. She hugged her arms closer to him. "We're still going to help you, Valen. All right? Let's unfuck this thing together. We'll help you dig yourself out."

He squeezed his eyes shut, hands still in his lap, seemingly afraid to accept any of the comfort being offered to him.

"Now, what is it that hurts?" said Ari. "Physically? What can we fix?"

"The – the – the si-silver dart is still – is still – "

Jerome and Bailey must have used one of the nonlethal silver darts to immobilize him. *Fuck.*

"Jesus, that hasn't worn off yet?" said Jerome.

"N-no," Valen said. "Please, it hurts, please, please."

Jerome got a stunned look on his face. "I ... I didn't know it hurt that badly. I'm sorry."

"Why *wouldn't* it hurt?" Valen wailed. "Why – why – "

Lex leaned into his field of vision, tilting his head to look at her. "All right, don't get worked up. Focus on what we can do now. How can we help you?"

He sniffled. "I – I – Please, pl-please just – knock me unc-uncon – knock me out again."

"Really?" said Ari.

"It – it'll wear off, I think – I think it will wear off."

"Okay," said Ari, squeezing him reassuringly. "Okay, we'll do that. What do you want us to do longer-term? Where were you trying to go? You went south."

"The – the border."

The *border*? Fuck, he'd been going in the complete opposite direction if that'd been his goal. Was he really that panicked, that he'd flee without making sure he knew where he was going?

"Do you want us to drive you to the border?" said Ari. It wasn't safe for them to drive him *into* vampire territory. But if he wanted ...

"Pl-please let me stay with you, ma'am, if – if – if you're still amenable to – to hosting me," Valen stuttered.

"Of course," said Lex. "Of course we will."

"Are you *sure* that's what you want?" said Ari. "Are you just saying that?"

"I c-can't be on my own like this," said Valen. "It – it already didn't work." He seemed a little more at ease now, though, by the offer to let him go.

"All right," said Ari. "Then we'll knock you out, and when you wake up, you'll be back at home. At our house. Nice and safe."

"In the ducky pajamas?"

Holy shit. Lex tried not to smile. "Sure, if that's what you want."

"We did it with a knife to the neck earlier," said Bailey. "Was that okay?"

"Y-yes," he said. "That's – that's the fastest way. But – but maybe make it bigger this time? So I – so I'm out for longer. Please? If that's – if that's okay."

"Of course that's okay," said Lex. "Are you ready?"

"Wait, b-before we do that … Can I ask something?"

"Yes, what is it?"

He flushed and looked down. "Can I … can I p-please hold the bird?"

The bird … ? Oh, he was talking about the pet cockatiel that Bailey and Jerome had. Lex hadn't even noticed; the cage was currently covered in a blanket, but she'd heard them talk about their pet bird often.

After a moment of silence, Jerome and Bailey both burst out laughing. "What, Princess D?" said Bailey. "The scream queen?"

Valen kept his eyes down, very red.

"Sure, man," said Jerome. "What the hell, sure, you can hold the bird."

Valen let out a gasp of delight, smiling despite himself. There were two huge gaps where his fangs had been, but Lex's heart warmed at the sight anyway. "Thank you."

Jerome walked over to the bird cage and slid the blanket off of it. The bird had moved to one leg with its beak buried in its wing, and it looked at the humans with half-lidded eyes, as though irritated at being woken up.

Jerome slid the cage door open and stuck his hand in, and the bird stepped up onto his fingers. "Hey, little miss, you wanna come meet someone new?"

Jerome came over. The bird's crest rose again, and it tweeted.

"Hold your hand out," said Bailey, taking Valen's wrist and manually positioning his fingers. Valen's hand fell again as soon as he let go, so he replaced his supports. Jerome set his hand so it was touching Valen's. The bird stepped up onto Valen's finger, and everyone cheered.

19

— • —

He looked completely like a corpse now, chest still, eyes glazed over and open, completely motionless. Rendered totally immobile and helpless at his own request. The amount of trust it took to let them do that ...

We've got you, sweet boy. Thank you for trusting us.

He really did look like a corpse. Maybe this was where the meritless idea of a vampire rising up from a coffin, of being undead, had originated. If Lex had come across him like this without knowing anything else, she probably would have assumed he was dead and buried him. And if he'd been at full strength, he might have been able to dig himself out. And Lex would have reacted with shock and horror when the corpse she'd laid to rest came back to life, even more so if it'd done it to come feed on the blood of the living ... no wonder humans and vampires had such poor relations. He was, objectively, a very scary and dangerous thing.

Lex wiped the blood off the back of his neck where they'd cut in to sever his spinal cord, then wrapped soft gauze around the injury, winding it all the way around his neck for good measure, to have something between the bare metal of the collar and his irritated skin. His neck was an inflamed red color from the metal constantly rubbing on it over the past months – it wouldn't be a problem if he was fully fed and healing quickly, but as it stood now, it must be really uncomfortable.

A lot of things about him looked really uncomfortable – he appeared to have somehow broken both his legs in his haste to get away, so now there was that on top of being severely underweight and still recovering from the ... everything else.

God, she felt so bad about him being stuck walking around with Nick's metal collar still padlocked on his neck. They'd have to figure out a way to get that off ASAP.

Jerome came in with a sleeping bag, suggesting they could slide him into it and zip it up. Like a little worm. It would keep the sun off him, as well as pad him against bumps. Not that he could feel it.

Ari unzipped the sleeping bag and laid it out on the ground, and she and Lex moved his body onto it. Jerome got a shit-eating grin on his face and crossed Valen's arms over his chest like one would for a corpse at a funeral, and Lex batted his hands away.

Ari zipped it up, then hauled him over her shoulder. "Thanks again for the help, guys. We really appreciate it."

"Maybe we'll come over to your place tomorrow to check on him, yeah?" said Jerome.

"Sure!" said Lex. "That sounds great. If you're willing to help feed him ... ?"

Bailey gave a thumbs-up. "Of course! My guy needs to put on some weight, fucking stat."

They waved goodbye one last time and took him out to the van. "I hate to suggest this," Ari said, "but maybe we just put him back in the coffin, so he doesn't roll around."

Lex grimaced. "Yeah ... there's probably not enough room up in the cab with us."

Ari stepped up into the bed of the van and opened the coffin, laying him gently inside and shutting the lid, but not locking it. "We need to give this thing back to Nick," Ari grumbled. "I'm getting tired of fucking looking at it. The coffin, I mean," she rushed to clarify.

Lex kept glancing in the rearview mirror all the way home. Every instinct in her brain was telling her that the person they had back there was dead, that something was terribly wrong with the situation, but she forced herself to engage her higher brain functions that knew what vampires were to calm down.

It was almost evening by the time they got home, but they weren't scheduled to work that night, so they had plenty of time. Ari removed Valen from the coffin and toted him up the stairs and into the house.

"There we go," she said, laying the sleeping bag out on the floor and unzipping it. "Nice and safe at home, just like we promised."

Lex looked at him, motionless and hurt, but alive, on the floor surrounded by his belongings Lex had been trying to figure out what to do with a few hours ago, flush with relief. "Thank God. If he'd actually died, I don't know how I could have lived with myself."

"Yeah ... " Ari said. She elbowed Lex. "If you still wanna talk about not being vampire hunters anymore, we can still have that conversation."

Lex knelt on the floor glumly. "Maybe. I don't wanna make decisions like that while we're upset. C'mon, help me lift him."

They got one end each and lifted him into bed. "Do you think he was serious about us changing him into the ducky pajamas?" Lex asked, trying to hide the eagerness in her voice.

Ari shrugs. "Dunno. He doesn't seem shy about being undressed, so maybe."

Lex sat on the bed and started unpeeling all the layers of clothes off him, wrangling his deadweight limbs until his shirt was off. She hesitated at the sports bra and eventually decided to leave it on. She did the same with his underwear and socks when she removed his torn pants and shoes, and then struggled to get the pajamas on him, buttoning them up.

"There," said Lex. "Cozy, right?"

Ari nodded from where she was sitting in the easy chair. "Looks good. Maybe we should leave a note, in case we're upstairs or something when he wakes up."

"Good thinking." Lex got a notebook and a Sharpie and wrote YOU ARE SAFE, YOU DO NOT NEED TO TRY AND RUN AWAY. YELL FOR US IF YOU NEED HELP. -LEX

She put it on the end table by the pullout couch, then dug in Valen's forgotten bag for the one book he'd apparently judged worth bringing with him, setting it out next to him. Then she pulled the comforter up to his chest, pulling a pillow under his head. "Good night, I guess."

***

They woke up later not to a yell, but a scream, the panic-induced wail of someone in mortal peril.

Lex was out of bed immediately, dashing downstairs to the living room. Two reflective discs of red light swung towards her as she stepped inside, and from the darkness there was the flash of fangs. "Get away!" snarled a monstrous voice.

The haze of persuasion fell over her. It was like someone dimming the lights in her brain. She twitched in place, fighting to take back control of her body, in full blown panic after almost dying the last time she'd been put under persuasion. Her body moved without her input or consent, pivoting on her heel and walking out of the room. Then the puppet strings on her body detached, and she slumped, falling over, pulse racing, far more scared than the mild nature of the experience merited.

She'd almost *died* the last time that'd happened. Her body locked up, and she fell to her knees. From the next room, Valen started to cry loudly.

Ari finally arrived, hustling down the stairs. "Lex, are you okay?"

She looked up at Ari with eyes wide and nodded.

Ari bent down and took her hand. "You okay?"

"Um," she said shakily. "Yeah, I – I'm okay. Sorry."

Ari furrowed her brow. "Did he use persuasion on you?"

She nodded tearily.

"All right. You're okay."

"It was an accident, Ari," Lex begged. "I think. He – he just got scared, it was a reflex, he released me right away. It didn't hurt me, I just – I just got scared."

Ari put both hands on her shoulders and squeezed. "All right. Breathe, Lex."

"Don't hurt him."

"I'm not going to hurt him, calm down."

Lex pouted. Ari sighed. "All right. Go make yourself some calming tea, okay?"

Lex padded into the kitchen, listening to Ari go into the living room and talk to Valen distantly. Her voice was low and soothing, and his shrill and nervous.

Lex wanted to go in and help too, but she'd lost her nerve, charging in and then getting rebuffed so thoroughly. She sat there as the water boiled, then poured herself a cup, staring into the tea bag as it suffused the water.

Valen sounded so scared, it broke her heart. But of course he would be scared. Why wouldn't he be? He was as vulnerable as a vampire could get – starved except for a few feedings gotten into him, unable to walk, surrounded by vampire hunters – the same ones that had put him in this situation, even. The only weapon he had to help himself could only be deployed as an absolute last resort, because it could be taken away at the drop of a hat if they decided he was somehow still too dangerous. All it would take would be to –

"Please don't put the muzzle back on! Please don't!" Valen's terrified cry came out of the next room.

Ari shushed him. "Calm down," she said firmly. "I'm not going to. Calm down. It's okay."

Lex padded into the room with her mug of tea to see Ari sitting on the edge of the bed, holding Valen firmly as tears rolled down his cheeks.

"I'm sorry I used persuasion on you," Valen sobbed. "I'm sorry, I didn't mean to. It was an accident, please believe me. I won't do it again. Please don't put the muzzle back on, I promise I don't need it to behave, please, please."

"It's okay," Ari said. "We just took you out of six months of being brutally tortured a few days ago. We understand you're scared. You understand why using persuasion is an issue, though, right? You know not to use it because it feels bad for us, not just because it'll make us mad at you, right?"

"Yes, I understand, I promise I understand."

"Okay. Just. Just calm down."

"What are you afraid of?" Lex prompted. "Like, what do you think is going to happen?"

Valen grabbed his chest, hyperventilating.

"Take it easy," Ari soothed. "You're safe. How do we make you feel safe? What do you want us to do?"

"I'm not sure," Valen said, tears springing in his eyes.

"Okay, that's okay," Lex said. She set her mug on the end table and sat on the bed next to Valen, putting a comforting hand on his thigh over the blanket. "Is there anyone you want to call? I know you said you didn't want your husband to come get you after all, but is there anyone else you trust? Family? Friends? So you're not just stuck here with us? We want to help you however we can."

"We're not trying to hold you prisoner," Ari said. "Just to make that clear again. We know you didn't do anything wrong, and we're trying to help you get better, that's all."

Valen drew his hands to his chest, quaking, eyes brimming with tears. "N-no, there's no one. I have no one."

"You have us," Lex said with a gentle touch on the arm. "You're not alone, I promise. I promise we're going to do whatever it takes to help you."

He took a deep, shuddering breath.

"Did you have a nightmare?" Ari asked. "Is that how you woke up?"

He nodded slowly.

"You look so tired," Lex cooed. It was true; the bags under his eyes were enormous. "Is there anything we can do to help you sleep?"

He wrapped his arms around himself. "I'm – I'm not sure. Be-because, um … No, I don't think so."

"It's okay, what is it?" Lex prompted. "Is there something that will make you more comfortable?"

He let out a soft whine. "The-the only time I wouldn't be hurt was when I was in the coffin, and-and now it f-feels like I'm in-in danger when I'm out in the open, so-so I don't-don't know if I'll ever be able to sleep again."

"So you feel like you can't sleep unless you're inside the coffin?" Ari asked.

"Please don't put me back inside there," Valen wept. "I can't, I *can't* go back in there no matter what, please, please – "

Ari held up a hand, cutting him off. "All right, all right, calm down. So the point is you feel like you need to be in an enclosed space to feel safe, and that's why you can't sleep out in the open, is that it?"

He nodded tearily. Ari clucked her tongue. "Lex, you stay here with him." She gathered her coat and keys and wallet.

"What?" Lex said. "Where are *you* going?"

"To the hardware store."

***

Ari came back about an hour later with several different kinds of wood and two-by-fours, which she promptly took downstairs where she kept her power tools. Valen kept nervously asking Lex what Ari was doing over the sound of the circular saw grinding and wooden pieces falling to the ground, and Lex promised she'd go check.

When she came down there, she immediately saw what Ari was doing: making a wooden box for Valen to sleep in. An actual coffin to replicate the feeling of being in a safe, enclosed space, without actually trapping him.

She stepped down with a grin on her face. "Oh, you're a genius."

Ari winked at her. "I know."

"What should I do to help?"

Ari had Lex help with measuring and cutting things, the coffin taking shape surprisingly quickly.

Lex came back up a while later, telling Valen they needed to fold the couch back in, because they'd need the space in the living room soon. Valen let himself be lifted gently and set in the easy chair. The sound of nails pounding into wood came next, and Valen sat with his hands clutched fearfully to his chest listening to it as Lex folded the mattress back into the couch, gathering the blankets and pillows in her hands and bringing them downstairs.

She also went upstairs and looked at her collection of plushies, searching for the right one.

"Oh, come on," Ari said when Lex brought a stuffed cat down. "I'm sure he doesn't want that."

Lex set it inside next to the pillows. "Well, if he doesn't, he doesn't have to use it. I'm just giving him the option."

Ari did not argue further. They finished it before the sun came up, lining the inside of the coffin with enough blankets and pillows and padding for it to be comfortable, then adding a lock and handles.

"All right, bat boy," Ari said, dragging the results of their work towards the stairs. "Get ready to get your tits blown clean off."

"Ari," said Lex, trying to suppress her laugh.

It was a struggle to get it up the stairs because of the shape. Huffing and puffing, they managed to shove it into the living room, dragging it by the handles across the floor, to where Valen was sitting in the easy chair looking scared and overwhelmed.

"How's this look?" Ari said proudly.

Lex pulled it open to show the inside. He leaned over, furrowing his brow, and he looked touched. "You made that for me?"

"Yeah, man," Ari said. "Here, you wanna try it out?"

He nodded.

Lex and Ari got one hand under him each, forming a sort of swing with their arms, and hefted him from the chair and into the coffin, laying him out gently. He settled into it, crossing his arms over his chest even though there was plenty of room inside.

"How's it feel?"

"It's comfortable," he said meekly.

Lex guided his hand towards the handle to pull it shut on himself. She could still hear his ragged breathing.

"What do you think?" Ari said.

"This – this is good." His voice was muffled and uncertain from inside. "Yes, I think this is good."

"Try the lock."

A clinking sound from inside. Ari grabbed the handle and gave it a little tug, but it stayed shut. "See? Nice and secure. Now, how about you open it back up?"

Valen pushed the lid open, and it flopped onto the couch beside him. "You wanna try sleeping in this?" Lex asked.

"Yes," he said politely. "Y-yes, I would like to try it. Thank you."

"Good." Ari patted him on the arm. "You can open it and close it however you want, and if you start to get a little freaked out, you can just haul yourself up over the edge to get out, yeah? And if you need anything, you can just yell for us, okay?"

"Yes," he said, slowly pulling the coffin closed, obscuring his face little by little. "Thank you."

20

— ◦ —

Lex wouldn't stop going to check if Valen was awake. She kept calling it his "nap," and Ari kept correcting her that he needed to get a full night's sleep – or day's sleep, or whatever. It was like trying to convince someone excited about baking cookies not to keep opening the oven to check on their progress and let all the heat out.

He slept so, so long. At one point Lex proposed that they check if he was still inside the coffin, for fear he'd somehow disappeared. Ari told her that was ridiculous, while simultaneously also secretly worrying about it a little bit. Lex confirmed that she could hear breathing and very quiet snoring when she put her ear to the coffin, though.

He was *out cold*. Lex and Ari went to bed, and when they woke up, he was *still* asleep, no sign of waking up, and still inactive for several hours afterwards.

The poor guy must have been fucking *exhausted*. No wonder he seemed unable to think clearly or make good decisions, on top of the expected anxiety and fear inherent to the situation.

They killed time by doing their quietest hobbies, and ended up calling Jerome and Bailey to come over later, anticipating that he would, hopefully, be awake by nightfall at the latest. All four of them made sure to call out of work, so they could give Valen their full attention for a little while. Lex and Ari were still considering a career change, all things considered, but best not to make any big decisions that quickly.

"We have to feed him when he wakes up," Ari said, crossing her arms and not looking happy about it.

Not hard to guess why. Valen had taken the last bag of blood nicked from the hospital with him during his ill-fated escape attempt. That probably wasn't a sustainable source of blood for him – it was doubtful they could talk the same people into letting it slide twice, so they had to manage getting the blood themselves.

But they couldn't let Valen feed on Lex, because she was still recovering from having half her blood spilled, and Bailey and Jerome weren't able to come until that night.

That just left Ari. Lex could honestly not think of anything Ari would like to do less than purposefully let a vampire feed on her. Bottom during sex, maybe. She hate hate *hated* being vulnerable and purposefully getting into a position where someone else could, or would, hurt her. Not that she had low pain tolerance – quite the opposite, in fact. It was more of a control issue. Unfortunately, the process inherently required giving some control to Valen, which was exactly why Ari really, really hated being the only one able to do it at the moment, because her sense of duty wouldn't let her make him go hungry for longer than necessary.

"I can do it," Ari said. Of course. In Ari's mind, she could do anything, until proven otherwise. "Just – just give me some time to ramp up to it."

Ari knew he deserved to be fed as soon as he woke up. He would be hungry after sleeping so long, and Ari knew what it was like to wake up and not be able to get coffee first thing in the morning, and maybe that was a similar thing. As she embraced the idea that she would have to let a vampire feed from her soon, she started listening for Valen to wake like waiting for a bomb to drop.

Eventually, Lex swore she could hear him moving around inside.

"Give it a rest, would you?" Ari said, keeping her voice low. "I'm sure he'll say something when he's awake."

There was a gurgle from inside the coffin, the tired call of someone who'd just woken up from deep, deep sleep trying to indicate they were awake.

Ari approached the coffin, but Lex rushed over and overtook her. "Can I open the door?" she blurted out, hand already on the handle.

"Yes," came his tiny, muffled voice from inside, followed by the sound of the lock clinking open.

Lex pulled it open to reveal Valen, looking disoriented and squinting against the light, eyes lidded heavily with sleep, hair wildly messed up on top of his head – and to Lex's delight, clutching the cat plushie.

"Good morning!" Lex said. "How are you feeling? How did you sleep?"

Eyes still encrusted with sleep, Valen rubbed his face. "Good morning ... How ... how long was I asleep?"

"Sixteen fucking hours," Ari said. "You just had a godly power nap, my dude."

"You deserve it," Lex said. "How are you feeling?"

"A little better," he mumbled.

"Did this thing help you sleep?" Ari said, nudging the coffin with her foot.

He nodded.

"Good. Do you wanna hang out in there a bit more, or come out onto the couch?"

"The couch sounds nice," he said quietly. It was impossible to tell what he was thinking.

Lex and Ari lifted him up and out, settling him onto the couch and piling up a fortress of pillows around him to make him as comfortable as possible.

"There," said Lex. "I know it probably still hurts, but how are you feeling?"

He wrung his hands, as though afraid to say, and then timidly said, "Hungry, ma'am. I-I feel a lot better, but – but I would be very grateful i-if there was more blood in the fridge, if I would be allowed to have it."

Yep, just like they'd thought. If he was hungry enough to ask for it while being so clearly scared shitless, definitely time to feed. Ari started, "Oh, we actually ran out of that stuff from the hospital."

"Oh. Wh-when will you – when will getting more be feasible?"

"Oh, um," Ari said, averting her eyes. "I don't think we can really get blood that way again, it was sort of a one-time thing, special circumstances. I think if I went back to the hospital and asked for more, that'd be pushing it and they might start asking questions."

Valen's face crumpled with despair, and he wrapped his arms around himself. "All right. I understand, ma'am."

The poor boy thinks that means we're not going to feed him, Lex realized with a jolt. *Come on, Ari, get on with it.* She nudged Ari with her foot.

"Yeah," Ari continued, too slow, painfully. "And, um, Lex can't really feed you, since – since she lost all that blood recently, not sure how long it'll be before she's fully back from that. So ... "

Valen's face heated up and he was clearly holding back angry tears. He shook a little, biting his tongue. *Come onnnnnn.* When Ari didn't keep going, Lex elbowed her, knocking the wind out of her. "What Ari is *saying* is that since there aren't other options, *she's* going to feed you."

Valen perked up, still shaking, cautiously hopeful. "Real-really?"

"Yeah," Ari said, absolutely failing to keep her unhappiness off every feature of her body. *Come on, Ari, you're going to make him too scared to eat.* "Obviously it's not ideal, but I'm really the only one here with enough blood for you to drink. So. So, have at it, I guess."

Ari just stood there. *Come on, Ari, you're the one who's always stomping around to stop delaying and get moving.*

Lex watched Valen's eyes trail up and down Ari, at a loss. "Um," he said, with all the bravery of someone approaching a live tiger. "How do you want me to – "

"Not on the neck," Ari said quickly.

"R-right ... " Valen looked like he was trying not to cry again.

"The arm would be good, I guess," Ari said.

"O-okay," Valen said.

"What?" jabbed Ari. "That not good enough for you?"

He clutched the blanket to his chest and looked up at her with wide, fearful eyes.

"Ari, you know that's not it," Lex said. "Come on. Relax."

Ari visibly untensed her shoulders. "Right. Sorry."

"You can't just tell him to feed and then stand there when you know he can't reach you."

Ari flushed, looking embarrassed and vulnerable. "Right. Sorry." She took a few steps towards Valen and held her arm out. "Well, there, g-go ahead then." She tapped the skin of her forearm. "Right about there should be good, right?"

Valen bit his lip. "I-I can't, I'm sorry. Bite you. I can't."

Sweet boy, even when we offer he feels like he can't.

"Sure you can," Ari said gruffly. "Gave you permission and everything."

"No, no, I – " He whimpered, sinking down into the pillows. "I-I don't mean to sound ungrateful, I really appreciate this, I-I really, really do, b-but – "

"What's the problem?"

"I don't have my fangs, a-and I don't know if I can really bite hard enough to draw blood with my blunt teeth, and – and – " *Oh.* His fangs had been pulled out, and he couldn't feed without them, not unless he just bit Ari with his whole mouth hard enough to draw blood, which definitely seemed like a worse option.

Ari's eyebrows shot up as she reached the same conclusion. "Oh. *Oh.* Shit. Fuck. Yeah, sorry." She retracted her arm. "Okay, how about this, then, I'll just make a cut on my arm for you to drink from, then when you're done, you just close it up with that super special vampire spit you got." Vampire saliva had wound-healing properties, so a vampire could bite a human, drink their fill, and then immediately close the wound again, as long as the wound was small enough.

Relief washed over his face. "Yes, th-that sounds perfect. Thank you, ma'am."

Ari withdrew her hunting knife, and Valen whimpered, averting his eyes. Ari made a small cut on her arm, then sat on the couch next to Valen. "*Bon appétit.*"

"Th-thank you," he wept. "I-is it really okay?"

"Yep. Now, come on, before it gets cold. Hah."

Valen leaned down and drank, movements soft and slow, like a cat lapping at a saucer of milk. Lex could tell what Ari was thinking: *I guess this isn't so bad.* She was doing a good job of hiding whatever discomfort was left. She brought her hand up and stroked the nape of his neck. "There you go," Ari said encouragingly. "Good boy."

He shivered and flushed hot in the face. Lex eyed him, keeping in mind what Ari had said about it. He just looked embarrassed.

After a few moments, he pulled back and swiped his tongue over the wound. The bleeding stopped instantly. Lex tried to hide her fascination. She'd never seen that done up close and personal before.

He raised his head. "Thank you," he said, voice thick.

"'Course," said Ari. "We can't let you starve now, can we?"

Valen dipped his head down, licking his lips. "Um, ma'am, have you been tested for diabetes?"

Ari furrowed her brow. "What?"

Valen's face snapped into wild panic, and he shrank back. "I – I'm sorry, I shouldn't have – shouldn't have said – said that, I – "

"Are you saying you can taste diabetes in my blood?" Ari snapped. "Or something?"

"I'm sorry," he wept. "I'm sorry, I'm sorry, pl-please forgive me, I – "

Ari stomped out of the room, huffing. Valen continued to babble and shake. "Alexis, I'm sorry, I didn't mean to – I don't know why – Please, just – "

Lex put her hands firmly on his shoulders, and he immediately shut up, quivering. "Did you taste something in the – "

"Yes," he said, tears streaming down his cheeks. "Her blood sugar seemed high, I was just worried for her health, but I shouldn't have said that, I didn't mean to offend her, or – or make her uncomfortable, I'm – "

"Okay," she said, giving him a squeeze, "Just calm down. Calm down, you didn't do anything wrong."

"I'm sorry."

"Okay, just. Just stay there a minute."

Lex followed Ari out into the dining room, where she sat stormily at the table, arms crossed. "Ari, what the fuck," Lex said.

"He can't – He said – Where does he get off drinking my blood and then *diagnosing* me?" Ari said. "He's being weird while drinking my literal fucking blood."

"Ari, what's your fucking problem? This whole situation is weird."

Ari's face spasmed. "I don't have *diabetes.*"

"Ari," Lex says, exasperated. "For fuck's sake."

"I'm not getting tested for diabetes."

Lex stomped over to Ari and slammed her hand on the table, pointing to the living room with the other. "You're going to march right back in there and explain to that boy that he didn't do anything wrong, and you just got upset because you have a complex about going to the doctor, because if you're just macho and independent enough, that means you don't get sick. You fucking idiot."

Ari flushed deep red. Lex had cut to the exact truth immediately, and it felt humiliating to be so thoroughly outed and embarrassed. "Okay, just give me a minute."

"No. Now."

Ari's face screwed up. "F-fine."

She got up and walked back into the living room, refusing to make eye contact with Valen. "Diabetes runs in my family," she said. "I get freaked out thinking about it. It wasn't anything you did."

"Oh," says Valen, looking a bit calmer. "Okay. That's understandable. I was just – just hoping to possibly be helpful if you didn't know. Getting treatment earlier can be – "

"I know," Ari said quickly, and Valen cowered again. Lex gave her a little kick in the shin. "Ow – I mean. Yeah, I know I *should* go to the doctor. Thank you for worrying about my health."

"And?" said Lex.

"And ... I hope you feel better."

"And you're ... ?"

"I'm ... hoping that you feel better?"

"You're sorry, Ari. You're sorry that you got upset with him and made him scared."

Ari rubbed the back of her head, finding her feet interesting. "Oh. Yeah. That, um, that too. You don't deserve to get scared or anything. I know I can be kind of intense sometimes."

Valen nodded. "Thank you. I understand."

"Now, then," said Lex, with a little clap. "We talked to Bailey and Jerome on the phone, and they're gonna come over tonight, all right? Unless you don't want them to?"

Fear flashed across his face. "What are they coming over for? Ma'am? If I may ask?"

"They're going to feed you too," Ari said. "You're gonna need more than just one feeding until you're back to a healthy weight."

"Oh," said Valen, expression unreadable. "Th-thank you. That sounds wonderful."

"They're bringing a board game too. Hope you like Monopoly."

21

— · —

"Do you have a moment to talk about our Lord and savior, Jesus Christ?"

Ari looked Bailey up and down, hand still on the doorknob, as though trying to decide if she wanted to just shut the door again. "You think you're so funny. You're gonna need Jesus to save you if you don't knock that shit off."

Bailey sauntered in. "You're right. We're actually here to deliver a pizza. You want an XL or a medium?" He hooked his arm around Jerome's shoulders.

"What is this, dinner and a show?" Ari shut the door.

"Nah, we're not doing standup. The show is what this is for." He gestured to his acoustic guitar, slung across his back.

"You think you're so goddamn funny."

"You know you love us."

"Only because nobody else will."

Bailey grinned widely, then turned towards Valen. "And there's the man of the hour! You're gonna eat like a king tonight."

Valen pressed himself fearfully into the back of the couch. Uh-oh, was he still scared of them? It made sense ... Although Jerome and Bailey had handed Valen back over to them, they *had* ... handled him a little roughly, not wanting to risk their own safety.

"It is *man*, right?" Bailey continued. "Jerome insisted it was man."

"You were all juiced up on T when you got here," Jerome added. "So I assumed. Sorry you haven't been able to get your juice while you've been here. It's clearly worn off by now."

Valen looked at them like a deer caught in the headlights. Lex's heart suddenly broke, realizing how foolish this must seem from his perspective. Referring to someone as *man* or *woman* must feel trivial when in a room with four people who you're afraid will torture and murder you.

"S-sir, with all due respect," Valen said, voice trembling, confirming Lex's suspicions. "I appre-appreciate the apology, but I worry more about having my personal structural integrity respected than my gender identity."

The four humans all looked at each other awkwardly.

"Right ... " Jerome said. "Listen. I know an *I'm sorry* isn't gonna do jack shit for something like ... this. But we really do mean it. We're sorry. That's why we're here to try and make up for it, even if it's just a little bit."

Valen burst into tears. "You left me there, you just *left* me there, all of you. You just watched. And you're the *kind* ones. What hope do I have, on either side of the border?"

Lex came over and wrapped her arms around him. "Shh, shh, you're okay," she soothed.

He wriggled away from her, sobbing. "I'm not okay! I'm very much not! I'm a starved and injured vampire in a room with four vampire hunters, who helped someone torture me! I would say this is as far from okay as one can be!"

Fuck. *Fuck.* Lex had been imagining it'd be smooth sailing from here, but ... obviously that had been foolish. Of course.

"Give him some space, Alex." Ari pulled her away and used the dreaded *Alex.*

Jerome sat down on the edge of the bed. Valen clutched the blanket to himself, tears streaming down his face. "I get it," Jerome said. "We suck. I know we suck. I'm sorry we suck. Please let us try and suck a bit less by helping you."

Valen loosened his death grip on the blanket.

"You're safe," Lex said. "I promise you're safe now."

"We realized how fucked up it was, what we did," Ari said. "And now we're trying to fix it. That's it."

"Okay," Valen said, voice wobbly. "Thank you."

"Do you want us to just feed you and leave?" Jerome said. "We were gonna, um, kind of hang out, but ... well, if it's just gonna make you feel worse, we don't have to hang around."

Valen made a visible attempt to calm himself down, closing his eyes. "You can go about your business. I won't – I don't mind. I'll stay out of the way. You won't even know I'm here."

"Er," said Jerome, awkwardly fiddling with one of his dreadlocks. "No, I mean, we were going to hang out here, with you, to try and make you feel better."

He looked positively *overwhelmed* by the prospect of being the center of attention of four vampire hunters. He shrank down. "I – I – I – "

"It's okay," Bailey said, sitting down and putting an arm around Valen. "Breathe, babydoll. It's okay."

Tears finally brimmed over in his eyes, and his lip lifted in a fearful snarl. "Why did you think it would be okay to do that to me even if I wasn't innocent? Why do you think anyone deserves that? I was in there for *six months*, locked in the coffin except to be taken out and tortured, and you didn't even give me a chance, you kidnapped me and tortured me, you didn't even *let me talk*, and – and – " His protest dissolved into wretched sobs. "Why do you think it's okay to do that to any living creature? You're *monsters*."

Fuck. *Fuck. This isn't going to work.* Lex's optimism crumbled. *It's not going to work. What we did is too big of a hurdle to get over. He won't ever trust us. Not after what we did.*

Bailey eased back, face dark. The humans all looked at each other awkwardly as Valen continued to bawl. Lex felt Ari's comforting hand squeezing her own.

"Listen ... " Jerome said, patting the blanket. "Like I said, saying sorry can only go so far. Trying to make it up to you can only go so far. I'm not saying it's right, or we should have let it happen. But maybe you'll be less freaked out if you understand. Most of us have lost family members to vampires. We know what happens to them. They just get taken and snatched up out of nowhere, thrown into the meat grinder. It's happened to us, and it can happen again, to anyone we care about, at any time. I don't know if you've ever been through something like that, but it ... does things to you. Makes you numb. Makes you care less about things you'd normally care about. Makes you think someone on the other side should have a turn suffering. Makes you think maybe you should just let the unthinkable happen if it means it can stop the flow of blood."

"It's fucked," Bailey said, tears welling in his eyes. "The whole thing is just fucked. Valen, man, please, you gotta understand. The only vampires we ever meet are the ones who cross the border, and they're usually the worst of the worst. We never met anyone like you before. We're on edge all the time, knowing every night someone wants to kidnap or kill us. Obviously I'm not saying it was right, but surely you gotta understand at least a little bit, right? We're not total monsters, I promise we aren't."

"You know what vampires are capable of," Ari added. "You know how they can be dangerous. But you don't *feel* it like we do. You've never been a prey animal."

Valen squeezed his eyes shut and took in deep breaths. "Yes," he said carefully, like he was trying to convince himself most of all. "I understand, in theory, the reasons behind your actions."

"I'm sorry it took us so long to realize," Lex said. "I'm sorry. I'm sorry we just ignored the way you were suffering." The guilt was eating her alive.

To her relief, his face softened, and he breathed in and out for a moment, calming himself. "Okay. I understand why you did it. I do. It's just difficult to feel safe."

Maybe we can still salvage this. Maybe we aren't unforgivable. "We've learned our lesson," Lex said. "We're not gonna let something like that happen again, to you or to anyone."

Valen nodded. "Thank you. Thank you, ma'am."

"There, see? Everything's okay." Bailey slung his guitar around and started to pluck a few strings. "Now, time for dinner and a show!"

Great, Bailey, I'm sure that'll make him feel all better. But to her surprise, Valen smiled, clearly amused. It still felt ... a little weird, to see a vampire be amused at jokes. As though before now she hadn't expected vampires to have any personality beyond wanting to hurt her. "Excellent," he said timidly. "I'll be sure to spread the word about the excellent service at your establishment, haha!"

"Oh, he's funny," Jerome said.

"Yeah, yeah, he's funny, but he's also fucking *hungry*, I bet. Time to chow down, big guy." Bailey rolled his sleeve up. "Ari said the arm is an option, yeah?"

"Um ... " Valen shrank back. "I can't bite – You – you pulled my fangs out."

Bailey blinked. "Ah. Shit. We did."

Ari wordlessly handed over her knife.

"Right ... " Bailey said. He took the knife unhappily. Jerome looked like someone had threatened to stab him, and took a step back without a word. Valen looked at him apprehensively.

"All right, here I go," Bailey said, looking queasy. He positioned the knife over his arm, in the spot where it seemed safest. He took in a pained, hissing breath as he made a cut with the knife.

"Jesus, you big baby," Ari said.

"Ey, ey, some of us don't see blood once a month, ya know. Only when something's the matter." He sat on the edge of the bed and held his bleeding arm out to Valen. "Eat up."

"Thank you, sir," Valen said politely, and bobbed his head in a bow. He leaned forward and took Bailey's arm delicately, drinking in small, dainty sips.

"There ya go," Bailey said, ruffling Valen's hair. "Bet that feels better."

Valen finished his drink, swiping his tongue over the wound to close it, then bringing his head back up, licking his lips. "It does. Thank you, sir."

Lex looked with concern towards Jerome, who was still cowering against the wall. "You don't have to if you don't want to," Ari said. "The two of us are plenty."

"Is everything okay?" Lex said. "Like, something up?"

"Um." Jerome swallowed and drew forwards, wringing his hands. "No, I – I want to help. I want to help him get better. I do. I just ... "

"Is getting fed from too much, even if it's from an open cut?" Lex said. "Blood loss affect you?"

"Um ... " Jerome nervously shook his head. "I – no, that's not it. I – "

"Don't feel obligated, sir, it's quite all right," Valen said placatingly. "I've had more than enough for today."

"I want to," Jerome said, sounding like he was about to cry. "I do, I'm sorry. I just can't, man. I'm sorry."

Bailey squeezed his shoulder. "You don't have to tell them, J-man."

"No, I ... Okay, yeah, I want to." Jerome sighed. He rolled up the sleeve of his hoodie, revealing a series of scars striped up his forearm. They looked old, but they were easy to see because they were raised and bumpy, and darker in color than his already-dark skin. "I just, um ... I just got some baggage about cutting myself," he said, swallowing thickly.

Fuck. As though Lex couldn't fuck up more than she already had, she'd asked a guy with a history of self harm – and a pretty bad one by the look of it – to cut himself. She hadn't even thought about it being hard for anyone besides Valen. "Oh ... Of course. Don't worry about it. Whatever you can handle. It's fine if you can't."

Valen looked at Jerome's arm uncomprehendingly. "I would never force you, sir. I promise. I don't know ... why, or who would make you do that, but ... "

What? He thought someone forced Jerome ... ?

Valen shrunk back fearfully. "I'm sorry, I'm sorry if that was rude, sir, I am – I just don't understand, I – "

Oh. *Oh.* Of course he wouldn't understand. Vampires didn't scar, and they probably didn't cut themselves in fits of mental illness either. Why would they?

Jerome laughed, his thick voice breaking up the tension in the air. "Of course. Oh my God. Vampires don't scar, so of course you wouldn't know. I can't imagine they self-harm either." He ran his fingers over his forearm. "I ... did this myself. When I was younger."

"What? Why?" Valen blurted out, sounding horrified, and then he cringed, as though realizing he shouldn't have been so forward.

"It's hard to describe," Jerome said. "I was ... in a lot of emotional pain. It felt like ... I didn't deserve to *not* be in pain, in a way, that I deserved it. Or maybe it was easier to have a bigger problem. A cut on the arm is easier to treat than feeling like shit, you know? You probably wouldn't get it, but it made sense to my brain at the time."

Valen looked down at his hands on his lap, before looking back up. "I ... do get it. More than I care to admit. I ... often starved myself for similar reasons. I felt too guilty to eat. Too guilty for existing. I never cut myself, but I often had self-inflicted pain. It was ... stupid."

Jerome let out a slightly choked murmur of pity, putting a hand on Valen's shoulder. "It wasn't stupid, man, neither of us were. I mean, heck, for you, it at least made sense, right? Because you felt guilty for drinking people's blood, yeah? That's only natural."

"No, I ... I still did that to myself even when I started drinking the imported blood."

The ... *imported* blood? It was becoming increasingly obvious from this conversation that, although they had certain things in common, there was clearly a huge cultural gap between them.

Valen picked up on their confusion immediately. "There are specialty shops on the other side of the border who import blood from overseas. Where there's infrastructure for collecting it from paid volunteers. Places where things are kinder, where humans and vampires aren't constantly at each other's throats like we are here."

"Penpals!" Lex declared. "I told you, I fucking told you! They get it from the vampire's penpals!"

"Yes," Valen said. "I've thought about trying to move there, but they're extremely stringent about immigration." He fiddled with the hem of his blanket. "But it's entirely voluntary, so I shouldn't have felt guilty for eating back then, but

... it still lingered." He looked up at Jerome. "I wouldn't have thought humans would have any reason to feel that way. You're innocent."

Jerome gave him a sad smile. "It's so much more complicated than that. We got ... things to cope with even though we don't have to drink blood, you know? Dunno if you want me to dump all this on you, but my ... I was depressed as fuck growing up. It's easy to fall into when things seem so hopeless. It's so hard to stay out of jail, when it feels like they're *trying* to get you in there. And my ... the first time doing it was when ... "

He put his head in his hands, starting to cry. Bailey sat down and put his arms around him. "It's okay. You're all right."

"When my daddy found out I was gay," Jerome choked out. "And I told him I was worried about – about catching GRID, or whatever that – that gay flu going around is that people are dying from, and he said – he said maybe it would be better if I did." He broke down into full-blown sobs.

Lex and Ari had been mostly casual acquaintances with Bailey and Jerome until this point, mostly just on the basis of them both being obviously in same-sex relationships and relating on those grounds. But now, Lex suddenly felt so privileged to be trusted with a story like this. She came over and sat on the other side of Jerome, adding herself to the hug. Ari followed suit.

"I'm ... sorry, sir," Valen's voice said from behind them. "That's unbelievably cruel. I'm sorry that happened to you."

Jerome sniffed and looked up at him, wiping his eyes. "Yeah," he said, voice wobbly. "But hey, I don't have to care about what he thinks anymore. Fuck him, haha. I got everyone I need right here."

"Yeah, man, yeah you do."

Jerome disentangled himself from the hug. "Well – well I don't care that my blood ain't good enough for the Red Cross – it's good enough for you, and you know blood better than they do. Come on, let's figure out some way to make this work, huh?"

The group tossed ideas around, and hemmed and hmmed for a while, before Jerome eventually agreed that it would be okay to make two pinpricks, like a bite, rather than a cut. It took a lot longer to get the blood out, but Jerome didn't mind, and good-naturedly played with Valen's hair while he did so.

Valen licked his lips when he was done, looking satisfied. "Thank you, sir. I feel much better now."

"Well, we ain't done yet!" Bailey jovially picked up his guitar. "Get ready!"

"R-ready for what?" Valen stammered.

"He's gonna play you a song," Lex said. *Oh boy, hopefully this goes okay ... Don't ruin a good evening, Bails.*

"It's supposed to make you feel better," Jerome said. "If you'd rather not, we don't have to."

Valen drew the covers further up himself. "Th-that sounds nice. That could be nice. Thank you."

"Right," Bailey said. His fingers started working at the guitar strings, plucking out a jaunty tune. "Now, I'm good on the guitar here, and Jerome's got the golden pipes, so I'm gonna let him lead, and I'll be the backup singer."

Jerome reached into his bag and pulled out a tambourine, shaking it. "And you ladies might know the words to this song, so feel free to sing along." He said this with a wink at Valen, which caused him to slide down into the couch.

Jerome started singing.

Oh it happened one night when the moon was bright
And full, but not as full as my heart

Ari let out a groan. "Of course you picked this one." This was an old joke of a song, a story about a guy being too horny for his own good, trying to court a vampire, and getting killed for it. It was lighthearted, so Lex pushed down her doubt about how it would be received.

Lex grabbed Ari's hands, dancing around a little bit and starting to sing along. "Come on, come on!"

When I saw her, I knew she could tear me apart

She was pale and dead and covered in blood but hey
Nobody's perfect
And she paralyzed me with a glance
No persuasion needed
And no sooner had my lips touched hers
Than all the blood had left my body
But it was worth it in the end as the feeling fled my limbs.

Valen went beet red, apparently getting the meaning of the song on this verse. Lex was about to check in with him if this was good-natured teasing or genuine bullying, before Bailey knelt down next to him, gesturing to him like a showman.

Oh you're so big and bad it's true
But that's what I like about you

Jerome knelt on his other side, shaking the tambourine.

It's true that you could snap me in half
But baby, maybe I'm into that

Valen tossed the covers over his head, mortified.

And if this ends with me getting all my stuff sucked out
Well, that's sort of what I was hoping for

They all pointed at him for the next part, which was an animalistic growl. He didn't see this as he still had the covers over his head, but he cautiously peeked out and saw them, looking like a student unprepared for a test.

"I'm sorry," he stuttered. "I don't know the words."

"Oh, this part is just a big growl," Bailey said.

Valen's eyes bounced around the room.

"Go on," Jerome said. "Give us your scariest growl."

Valen nervously gave a squeak, which could be called a growl if you were feeling generous, which they were. He was clearly too nervous to give a real growl, the kind they'd heard from the basement before they'd come to their senses.

They all cheered for him, like he was a celebrity. Possibly the first iteration of the song that had a real vampire give the growl part, and it was fun despite the lackluster contribution on Valen's part.

And more importantly, Valen looked delighted, looking around at the four of them like he hadn't expected them to value his contribution.

He looked over to Lex and Ari, expression unreadable.

"There," Bailey said, setting his guitar to the side. "Now that the performance is over, how about some Monopoly?"

Lex groaned. "Only if you don't go as hard as humanly possible."

"Not my fault if I play to win."

22

— ◆ —

"All right, up you go."

Still in his pajamas, Valen tentatively stepped up onto the bathroom scale.

Ari scrutinized the numbers. "All right, seventy-three pounds! You're getting there, big guy!"

"How much did you weigh before all this?" Lex asked.

"A-about a hundred and ten pounds, I think."

"That's still on the light side," Ari said. "We've gotta fatten you up."

"He's already gained ten pounds."

"Yeah, it's a wonder what three square meals a day can do to ya."

"Thank you," Valen said cryptically. As usual, it was impossible to tell what he was thinking. He sounded like he was about to cry.

Ari asked, "Everything okay?"

"It's just – it's just been a lot."

"Of course ... You just take it easy. You don't have to worry about anything anymore."

They'd needed to wait a while for his legs to un-break themselves, but that'd been sped up considerably now that he was no longer starving. He'd been getting more steady on his feet, and seemed to actually have some energy, and maybe, if you squinted, even started to develop some muscle and fat back.

Ari helped Valen back down the stairs and into the living room. She eyed the coffin. "Um ... So ... I promise it's okay ... but ... "

Lex followed Ari's gaze and immediately knew what she was thinking: Valen had once again torn up his pillow. Both the pillowcase and the pillow itself had bite marks all over, the filling spilling out. "Oh. We can replace it again, don't worry."

Valen wrung his hands. "I'm sorry. I'm sorry I keep ruining them." His eyes watered. "I'm trying not to, but I do it in my sleep."

"It's okay," Lex said, taking his elbow. "It's not a big deal."

He broke eye contact, looking down, face red.

"I noticed that you grind your teeth and bite things when you're awake too."

"I'm sorry," he said, tears spilling over. "I'm sorry, I'm sorry, I promise I'm not – I'm not – "

"Relax," Ari said, putting her hands on his shoulders as though to push him back into his body. "We're just trying to figure out how to fix whatever problem you're having."

He sniffled and wiped his cheek with the back of his hand. "It's an anxious habit. It was – chewing on the muzzle was really the only thing I could do sometimes."

Lex's heart broke imagining all the times he'd been in massive pain and unable to move, the only activity available to him grinding his teeth on the metal bit in his mouth. That would ... also explain why all his teeth had been a little bit worn down, from the constant wear against the metal surface. "It's okay that you do that. I don't think you should try and make yourself stop. Can you open your mouth for me for a minute?"

He did so, still not making eye contact. Lex noted his fangs were fully grown back in. His teeth didn't look damaged at all – having restored themselves from their ground-down state – but there *were* threads of fabric stuck in them here and there.

"Do you want us to get you a chew toy?" Lex asked.

Valen shut his mouth. "A chew toy ... ?"

"I bet the kind they make for dogs would stand up to your chewing better. Or we could try and find a binky, or something along those lines."

"Yes, I would like that."

***

Lex and Ari had continued to go on patrol – they'd taken a few days off work to help Valen, then once they'd settled into a routine and felt comfortable leaving him home alone, started to go back to work. They did need the money and couldn't just *not* go back to work ... but they *did* try to avoid running into any actual vampires, the situation at home weighing heavily on their minds.

They stopped at the store on the way home, in the hours when the sunrise was still young, and bought several dog toys that looked like they could take some serious biting. They also tried to find the biggest pacifier they could.

While they were in the children's section, Lex noticed the books.

"You can't be serious," Ari said, as Lex picked up a few nonfiction books that looked to be for middle schoolers. "The man was practicing advanced biochemistry when we found him."

"I've seen him reading, but he never turns the pages and just kind of stares at it blankly. I think he needs something to ... ease him back in."

" ... Well, it couldn't hurt to offer, at least. Keep the receipt, we can just return them if he doesn't want 'em."

***

When they got home, Valen was in fact doing the exact thing Lex had noted. He had a virology book open on his lap, but he was just staring over it at the window, where the curtains glowed from the sunlight they were holding back.

"Hey," Lex said, kneeling by the coffin where he was lying down. "We got some things for you."

The paper bag crinkled as he dug inside it. "Oh. Thank you." He picked up one of the books and flipped it open. There was a picture of an elephant, with simple text next to it telling elephant facts. His eyes drifted over the text. He slowly ran a hand over the picture, then grabbed one of the pacifiers and put it in his mouth, chewing it quietly. Once again, it was impossible to tell what he really thought, but he seemed to make heavy use of the gifts over the next few days, which seemed like a good sign.

***

Lex was now recovered enough that she felt confident to help feed Valen, so he now had four people feeding him. Ari seemed to warm up to being fed from a little bit more, and Bailey and Jerome came over as often as they could too. He was still massively underweight, but he started to lose the sallow, skeletal appearance fairly quickly with the amount of support he was getting.

Valen was still visibly *nervous*, though. He was reserved and still didn't seem to trust Lex and Ari fully. Which was completely understandable, but if there was anything they could do to speed that up, that would probably help Valen feel safer.

Once, when Ari was talking on the phone with Nick, Lex saw him physically flinch. His hearing was good enough that he could probably hear Nick's voice just as well as Ari, and he immediately climbed back into his coffin and hid, a mass of quivering blankets.

"You're okay," Lex soothed, rubbing his back through the blanket. "He's not here."

"D-does he know where you live?"

"No," Lex said. "No, he doesn't, remember?" Lex had reassured him of this probably about a dozen times by now.

Valen huddled under the covers, two red, watery eyes peering out from under the blankets.

Ari quickly finished her conversation and hung up the phone, coming back in. "Nick is still trying to rope someone else into getting a live capture. I think he's getting desperate, because he called just to tell me the bounty's gone up again."

Valen let out a terrified whine.

"We're not giving you back," Ari said firmly. "We're not letting him find out you're still alive, and we're not letting anyone else take you. You say the word, and we take you straight to the border."

Valen peeked out from under the blanket. "You were talking to him." He said it in an accusatory way.

"Nick? Yeah, on the phone," Ari said, not seeing his point.

"And at work sometimes, yeah," Lex added.

"You were talking to him like he's a person and not a monster."

Lex and Ari looked at each other, then back at him. "He's fucked up," Ari said. "But everything he did, he had permission for."

Valen burst into tears. Lex's stomach sank.

" ... Right?" Ari said, suddenly alarmed.

"No," Valen wept. "No, no, a thousand times no. He came back at night when the compound was empty because everyone was out on patrol. He opened the coffin when he was alone, he broke the rules all the time."

"What?" Ari growled. "What for?"

"Ari," Lex said. Fuck, *fuck*, she almost didn't want to know the answer to Ari's question, but she also thought it was unfair to ask ... Especially since Valen was now crying so hard that he couldn't even get the words out to answer.

Ari knelt, steadying him and supporting him in her arms. "Breathe, breathe, you're okay."

Lex handed him a tissue. He took it, but was still crying too hysterically to use it.

"Let it out, baby," Ari said. "You're okay."

Valen took in great, sobbing gasps, wiping his eyes, then blowing his nose. He wiped his cheeks, which were flushed with black blood. "S-sorry."

"You're okay. Let it out."

His lip wobbled. He grabbed the stuffed cat Lex had put in the coffin, hugging it. "Nick has a shocking sadistic streak that he knows how to keep hidden."

Ari stood, palming her mouth. "All right. Fuck."

"I'm sorry," Lex said. "We didn't know." She was still lying to herself. They'd *suspected*. But none of them had cared enough. It'd bothered them a little, but they'd still been in the "he deserves it" phase.

"He did it all the time. When we were alone. He – he – he would do anything he couldn't get away with during the day under supervision. Things that – that could have no possible justification. Humiliation, senseless torture, rape – "

"What the *fuck*," Ari said. She was turning a cartoonish shade of red with her anger. "I'm going to kill him. I'm going to fucking kill him."

Lex felt *sick*. The things Nick had done with permission were fucked up enough, but there had at least been *reasons* for those. Not even the director would approve of meaningless torture and *rape*. And oh God, Valen hadn't even been able to tell anyone that this was happening, this *whole time*. Nick had known he could get away with it, because letting Valen talk had been the one thing they'd all known to avoid at any cost. "We need to tell the director. He needs to know."

"We can't," Ari said through gritted teeth. "We can't do anything with this information without everyone finding out Valen is alive."

Valen took one of the chew toys and put it in his mouth, grinding anxiously.

"I'm going to fucking kill him. I'm going to shoot him as many times as bullets I have, and then I'm going to get more bullets and shoot him some more. They're going to be scrubbing him out of the carpet for months afterwards."

"Ari, shut up," Lex said. Valen had pulled the blanket back over himself, still shaking with fear. "You just said we can't do anything to let anyone know Valen is alive. And getting yourself arrested isn't going to help anyone."

Ari left the room. Lex could hear the punching bag Ari always used when she needed to let off steam being beaten half to death.

Lex knelt down. "What do you want us to do, Valen?"

Valen breathed heavily for a few moments, looking positively overwhelmed. Then he finally admitted, "I don't know."

Ari came back in, still breathing heavily. She had a foil package in one hand. "Take this. All of it."

Valen hesitated, then took the package. It had several small white pills inside. "What is it?"

"Emergency contraception."

Valen's eyes widened. "You don't think – It isn't *possible*, surely, for a human and a vampire … ?"

"I don't know. But I'm not taking any chances. The whole pack."

"Will it even work?"

"It's hormones, so if testosterone injections work on you, then maybe."

Lex was so horrified that for a moment, she wanted to protest that this wasn't necessary, that surely Nick hadn't …

But if Nick *hadn't*, then Valen would have said they weren't necessary. But instead, Valen just looked grim and started pushing the pills through the foil to swallow them.

***

"Try the bolt cutters again."

"We're not trying the fucking bolt cutters again. We already saw that didn't work."

"I don't think we're going to make any progress this way."

"We might if you give me longer than ten seconds!"

"We might have to use the saw."

"We're not using the fucking *saw*. You're going to take his damn head off."

Valen clearly looked nervous about the turn the conversation was taking. He was currently bent over the workbench among a nest of tools and books spread out around him. Ari gripped his head with one hand, pushing him down a bit painfully on accident, and he winced. "Fuck me, I didn't expect this to be so hard."

Ari continued jamming the lockpick into the padlock keeping the metal collar on Valen's neck, grunting in frustration, consulting the books on the table, which all had diagrams of locks. It'd been years since she'd picked a lock, but she was *determined* to get this stupid thing off Valen's neck *today*. She'd suddenly decided it was urgent to get it off, and now had the energy of an irritated, tired father on a road trip as his family sits in cowed silence, afraid to worsen his mood as he drives.

Ari took a step back, letting him stand upright. "And you're *sure* you can't break it now that you've gotten some strength back." Ari had already asked this a good three or four times. Lex had stopped bothering to remind her that the equipment was vampire-proof and therefore Valen would never be able to break it no matter how strong he was. That was the point.

Valen indulged her, hands pulling on the collar, then at the lock. "Yes, ma'am, I'm quite sure."

Ari scowled. "All right. Lex, hold the light." Valen craned his neck upwards, wincing away as Ari went at it with the lockpicks again.

"Maybe we can try and get the key off Nick – "

"No, I'm not doing *anything* that could clue that maniac in to the fact that we have Valen."

Valen's breathing sped up noticeably.

Ari started to huff and puff angrily, motions becoming agitated. She eventually broke a lockpick and tossed it to the ground, cursing.

"All right, let's take a break," Lex said.

Ari plopped down onto the chair next to the workbench. "Fuck. I can't – I can't – I still can't believe he did that." *I can't believe we let him do that.* She hated

Nick, and she hated herself. There was only one thing that could make her hate herself a little bit less. She stood back up and attacked the collar again.

"Ari, stop, take a break."

"I'm *fixing* this," she snarled. "I'm getting it off, I'm fixing it. Give me the saw."

"Ari, you're scaring him."

Ari looked up and realized Valen was cringing back, frightened by her intensity and anger, eyes squeezed shut.

Ari dropped the lockpicking stuff. "I'm sorry," she said, finally letting the tears well up in her eyes. "I'm so *fucking* sorry we did this to you."

Valen looked at her for a moment, then his face softened. He reached out to touch her elbow. She pulled him into a hug, burying him in her ample bosom and broad arms, and cried into his hair. "F-fuck. I'm sorry, I'm *so* sorry."

His arms tentatively came around her. "I'm ... not going to say it's okay," Valen started. "Because it isn't. But when we make mistakes, what matters is what we do after that. And you've chosen to do everything within your power to fix things, even though it meant confronting your own feelings of shame and guilt. Looking uncomfortable truths in the eye takes courage and integrity, and for that I admire you."

This was the moment at which Ari fell a little bit in love with him. She decided to handle this by choking out, "Wow, okay, Aristotle."

Lex let out a laugh, slapping Ari on the arm lightly. "You goofball. Come on, sit down, let me try for once."

Ari sat down, wiping her nose on the back of her hand.

Lex, considerably more calm and steady-handed than Ari currently was, gave it a try. Valen seemed visibly more relaxed now that it was Lex's hands on him, and she spent a minute examining the diagram of the lock with all its pins. She took the lockpicks and started fiddling with it. The lock popped open. "There, see? Nothing we can't fix."

23

—•—

There was a knock at the door.

That was bad. Jerome and Bailey hadn't mentioned coming over. They weren't expecting anyone. They hadn't gotten any phone calls.

Except …

Except Nick had been calling them. And they'd told him to stop calling, knowing how uncomfortable it made Valen, so they'd stopped taking calls from Nick.

But no, Nick didn't know where they lived.

Right?

Ari was still in the kitchen, so Lex walked into the living room. She glanced at the coffin on the floor. Valen was inside napping, and it was closed.

She peered through the peephole. It was Nick.

Ah. Fuck.

Well, she just needed to get him to leave. She cracked the door open. "How did you find out where we live?" she hissed.

"Ah, Alexis. Well, I needed to talk to you about something work-related, and you wouldn't take my calls, and none of the others would get a message to you. I had to get your address from the director so I could come over."

"What do you want?"

"Can I come in?"

"No."

Nick literally stuck his foot in the door to keep her from closing it. "It'll just be for a minute. I just need to talk to you."

Lex briefly considered slamming the door on his foot as hard as she could. But that would make things worse, right? Their priority *had* to be to keep Nick from finding out they had Valen here.

But Valen was *right there*.

In the coffin. With the lid shut.

And Nick would just walk by and see a big wooden box and, what? Not assume it had a vampire inside it?

She was so caught up in her indecisive spiral that Nick was able to just push the door open from under her hands and stroll in. "Thank you. You two are *impossible* to get ahold of."

Fuck. She'd let him in the house! Oh, this was bad, bad, bad. Lex and Ari had already established themselves as very bad liars. He was going to figure it out for sure.

Fuck.

Ari came into the room, her arms full of the snacks she'd been retrieving for movie night. She frowned stormily as she saw Nick. "Ah. Nick."

"Ariana," he said, nodding to her. He moved past Lex and thus caught sight of the wooden coffin in the middle of the damn room.

His face just froze for a moment. "Um," he said, peeling one finger away from his fist to point to it. "What is that?"

Ari dumped her snacks on top of the coffin. "It's a coffee table," she said. "I've been trying my hand at woodworking. Been thinking about quitting vampire hunting, so I need some other skills."

Lex sat down next to Ari on the couch, trying her hardest to be nonchalant. Sure. It was just a coffee table. She could pretend that, right?

"It's ... an interesting shape," Nick said.

"Bit of a joke," Ari said. "Thought it would be funny. It's kind of shitty, though." She retrieved a bag of walnuts and started cracking them open, letting the shell fragments scatter all over the top of the coffin. "So, what the fuck is so important you had to come find our house?"

Nick sat in the chair across from the couch, still looking at the coffin. "My eyes are up here," Ari barked.

Nick's eyes flitted up to her. "Right. Sorry. Ariana, I – "

"Don't fucking call me that." Ari cracked another walnut open. She hadn't even eaten the nut from the first one.

"Apologies. Well, it was about live captures."

"We're not doing that again," Lex said.

"Oh, don't misunderstand. I'm not here to *ask* you to do another live capture. I've already got one, you see."

Ari narrowed her eyes at him. "What?"

"Yeah, Isaiah and Cyril just managed to get one last night. It's strung up in my lab right now. I came over because I need the coffin." He glanced down at the "coffee table." "The, um, device made of metal bars, not your, ah, woodworking project."

Crack went another walnut. "You didn't have to come into the house for that."

Nick rolled his eyes and gestured exasperatedly. "Oh my God, I was just trying to have a conversation with you like a normal person. Isn't that what you want? For me to act like a normal person?"

"I can think of a few other things I'd like." Ari fed two walnuts into the nutcracker and crushed them.

"Can we drop it off tonight?" Lex asked, trying not to panic. That would give them more time to decide what to do ... and if the base was empty, they could theoretically just attack Nick to get this new vampire away from him. "It won't fit in your car, so we'll have to drive the van all the way there. We don't have time to do that today."

"Oh, busy, are we?" Nick said.

Ari kept cracking walnuts without eating them, maintaining direct eye contact with Nick.

Nick looked like he wanted to argue that the coffin *would* fit in his car, but then thought better of it. He leaned over. "This coffee table is very interesting."

"It's shitty. It was my first attempt at woodworking."

"Mm-hm. It's very large."

"It's a shitty coffee table. Made it too big."

"One could even say it's large enough for someone to hide in."

Ari took two walnuts and cracked them against the coffin lid with her palm. "It's a *really shitty coffee table.*"

Nick stared at her. She stared back.

There was a loud squeak from inside the coffin, the sound of one of the dog toys they'd gotten Valen.

Nick raised an eyebrow. "Do you have a dog?"

"Yes," Ari said, without missing a beat, without the expression on her face changing despite the panic mounting on Lex's.

"I don't see it around."

"She's in her crate. We have to crate her when a man comes in the house. She hates men because of her previous owner."

Nick smiled. "She sounds like you, then, Ariana."

Ari looked at him with burning hatred, hands full of walnut shells. Lex leaned in to block their eye contact. "So, we'll see you tonight, then? We'll bring the coffin over before we head out for our patrol?"

"All right," Nick said mildly. "The specimen can be secured in other ways until then."

"Yeah, I bet," Ari muttered.

Nick stood. "Well, see you tonight, then. Give me a call before you're on your way over."

Ari hovered behind him until he was out the door. She stood there hawkishly at the window, watching until Nick had gotten into his car and driven off.

She pulled the curtains closed and came back over, where Lex had already knelt and pulled Valen out of the coffin, dumping all the walnut shells onto the floor.

He was rigid in her arms, tears streaming down his face. "I'm sorry," he wept. "I'm sorry, I forgot that was one of the toys that had a squeaker in it. I'm sorry."

"You're okay," Lex said, and Valen's eyes rolled around the room as he continued to weep, that one particular phrase from Lex uniquely terrible at making him feel better.

Ari clenched and unclenched her fists, breathing heavily. "I'm going to fucking kill him."

"What do we do?" Lex said nervously. "I feel like he definitely figured it out. He definitely figured it out, right? And he has another vampire. We have to do something, right?"

Ari ground her teeth. "We have to get Valen out of here. Across the border."

Valen let out a scared sound.

"Can you run?" Ari asked. "Are you going to be okay on your own?"

"Yes," Valen answered. "I-I think so."

Ari came over and wrapped her arms around him. "Good," she said softly. "I don't want anything to happen to you." She lingered in the embrace for a few moments before pulling away. "Which is why you're going home at nightfall."

Valen looked very scared, but nodded resolutely. "Okay."

"What about the other vampire?" Lex asked.

"Valen, can you hang around long enough for us to bust them out? I'm thinking we just ... go grab them and dump them in your lap, and you both go home. Nick is gonna be pissed, but I bet we can finesse this in a way that we don't get in too much trouble. We might lose our jobs, but Lex and I were thinking of quitting anyway. I'm not putting my job over my humanity. And it *does* come down to that, thinking about letting someone else go through that. Even a vampire that was here to catch a human."

Valen nodded. "Yes. Thank you. Yes, we can do that."

Ari ran her fingers through her hair, huffing. "Okay. Guess we just need to figure out what we're gonna do, then."

24

‒ ◆ ‒

They decided Valen should stay home while they went to the hunter's base. That seemed safest, since it would keep the most distance between Nick and Valen. Bailey and Jerome would stop by to check on him later, just in case. They gave Nick a call to say they were on their way over and headed out.

The problem was when they arrived at the base, there weren't any cars parked out front. "Where's Nick's car?" Lex said, immediately panicking. "Where's Nick? He's here, right?"

Ari cursed and got out of the car. "We need to get unlucky vampire number two and get back home *now*."

They briefly considered racing back home immediately, but if Nick had left the base to go terrorize Valen, the *only* upside was he'd left his new catch undefended. Because of course he didn't tell anyone else he was going and have them watch his new catch, because of course he loved doing nasty shit under the table without witnesses.

Did he think they weren't ballsy enough to just snatch the unguarded vampire? Was he counting on them not being able to pass this one off as dead?

... Was there actually a vampire here, or had it been a ploy to get them out of the house?

They had to at least check. They needed to do it now. They wouldn't get an opportunity this good again.

Ari kicked the door in and stomped down the stairs without shutting it behind her. They half-expected the basement to be empty, the second vampire a total fabrication to get them away from Valen. But no. There was a vampire in the basement and – oh God, it was a *kid*. Well, not a kid, explicitly not a kid, but only by very recent developments.

He must have just turned eighteen by the looks of him. Baby-faced, but trying very hard not to look it. His fancy clothes were torn in a heap on the ground.

He was clearly a member of the nobility. It was a coming-of-age ritual for a newly minted adult vampire nobleman to go catch their first human upon entering adulthood.

Of course the second live capture had been the inaugural hunt of a newly adult vampire. Here in the basement, they only found the most innocent vampires to torment.

He was chained with his wrists hanging from the ceiling, feet likewise secured to the floor. Gagged, muzzled. He was naked with his pants pooled around his ankles, because of course he fucking was.

He'd been staring at the ground, crying hot, angry tears, but as the two women appeared on the stairs, his gaze snapped to them and he growled savagely and thrashed.

"Give me a fucking break," Ari snapped. "We're here to help you, believe it or not."

"Let's get you out of here," Lex said, trying to be comforting despite the time ticking by painfully.

When they approached to get him down, he kept squirming, chains going taut with the force of his struggling.

"We don't have time to piss around here," Ari shouted with such force that the vampire stilled out of fear. "This is taking less than five minutes one way or the other, so it's up to you if we do that by just blowing your head off, got it?"

Lex reached down and pulled his pants up, restoring some semblance of dignity. Replacing the shirt would have to wait until later. He remained still as she undid the shackle on the floor then reached up and disconnected him from the ceiling. He immediately tried to lash out, but he ended up losing his balance and falling on account of his limbs still being restrained.

"Hey," Ari growled, and she withdrew her revolver and pushed it against his forehead. His watery eyes crossed to follow the barrel. "Last chance, motherfuck-er."

He kept growling and baring his teeth as much as he could, but stopped trying to hit them as Ari hooked her arms under his biceps and started dragging him up the stairs. "I guess it's a good thing we still have the fucking coffin. Not that I'm too happy about it."

***

They hoped Bailey and Jerome had gotten there at a convenient time to stop whatever Nick was trying to do to that sweet boy.

The not-so-sweet boy in the back of the van growled and screeched and thrashed, chains jingling inside the coffin. He refused to stop posturing about how tough and dangerous he was despite the fact that he became scared and pliant as soon as either of them threatened him. It was like a dog barking at someone through a door only to then retreat in embarrassment once the door was open.

"Just hang in there," Lex said over his enraged noises. "You're safe now."

He seemed less concerned about safety and more about wanting to take her head off. His nostrils flared as they made eye contact.

"Just glad he's not gonna be our problem for long," Ari muttered.

Their stomachs dropped when they finally got home and saw Nick's car parked out front of their house – but thank God, Bailey and Jerome's was right behind it

"Fuck," Ari said. "Fuck fuck fuck." She screeched to a stop, slammed the door open, and sprinted up and into the front door, which was standing open. Lex gave one last glance at the captive vampire behind her before deciding he wasn't going anywhere and joining her.

Valen could be heard crying loudly even before they'd gotten inside the house. Ari came into the living room and stopped dead. Lex bumped into her back, came around her, and saw what had caused the reaction.

Nick was on the floor – or rather, all over the floor. He was dead as dirt, covered in blood and gore, a huge, ragged bite taken out of his neck.

"We're in here." It was Bailey's voice from the dining room. Lex was eager to get away from the corpse. She dashed into the dining room. Valen was there, between Jerome and Bailey. He was clean and surprisingly not covered in blood. She didn't have time to question it, rushing to get Valen in her arms. Safe in her arms. "Valen. Valen, oh my God, oh my God, I'm so glad you're okay."

Ari came in next, putting her arms around both of them. "Holy shit," she whispered.

"I'm sorry," Valen sobbed. "I'm sorry I killed him. I know I shouldn't have."

How to even *begin* making him understand how much they didn't care about that? "It's okay," Lex said. "You had to. You had to defend yourself."

Valen let out a cry like she'd just told him the exact opposite, that he was horrible for killing him. He leaned into her, crying inconsolably.

You're safe now. You're safe, sweet boy. She looked over his shoulder at Jerome and Bailey and mouthed, *Thank you.*

The two men came over and hovered over them, almost but not quite making a five-person group hug around the vampire.

"I'm sorry," Valen said again, voice hoarse from crying. "I'm sorry I killed him."

"It was self-defense," Bailey said. "I'll say it however many times you need to hear it."

Please, please, please understand. It's not your fault.

"It wasn't," he whispered with terror. "It wasn't self-defense. I had him under persuasion. He couldn't hurt me. I killed him anyway."

Lex drew back slightly so she could look him in the face. He scrunched his face up, as though expecting retaliation at any moment. "I'm a monster. You need to execute me. I'm a murderer."

None of them could bring themselves to think of killing Nick as *murder*, not from Valen and especially not when Nick had actively broken into the house to come after him. Nick had, as they would say, fucked around and found out.

Ari squeezed his shoulders. "You are not a monster or a murderer," she said firmly.

"It was self-defense," Lex reiterated.

"He broke into the house to come after you," Ari continued. "That's self-defense."

Valen looked at her incredulously through tearful eyes. "But – but I killed someone who was defenseless and I – I – I – it made me feel good."

"It made you feel good because he's a monster that tortured and abused you, and you were putting an end to it. You have the right to do that."

"But ... but I liked it," Valen said, swallowing. "I liked killing him. I'm a monster."

"You are not going to do that to just any random helpless person," Lex said. "You're just not. Nick doesn't count. There are circumstances." The idea of Valen being a malicious murderer who killed for fun just because he could was too ridiculous to entertain, now that they knew him.

Ari spun him around, squeezing his shoulders. "Look at me," she said, very serious. "You are not a monster. I don't fucking care. I don't care about the details about what happened here. I don't care if that spineless rat was on his knees saying sorry and begging for mercy. He broke into the house to come after you. That's self-defense."

Valen put his face in his hands, still crying. Bailey and Jerome came closer, encircling him. "Okay," he whispered. "Thank you. What do we do now?"

Ari sighed, palming her face. "Okay. So. What we do now is figure out what the fuck to do with his body. And with the pissed off teenager we have locked in the van."

25

Valen watched with amazement as the four vampire hunters pivoted from comforting him to very quickly plotting how to cover up his murder. It turned out that the two problems they had – a fresh corpse and an angry vampire in their van – were the answer to each other.

Because the pieces all fit together perfectly. The corpse was of a man recently killed by a vampire. A man who was known to skirt around safety rules to go taunt vampires alone, playing with fire.

And the vampire was his most recent victim, last seen improperly secured and growling at him savagely, threatening to kill him.

"More," Jerome said.

Bailey squeezed his cut, more rivulets of blood pulsing out and into the container. Jerome palmed his mouth. "Valen, man, how much blood is in the human body?"

"About a gallon," Valen answered. He was sitting curled up on the couch, under a fortress of pillows, as though to ward off the grisly scene he'd caused.

"I ain't got a gallon, man," Bailey said. "I got a lot of blood but you can't have all of it."

"We don't need a whole gallon," Ari said. "They're not gonna get suspicious just because there's not a whole damn gallon."

"Looks like we've got a quarter of a gallon, maybe," Lex said, peering at the jug they'd been filling up.

/

"Won't they be able to tell it's not his blood?" Valen said, and then got embarrassed when all eyes fell on him.

"How would they be able to tell?" Lex asked.

"By ... by the s ... I forgot humans wouldn't be able to smell the difference."

"Here, I think I can give some more," Lex said. She came over and took her bandage off, adding more blood into the jug.

"I think that's enough," Ari said. She paced the room nervously. "Okay. Tarp. Okay, we need to get the shithead kid out of the van first. We can't bring him back there in case we get caught."

Lex retrieved a tarp from the basement. All four of them went down, opening the van and swarming on the coffin. The new vampire's eyes wheeled around, too intimidated by being hauled around by four vampire hunters to even posture and growl.

They secured the tarp over him just in case any nosy neighbors were nearby. Not perfect, but it'd have to do for now. They had to do this as fast as they could.

They set the coffin down on the living room floor with a heavy thud.

"Valen, get in your box," Ari said. "Don't get out of it till we're back. Both of you just sit tight. You hear? Sit tight. Don't move until we're back."

Valen complied, folding himself up and pulling the wooden lid of the coffin over himself. After a moment, the lid slid to the side and his hand could be seen reaching out to grab some more of the pillows off the couch, pulling them in like a predator dragging prey back into its lair.

"Okay." Ari huffed, still pacing around. "Second tarp."

Lex went down and retrieved a second tarp. "Now the hard part?"

They wrangled Nick's corpse onto the tarp, rolling it up. As quick as they could, hoping to God none of the neighbors were watching, they ferried it down into the van.

They came back into the living room. "Okay," Ari said. "Uhhhh. Cover the blood. Cover the couch."

They dragged the couch over the biggest stain on the floor, then unfolded a blanket over it to hide the grisly scene. There, if anyone peered in the window, they'd just see a wooden box and a tarp over a mysterious object.

"Okay." Ari's keys jingled as she locked the door behind her. "Sorry, kid, just hang in there for like an hour."

***

It was a good thing Valen had drunk so much of Nick's blood, because they were pouring all four of his rations onto the basement floor.

They poured it from a few inches away, and slowly, so it would form a creeping puddle. Then they dumped Nick's corpse on top of it, so his throat was positioned over the puddle, to make it look like he'd had his throat ripped open and then bled out.

They took the restraints that had been on the new capture and laid them out in the room, empty, so that the natural thought would be, "Why did Nick take the restraints off?" or "How did it get the restraints off?"

They trashed the room, throwing things on the floor to make it look like there had been a fight. Bailey smashed into the door to make it look like it'd been knocked off its hinges in the escape.

A close examination would surely reveal the truth. They could test the blood on the ground and find out it was a different blood type or something. It wasn't airtight.

But it didn't need to be airtight. It just needed to be enough to make sense to everyone at the compound, because why would they suspect anything other than the extremely obvious cause of death that the vampire he'd brought down had torn him apart and escaped?

Nick had wanted there to be no witnesses so he could get away with it. For nobody to know exactly where he was so he had plausible deniability. Well, *someone* was going to get away with it. Just not him.

They left the front door open and drove away. "Burn in Hell, you rotten piece of shit," Ari said.

***

They got back just before sunrise, which was when they realized they were now stuck with this second vampire until sunset.

Well, more time with Valen too.

"Valen?" Lex called out as they came home. "We're back now. You can come out."

The coffin creaked open, and Valen shuffled over for more hugs. "How did it go?" he asked nervously.

"Just fine," Jerome said. "The next person who finds him is gonna think your new friend here killed him and then ran off. So now all we have to do is wait until sunset and you two can get over the border to safety."

Valen looked relieved. "Thank you," he whispered.

"Of course," Lex said. She sat him down on the couch, sitting next to him and putting a comforting arm around him. "Are you doing okay?"

He nodded. "Thank you. Are all four of you going to stay?"

"We might need to take turns taking naps," Bailey said. "Since we were out all night. But yeah, we're all gonna make sure you get home safely."

"Thank you," Valen said bashfully. "Thank you so much."

Ari let out a breath. "So ... now we wait."

There came a disgruntled sound from the metal cage under the tarp.

" ... Right," Ari said. She was half-tempted to just leave the kid locked in the coffin and give the whole thing to Valen to take care of. But no, they had to do this properly. "I guess it wouldn't be right to keep that kid locked in there all day if we don't have to. There's four of us here, plus Valen, so I'm sure we can keep him under control." She looked to Valen. "I'm trusting you to keep an eye on him, got it? We're vampire hunters, so if we let this kid go, anybody he hurts is on us. You need to make sure he gets back over the border without taking anyone, or we failed to do our job."

"Yes," Valen said very seriously. "I'll make sure he doesn't hurt anyone else."

"Okay." Ari withdrew her keys and knelt, peeling the tarp back. The vampire inside glared daggers at her, teeth peeled back in a snarl around the bit in his mouth. "Hey, listen. We're gonna let you out. We're gonna all be civil, no fighting, no persuasion, no hurting, and then at nightfall, you're going home. You don't need to try to get away. It's daytime now, so you got nowhere to go anyway. Sound good?"

The vampire growled at her. "Hey," she said, like talking to a naughty dog. "Come on, kid. I know you're tough and scary. I know, all right? I'm saying I'm going to let you out. Literally all you have to do is nothing. Just sit there and let us take you home. Easy as pie."

The vampire fell silent, glaring at her. Ari undid the tarp and pulled it all the way back.

Valen approached tentatively. He let out a gasp. "Sebastian?" he exclaimed.

"What, do you know him?" Ari said.

Valen nodded, looking tearful. "He's my husband's cousin. So my cousin-in-law, if that's a thing."

Oh, related to Valen's husband ... meaning part of the magnate family that ran the blood farms.

Valen was heartbroken. "Oh, Sebastian, I'm so sorry." He looked so much more grown up than last they'd met – but still so small and scared in the coffin, the nightmare device Valen was eager to get him out of. "I forgot he was old enough to be coming of age soon. Don't worry, Sebastian, I'm here, I'll help you."

Sebastian was clearly trying to hide how relieved seeing Valen made him feel. He stopped posturing and looked at Valen with big, wet eyes.

"Here," Ari said, holding the keys out. "Why don't you handle this?"

"Thank you." Valen slipped on a pair of gloves so he could handle the silver, then took the keys and unlocked the coffin. He unwrapped all the chains securing Sebastian inside it, lifting him out. "I'm so sorry this happened to you, Sebastian … I suppose I should say happy birthday?"

Sebastian glared at him.

"Sorry … " Valen undid the muzzle, pulling it out of his mouth.

The four human hunters fidgeted nervously, hands moving to their weapons, as Sebastian licked his lips. "Valen, what on earth are *you* doing here?" Sebastian demanded. "You ruined everything!"

Valen was taken aback. "What? How did *I* ruin it?"

"I came here to catch my first human and make my family proud, and now I'm stuck here overday! Again!"

Valen waited for him to elaborate, but nothing further came. "And how is that my fault?"

"Erm." Sebastian looked caught off guard. "Well, I don't know. You're the only vampire around, so I just assumed you were running things."

Valen let out a laugh. "No, no. Here." He undid the cuffs around Sebastian's wrists and ankles, freeing him from the last of the restraints. Sebastian stood and rolled his shoulders, prompting another round of nervous fidgets from the humans.

"Thank you," Sebastian said brusquely. "I need a shirt."

"Oh, uh … " Valen went over to his wardrobe and pulled out the biggest shirt he had. "Here."

Sebastian eyed the shirt with disdain, as though judging it not fine enough. But he put it on without complaint. His eyes swept over the humans. "Can I drink from one of your thralls?"

"Oh, ah … " Valen turned back to look at them. "They aren't my thralls."

223

"Oh. Whose thralls are they, then?"

"Nobody's."

"Oh, so they're fair game, then?"

The four hunters all backed up, drawing weapons defensively as Sebastian eyed them. Valen very quickly stepped in front of Sebastian. "No, no, you misunderstand."

Sebastian stared at him with hackles raised. "Well, I'm not leaving without a thrall."

This was going to be a hard sell. "Yes, you are, unfortunately."

"Come *on*, you don't need *four*, surely. Can I have one? Mother and Father aren't going to be pleased with me for coming back so late, let alone empty-handed."

"Sebastian," Valen said, exasperated. "You have no *idea* what horrible fate you narrowly escaped. You are going home unscathed and empty-handed, and you will learn to appreciate that as a victory."

Sebastian scoffed. "Why, because I was told so by my cousin's commoner-born sex-pervert wife?"

Valen's shoulders stiffened, and he went bright red. "Sebastian, you – "

"My name is Sebastian Vorigan Kithrara, son of Mordecai Asmodeus Kithrara, secondborn of Viscardi Maxwell Talon Kithrara, third in line to control the blood harvest web. My family feeds the entire enclave. I'm an *apex predator*. I'm not going hungry, ever. And I'm not leaving without a human. This is my time to prove I'm worthy of my heritage, to fully step into my role as – "

"Sebastian!" Valen interrupted. "I was there when you threw a fit about not getting the right number of ponies or whatever on your eleventh birthday! You're not a fearsome predator! You're a spoiled child!"

It was Sebastian's turn to flush bright red. "There needed to be a dozen of them and there were only ten! Those last two missing ponies were crucial for the whole event!"

"God above, you've never been told *no* in your life, have you?"

"So, can I feed on one of them or not? I haven't eaten in two days. I'm starving."

"You do not know the meaning of the word *starving*," Valen snarled with such ferocity that Sebastian's eyebrows shot up and he stepped back. "You impudent whelp."

"You can't speak to me this way," Sebastian said. "You have to show me proper respect."

"Sebastian, listen to me. You need to stop being foolish and value your life over your pride. You were caught by vampire hunters. They already proved they can beat you. Please, if – "

Sebastian looked away from Valen and eyed Bailey. "You, come over here and bare your neck."

Bailey's face went into the telltale slack expression of a human under persuasion and he shuffled forward.

Valen seethed, letting out a serpentine hiss, and stepped forward, slapping Sebastian across the face and raking his claws over his cheek. The persuasion broke, and Bailey fled back to the other side of the room.

Sebastian reeled back, black blood seeping through the fingers clamped over his cheek. "You – you struck me!"

"I'll do much worse than that if you harm any of these humans."

Sebastian seethed. "What is *wrong* with you?"

"I could ask the same of you, but I already know the answer!"

Sebastian lunged at Valen with a growl, and Valen rolled back, head slamming into the ground. He kicked Sebastian off of him, shocked at his recently returned strength and overshooting to pummel Sebastian all the way into the ceiling. Sebastian fell back down with the sound of splintering wood, snarling and seizing Valen by the neck.

Valen kicked again, raking his talons over Sebastian's arms to shred the shirt he'd just been given. This time, he couldn't get him off, and Sebastian squeezed, cutting off his air. Valen flailed and tried to gasp in breaths that didn't come.

Well, *this* was embarrassing. Was Valen really not stronger than an eigh-teen-year-old boy?

Ari appeared behind Sebastian, plunging a silver knife into his back.

Ah. Right. There were four vampire hunters in the room.

Sebastian screeched, getting off Valen and clawing at his back to remove the knife. Lex appeared on the other side, plunging a second knife into his exposed belly as he lifted his arms up. Jerome was third, sweeping Sebastian's leg. Sebastian stumbled back and into the arms of Bailey, who had the muzzle. It went back on. Sebastian let out a muffled wail, perhaps realizing he was in over his head, and tried to pull it back off. Jerome and Ari pulled his arms away to cuff them together while Bailey stifled his wriggling.

"Feet next," Lex said.

Bailey let go of Sebastian, who fell flat to the ground. He started crying again as Jerome secured the second pair of cuffs onto his ankles. "Sorry, kid."

Valen got up, coughing.

"You okay?" Ari said.

He nodded. He was … very uncomfortable watching another vampire be over-powered and rendered helpless the same way he had been at the start of this whole ordeal. *It's not the same. He'll be set free in a bit. It's just for safety. It's strictly necessary.*

Valen pulled his glove back on and approached. Sebastian was standing now, held by Bailey under the elbows. He eyed Valen angrily.

"I'm sorry, Sebastian," Valen said. "This is for the humans' safety. I promise it'll be okay. I'm sorry they had to hurt you." He reached forward and took out the knife in his stomach, prompting a muffled scream from Sebastian. "I'm sorry."

Valen's heart nearly stopped. He hadn't noticed until now, but when they'd been fighting earlier, they'd cracked the wood ceiling. Part of which was now lodged in Sebastian's chest, off-center from his heart.

Sebastian seemed to notice it at this point too, going very still and breathing in rapid, panicked breaths. The wood fragment wasn't very large, but it was certainly large enough to kill him had it gone into his heart.

"You're okay," Valen placated, holding his hands out. He vaguely noticed they were shaking. "I'll – I'll just – I'll pull this out. You're okay."

Sebastian was crying in genuine fear now, too scared to move. Valen could hear his heartbeat thudding wildly in his ribcage, and Bailey's support was clearly the only thing keeping him from collapsing on weak knees.

Valen gingerly took the piece of wood and slid it out slowly. Sebastian didn't dare move or breathe until it clattered to the floor, at which point he sagged with relief into Baileys' arms, shaking.

"You're okay, lil guy," Bailey said. "Valen is gonna take you home tonight."

Sebastian didn't even struggle this time as Bailey laid him down into the coffin and locked it.

Valen had stepped into the next room, facing the wall, hands on his chest. His own heart was pounding.

"You okay?" It was Lex, appearing at his elbow.

He shook his head. He tried to speak, found words escaped him, tried again. "I almost killed him," he said in a horrified whisper.

"But you didn't," Lex said. "He's okay."

"But I could have." He hid his face in his hands, tears leaking out. If he'd accidentally killed Sebastian so close on the heels of killing Nick, he wasn't sure if he could have taken that. He couldn't take being a murderer twice in one day. "I-I don't want – I don't like – I don't want this. I don't *want* this. I don't want to kill."

Ari came up from behind him, wrapping him in a bear hug. "We know you don't, big guy." His feet left the floor as she picked him all the way up, sandwiching him between her and Lex. "Come on. Honest mistake. You were defending us. You did the right thing."

Soothing his conscience was always a surefire way to calm him down. He swallowed. "Okay. Thank you."

26

"Can we at least turn the television on, so he's not just alone with his thoughts all day?"

Ari looked from Valen, sitting on the couch with a look of concern on his face, to Sebastian, still locked in the coffin nearby. She sighed. "All right, fine."

Valen gave a joyous little wiggle, as though he really wanted to watch TV. Ari took the remote and flipped the TV on. It was on a news station.

"Do you have access to any nature documentaries?" he asked, excited.

Ari handed him the remote. "Knock yourself out. Just don't buy any of the pay-per-view shit."

She left the two vampires in the living room to go talk to the other humans in the dining room. Bailey and Jerome had changed into their pajamas. "We're gonna hit the hay, okay?" Bailey said.

"Yeah," Ari said. "We all had a long night, but you two went on patrol, so you go first. I'm gonna wake you up around four so me and Lex can take a turn, though."

The two men absconded to use Lex and Ari's bedroom. "So, I guess we just have one more day with Valen," Lex said, sounding sad.

"Yeah," Ari said, trying not to care. She bumped Lex with her elbow. "Come on, let's go make the most of it."

Valen was flipping through the channels when they came back in. Sebastian had been watching the TV, but as soon as they came back in, he turned away, pretending not to be interested.

Ari plopped down on the couch, putting one arm around Valen. "How ya doing, buddy?"

Valen gave a quick, nervous nod. "I'm doing well. Thank you, ma'am."

"Good." She gave him an awkward pat.

Valen fidgeted with the rubberized buttons on the remote. "So, Nick … "

"We took his body back to the base," Lex said. "We made it look like Sebastian killed him."

Ari glanced at Sebastian. "You don't mind, right?"

Sebastian rolled his eyes.

"Thank you," Valen said, hugging his arms around himself. Lex scooted closer.

The phone rang. Ari groaned. "All right, here we go."

She got up and answered. Valen clung to Lex and listened tensely.

"Yo." It was Cyril, one of the other hunters at the base. "What the fuck happened to Nick?"

"Huh?" Ari said. She'd been practicing the lie. Just to make sure. "I dunno, he finally grow some balls?"

"He's fucking dead!"

"God, I wish."

"Bitch, he's dead for real!"

"Really?"

"Yeah! What happened last night when you came to drop off the coffin?"

"Oh." Ari let out an audible grimace. "We didn't actually go out last night to return the coffin. We just told Nick we would to get him to leave. He showed up at our house, and – "

"The fuck you mean you didn't go out?"

"We didn't go out, shithead! Nick came over to harass us at our house, we told him we'd come over later to get him to leave, then we stayed home because fuck him." This was perfectly in character with the way they typically interacted with Nick and shouldn't draw any suspicion. "I didn't fucking kill him, although I kind of wish I had." This with a wink at Valen that made the vampire flush and sink deeper into the couch.

Cyril could be heard cursing on the other end. "So, you didn't see what happened?"

"We were at our fucking house, dumbass. We didn't see anything that wasn't at our goddamn house. I was fucking my girlfriend last night."

"Jesus Christ. You dumb cunt."

"How'd he die? Like what happened?"

"How do you fucking think? The damn vampire he wanted to play with killed him. I guess after that old one was weak for so long, he forgot a fresh one would be, uh, dangerous."

"Right." Ari stood stone-faced for a minute. "Well, anything else?"

"Uhhhhhhh – "

"I'll take that as a no. Don't bother me again." She hung up.

Valen dashed forward into her arms, and she hugged him.

"Put a hold on the waterworks," Ari said, and Valen wiped his eyes. "You're okay."

Valen went back to the couch and sat primly, hands on his lap. He looked over at Sebastian, looking pleased with himself. "That man who hurt us is dead, and we don't have to worry about him anymore."

Sebastian looked relieved despite himself.

They passed some time watching a nature documentary with Valen before the phone rang again. Ari let out an even more exasperated groan.

She ripped the phone off the hook. "*What*?"

"Ariana," said a very serious voice. "This is Director Griswald."

Ari straightened up. "Ah? Hello?"

Valen clung to Lex once again. Lex patted his back. "You're good," she whispered.

"You've heard about what happened to Nick?"

"Yeah," Ari said, more nervous than she had been lying to Cyril. "Hear he got burned playing with fire."

"I've been informed you were expected to see Nick last night to drop off some restraints for the new vampire."

"Y ... yeah, we were supposed to, but we ended up not doing that."

"Why not?"

"We ... I'm sorry, Director G, we just really don't – didn't – like Nick, we didn't think it was very important." She waited tensely for his response.

"All right," he said, finally. "It's not like Nick didn't have any restraints, and he knew how to keep the new research specimen secure. So, you didn't see anything last night? No other information to give me?"

"No, sir," she said. "We were home all night. We weren't scheduled to go on patrol. We had a night in."

The director hemmed and hmmed. "All right, Ariana. Thank you. Please call me if you think of anything or remember anything else."

He hung up. Ari replaced the phone, hand hurting from gripping it so tightly. She let out an exhausted breath and came back over, sprawling out on the couch. "Well, I think we might have really pulled it off."

More waiting. More nature documentaries. Valen couldn't seem to get enough of them. He chattered over the narration at length to offer his own contributions, which he seemed to think were more interesting. And then the phone rang again. Ari groaned, screwing up her eyes. "For the love of – " She trundled back over and picked it up. "*What?*"

It was Franklyn, another coworker at the hunter's guild, one they liked better than Cyril. "Ari, dude! Director G is on the news! Flip over to channel four!"

Valen, hearing the conversation, fumbled with the remote and changed the channel. Sure enough, the director's stony visage was visible in front of a mic, as though he were being interviewed. The banner at the bottom of the screen read *DALTON GRISWALD, DIRECTOR, DEPT. OF NOCTURNAL SECURITY,* which then advanced to the headline *EXPERIMENT GONE WRONG?* Underneath that was the ticker tape showing which counties had the most recent V alerts – it was always the same handful near the border.

"Thanks, Frankie," Ari said distantly. "I'll call you back." She hung up and went to stand in front of the TV.

" – save many lives," the director was saying, and Lex used the remote to turn the volume up. "The experiments were certainly controversial, but we had a strong justification."

"And why didn't you make the public aware of it?" the interviewer asked.

"There was minimal danger," the director claimed. "Except to the staff members handling the vampire, obviously."

"But how can you claim there isn't any danger when there's a vampire running around loose out there now?"

"Our guild members work tirelessly to protect the people we serve. We're spending the day checking all the places where the escaped vampire could have gone. It's no more risk than the usual presence of – "

"Mr. Griswald, how can you – "

"Please let me finish – "

"But how can you – "

"No, no, let me – "

"Director, how can you – "

"Please stop interrupting me, Nancy, I'm trying to answer your question."

The headline at the bottom changed to *GUILD SCIENTIST SLAIN*. The director took a deep breath. "The tragic loss we experienced today was the result of personal negligence, not our program with live vampires. Nick was a very close, longtime friend of mine, and our work will certainly suffer without his contributions moving forward. However, I can't deny the risk inherent in such work, and even if I believe we have a firm justification and the ability to work safely with enhanced security, I can't deny the public has all the reason to be nervous about it given what's happened. Therefore, that's why I've decided, starting today, I'm shutting down that work."

"Yes!" Lex and Ari stood, giving each other wild high-fives. "Yes!"

"*Yes!*"

"There will be no more live captures," the director continued. "No one in our organization is prepared to continue Nick's work, and the risk has proved itself to be too great."

The interviewer made a face. "There you have it, folks. We'll be right back with more after the break."

Ari flopped back onto the couch. "Fuck yeah. Fuck. *Yeah.* We did it. Those jackasses really think Sebastian got loose while Nick was alone and killed him and ran off. *And* they're not going to torture anyone else because of it. Fuck yeah."

Valen gave a few excited wiggles. "We did it! Haha!" He glanced over at Sebastian and then shamefacedly turned in on himself, hands on his knees. "Um, Ari?"

"Yeah?"

"Do you think ... we could try letting Sebastian out again? He looks a lot calmer now, and he still has stab wounds. That can't be comfortable. He's just been sitting there with them the whole time."

"Oh. Uhh, yeah, sure, I guess." Even she had to admit Sebastian looked kind of pathetic. "Long as you can keep him under control like you did before."

Valen nodded. "I'll handle it. Leave it to me."

Valen once again unlocked Sebastian, and the younger vampire groaned and whined pathetically as Valen stood him up and helped get him out of all the restraints.

"This is so undignified," he muttered.

"You're all right," Valen said, and he propped Sebastian up to take him upstairs to the bathroom.

Ari let herself untense, melting on the couch. "Fuck. It's really over, huh?"

Lex sprawled onto Ari's lap. "We didn't do perfect, but we did our best, I think."

Ari let her eyes unfocus on the TV. The current documentary had started talking about mushrooms. "Yeah. Maybe."

A few minutes later, the pair of vampires came back. Sebastian was cleaner and had been bandaged. His face was still very red.

"Sebastian has something he'd like to ask you," Valen announced.

Lex turned off the TV. Ari sat up straight.

"This is humiliating," Sebastian mumbled.

"Go on," Valen said.

Sebastian turned even redder, but he finally looked at Lex and Ari. "I am very hungry. May I please have some blood?"

Woah. *That* was an improvement. "Of course!" Lex blurted out. "You can have some of mine!"

"Uhh ... are you sure that's a good idea?" Ari said, even as Lex slid off the couch towards Sebastian. "Considering how much we dumped on the floor?"

"It's just one time," Lex said, waving her off. "I'll be fine."

Sebastian reached out to grab Lex's hair, and Valen smacked his hand away. "Ah-ah-ah. That's not how it's done."

"That's how it's done where *I'm* from."

"Well, we aren't *where you're from*, are we?"

Sebastian lowered his hand, once again looking chastised.

Lex extended her arm out. "Go ahead and bite my wrist. It's okay."

Sebastian looked offended, his facial expression struggling to remain neutral. Lex remained tense, ready to step away if he tried to go for the neck instead, which he clearly wanted to.

His face broke. He visibly gave up. He bent his head and bit her wrist.

"A bit gentler," Valen said, and wonder of wonders, he actually listened.

***

Sebastian was still behaving himself at sunset, so they didn't shove him back in the coffin for the drive to the border.

Valen leaned into the window and watched the trees fly by as though it were a fascinating movie. Sebastian did so boredly.

The van's tires rolled to a stop in the dirt at the expanse of trees that filled the border. Valen's boots crunched over sticks, and he slung his backpack over his shoulder as he stepped out. Sebastian had been bundled up in a hooded jacket to hide the bandages and wounds he seemed self-conscious of.

"Well, here you are," Lex said.

"Go on, get outta here," Ari said.

Sebastian started walking towards the border. Valen hesitated.

"One more hug for the road?" Lex suggested.

Valen nodded.

Lex came over and hugged him. After a moment, Ari came up and did as well.

"You can come back, you know," Lex said softly. "I know it's been ... rough, but – you're always welcome here." Stupid. It was stupid to say that. Why would he *ever* want to come back?

And yet, he patted her back.

Ari finally broke the hug. "Hah, I doubt he wants to see our sorry asses ever again. Go on, big guy."

Valen adjusted his backpack, looking unsure.

"Hey!" Sebastian shouted in the distance. "Are we going or what?"

"I'll call you to let you know I've arrived home safely," Valen said. "And I'll ... think about it, Alexis. Thank you, both."

With that, Valen turned and ran off, far faster than a human could ever hope to catch up. Lex and Ari turned and wordlessly continued to hug each other, letting themselves cry now that no one was watching.

27

—·—

Valen called to let them know he and Sebastian had gotten home safely, but he didn't come back. It wasn't surprising, really, but it still hurt.

What *was* surprising was the fact that he didn't answer his phone after that first call. Did he really not want to talk to them? Had he been hiding his disdain for them that well?

Lex cried about it. She knew in her heart Valen had no real reason to want to stay in touch with them, but she'd thought *maybe* they could have at least fixed the situation a *little*, to show Valen humans weren't *complete* and total monsters to him. That maybe they could at least have a phone call every once in a while. It was hard to tell if she was more upset about not ever seeing Valen again, or if the guilt of what they'd done was just too much to bear now that there was nothing more that could be done to fix it.

Lex left a frankly absurd number of voicemails, calling him almost every day for the few weeks after his departure. Ari kept telling her not to, that he would call back if he wanted to, and Ari channeled her own negative feelings into getting frustrated at Lex for not leaving it alone.

Ari knew she was a piece of shit deep down, and Valen not wanting to see her again just confirmed that. There wasn't anything to be surprised about, but it still hurt.

They tried to soldier on. They kept on as usual. Neither of them really wanted to be vampire hunters anymore. Not only did it feel bad, but they just weren't good at it anymore.

Pretty much every single time they answered a V alert and it turned out to be a young adult vampire undoubtedly on their first hunt, neither of them could bring themselves to kill them. They just didn't try very hard and let them get away, settling for hoping they'd been scared off.

It was horrible. Neither of them wanted to think about how many humans had been harmed or taken because they were falling down on the job, but neither of them had the guts to quit. Not to mention they sort of couldn't, because they needed the money, and it was ... difficult to find another job, sometimes, when vampire hunting had been your main career for years and people had expectations about what kind of work people like you were suited for.

They started arguing more often. Ari's stress eating picked up. Lex cried more easily. They packed up the belongings Valen had left behind and hid them so they didn't have to look at them. It felt like there was a Valen-shaped hole in their life.

Until one day, the phone rang. "What?" Ari answered gruffly.

"Ariana." It was Valen's voice, and Ari had never *not* been pissed to be called Ariana before now. "Please help me. I don't know what to do. I'm with my husband and I don't know what to do. Please help me."

Ari's heart leapt in her throat. Lex saw her expression and came over to put an ear up to the phone. "Valen?" Ari said, alarmed. "Where are you?"

"The Kithrara estate, I – " He abruptly went silent.

"Valen?" Ari pressed. "Valen? Talk to me, baby, what's happening? Valen?"

The line went dead.

Ari slammed the phone back in the cradle. "Fuck. *Fuck.*"

"Star-sixty-nine it," Lex said desperately.

Ari dialed to ring back the last call number. The phone didn't even ring. "Fuck!" Ari slammed the phone back into the wall.

"The Kithrara estate," Lex said. "That's his husband. His – "

"His scumbag shitbag abusive husband," Ari said. "Who isn't even letting him use the phone freely."

"What do we do?" Lex said, sounding small and lost.

Ari ground her teeth. She picked the phone back up and dialed Bailey and Jerome's number.

28

Ari rolled the map out onto the table, all four of them leaning over it.

"Okay," she said, planting a finger on the map. "I got this from Patrick and he said it's using the most up-to-date flyby data of vampire territory, and the Kithrara estate is here. This is the main estate, where the head of the family is. Valen mentioned that his husband is the oldest son of the current head, which means *that* estate house would be over … here." Her finger slid along the border.

"It's so far in," Lex said, dismayed.

"Not as far in as most of the noble houses, apparently," Ari said. "Apparently this is considered close to the border as far as vampire estates go."

Lex leaned over, hemming and hawing. "If we set out around midnight, we'll get there as the sun rises."

"This is crazy," Bailey said. "This is suicide. We all know that, right?"

All four of them looked at each other.

"I'm going to help Valen," Ari said. The same simpleminded, utterly stubborn Ari who'd simply driven over to get Lex in vampire territory all those years ago, as though it really were just that simple. "It's my fault he got put through hell and back, and I'm going to make sure it never happens to him again. Anyone who wants to bail … I won't think less of you."

The overhead lights buzzed in the silence.

"Right." Ari took a deep breath. "The most crucial advantage we're going to have is that we can be out and active during the day. It's key that we hunker down at night and don't get spotted. As long as we can manage that while getting Valen's attention, all five of us can get out of there alive."

"We need to get a message to Valen that the others won't notice or won't understand," Jerome said. "Something that will mean something only to him."

Ari smirked. "Lex, go rifle through your plushies. We have a very important cat to bring with us."

***

They loaded the van up with supplies. Hunting gear, food, water, sleeping bags. Toilet paper. Bottles to piss in.

This was going to be a long road trip.

They drove towards the border while it was still night, to give them as much time as possible in vampire territory while the sun was up. Sunrise happened right about as they passed over the border, streaking past the skull-laden sign that demarcated the two territories.

Ari saw the back of the sign in the rearview mirror, the side declaring HUMAN TERRITORY, VAMPIRES WILL BE KILLED ON SIGHT. "Here we go."

They went over bumpy, unpaved roads for a while. Ari bitched nonstop about the effect on the van's suspension.

It only stopped when they got back onto a paved road, at which point all four of them waited in tense silence with bated breath, as though afraid making too much noise would summon a hoard of vampires immediately.

"Okay," Ari said. "We're in vampire territory, and nothing bad has happened yet."

"Okay," Bailey said.

"Okay," Jerome agreed.

"Yeah," Lex said. "We're doing it."

They passed by a house, the first vampire-made architecture of the trip. It had no windows. Everyone's skin crawled.

It looked like a farm of some sort. There was a barn, again without windows. There were horses and cows standing in the field. All four of the humans had no idea what to say.

"I didn't know they *farmed*," Jerome said. "The fuck they need to *farm* for?"

"To feed human captives?" Lex suggested.

"Maybe they just like horses," Bailey suggested. "A horse girl can be a vampire, I guess."

They realized the breathtaking scale of the farm as they drove past it, way, way larger than a human farm. Made sense, for a species that could heft a horse with their bare hands and run the entirety of the farm in under a minute.

It was almost easy to forget, here in the rural part of the territory during the day. There were birds and animals out and about. There were plants and roads and water towers and powerlines. There were buildings, always without windows, in case any of them *were* close to forgetting.

The idea that the monsters they fought nightly just had their own society over here was surreal. They'd always known, in an abstract way. But actually seeing it was different.

Lex got out the map and started navigating. The buildings started getting closer together. The sun climbed higher in the sky.

Ari turned down a road that had a row of houses. All four of them buzzed with anxiety, knowing the only thing keeping them safe from a hoard of bloodthirsty vampires was the time of day.

The panic faded as they went along and it just looked … normal. There was a stray cat on a lawn. Someone had a gnome by their mailbox. There was a corner shop – the first building they'd seen that had a window, which was shuttered with a heavy metal sheet and bars. There were absolutely no people around, the streets utterly empty, everything standing abandoned in the light of day. It was ominous.

A blur suddenly ran past in front of them, a ways up the road. All four of them let out startled yelps.

"No way," Jerome said. "Is someone out and about during the day?"

The blur slowed down and resolved into the shape of a person, swathed in a thick suit that looked like a hazmat suit, complete with darkened lenses, every inch of their skin covered. It was emblazoned with what appeared to be the logo of a company of some kind, and they were pulling a cart behind them full of packages.

It was hard to tell what the vampire was looking at, but it was definitely facing their van. Ari rolled to a stop. They waited there, hands creeping towards their weapons.

The vampire tilted its head at them, as though it wasn't sure what it was seeing. Then it raised a hand and pointed.

It took a second to figure out towards what. But then they realized.

Towards the border.

"Oh," Ari said. "Ah. No. No, we're – " She pointed down the road, where they'd been heading. "We're going that way. That way."

The vampire lowered its hand slowly, then gave a shrug. *Your funeral.* It ran off, becoming a blur of motion to take its cart off to who knows where.

"They have a special service that comes deliver shit to you during the day," Bailey said. "What the hell. I wouldn't have guessed."

"Probably costs an arm and a leg," Ari muttered. "It's fine as long as they don't come back, I guess."

This was putting them in a weird headspace, this display that vampires here at home were just … normal people. Living their lives. Never even interacting with a human. Being fed blood bottled by the ones who *did* come over the border as a job. Vampires had jobs and houses and hobbies and pets and *it was weird.*

It was about half an hour more of navigation until they came up a long driveway towards an iron gate squatting in the middle of a huge stone wall. The gate had a decorative letter *K* on it.

"Okay," Ari said. "Nobody get out of the car yet."

They drove slowly around the perimeter of the estate. When they could see over the wall or through hedges, they caught glimpses of an immaculate, manicured lawn, rose bushes, flowers, fountains. Ari slammed on the brakes at the shock of seeing the huge stone water fountain running with blood, before they realized it was just water lit by red lighting to *look* like blood.

Their scouting revealed an area on a hill nearby where they could park the van and stay out of sight, but be able to see into the estate over the fence.

That just left the thing they had to get out of the van for. Ari pulled back up to the front gate. "Okay, we need to leave the cat somewhere either Valen will see it, or someone will see it and bring it to him. Maybe on that patio. Jerome, get out and leave it there."

"What! Why do I have to do it?"

"You have the longest legs. I bet you could get over the fence the easiest."

"So I have to die to vampires because I have long legs?"

"Two of the people in this van are fat fucks, and you're the fastest runner and have better upper body strength than Lex. Get the cat and give it to him."

Lex rifled around in her backpack and pulled out the stuffed cat that had been in the coffin, the one that had helped Valen sleep.

"I've seen this movie," Jerome said, taking the stuffed animal. "If I die first, I'm coming back to haunt your asses."

He opened the side door, the first time the door had been opened in hours. They all cautiously peered out. Jerome hopped out and approached the fence. He gave a mighty leap, but there weren't any handholds on the gate. He slid down the slick metal and plonked back on the ground. "It's no good, boss, I need some help."

Bailey got out and knelt down, hefting Jerome onto his shoulders and tossing him over the gate. Jerome landed with reasonable grace and took off, running the cat up to the patio. Bailey peered through the bars, watching him with worry.

Jerome appeared back at the gate. "Got it. Uhh." He eyed the gate. "Little help again?"

Bailey tried to give him a boost through the bars, but it didn't really work. "Just a second," Bailey said. "Lex, toss me some rope." Under less dire circumstances, he might have made a joke about leaving Jerome behind, but they were all swamped with so much anxiety about being in the open on the estate of the family responsible for thousands of kidnappings and murders, that it was all they could do to stay functional.

Lex complied, digging out some rope. Bailey unfurled it and tossed it over, then pulled. Jerome used it to rappel up and over the gate, landing in Bailey's arms on the other side.

After a moment, Jerome playfully sunk deeper into Bailey's arms, feigning bashfulness. "Well hey, handsome, how you – "

"Later," Ari interrupted. "Get the fuck in."

Bailey carted Jerome back into the van, and Ari floored it to get away from the gate and back to the hiding spot they'd identified earlier.

She killed the engine. All four of them got out and pulled branches and leaves and bushes over to camouflage the van a bit more. They then got back in and locked the doors.

"Okay," Ari said. "Now ... we wait."

They took turns sleeping. The ones who were awake were bored as hell, but they'd brought some books to read. When the sun started to set, they took turns watching the patio through binoculars.

"We got movement," Lex said when some of the doors in the estate began opening. The sun was completely down now. The vampires were starting to wake up.

They were in vampire territory after sundown in the dark. Whatever laughing and joking there had been stopped immediately. Nobody could focus on reading. The minutes crawled by so, so slowly. They jostled to watch through the binoculars.

"Someone's picking it up!" Ari said, tugging Lex's sleeve. Someone who appeared to be a groundskeeper had been in the middle of doing something with the hedges when he saw the stuffed animal and walked over to the patio. He scratched his head, picked it up, and walked back into the house. He came back outside a minute later, empty-handed.

Ari let out a tense breath. "All right. Valen will recognize it and hopefully make the connection that we're here, so hopefully it's been put somewhere he can see it."

"What's the next step, boss?" Bailey said.

Ari ground her teeth. "I'm not sure. Valen is a smart guy, so I was hoping he'd figure out some way to just come out to us."

Bailey wrung his hands. "We should figure out something else in case he – "

"Yeah, yeah, I know, I know."

They passed the time tossing ideas to each other and hoping no vampires stumbled across them. They were behind the estate, with no reason for anybody to be coming by, so they *should* be in the clear. But –

"Hey, hey, hey, hey, someone's coming this way," Jerome said, rapidly tapping Bailey on the arm.

More pairs of binoculars were lifted up to check. The *someone* was dressed in a maid outfit, and she was taking a sort of meandering approach up the hill behind the estate.

"Why the hell you coming over here, girly?" Ari muttered. "Get back."

"Wait, maybe it's – " Lex started, and they all froze as the vampire started running through the vegetation on the path leading up to where they were parked, disappearing from sight.

"Shit, shit shit shit shit."

"Fuck."

"Shit and fuck."

Weapons were drawn, guns were loaded, stakes were readied.

The sound of light footsteps rapidly pattering nearby ramped up very, very quickly before there was a huge *THUD* and the van shook. There was also a surprised *oof* and the sound of someone tumbling to the ground.

All four of them waited with hearts hammering, not opening the doors just yet.

The vampire's face popped up in the windshield, her hands on the hood of the car, bouncing excitedly. "I found you!"

The doors flew open and all four of them came out with weapons drawn.

"Ah!" the maid cried, stumbling backwards. "No, no, it's okay! It's okay! Don't!"

They slowed down, cautiously lowering their weapons.

"Mistress Kithrara sent me out to find you!"

"Mistress – " Ari said. "Valen?"

"Yes! Don't worry, I won't tell anyone you're out here!" She sounded delighted to be in on a secret.

They all looked at each other.

"Okay," Ari said. "Great. What did ... uh, Valen, send you out here for?"

"She was worried about you sitting out here all alone! It's dangerous for you to be here!"

"Yeah, we know," Bailey muttered.

This was incredible. They were talking to this random vampire, who was just ... a normal person. The only vampires they ever interacted with were the ones who came over the border, which they usually only did for one reason. It was weird to see that most vampires were just kind of ... normal.

Ari turned to the van. "What the hell! You put a huge dent in the side of my car!"

"I'm sorry!" she said. "I didn't see it! I could smell it was around, but you covered it up!"

Ari sighed, rubbing her scalp. "All right, no use crying over spilled milk."

"No use ... ?" the vampire said.

"Don't worry about it. Hey, do you think you could pass a note to Valen without anyone else seeing?"

***

They wrote a note that told Valen to bundle himself up and walk out of the house at sunrise. If he could do that, maybe it really could be that simple. The vampire took it and ran off.

So they waited, hoping she was being genuine about not alerting anyone else.

Luckily, the only incident for the rest of the night was Bailey farting in the van, and everyone else being too scared to roll the windows down for fear of being heard.

The sun rose once again, and they all breathed a little easier watching the figures at the estate down below scramble to get back inside, shuttering doors behind them.

Once the sun was fully out, Ari pulled the van up again, nosing it towards the front gate. They waited.

The front door was hidden by the angle of the stone wall, but soon a ghostly figure clad in white – a wedding dress – wrapped up head to toe, appeared cautiously crossing the lawn. There was a second person behind them, following along obediently. A human under persuasion.

That raised an eyebrow, but nobody said anything. Valen picked up his pace when he caught sight of them.

"Come on, baby," Ari said under her breath. "Give me my boy."

Valen opened the gate by pressing some unseen button behind the wall. Bailey and Jerome opened the side door wide, hanging out and urging Valen to come in. The vampire did so, crying as he stepped up.

"We got you," Bailey said.

"No need to worry now," Jerome added.

Ari and Lex turned around to see him. He was a mess, crying limply in Jerome and Bailey's arms. The human behind him stepped up to follow – she was holding a cat carrier.

Well, whatever. They came to rescue a vampire, they could rescue a vampire, a human, and a cat. Bailey shut the side door as soon as everyone was in.

"Let's blow this popsicle stand," Ari said, slamming the gas.

29

— • —

Valen just stayed in Bailey and Jerome's arms and cried for a while, everyone in the car swaying as Ari drove like hell to get them back over the border.

"We got you," Bailey said. "We got you, sweet boy. Here, here, why don't you sit over here so you're further away from the sun."

He shifted Valen into a corner further away from the window. Valen kept crying, still not removing all his wrappings.

Lex had twisted around in the passenger seat to look back at him. "Are you okay? Do you – here." She took her seatbelt off and clambered over the center console.

"Hey, hey!" Ari growled with annoyance. "I'm driving!"

Lex fell over into the back of the van. Jerome laughed at her.

Ari held up the roadmap. "Hello? Navigation?"

"You'll be fine, right?" Lex said. "Just keep going south."

Ari muttered, watching them in the rearview mirror. Under any other circumstances she would have already pulled over to also give Valen a hug, but the urge to hightail it out of vampire territory was too strong.

Lex came over and put her arms around Valen. "There you are. Hi. It's good to see you again."

"I can't believe you came here," Valen said tearfully. "I can't believe – you – you did that for me. Risked yourselves like that."

"Yeah, well," Ari said gruffly. "You call me and I come running. Just how I am."

Lex held his hands. "You deserve the world, Valen."

"We gotta make up for what we did somehow," Bailey said. "We're your guys for life."

Valen's lip wobbled and he burst into tears again.

Ari kept driving as the four in the back dissolved into a pile of hugs around Valen as the vampire just kept sniffling and crying.

"I'm sorry," he said, finally. "If I'd just not been such a fool, I could have helped myself without you having to put yourselves in such danger."

"I don't wanna hear any of that," Ari said. "Can it."

Valen's eyes drifted down.

"So ... " Lex said. She cleared her throat. "The, um. The cat is nice. And, um. So ... who's this?"

She pointed to the human, still sitting in the opposite corner watching the whole thing with the same eerie blank expression on her face.

Valen hid his face in his hands. "I'm sorry," he said quietly.

Lex patted his hand. Softly, despite the dread building in her stomach. "Hey. Valen. Who is this?"

"My thrall," he answered, voice scarcely above a whisper.

There was silence in the van for a moment, the vehicle rocking and creaking. "That doesn't sound like you, Valen," Jerome said. "Not at all."

"I'm sorry," he said again, still hiding his face. "I'm sorry. I didn't want this."

Lex ran her hand around the nape of his neck, stroking softly. "Okay. It's okay. We'll figure this out."

"It was either this or starving again," Valen said. "I'm sorry. It was too much for me. I couldn't. I'm sorry."

"Okay," Lex said. "Okay. We'll figure this out. Don't worry."

"Can she be saved?" Jerome said, waving a hand in front of her face to no response. "She looks braindead." The humans repeatedly exposed to persuasion every day became completely mind-wiped husks within months, brains melting under the stress.

Valen hid his face in his knees. "Yes," he admitted. "Yes. She hasn't been here long. She's just under persuasion right now."

Bailey looked at Valen sharply. "Valen!"

"I'm sorry," he sobbed. "I'm sorry. I'm sorry."

"Let her go," Ari said. "We'll deal with it."

Valen curled himself up in a tight ball, and everyone knew the persuasion was gone as soon as the look on her face changed dramatically.

The human gasped and shook her head, disoriented. "Please," she said, scared.

"Hey, hey, you're all right," Bailey said, holding her firmly. "You're safe. What's your name?"

She put her arms around herself. "Sarah."

"Hey, it's nice to meet you, Sarah. My name's Bailey. We're vampire hunters. We're gonna take you home."

"Why is *she* here?" Sarah demanded, tears in her eyes. "What's going on?"

Bailey followed her gaze to Valen, who had broken down into fresh sobs. "We were picking – ah – Valen is a *he*, okay?"

"I don't give a fuck!" Sarah shouted. "Fuck off! Whatever they are, they're a monster! Why haven't you killed her?"

Everyone fell silent as Ari pulled the van off to the side of the road, then put it in park.

"Um, Ari," Lex said, and Ari stepped out and opened the side door of the van, yanking Sarah by the arm.

"Don't say that shit about him in front of me," Ari hissed. "Fucking don't."

Sarah sobbed with fresh fear. "She bit me. She made me her slave. She treated me like I wasn't a person. How can you defend that?"

Valen's crying picked up.

"Fuck *off*," Sarah said, voice breaking. "Boohoo, you feel guilty about – "

"*Shut up*," Ari said, yanking Sarah forward.

"Stop!" Lex said, shoving Ari away. "Stop it, Ari."

Ari looked about to explode. "We just got Valen away from his abusive husband. That's why he treated you like that. You don't get to – "

"I don't get to – " Sarah cried. "Boohoo, Valen had an abusive husband! I had an abusive *vampire* biting me and brainwashing me!"

"It's not a competition," Lex tried.

"Apparently it is!" Sarah shouted. "Because otherwise you won't even acknowledge I'm entered!"

"I'm sorry," Valen whimpered. "I'm sorry. I'm sorry."

"Get out," Ari shouted. "Get out of my fucking car."

Sarah looked to Valen before she realized Ari was talking to *her*. "What?"

"Ari," Lex said, stepping in front of Sarah. "If we kick her out, she won't make it back on her own."

"I don't care. We're here for Valen."

"Ari," Lex hissed, and she stepped forward to the edge of the van, leaning out so she hung over Ari. Ari had to look up at her to make eye contact, and Lex reached a hand out and put one finger on Ari's chest. "Stop acting like this."

Ari broke eye contact and her face went red. She folded her arms around herself and muttered.

"I will handle Sarah and Valen. Go drive the fucking van."

Defeated, Ari got back in the driver's seat and pulled back onto the road.

Lex slid the door shut. "Everyone calm down," Lex said. "Take a breather. Everyone is safe right now. That's what's important."

"How can you say that?" Sarah sobbed. "She's *right there.*"

"Okay. Sarah." Lex took Sarah's hands. "Listen. Take a deep breath with me now. Okay. You're safe. Valen's not going to hurt you."

"She – "

"Just let me talk for a minute. Valen is someone who's very important to us, and he needed our help. So we came to help him. He's a very noble and compassionate person – "

"She didn't even ask my name!" Sarah wept.

Valen's face flushed with guilt. "What difference would it have made!" he cried. "Would it have made the bites hurt less?"

"I don't know!" Sarah snapped. "Maybe!"

"Okay, listen," Lex said. "It's okay to be scared and it's okay to be mad at Valen. It's only natural."

Valen crumpled, crying softly.

"He isn't like that when he has a choice in the matter. What's done is done, but he's not going to do that anymore. Trust me. He's with us now. Okay?"

"No, it's not okay! I thought I was going to be there for the rest of my life!"

"He could have left you behind, you know," Ari snarled. "I'm sure he didn't *have* to take you."

Sarah looked cowed, shying away. "Sorry, I'm sorry."

Lex glared at Ari, then hugged Sarah again. "It's okay. It's over now, that's what's important. Okay?"

Sarah looked very much not okay with it. "Okay. I guess. Can I go home?"

"Yes," Lex promised. "Yes, we'll take you home first thing, I promise."

***

In the end, Sarah wanted out of the van before getting her *home*, demanding to be let off at the first sign of civilization on the human side of the border. They let her off with enough change to make multiple phone calls, wishing her well, which she didn't return.

Valen remained curled up in the corner. The cat had been taken out of the carrier and hadn't left his arms since then, though whether that was willingly or because Valen desperately clutched her for comfort was unclear. She was a puffy white thing, with long hair that coated everything she touched. Valen stuck his face into her to hide his tears.

"I'm sorry," Valen wept as soon as they drove away from Sarah. "I'm so, so sorry. I didn't want to. It was either that or starving again. I wouldn't have if – "

"You were asked to make an impossible choice," Jerome said. "The latest in a long line of impossible choices. We know what that's like. We're not going to hold it against you."

"I'm on your side forever," Ari said. "We owe you that."

Valen finally pulled his face out of the cat's flank. "Thank you," he said tearfully. "I-I-I don't know what I would do without you."

"Well, you got a few decades before we die and you gotta figure it out," Ari said.

It was late afternoon by the time they got back to Lex and Ari's house, and they were all ready to drop dead from exhaustion. Valen coaxed Snowball – apparently the cat's name – back into the carrier, then made sure he was all wrapped up to be escorted back into the house.

"You still have the coffin," he said, eyeing the wooden box on the living room floor.

"Yeah," Lex said. "We figured you'd need it if you ... ever visited."

Valen took her hand and squeezed it. Ari came up behind him and put a hand on his shoulder. Bailey and Jerome came in, haggard and worn out.

"We crashing here?" Bailey said hopefully.

"Sure," Ari said. "We'd appreciate the extra eyes to keep Valen safe. Last time he was here didn't go so well, after all."

Jerome nodded. "I'm gonna use the bathroom before we hit the couch, then."

The two men went upstairs. Valen let the cat out of the carrier, and it bolted behind the easy chair. "She'll adjust, I'm sure," Valen said tiredly. He eyed the coffin.

"You ready to rest?" Lex said. "Should be safe, right?"

Valen nodded. "I ... doubt my husband would follow me all the way over the border, and he doesn't know where we are anyway. I ... I think this is as safe as I can get."

"Right." Ari motioned to the coffin. "Good night, then. Let us know if you need anything."

Valen shuffled towards the coffin, then hesitated. "Ahm, if I may ... ?"

"You may," Ari said. "What is it?"

Valen flushed. "I ... I found that sleeping with someone's arms around me helped me sleep better than being in the box, actually."

No way. He wasn't asking for ... Was he?

"Oh?" Ari said. "Oh!"

"Our bed is big enough for three, if that's what you're asking," Lex said.

Valen flushed red. "It would be ... inappropriate for me to share a bed with anyone who wasn't my husband." This said with barely-repressed yearning. More like he was asking for permission than objecting.

"Your husband, huh." Ari ran a finger over Valen's shoulder, on the lacy fabric of his wedding dress. He was still wearing it. Presumably it had just been the garment that covered most of his skin the best. "Do you love your husband?"

"No."

"Do you want to go back to him?"

"No!"

"Do the vows this dress represents mean anything to you anymore?"

Valen gripped the fabric of the dress, knuckles white. His face snapped into a wicked expression. He gripped both shoulders and tore the dress off. "No!"

He started tearing the dress apart with animalistic fervor, ripping it to ribbons. Lex and Ari stepped back to give him more space as he shredded with wild abandon.

When the expensive garment was no more than a pile of frayed white fabric at his feet, he became self-aware and flushed with embarrassment. He was standing there in just a slip now. "Er," he said, chest heaving. "S-sorry, I got a bit carried away."

Ari grinned wolfishly and swept him off his feet. "Come on, then. Let's go upstairs."

30

— • —

Ari carried him gently up the stairs bridal-style, and he spent the evening in their bed squished between them.

He seemed happy. Shockingly so. Lex's heart fluttered. Ari pretended not to care, but her arms never left Valen, not once the whole night.

Maybe they'd done it. Maybe they'd fixed things.

The phone rang the next morning at sunrise. Ari grumbled out of bed to go downstairs and answer it. Valen remained clinging to Lex, looking worried.

Ari came back up, still in her bathrobe and slippers. "We have a situation," she announced. "That was Franklyn, calling to give us a friendly heads up. Sarah called the guild and told them what happened. That, combined with the fact that we used official guild resources to get the maps of vampire territory, tipped the higher-ups off to what we did and now the director himself is out looking for us."

Valen went rigid, then burst into tears. He just looked so *scared*. It was heart-breaking.

"We'll run away," Lex said. "We'll keep you safe."

"Hold on," Ari said. She ground her teeth. "Let's not jump to that yet." She sat down on the bed, hand on her chin. "Franklyn called to tip us off. From the sound of it, the other hunters might be on our side too. If we gather them all up to stand with us, the director will *have* to take us seriously. Getting permission for Valen to be here would be way better than just making him be on the run for the rest of his life."

Valen eased his death grip on the blanket, lowering it down. "A-are you sure?"

"I know not *everyone* is going to take our side," Lex said. "What about Cyril and Isaiah?"

"We can just shoot them."

"Okay, well, let's not jump to *that* yet."

"Everyone already feels bad about letting Nick have Valen for so long," Ari said. "Everyone except Cyril and Isaiah ditched Nick after not too long. All we have to do is let them meet Valen and tell them all what he was doing here to win them over."

Valen wrung his hands. "Ari, I-I'm scared."

Ari came over and put her strong arms around him. "We will take care of you," Ari said into his hair. "I promise. No matter what. We went all the way to your husband's estate to get you. We'd do it again."

Valen melted in her arms. "Okay," he whispered. "I trust you."

Ari kissed him on top of the head. "And I'm not gonna take that for granted." She plopped him back into Lex's arms. "Lex, you and Bailey and Jerome keep an eye on him. I've got some phone calls to make and some running around to do."

***

The director could be convinced, if the circumstances were right. It was now her mission to make those circumstances happen.

She had to gather up the rest of the hunters from this base. She could get them all on her side if she said the right things.

It was a good time for it, since all the hunters on patrol that night had just come back at daybreak. There were a few pairs that were off duty tonight, who Ari managed to get ahold of by phone or just driving over to their house.

Even the ones who were not particularly enthusiastic about it knew something was going on, and that was enough to get them all to gather at the base.

Even Cyril and Isaiah were there. She knew they were going to cause problems, but best to have it happen now while everyone was there.

She told them everything. She told them why Valen was here, who he was, what he'd done. What Nick had done to him. How Ari would do anything to defend him. How they *all* bore responsibility for this, and how they had an opportunity to fix it now.

There were arguments and questions. There were skeptical people being convinced. There were fistfights when Cyril and Isaiah were, as predicted, the last holdouts who were furious with Ari.

The tide turned when the rest of the hunters kicked Cyril and Isaiah out, and that was when Ari knew she'd done what she needed to do.

Ari told all the other hunters to get ready for her to bring Valen over, expecting the hunter's HQ to be the best place for the confrontation with the director to happen. She then sped back home.

***

After Valen had gone over the border, they'd made a special trip back to Valen's house in human territory to pick up some of his things that'd been abandoned. Lex had wanted to make sure they didn't get stolen, and it was convenient to have them in case he ever came back, her reasoning had gone.

So they had an outfit for Valen to wear to go out in the sunlight despite the very destroyed wedding dress. They wrapped him up, long sleeves and billowing cloak and laced-up boots and a hood over a mask and another hood.

They'd done everything in their power to make him safe – make him *feel* safe. It hadn't been enough.

Lex and Ari and Bailey and Jerome had all gotten out of the van, standing in the parking lot of the hunter's base, trying to coax him to come out. Valen stayed huddled in the corner. His mask hid it, but they could all hear him crying. "Are you sure I can't just stay in the van?" he tried.

Lex's heart broke. He deserved so much better than this, being so scared even when surrounded by people who wanted to help him. "It'll be okay," Lex said. "For real this time." She held her hand out for him to take. "If you trust me one more time, I promise I won't let you down again."

Valen took her hand with a shaking, be-gloved hand of his own. He stepped out and let himself be steered into the hunter's compound.

There were a few moments where Valen's legs seemed to stop working and the humans had to half-drag him to keep going. He said nothing.

They stepped into the building. All the hunters were gathered in the main room, and they all turned to face him. Valen let out a whimper and clung to Ari's side.

Ari put an arm around him, drawing him forward. "Everyone, this is Valen. You all know who he is, but let's meet him properly this time."

Franklyn stepped forward, rubbing his arm and looking embarrassed. "Hey. Um. My name's Franklyn. Um ... I wanted to apologize. I think we all ... know what we let happen to you wasn't right. I'm sorry. We let you down. Ari tells us you're here to try and make things better between humans and vampires. If you're still down for that, we'd like to help."

Valen slowly uncurled himself from Ari. "Really?"

"Yeah, man."

Valen took his mask off, dangling it from one hand, feeling okay looking at them eye to eye now. Despite their declaration, a few of them shuffled nervously as he made eye contact with them.

"I've stood by and witnessed my fair share of atrocities that I didn't stop," Valen said. His voice shook, but only a little. "What's important is that we forge a better future together."

His face contorted into panic as the hunters crowded in on him, but it was because they were cheering and slapping him on the back. Ari started swatting them away, noting his discomfort.

"The boys have been working on something for you," Ari said, to deflect. "In the basement."

His trembling started up again.

"It's okay," Lex soothed. "Ari took care of everything. You can trust us."

They half-dragged him again. He kept his eyes squeezed shut until they got to the bottom of the stairs.

The basement was ... empty. Of all the things that had been in it last time he was here. The blood had been scrubbed away; there were no longer silver implements scattered about.

There *were* a few lab benches with some scattered labware on top. Valen slowly uncrunched himself. "Um, I'm not sure I understand."

"We're offering to make this *your* lab," Ari said. "'Course, you went through some pretty fucked up shit here, so if you don't want that, you don't have to take it. It's your space now. If you tell us to fill it up with cement, we will. But everyone agreed that's what should happen now. We're all on your side here, and we want you to stay here with us where we can protect you."

Valen slowly turned around in the space, looking conflicted.

"We're going to pitch it to the director when he gets here," Lex said. "He's a very strategic man, so he'll be able to see that you're an asset."

Valen turned and planted his face in Ari's chest. "I'd like to try," he said tearfully. "Thank you."

He suddenly pulled away, ears twitching. It became obvious why a moment later when Lex and Ari heard the sound of car doors slamming – the director must have arrived.

Despite Valen's vote of confidence, he moaned in terror and hid under one of the lab benches.

"Okay, that's okay," Lex said. "It's gonna be okay, but if it makes you feel safer to hide down here for a bit, you can do that."

All four of the humans went upstairs.

The director was standing in the entryway. Ari shut the basement door and stood in front of it protectively.

"Director Griswald," Lex said. "We need to talk."

"Yes, we do." He looked to the gathered hunters. "We *all* need to talk, then?"

"We *all* have a proposition," Lex said. "The vampire whose torture you sanctioned is innocent of any wrongdoing. He wants to help."

"He ... wants to help?"

"He's a scientist too. He's trying to make artificial blood. That's why he was here in the first place. That's why we rescued him and kept him hidden from you. That's why I don't care if you fire me or put me in jail. That's why I'm willing to die defending him."

The director's jaw clenched. "I've been told this secondhand. I only half-believed it until I heard it from your mouth, Alexis."

She stood firm.

"If what you say is true, then ... he could be very valuable, yes." The director was a politician at heart. It was obvious they'd won. There was no way to deny what they were saying, not with all of them gathered here like this. "I'd like to meet him."

"Yes," Lex said. "As long as you understand ... "

"As long as you understand," Ari finished for her, "that we're on his side first. Got it?"

The director nodded.

Ari opened the door and escorted him down. The basement was ... empty.

Ah, he must be in the darkroom. Lex crept towards it and pushed the door open. A rectangle of light fell on his face, eyes blown wide. He'd jammed himself under the sink.

She tried not to laugh. "Hey. It's okay to come out."

Valen shakily took her hand and let her pull him out.

"Director," Ari said courteously. "This is Valen."

Valen gave in to his nervous instinct to curtsey. "Hello, Directly – Director Hunter – "

The director's stony face broke into a laugh. "Yes, I'd expect that reaction from anyone in your position." He extended a hand. "Better late than never on proper introductions, right?"

Valen shook his hand, still looking wary.

"Firm grip!" the director exclaimed, as though anyone could possibly care about that. "Alexis and Ari have informed me of the proposition the hunters at this base came up with for you. I wasn't aware you possessed your own scientific training. I admit I was a bit hesitant about the idea at first. It's unconventional, but it would be a waste to not have you take Nick's place."

The hair on Valen's neck stood up. "You want me to – "

"Not experiment on live vampires, if that's what you're worried about. No, I think it's obvious by now that was ... a mistake. It was wrong to let that go on, and now we should move past it for the common good." That was something, at least. "Which is why, along with the job offer, I want to extend to you the offer of safety within human territory. You'd be under my personal protection. I've been informed of your experiments to try and create artificial blood, and I'd like you to continue them here with Lex and Ari."

Everyone could see the longing in his eyes. He wanted it bad, even through the fear. Even through everything.

"I'll do it."

The director smiled. "Then let's get your lab set up so we can start making a better future together."

ACKNOWLEDGEMENTS

I've borrowed and drawn inspiration from some others' writing for this universe, particularly the writing of my friend Mill Cohen. Thank you for sharing your ideas with the world!

— • —

ABOUT THE AUTHOR

Nox is a lover of all creatures and people in sci-fi and fantasy and loves stories about persevering through horrors to come out better on the other side.

MAGNANIMOUS MOONRISE

NOX SPACEY

THE WHUMPY PRINTING PRESS

CONTENTS

— · —

CONTENT WARNINGS

This story contains dark content, including torture and sexual assault.

Below is a list of content warnings by chapter.

Prologue: Mind control, casual misogyny

1. Knife violence, blood, broken bones, nonconsensual bondage/restraint, gag/muzzle, implied past sexual assault

2. Nonconsensual bondage/restraint/being trapped, gag/muzzle, heavy emotional distress, mentions of mass human rights violations

3. Nonconsensual bondage/restraint/being trapped, gag/muzzle, referenced past sexual assault

4. Nonconsensual bondage/restraint/being trapped, gag/muzzle, broken bones/broken nose

5. Nonconsensual bondage/restraint/being trapped, gag/muzzle, "it" as a dehumanizing pronoun, transphobia, violence against a transmasculine character, forced nudity/stripping, sexual assault

6. Nonconsensual bondage/restraint/being trapped, gag/muzzle, heavy emotional distress, references to torture, burns, violence against a transmasculine character, sexual assault, rape

7. Knife violence, misgendering, drowning

8. Nonconsensual bondage/restraint/being trapped, gag/muzzle, aftermath of torture, cuts, burns, nonsexual nudity, heavy emotional distress, suicidal ideation/euthanasia discussion

9. References to torture

10. Nonconsensual bondage/restraint/being trapped, gag/muzzle, aftermath of torture, starvation, nonsexual nudity, heavy emotional distress, mind control, violence against a female character

11. Nonconsensual bondage/restraint/being trapped, gag/muzzle, aftermath of torture, starvation, nonsexual nudity, heavy emotional distress, mind control, violence against a female character, lots of blood, unsanitary/vomit, brief eye injury

12. Aftermath of blood loss

13. Aftermath of torture, starvation, heavy emotional distress

14. Nonconsensual bondage/restraint/being trapped, gag/muzzle, aftermath of torture, starvation, heavy emotional distress, mentions of off-screen rape, cuts/broken glass, burns

15. Nonconsensual bondage/restraint/being trapped, gag/muzzle, aftermath of torture, starvation, heavy emotional distress

16. Nonconsensual bondage/restraint/being trapped, gag/muzzle, aftermath of torture, starvation, heavy emotional distress

17. Aftermath of torture, starvation, heavy emotional distress

18. Aftermath of torture, broken bones, heavy emotional distress, nonconsensual bondage/restraint/being trapped, gag/muzzle, suicidal ideation,

homophobic slurs (reclaimed usage), teeth pulling (off-screen)

19. Aftermath of torture, starvation, heavy emotional distress, mind control, violence against a female character

20. None

21. Discussion of disordered eating/self-harm/cutting/homophobic parents

22. Weight discussion, mentions of rape and torture (off-screen)

23. Heavy emotional distress

24. Nonconsensual bondage/restraint/being trapped, gag/muzzle, character death

25. Blood, corpse, knife violence, casual misogyny, prejudiced vampire

26. References to character death

27. Guilt, references to abusive spouse

28. Tension

29. Mind control, misgendering

30. None

PROLOGUE

"Mama, who's that?" Valen pointed to the blank-eyed human standing behind the person on the bench.

"Oh, that? That's that man's thrall."

Valen stared, keeping one finger in her mouth to chew on. "Why's she like that?"

"The human? Like what?"

"She's just standing there?"

"She hasn't been given an order. She does whatever her master tells her to."

"Like a servant?"

"Sort of."

The ears of the vampire on the bench twitched. He'd been reading a newspaper – newspapers were still a relatively new technology, and some vampires were slow to adopt them, especially in more rural parts of the country, but this man was obviously a cultured, wealthy vampire if the thrall was anything to judge by. He folded the newspaper up to eye Valen and her mother. "Have you never seen a human before, young lady?"

Valen shook her head. It was rare for vampires with human thralls to visit this park – it wasn't a wealthy part of town.

"This is where your food comes from," her mother informed her. "They take blood from humans like this and put it in bottles for you."

"Want to come take a closer look?"

Valen looked to her mother.

"Sure, why not? It's educational."

Valen scampered over, the red ribbons on her dress fluttering behind her. "I didn't know they looked like that."

"Like what, Valen?"

"Like us?"

"Humans are not like us," the man said. "I assure you. They're for food."

Valen peered up at the human with wide, curious eyes. "Is that why she can't talk?"

"Yes, child." He reached down and stroked Valen's hair. "You have such pretty, curly hair. It's a shame, though. White hair is distinguished on men, but it ages girls. Have you considered dyeing it?"

"I'll worry about that when she's old enough to worry about such a thing," Valen's mother snapped.

The man withdrew his hand. "I was just offering a bit of advice. I have a friend with white hair running in his family, and all the women bemoan how they look like old maids by the time they're only four hundred."

Valen had continued to stare at the human, oblivious to the whole conversation about her hair. She was confused, because this human looked ... sick, in a way. All the animals in the picture books she loved so much were always depicted in motion and full of life. The human had inflamed bite marks on her neck, and she had no visible inclination for any emotion or action whatsoever. Even a prey animal, as humans supposedly were, was still an animal that moved around. "What's wrong with her?"

"You're very full of questions," the man with the human said. "They say young vampires with inquisitive minds grow up to be scientists."

Valen's mother picked her up, mood for a nice walk to enjoy the night sky now gone sour. "That's more suitable for boys."

"Yes ... something like art is more suitable for girls," the man agreed, and they both seemed to think it made a lot of sense.

"Well, good night, sir."

Valen looked over her mother's shoulder as she was ferried away, still staring at the human, still curious.

"What do you think, Valen? We'll go home and play with the fingerpaints? You can make some pretty pictures of everything you saw today."

1

— • —

Valen hated going out during the day. He'd never felt direct sunlight before, and he had no intention of changing that. Sunlight was supposed to be one of the worst things a vampire could feel. He'd seen pictures of burns in school. He had no desire to risk that.

But he couldn't *only* come out at night. The neighbors were already way, way too suspicious of him. And the particular mushroom he was here to collect thrived in the heat of the day, withering at night and making them less ideal for harvesting. The *only* reason he was here, in the heart of human territory, was for these stupid mushrooms that were so picky about where they grew.

It was fucking terrifying, being this far away from safety, surrounded by people that would view him as a dangerous apex predator if they knew his true nature. But what he needed just didn't grow in the cold of the northern vampire territory, especially not in the fall when the sunlight was getting weaker and the days shorter. Fall and winter were most vampires' favorite seasons for that reason, but there was no way he could get the ingredients he needed anywhere in vampire territory at this time of year, and probably not even in the summer, with the latitude ...

He'd already been here for a few weeks, which was longer than he'd wanted to be, but the mushrooms had been surprisingly hard to find. Maybe it was the season change.

He missed his little apartment. It was small and crappy compared to the luxury his husband had provided him, but it was *his* space. It was cozy. He was looking

forward to the day he could go back – which would be when he'd made enough progress on his research project that he no longer needed free access to these mushrooms.

The mushrooms were probably a stupid idea to begin with. It was hard to tell, when everyone told him most of his ideas were stupid. The only idea everyone had told him was a good one was marrying his husband, and that had turned out to be a *terrible* idea.

He walked home that day empty-handed, heart heavy as he came back without anything to show for his brave excursion into the sunlight. Even with all his wrappings covering every inch of his skin, and the mask with the darkened lenses, it was nerve-wracking. He'd been a huge ball of anxiety ever since coming here, which was making it hard to work and get done what he needed to get done so he could *leave*.

His feet dragged as he unlocked the door and trudged inside. Maybe he should just give up. Maybe this was a fool's errand, just like his entire family had said. Just like his in-laws had said.

Well, if they were right about anything, it would probably be entirely by coincidence.

He pulled the mask off his face as he strode into the kitchen. It was an old-fashioned mask with a beak, which he'd stuffed with herbs – that had, in fact, been the original usage of such masks when humans first used them. To block out smells.

He tried to avoid humans, but he sometimes saw them. And Valen didn't want to smell humans when he was thirsty. He didn't want to even be tempted.

His mouth was so unbelievably dry from the heat, and he'd been out all day without feeding. He removed his gloves and wiped the sweat from his brow, shedding his protective layers, then leaned down and took a bottle from the fridge.

The fridge was filled with artificial blood he'd brewed from the ingredients he'd gathered. This last batch had been … acceptable, but not ideal. He needed to work on it until it was perfect. It had to either be cheaper than real blood, or taste better, or both, or no one would buy it.

There was already ethical blood shipped from parts of the world where there were plenty of volunteers willing to give it up for pay, but nobody here bought it because it was more expensive and tasted worse because of how old it was by the time it arrived. There was no infrastructure for such a thing here, and there likely wouldn't be for centuries given how poor relations between humans and vampires were. If Valen wanted to shut down the mass-scale horror that was the blood farms, he needed something that would fill the demand for blood better than real blood. Which was ... quite a challenge.

His concoctions were often foul, but they did the trick. It wasn't easy to figure out exactly what it was in the blood vampires needed, but with some guesswork he usually managed to feed himself adequately. He'd been weaning himself off real blood gradually, now at the point where he only needed genuine human blood once a month or so. The rest of the time, he could sate his bloodthirst with the strange, artificial-tasting pseudo-blood he cooked up. The mushrooms he'd been harvesting had some component he had yet to isolate that added something more satiating to it, but it still had a long way to go before he could do anything with it.

Valen tilted the bottle to his lips, trying to let the nourishment slide down his throat without tasting it too much. This particular bottle was ... bad.

He was so focused on his thirst, and the smell of the artificial blood, that he didn't hear or smell the humans until it was too late. He *would* have smelled them if he'd not been wearing his mask when he walked past them earlier, but he wore the mask while out and about *specifically* to block out the scent of humans.

He heard the footsteps rapidly approaching and tried to turn, but couldn't do it fast enough. Something slammed into his mouth as two bodies made contact with him, and he realized with horror a bit had been forced into his mouth, wedged under his fangs and pinning his tongue to the floor of his mouth.

One of the interlopers used the surprise to push him to the ground. The strap on the bit tightened, and he fought a wave of panic as he felt it being secured to his head. He had to get it *off*. They did it because they didn't want him to use

persuasion, of course, but it also meant he couldn't tell them he didn't want to fight them. He tried to talk, to say something, to get *any* word out before things went too far, but his tongue was locked firmly in place, his jaw immobilized, and only frustrated sounds came out. They'd known to go right for his biggest asset and lock it down tight.

The practiced ease with which they were wrangling him told him everything he needed to know about who they were: vampire hunters.

He'd come all the way out here, to this remote location, purchasing a house no one cared about, staying inside and slinking around to avoid the neighbors, staying away from every human he came across *specifically* to avoid vampire hunters.

Fuck. Fuck fuck fuck fuck fuck fuck. Forget not wanting to fight them. He had to if he wanted to get out of here alive. He didn't want to kill any humans, but if they were going to make it him or them, he would choose himself.

He finally let his full strength loose, shoving the human on top of him back into the wall. He winced as he felt her bones crack – but he had no time to regret being so rough, because the second human came at him with a knife. He'd never felt the touch of silver before. *Fuck*, did it hurt, especially when it was on a blade being plunged into his abdomen. He couldn't suppress the hissing scream that erupted from him like a whistling tea kettle. He used one hand to fumble with the bit, extending the other out to try and keep his attackers away from him.

Fuck, he should have just used both hands to take the bit off, because the human whose bones he'd just broken came at him again. He couldn't fight through the burning, sizzling, stabbing pain of the silver knife enough to stay standing under her weight, because she slammed him into the ground, jamming the knife further.

"The cuffs!" yelled the human on top of him. "Get the cuffs!"

Fuck fuck fuck FUCK FUCK FUCK. Valen would probably be embarrassed about the undignified, incoherent noises he was making under less dire cir-

cumstances, unable to suppress the instinct to hurl out pleas for a nonviolent resolution.

He felt warm hands on his wrists, wrenching them into a position to cuff them together. *No no no no no, please.* The throbbing pain of the silver in his core burned and drained his energy to fight back. His heart sank as the cuffs successfully closed, pinning his hands behind his back.

It felt like this shouldn't be working. It seemed like humans shouldn't be able to do this to him, a vampire. Surely they were too weak to pose a real threat, even with the right equipment? Surely his earlier worries had been his overly anxious mind being paranoid again, right? Why was attacking him *working*?

"I have ankle cuffs on my belt," said the first human.

Ankle cuffs! This doesn't seem excessive to you at all? He felt the hands on his ankles, and he took the opportunity to try and do *something* while he still could, kicking out savagely and blindly. He felt soft tissue crunching under the blow, and both humans erupted into a chorus of curses.

The hands holding him down lifted him up. He flailed around, disoriented. "Stop struggling!" said the gruff voice.

And just let you do God knows what to me?? He was about to wonder why they were taking him alive instead of just staking him through the heart, but he ran out of time as he was slammed into the wall.

He felt the warm body pinning him to the wall. *Oh no. No no no.*

This was too much. Restrained, pinned, handled roughly. It was too much. He whimpered as his assailant's legs came up and pinned his own to the wall, surely out of practicality but nevertheless pressing them intimately close together.

The sensation of a hostile presence squeezing him, chest-to-back, crotch-to-ass, mouth-to-neck. It was *too much*. Too much like *that time*.

He wheezed, eyes wheeling, trying to scrabble out of the hold, but the throbbing silver knife penetrated him, pinning him in place.

Legs shaking, he just let the ankle cuffs come on and snap shut. Maybe if the ankle cuffs were on, they would let him out of *this* position. They didn't. His

limbs were all fastened together to render him immobile, and they still held him there. He did his best to let out a pleading cry, but he felt hands around his neck.

Stop, please stop, please, please ...

It was a muzzle, coming over the lower half of his face. A *muzzle*, on top of a bit. *What did I do to make you want to truss me up this much?* He tried to suppress his terrified shaking. The hands were gentle as they fussed with the leather strap, not even catching it in his hair, but he so, *so* acutely felt the further locking down of his ability to speak.

The human behind him *finally* pulled away and, with nothing to support him, he collapsed to the floor. He couldn't suppress the sounds as he jolted the knife sticking into him yet again, wishing more than anything for it to be removed.

His vision started to blur from the pain. His unfocused eyes saw nothing but the floorboards as the two humans talked somewhere vaguely above him.

"Fuck. He got me good ... Are you okay? ... Here. Just take it easy. We'll see the medic when we get back to base."

"Shit."

Footsteps towards him, then: "Hold still."

It took Valen a minute to realize the human was talking to *him*. He let out a terrified growl, but it died in his throat as she grabbed the knife handle. "I said *hold still.*"

He complied. It was a mixture of relief and agony when the blade was removed. The horrible sensation of the silver faded, and he went limp on the floor.

"All right. I didn't think this far ahead. Now what do we *do* with him?"

He had answers, but he couldn't give them. They wouldn't let him, as long as he had the option to just overpower them with persuasion as soon as he opened his mouth.

The other human answered after a long pause: "Let's put him in the coffin, then search the house."

"Are we going to take him back to base? To Nick?"

"I mean ... what *else* are we going to do with him?"

He tried to control his breathing. He didn't know what they were talking about, but it filled him with dread. It didn't sound good for him in the slightest. Why did they take him alive? What were they going to do to him?

He couldn't ask, so he just lay there, letting out a miserable whine.

"Oh, shut up," the larger human snapped. "You tried to kill us. Don't expect us to feel bad for you." *What the fuck would you expect me to do? Anyone to do? Just happily get tied up and stabbed? You attacked me.*

"Let's do it, then." Oh God, they both walked towards him, and hands were grabbing him and hauling him up. He went limp. What could he do? Everything they'd restrained him with was silver, and he couldn't break it.

Then he saw they were taking him outside. Out the front door. He couldn't do anything, but that didn't stop him from trying. He wriggled again, trying to lock up to avoid going through the door.

This just earned him a push, sending him tumbling out onto the porch. "Fuck *off.* You're

going outside to the van."

He fell *terrifyingly* close to the line that demarcated the safe shade from the blazing intensity of the sun. He could almost feel the solar radiation on his cheek. He wormed away, trying desperately to stay away from it.

"He's scared of the sun," said the smaller human.

Valen went limp. *Of fucking course I'm scared of the sun. I'm a* vampire. But why on earth would he expect vampire hunters to care about that?

"Yeah, and I'm sure all his human victims were scared of getting all their blood drained out of them. I'm not coddling a monster. Let's *go.*"

Fuck. *Fuck.* Valen suddenly realized what the fridge would have looked like to anyone who didn't know the blood was synthetic. It didn't taste or smell the same to a vampire, but to a human eye it would *look* basically identical, and their sense of smell wouldn't be nearly good enough to sense the difference either. Oh God, there had been *so* much of it. If they'd seen that, they must have assumed he was a mass murderer, the worst among his kind.

He frantically shook his head, making desperate eye contact, something, *anything* to try and save himself from whatever was about to happen to him. The smaller human looked at him doubtfully, but then she left his field of vision as he was dragged backwards by the ankle.

No no no no no! Stop! Please!

"Hey, if we throw your cloak over you so you don't get burned, will you stop fucking struggling? We just want to get this over with so we can get first aid."

He sagged, trying to stop hyperventilating. He didn't dare make eye contact with the human who'd spoken, but he managed to get out a nod.

The boots in his field of vision walked back into the house, then came back with his cloak dragging on the floor. Thank God. Thank God. That was so much better than nothing.

The world disappeared as the cloak went over him. He heard them discussing the logistics of getting him to their vehicle, and he let it happen, terrified of the possibility of the cloak being removed midway as punishment for struggling. He felt their hands on him, carrying his weight with surprising gentleness. Then he felt the hard surface of a vehicle under him and heard bootsteps walking near him. Then the jingling and clanging of metal.

He tensed. That didn't sound good. That *didn't* sound good.

"Okay. Just lay him in there."

He wasn't sure what he expected to see when the cloak was removed, but it wasn't a goddamn *cage* just big enough to lock him in, just forcing him to lay there like a corpse in a coffin.

He was seized with the overwhelming dread of a premonition that if he let himself be put in there, that was it. Terrible, terrible things would happen to him, which he would be powerless to stop, and *he could not let himself be put in there.*

He kicked out and broke more bones, prompting more panicked cursing and scrambling from the two hunters. He pushed himself up and against the wall to stand, ineffectual with his legs secured together but it was enough to let him slam into his assailant when she came at him, denting the metal wall behind them both.

More curses, and the silver hunting knife was back. *Mistake! Big mistake! The knife is back!* It scraped his clavicle this time, sinking into the meat of his shoulder and pulling down. The explosion of burning pain was accompanied by the smell of cooking flesh and wisps of smoke curling off him. He ground his teeth against the bit, electrified screams spraying out as best as they could around the intrusion.

The smaller human was back on him, forcing him down, into that horrible contraption. "Fucker. Goddamn. Just – just get in there."

No! he tried to shout. *Fucker, no, absolutely not.*

But despite his best attempts, he found himself thrust into the metal-barred box. He still thrashed wildly, his movements weakened by the restraints and the injuries, but he had to *try*. He was rewarded by the sensation of skin and clothes shredding under his talons, before the humans' hands turned him over, supine, and buckled him in with chains, rattling over the metal and resting over his torso. He could not help but notice that these ones were uncovered silver, without the outer steel layer that prevented burning that the shell of the device was made of, and the only thing stopping the chains from burning into his chest were his clothes.

There was *still more*. She moved towards his feet and slid his ankles into restraints that kept his legs pinned to the floor. Then she shut the lid, carefully avoiding eye contact through the bars as she locked the padlock and hobbled away.

For some reason, that last part was what broke him. Tears welled in his eyes, and he went limp in his new prison. He hadn't even done anything, hadn't even attacked them until he was *under* attack, and they still thought all this was necessary, a gag *and* a muzzle *and* wrist and ankle cuffs *and* being shoved into a locked cage *and* secured to the inside of the cage. As though they were binding some sort of demi-god they were sealing away.

He supposed they didn't have any reason to think otherwise; these were all reasonable precautions given what some vampires were capable of ... but he was *Valen*. He still cried every time his parents yelled at him. He couldn't have pets even though he loved cats because he got too sad when they died. He put bugs

outside the house instead of squishing them. He had always, always tried to choose kindness when he could. He'd always accepted the scorn *trying* to be soft earned him in a culture that expected and demanded violence of him, because it was always worth it to know he was doing his best to decrease the amount of pain and suffering in the world as best as any one person could. And his reward for trying to live that life was *this*.

He was vaguely aware of the two hunters talking to each other, voices getting fainter as they slid out of the back of the van. He sobbed, crying out as loudly as he could. *Don't leave me here like this. Don't. Don't. Give me a chance. Please.*

The doors of the van slammed closed, plunging him into darkness.

2

— · —

Valen lay there in the dark. He could do nothing else. His heart was pounding, and his body was finding other fun ways to manifest his anxiety, like sweating.

And he cried. Oh, did he cry. He hadn't cried this hard since his wedding night.

He heard the humans talking again, muffled through the vehicle. He half-heartedly pulled at his restraints one more time for good measure.

The doors were thrown open, startling him. He tried to shy away, but he was absolutely locked in place. The threat of sunlight felt *so* much worse now that he was so thoroughly immobilized. They could just drag him out and toss him into the sun if they wanted to.

"Hey, you," said the taller human.

"His name is Valen," said the shorter one. "I found his wallet." *You took my wallet? Am I being* mugged *by vampire hunters?*

"Fine. Valen."

His name was enough to get him to turn his head. It was too bright to look directly at either of them, but he saw their featureless silhouettes lit from the back. He tried to curl up to protect himself, trying to control his trembling. He just kept imagining them dragging the whole cage out and into the sun, forcing him to just lie there and take it, unable to even writhe or bargain or do *anything.* The metal bars would probably make a grill pattern on his skin.

"Don't give me that look. Stop being a baby. We're not even hurting you. The muzzle is padded, the cuffs aren't bare silver. We could be being a lot meaner."

I'm supposed to be grateful for this??

"We did stab him," piped up the other human.

"My point is." There was a pause as the human clambered up into the van with him. Valen's eyes were mostly shut, so he couldn't see her until she leaned directly over his metal prison. "My point is, if you want us to *continue* not being mean, maybe you can help us out."

... And how exactly do you expect me to do that?

"Where did all that blood come from? There weren't any people in the house."

... And how exactly do you expect me to answer you?

"How do you want him to answer?" He was relieved to hear the other human echo his thoughts. Maybe, *maybe* they could be reasoned with ... somehow. And this whole daymare could be over before it truly started.

The taller human shushed the shorter one. She turned back. "They aren't in the house?"

I guess we're doing yes or no questions. He shook his head. Even that much movement was difficult with how he was strapped in.

"Are they nearby somewhere? Outside?"

He shook his head.

"Do you have captives at home?"

Oh God, she was getting mad. She wanted a yes, clearly, but surely *that* would make her angrier. He shook his head. *Please, please, please don't hurt me. I'm trying. I'm trying to help. Please don't drag me out into the sun.*

The human peeled her lip back. The gesture couldn't be threatening from someone with no fangs, but the anger behind it scared him. She could hurt him quite a lot even without any fangs. "Then where the hell did it come from? Is it animal blood?"

Animal blood. *Animal blood*, yes, that was safe, if he just told them it was that, they would take that to mean he hadn't hurt any humans, only animals. Neither of them would be able to smell the difference. He nodded. *Yes, God, please, it's animal blood, I'll tell you it's whatever you want it to be if it means you'll let me out.*

"So you're some special vampire that can drink animal blood instead of human blood?"

Well, that lie had fallen apart immediately. If she'd be mad at him for answering either way, why was she asking in the first place? He quivered, unsure of what to do, the only actions afforded to him either *Say yes* or *Say no*, and he could imagine consequences for either and both.

"Erm, babe." The other human came closer. "I'm not sure if this is really going to go anywhere. Listen, do you think that maybe ... I don't know, do you think he made it somehow?" Relief flooded through him. His legs shook, his spine going limp. *Yes, yes, yes, God yes, oh my God yes, somehow you got it, thank you, thank you, thank you.* He nodded and fidgeted aimlessly in his restraints.

"Well, which is it, then?" snapped the taller human, the grumpier one. "Is it animal blood or did you make it somehow?"

Do you not understand the concept of a yes or no question? He nodded. This was progress, right?

"Okay, this is pointless. We're not gonna get any real answers out of him until we can find some way he can communicate without using persuasion."

Just take it off! Just take the muzzle off! Please just take the muzzle off! Please just take it off! I promise it'll be fine! Frustrated tears spilled from his eyes.

"No, no, listen, the stuff in the basement, it looked like ... Well, I don't know, I'm suspicious it might be that one."

"Why would any vampire come all the way out here, set up camp in the middle of human territory, to *make fake blood*? Like, why would any vampire make fake blood at all when they can just get it from humans, let alone come all the way out here to do it?"

He groaned, eyes rolling back in his head. This whole situation – it did look strange, he really couldn't blame the humans for not understanding what was going on. It did look suspicious as hell, it *did* look like he'd killed a bunch of people, they had no reason to believe he hadn't, but he *hadn't*.

"Well, I – I don't know. I'm just guessing. There's – there's some notes, but I can't really read the handwriting."

Valen cursed his illegible handwriting. His penmanship teacher had been right for all the times she'd scolded him.

"Well, let's just hand it all over to Nick and see what he can make of it. And maybe someone there will have an idea of how to safely talk to him. We can get some pen and paper, maybe." The van dipped as the humans moved away, boots thumping on the dirt outside.

No, no, no, where are you going? Come back! That was it! You got it right! That was it!

He writhed, agitating the cage.

The smaller human turned back to look at him again. He tried to beg with his eyes. *Please. Please don't do whatever you're about to do to me.*

She came over and leaned above him again. It was unnerving, the way it let them loom over him when they did that. "Hey," she said, with startling softness. "It's gonna be all right. Okay? We're just trying to keep everyone safe."

Me too. I am too. She had no way of knowing that, of course, and why would she believe it? His head swam with anxiety, desperately trying to trust her words, the only lifeline he'd been thrown. The two humans chatted distantly, shutting the van door once again, returning him to the relief of darkness. He felt the van dip again as they climbed up into the front seats, then the engine turning over and humming to life. Then they drove off.

3

— · —

Valen couldn't see out the window from the position he was locked in; he couldn't see the scenery whizzing by to try and guess where they were going. He could only guess at how much time was passing by the shifting of the sunlight, indicating the sun crawling across the sky, and by his legs starting to ache from being forced into the same position for however long.

He didn't know where they were going, but it was evidently quite far away.

They made a rest stop. The taller, crankier one stayed in the van, hobbled by the way he'd slammed his boots into her shin and apparently broken her leg. He felt neutral about that, neither guilty nor particularly victorious. They were humans. They were behaving naturally for such an animal, just as Valen behaved as natural for a vampire. Nature had pitted the mongoose and the snake against each other, but they held no real malice for each other.

The shorter, peppier one came back with two drinks. Valen was able to see flashes of her hair through the window, her smile, the frightening light of the dreaded sinking sun illuminating her from behind, hurting not a hair on her head. She seemed supernatural in that power. Like a goddess. A creature capable of walking out in the middle of the day and absorbing all that accursed radiation and coming out unharmed, happier for it even. He'd always been terrified of humans, despite his supposed supremacy over them. Terrified both of what they were capable of, and how easy it was to break them, a puzzling dichotomy.

She paused by the window and peered in. Valen quickly averted his eyes, hoping she hadn't caught him staring. Despite his fear, his eyes flickered up to meet hers once or twice as he fought with himself.

Moving his eyes and *barely* moving his head were really the only things he was capable of in his current state. Surely they wouldn't get fussy about him *looking*? She retreated, and Valen heard her opening the door and settling into the front seat. He heard her asking if everything was okay, about how the taller one was feeling, about how much longer they had to go.

Through eavesdropping over the course of the trip, he was able to deduce a few things. The tall one was named Ari, which he presumed was short for Ariana. The shorter one was named Lex, which could be short for any number of things. Alex, Alexandria, Alexis, Alexa. Alexander, he supposed. He rolled the puzzle over his tongue like a savory treat, trying to occupy himself, trying to ignore the bit shoved and locked in his mouth.

He deduced they lived quite far away and wouldn't be getting home until late tonight, from the way they debated just staying "there" for the night, although he could not figure out where "there" was. It seemed they lived together. It seemed they'd known each other quite a long time. It seemed they cared about each other quite a lot.

It seemed they were dating.

Despite his predicament ... jealousy prickled at his heart. He'd always yearned for a love like that, soft and authentic in defiance of societal expectations, and it'd always been denied him.

Instead, he'd gotten –

Flashes of images in his mind, bloodied sheets and clawed bedposts, bruises where there should be hickeys, torn clothes and shaking hands. Threats of violence if he didn't wear the dress, if he *did* cut his hair. Knowing he was there to do something everyone expected, which would take a million agonizing tries because fertility was so low for vampires, in their cursed state. It could take decades to conceive a child.

He squeezed his eyes shut. *Don't think about it, don't think about it.*

He let his thoughts drift to the fantasy of someone like Lex. What it would feel like to be touched gently by someone whose hands were soft, yet so strong. He let himself be carried away by the idea, imagining that instead of body-slamming him and muzzling him, Lex had just gently put a hand on his shoulder and turned him around with a smile, bidding him to come talk, or do more than talk.

It was a wholly inappropriate time to be thinking about such things, a ludicrously bizarre thought to have about his kidnappers ... but it wasn't like he had anything better to do to kill time. He was lucky he couldn't get visibly aroused, at least not in a way they would notice. He was sure having a visible erection would make things worse, or at least very awkward. He'd never been *happy* about the empty space in his pants between his legs before now. Especially not when thinking about sex.

But he tried to snatch glances of them for more than just trying to figure out his fate. He loved looking at Lex. Hell, even *Ari*, who was scarred and jaded and rugged and gruff, the complete antithesis of soft feminine beauty. He found himself yearning for her to touch him softly, wondering what those calloused hands were capable of.

He was a little bit in love with them both, despite himself. He knew it was a pathetic way to cope, but they were terrifying and powerful and violent and soft and gentle and kind. He wished desperately he was the kind of person they would show that softness to. In that moment, he wanted nothing more than for them to pull over, come to the back, unlock him and help him up with the same gentle touches they used on each other. He could see the love they were capable of. He knew they'd become vampire hunters because of that love, to stop people from getting hurt; he could see it and feel it. It was the same reason Valen had been scheming to shut down the blood farms ever since he found out where his food came from.

It ached and burned that they hadn't given him a chance. Just a few sentences would have been all it took to see that they were kindred spirits. Just a few

sentences would have also been all it took for him to kill them, and they all knew it, and he couldn't blame them for securing him this way when he knew the horrors his kind was capable of.

But it still hurt. He knew that softness wasn't for him. It was only for other humans. For good people, people whose existence didn't depend on violence for their most basic sustenance. He was fooling himself to imagine such things, salting his own wounds. They clearly didn't care for his well-being – and why should they?

Ari's annoyed face appeared over the passenger seat. "Hey."

Valen suddenly realized he'd been crying and letting out soft sounds this whole time. He flushed, fidgeting, refusing eye contact, as though he were afraid Ari would know what he'd been thinking.

"Look at me."

It took all his willpower, but he wrenched his eyes up to look at Ari through vision blurred with tears.

"Are you in pain?"

What? Why would you care about that? He didn't know what to answer. Was she mad at him? If he said yes, would she rub it in and make it worse? Would she laugh and say *good*? If he said no, would she say *I can fix that* and bring the knife back out?

He squeezed his eyes shut.

"Hey."

He kept his eyes shut.

"You're making sounds that sound like you're being hurt somehow. Is there bare silver touching you?"

He kept his eyes shut.

"Just nod your head if it is. I'll come fix it."

Fix it? Did she mean she would come take it off his skin if it was ailing him? He wasn't currently experiencing any physical pain they could fix – only the

21

general ache from being locked into position for so long. Was he misinterpreting somehow? Why would they care about his comfort after locking him in *this*?

He was frozen in fear. What was she getting at? Did he dare let himself believe she was trying to be kind to him? Now? When he was locked in this stupid thing, off to God knows where? After he'd tried so hard to resign himself to the fact that they didn't care about him?

"He's probably just scared," Lex said.

Scared. How could I be anything else?

Ari snorted and turned back, sinking into her seat. "Whatever it takes to make him shut up."

Ah, there it was. She just wanted him to be quiet. Maybe she would have helped him if he'd needed it, but maybe she'd have just made things worse as long as it meant she got her silence.

Valen managed to stay quiet for most of the rest of the trip ... until the van rolled to a stop, and Lex killed the engine, apparently having reached their destination.

"Finally," one of them moaned.

There was silence for a moment. Valen stared up out of the window he could get into his field of view.

They were outside a house with silver bars on the windows. *A house with silver bars on the windows.*

Panic swirled in his chest, drowning out whatever the two women were saying up front. This looked bad. Really, really bad. This looked like ... a hunter's nest.

Why did they take me alive? Why the fuck *did they bring me here? Why didn't they just kill me? What are they going to do to me?*

4

— · —

Valen heard voices outside, more voices. Men's voices. That raised his hackles.

"Ari, you son of a bitch! You actually did it?"

Valen felt the van dip under him as presumably Ari got up. "What, like it's hard? How come you all haven't managed it yet?"

They were talking about him like he was a particularly wily rabbit in their snare. They were *laughing* and congratulating each other. *I'm going to die here. Die, or something worse.*

"We sent your girl straight to the infirmary when she came in," said one of the men. "Her face was busted, man."

"Don't call my girlfriend's face busted. Even with a broken nose, she's easier on the eyes than your ugly mugs."

"We get it, you're gay."

"Bisexual."

"Same thing."

Valen winced as the back door was thrown open, three human silhouettes outlined by the terrifying sun behind them. "Shit," said one of the men. "You really do just have a whole ass vampire in your car, huh."

"What did you fucking think? That we just brought back his leg or something?"

"Damn, woman, don't bite my ear off." Valen watched in terror as one of the men clambered up into the cargo space next to him, leaning over to look at him.

"Don't look him in the eye," said the other man. "They can use persuasion that way."

"Some of them," said the first man. He blinked at Valen, but he had already averted his eyes, gaze glued to the man's shins a foot away from his face.

"I guess this one can't," said Ari. "Or he would have done it already."

"Unless he's just biding his time."

Valen squeezed his eyes shut.

"So, are you lazy fucks gonna help me move him inside or did you just come out here to gawk at him?"

"Geez, fine. This thing got handles on it?"

"Yeah, on the sides. I think it's a two-person job."

No no no no no. They were going to drag him out into the sun while he was locked into place, unable to even throw his hands up to shield his face or open his mouth to scream and plead.

His chest heaved in terrified gasps as hands grasped the handles, starting to drag him forward. He felt heat on his boots as they came out into the sun.

"Oh, hold on a minute," said Ari's voice, and mercifully the sliding stopped. The sound of her footsteps on gravel. Cloth rustling. He kept his gaze trained on the ceiling, his quaking rattling the chains slightly.

He saw Ari's hands tossing something on top of the cage. His cloak. She pulled it across until the top half of the cage was covered, his exposed skin enveloped in shadow.

Thank you, he thought, almost crying at how low he'd sunken that *this* was a relief for him. *Thank you, thank you, thank you.*

"What's the matter? You afraid of hurting it?"

"I don't give a shit about its feelings," Ari snapped. "I'm just doing it because Lex would be upset if he got burnt."

"Sure, sure. Softie."

"Hey, this is just like when I put a blanket over my birdcage. It makes them go to sleep. They think it's night."

You have a bird? Valen thought. *I want to see the bird.*

There was a round of laughter. Despite his terror, he felt a twinge of jealousy again, wishing he were in a position where he could partake in the camaraderie.

The world tilted as they lifted him down and out of the van.

"Shit, he's heavy."

"It's the cage, dumbass. It's gotta weigh like a thousand pounds."

Valen closed his eyes against the filtered sunlight coming through the cloak – it was mercifully scant, but it stung. Just a little.

He heard the sound of a garage door opening, then the sun faded. He shuddered in relief.

More metal rattling, the sound of reinforced doors being unlocked. The hands carried him deeper into the belly of the beast, into the heart of the den.

He felt his prison being lowered to the ground, then come to a stop with a thump. More voices.

"Woah, shit, it actually worked."

"Oh my God, you actually got one."

"Holy shit, Ari. Let me see it."

All men's voices. Valen's face twisted into an unseen snarl, and with savageness that surprised even himself, he let out a rolling growl, slamming his head into the top of the cage so hard it banged off the floor for a brief second.

The cloak slipped off the cage and pooled onto the floor, letting him see the full view of all the hunter's shocked faces as they took a step back. His forehead felt warm, dark blood leaking from his skull, visibly soaking his white hair. He ground his teeth on the bit, hackles still raised.

"Je-jesus," said one of the men. "B-be careful with that thing."

He peeled his upper lip all the way back, exposing the full length of his fangs. *That's right. Be afraid of me. You fucking bastard. I'll kill you if I get the chance. Stay the fuck away from me. I hate you. Don't touch me.*

His eyes flitted over to the doorway as Lex came back in, now with a bandage on her nose. Her eyes fell on Valen. She looked *worried*. She apparently thought better of offering a comment, though. "Where's Nick?"

"He's on the phone with the director."

Valen's ears perked up, straining to hear the noise in the background. With his preternatural hearing, now that he knew to listen for it, he could faintly hear the sound of a voice talking on the phone.

Oh boy, whoever was on the other end of the line sounded *angry*.

"Oh boy," said Ari. "I bet he's just *thrilled* with this new development."

"I thought he gave Nick the okay to do this?" said another hunter. "He authorized Nick to put a bounty on bringing a live vampire back."

The other hunters laughed.

"Yeah," said one wryly. "To get him to shut up. He didn't think anyone would actually *do* it."

"The director was bluffing," said Ari. "Because vampires are so damn *hard* to catch live, he thought none of us could do it. He doesn't *actually* want a vampire in the building."

A glimmer of hope. Maybe if whoever was in charge wasn't happy, that would mean he could get out of here. But ... no, the human would probably just want him to be killed instead.

Valen's attention snapped back to Lex as she braced herself on the cage. "Hah! That'll show *him*. And he's contractually obligated to pay out the bounty."

A man's hand came into Valen's field of view. He headbutted the wires above him again, bearing the brunt of the stinging silver if it meant getting a chance at scaring him off. *Don't fucking touch me.*

The hunter jerked his hand back without actually putting any of his fingers through the bars enough to reach. A pity. "Yeesh ... Well, Nick can have him."

"Speaking of," said Ari.

Another man had appeared in the doorway, an unhinged smile on his face. "You *did* it. Thank you! Thank you!"

Oh, thought Valen. *Oh no.* He didn't like the look of this guy at all. Unlike the others, he seemed *excited* to see him, not scared. He shuddered. That ... didn't seem good.

The other hunters reacted to his presence as well; they all looked slightly less at ease. Lex tugged at Ari's arm. "Come on, Ari. You have to get your leg seen to."

No no no no. Don't leave me here with them.

"Wait, ladies, I have to give you the bounty for your hard work!" The newcomer circled the cage like a shark. "And, everyone, after some ... heated discussion ... with the director, he has simply given me the guideline that, for safety, we can only open the coffin when at least two people are present."

This wretched device they'd locked him in was called *the coffin*. Fitting, but it made his blood boil. *Is this a joke to you?*

"So, who wants to be the lucky volunteer and help me take this specimen downstairs?"

"I will," Lex said quickly.

Was Valen imagining this? Was it wishful thinking? Was he projecting, or did Lex seem to actually care a little bit?

"I see how it is," said Ari. "Rather spend time playing with Nick in the basement than helping your poor, hurt girlfriend to the nurse."

Lex stammered, "We can – we can do that together and then go help Nick right afterwards."

"Well," said the upsettingly enthusiastic man, "I don't hear any other volunteers, so ... " He beamed. "I'll wait right here for you to get back!"

Valen watched their boots squeak out of sight, further into the compound. He kept his eyes fixed on them, purposefully ignoring the man hovering above him.

The other hunters dispersed slowly, until Valen was alone with Nick.

Valen felt Nick's eyes on him. His fearful trembling started back up. He refused eye contact for as long as he could, until he couldn't stand it anymore.

Nick was just grinning at him. He wished he hadn't looked. "We're going to have *so* much fun together."

5

— · —

The coffin fell down the stairs when they moved him to the basement. It didn't matter whether or not it was an accident; it hurt all the same.

"Oops," said the voice of the man above him, the man that Valen now hated unconditionally.

"All right, Nicky, how about you slow down a bit." It was Ari who said it.

"Of course. Sorry."

You're not sorry at all. You piece of shit.

Nick came into his field of view as he leaned down and dragged the coffin away from the stairs. Valen craned his head to see where they were going.

Oh. It was an unfinished basement turned into a workspace of some sort. Bare concrete floors, cinderblock walls, a variety of tools that could be for DIY projects or metalwork … The thing that really raised his hackles was the sheer amount of chains in the room. The first one that caught his eye was the one hanging from the ceiling in the center of the room, but he gradually spotted more and more, mounted in various positions.

I'm fucked. I'm so fucked.

"Okay, before we do anything else, I wanted to get your thoughts on all this stuff." Valen craned his head to see Lex putting a cardboard box on the workbench. It appeared to contain various things from his house. He furrowed his brows.

"Hmm?" said Nick. "What is that?"

"Stuff we collected from his house. He had a *lot* of blood in the fridge, but we didn't find any signs of violence or any human captives."

Because there weren't any! THERE WERE NEVER ANY!

"Oh?" Valen's vision was blocked as all three humans crowded around the box, backs towards him.

Valen let his head loll as the humans chatted amongst themselves, commenting on the various things they'd collected from his house, musing about what they could be for, arguing with each other.

Hot tears of frustration pooled in his eyes. It would be so simple, so easy to explain himself if he weren't muzzled. But the only thing he could use to convey his innocence, his voice, was also his most destructive weapon and therefore had to be kept locked down tight.

Please, please, please, please. I know you have no reason to, but give me a chance. Please.

His ears pricked up as he heard the humans discussing what *sounded* like trying to figure out a safe way to talk with him – he heard snatches like *pencil and paper*, and tuned back in to their conversation. Just in time to hear Nick say:

"No! Absolutely not! Vampires can use persuasion through *any* mode of communication! Even writing! It kicks in as soon as the victim understands the message imbued in what the vampire was communicating. So long as there's a shared language, it'll work. Some can even do it with nothing but eye contact!"

Some could, yeah. Valen had never managed to figure out anything besides the standard vocal commands – he'd tried to avoid using persuasion whenever he could. It was an atrocious violation of human rights. Lord knew he'd been *trying* eye contact persuasion more than he ever had in the past few hours, though, but to no success. He just did not have that ability inside of him.

Lex made eye contact with him. That was, in his opinion, a little stupid given the topic of conversation, but he forced as much pleading into his eyes as he could.

"O-okay then," said Lex, turning away.

No! Come back! Look at me!

29

They went back to examining Valen's belongings. A bottle of blood, which Nick held up to the light and swirled around. Valen didn't dare get his hopes up too high that Nick would be smart enough – or suspicious enough – to figure out that it wasn't real blood.

After all, Valen had been trying to make it as similar to real blood as possible.

"Looks like blood to me."

" ... Right, but is there, I don't know, some tests you could do on it?"

"To ... ?"

"To see if it's actually blood?"

"What else would it be?"

"I don't know!"

Let me tell you what it is! For fuck's sake! He tried screaming, but he could only get his mouth open so far. He chewed on the bit.

"The mushrooms are the weirdest part to me," said Ari. "I can't *imagine* what he was doing with them."

"I don't know if this is a fruitful avenue of investigation," said Nick. "When I asked you to bring me back a vampire, I wanted it to do experiments on, not ... whatever this is."

"Can't you at least *try* a little bit?" said Lex. "There's something unusual going on here." Lex. Lex was the closest to figuring it out. *Please, Lex, please.*

Nick sighed and put down the bottle. "All right. If you really want to know." He tapped his chin. "Well, a large volume of blood, with no human victims in sight ... The simplest explanation would be it was harvested elsewhere and brought with him. Having access to this much blood this fast, I would guess that this vampire is affiliated with the blood harvesting facilities, and was granted this large portion to feed him as he came deep into human territory to do something."

No! No! Holy fuck, they were looking at all his research and coming to the *exact* wrong conclusion. With some chagrin, he realized that even if they could read his handwriting, it probably wouldn't be obvious what any of his notebooks actually meant. They were too granular. The pages all held notes like, *Today I*

tested chemical compound #156 but it was unsuccessful as the iron content was too low. He hadn't thought it would be necessary to write "RESEARCH NOTES FOR MAKING ARTIFICIAL BLOOD" on the top of every page.

He desperately pulled at the restraints, hoping against all logic that maybe on *this* try he would be able to free himself. He couldn't just *lie there* and listen to this. Alarm bells blared in his head. This was getting worse for him, quickly, which he hadn't thought was possible.

He howled and struggled as all three ignored him, talking with each other in low voices. Nick was turning over a mushroom in his hand. Ari fruitlessly examined Valen's notes. Lex flicked at an empty beaker.

"Here it is – ah, this is illuminating." Nick had a book open. "This mushroom species only grows in warm climates, which means it couldn't grow in vampire territory. Hence he must have come here to collect it."

Yes. Yes, that one's true. You're getting closer. Please.

"But what could he use it *for*?"

Nick held the book out. "Well, this mushroom species apparently produces a potent tranquilizing poison."

It also has a freakishly high iron content, and might mimic the taste of hemoglobin ... Vampires are immune to the poison part. That's just a coincidence.

"If we assume this vampire is affiliated with the blood farms, then we can guess that maybe he's here on a sponsored trip to research more effective ways to hunt down humans. His notes support that – there's a lot of drawings of chemical compounds, and notes on combining things in different ratios. Perhaps it was to develop a tranquilizer that would be easier to use than hunting down humans manually."

Valen was so stunned for a moment that he just lay still. That was ... the dumbest thing he'd ever heard. Why would vampires need *tranquilizers*? Most of them could stop a human in its tracks with a single word. *We don't need to make it easier!*

He started growling now. He had to do *something*. *Don't you fucking dare. You have* no *idea what you're talking about. You dumb fuck. You think you're so smart.*

To his horror, Lex and Ari seemed to follow this train of thought. Lex looked … disappointed. "Oh … "

Ari took Lex's hand. "Come on, Lex, we kind of knew he must be here for something no good."

"Right, but … I dunno, I guess I thought maybe … "

Nick snapped the book shut. "Well, I will let you know if I discover anything else, but I think for now this is the most likely explanation."

Holy shit. No, no, no, this couldn't be happening. They thought he was with the vampires who hunted humans down and dragged them back to be drained and killed. Oh God, they'd assume he was the *worst* kind of vampire if they believed that. Most vampires were at least a *little* bit squeamish about where their food came from, but the ones who captured humans to bring back for a horrible death were some of the most sadistic fucks he'd ever met. It took a special kind of person to do that job, and anyone with a heart dropped out quickly.

They sometimes played with their food before turning their captures in. Some humans arrived at the blood processing facilities already half-dead. He'd seen it firsthand.

They thought he was like *that*?

He tried to control his breathing. The humans were talking again, but he couldn't hear them over his crashing heartbeat. Terror overwhelmed him. If they thought he was like *that* –

"I don't need help!" Ari was partway up the stairs for some reason. He watched as she exited the basement, leaving Valen alone with Lex and Nick.

Lex. Lex, please. For God's sake. Please, please, you have to realize.

Nick turned back to the coffin with a terrifying smile on his face. "Well, now we can, perhaps, get on with it."

Not you! Fuck! Get away from me!

Lex approached him. *Lex, please, for God's sake. You have to figure it out.* "Okay ... Well, I guess I count as a second person here, so it's not against the rules to open the coffin. What exactly are you going to do?"

"Well, I need to document everything, so we should start with photographing its condition when it arrived." He gestured to the chunky camera on the workbench.

"O-okay. Um, what are you going to do – to – that will affect his *condition*?"

"Well, the first thing I wanted to try out was to establish the optimum percentage of silver for an alloy to still be effective for vampire hunting. We've been using pure silver, and we go through a *lot* of it. If, say, fifty percent silver is just as effective, we could be much more efficient."

"Okay?"

Lex! For God's sake! He's saying he's going to burn me with silver over and over again, to see which one works best! Doesn't that sound fucked up to you? Don't you think you should put a stop to this? Don't you think you should UNMUZZLE ME RIGHT NOW FOR GOD'S SAKE?

Nick was in his face as he knelt down, unlocking the coffin.

Valen expected to feel some sense of relief when the coffin opened, to not be locked in so tightly, but instead, the opposite happened. Now there was *no barrier* between him and Nick, and that was terrifying. He thrashed, once again knowing it was futile, but needing to do *something*.

Nick stood at the foot of the coffin like a sleep paralysis demon. "Go ahead, get it all out of your system."

Valen fell back, limp, chest heaving.

Valen's eyes followed Nick as he pulled out a pole from his workbench, one with a noose on the end, the kind used to handle a struggling animal while keeping it at a distance. As though Valen were an aggressive dog. He would be offended, but he had a bad feeling the humiliation was only going to keep getting worse.

Valen had no way to avoid the clasp being slipped onto his neck, but he tried, jerking his head away. The wire cinched closed. "Feisty, aren't you? Lex, will you please undo the restraints?"

Lex removed the chains from his chest, then strained to remove the chain keeping his shackled ankles secured to the coffin, keeping her face well out of kicking range.

Nick lifted the pole. The cord around his neck choked him, of course, because he wasn't in any position to support his own weight until he'd gotten his footing. His chest heaved in relieved breaths once his weight was on his feet and not on his neck. He was pretty sure this was not the intended use for such a device – of course, it was usually used on quadrupedal creatures.

"Now, Lex, we're going to use those chains in the center of the room, if you'll please attach them to its arms when I get it over there."

Valen groaned, because he could immediately see where this was going. He hissed and spat as fiercely as he could as Nick used the pole to guide him to the center of the room. He clumsily stumbled over his shackled ankles as Nick pulled him faster than he could walk, falling to his knees in the center of the room.

Lex came over and gently took his wrists, pulling the chain down to attach it.

"No, no, in the front, if you please, so we can have his arms above his head."

Lex froze. "Er, how do you want me to do that?"

"Unshackle the wrists and move them to the front."

Go ahead and try it. See what happens.

Lex gave him a frightened look. "Er ... I don't think I can do that without him being able to claw me."

"You're the one who managed to capture him in the first place. I'm sure you can figure something out."

"Okay ... Um ... "

Valen watched her with burning eyes, curious as to what she would try.

She reached a hand out towards his face, gently stroking his cheek. "Shh. It's all right."

Well. *That* wasn't what he'd expected. It was pathetic, but he found himself comforted by the touch, letting himself lean into it slightly.

"Listen ... I know that this ... isn't fun for you. But I think you know fighting back isn't going to do anything, yeah?"

He couldn't look her in the eye. The emotions swirling inside him were too complicated. All at once he was thinking *How fucking dare you* and *Please help me* and *Please keep touching me* and *Don't fucking touch me* and *Why are you doing this?* and *I don't deserve better than this.*

"It's gonna be all right," she soothed. "Easy, now, shh, shh. There, you're okay. It's gonna be okay."

He knew it wasn't true, it *couldn't* be true, but he let himself get lost in the fantasy for a moment, that it *would* be all right in the end. His only movement was to shake as she unlocked him and maneuvered him into the desired position, re-locking him and securing him to the chain.

"Brilliant!" said Nick.

Brilliant. It was brilliant, in a way, the way she'd just expertly manipulated him into being docile. It was a heartless trick on him, and it would work if she did it again.

"There we go," she said, her voice sweet, her voice poisonously sickly sweet. "See, it's not so bad."

Maybe if she said it enough, Valen would believe it. *It's not so bad.*

It abruptly got worse as the chain around his wrists lifted off the ground, up to the ceiling, stretching him up, up onto the balls of his feet. Vulnerable, unable to curl in on himself any longer.

Nick stepped into his field of view. "There. Now, we can – "

Valen's explosive hatred came back instantly, and he made use of the new weapon the humans hadn't realized they'd given him: he used the chain in the ceiling to lift his weight, fists tight in the chain, and mule-kicked Nick dead-center.

He felt just a smidgeon of pride and control over the situation now, even as Lex caught his feet to stop his movement. "All right, what did we just talk about?"

She brought his feet down and attached them to a mount on the floor, which secured the shackles to the ground and limited his range of movement. Valen trembled, knowing he'd probably just made things worse, but he didn't care. It was worth it. Nick hacked and put a hand to his chest, trying to recover from the surprise attack.

"Ah, yes," he said, clearing his throat. "This is why – why it's important to – to have two people to handle it, I suppose."

"Right ... "

He clucked his tongue, now examining the blood on Valen's forehead. "You've already been damaged." He got out a soft cloth and dabbed Valen's face. Valen tried to jerk away; even when he was trying to be gentle, Nick prompted disgust and fear that made Valen recoil.

"Now, now, we'll have time for that later. Right now ... " He removed an enormous pair of scissors from his workbench.

Ah. Now we're starting, I guess. A thrill of terror coursed through Valen, and he thrashed again. *Where are those going? What are you going to do with those?* Was he going to clip Valen's fangs? Cut off his nails? Something worse?

"Stay still," Nick hissed, moving out of sight. "It'll only be worse if you struggle."

Valen's eyes fell to the furnace and the molten silver next to it, imagination now running wild with all the possibilities that things being *worse* could entail. It was enough to make him fall still. He felt the touch of cold metal on his back, and he almost jumped. But it wasn't cutting his skin, only his shirt.

Wait – *it was cutting his shirt?* Nick was *undressing* him?

No no no no no NO NO NO. This was too much, having his clothes peeled off by a sneering man telling him to behave. Oh no, oh no, oh no, they were going to *see*, they were going *see him*. He froze up, knees locked, learned helplessness kicking in, hoping against hope it would just stop.

"Is this – is that really necessary?" said Lex, with some obvious discomfort.

Valen felt the scissors snip his sleeves off. "What did you think I meant by photograph his condition? I can't very well do that when he's all covered up."

Stop touching me! Get away from me! Fuck you! Stop it!

Lex looked conflicted. *Lex, please, you know this is wrong, please, please stop him.*

Valen felt his dissected shirt fall to the floor, exposing his chest, naked except for his binder. *No no no.* He wept, fresh humiliation and vulnerability welling up. *They're going to see, they're going to see and it's going to get so much worse after they see, somehow they'll make it worse –*

"Hm?" said Nick.

"Uh?" said Lex.

Valen sobbed as he felt the scissors again, snipping off his precious binder, the one he'd had to fight so hard to sneak past the people in the house who told him he couldn't wear one.

Please just leave it on, please please please just leave it on, I'll do anything you want if you just leave it on.

The binder broke and slid off, thumping softly to the floor, leaving him un-equivocally exposed, unable to even curl up and shield himself with his arms.

"Well, well, well!" said Nick. "It seems this vampire you've brought me is actually a *vampiress*."

Fuck you! He'd never wished more than he did right now that he could get his breasts removed. But even if he had surgery, his vampiric healing factor meant that they would just grow back. He could never escape this, this chest he had never consented to have and which seemed to belong to everybody except him, which everybody saw instead of seeing *him*. *Fuck you fuck you fuck you fuck you fuck you fuck you –*

"I ... I didn't know vampires could be transgender," said Lex, which was less rage-inducing, but still concerning. Why ... why *wouldn't* they be able to be transgender? What did Lex think about vampires that she hadn't considered that possibility?

Nick scoffed. "Don't be absurd. I'm sure vampires have no use for such non-sense."

Valen watched as Lex withdrew Valen's stolen wallet from her pocket, opening it, presumably re-examining his ID card. She looked back up, face furrowed, scrutinizing him. Then her face softened with pity.

His attention was yanked away as he felt Nick's hands on his pants, unbuttoning them and undoing the zipper.

What the FUCK, what the fuck what the fuck – He tried to back away, to get as far away as possible. It was too much, too much, too much.

"Come *on*," said Lex. "You can't be serious. What could you possibly need *that* for?"

"I already told you," Nick snapped. "I need a nude photograph for comparisons later. I'm positive vampires have no concept of nudity being shameful, so stow your antiquated sensibilities."

Come on, Lex, you know this isn't right. Stop him, stop him, don't let him. He felt himself flushing, face heating up. These two strangers, who didn't even see him as a full person, thinking him incapable of base emotions like embarrassment, were going to see his entirely uncovered body, laid bare before their harsh, judging, non-understanding eyes for their own purposes.

His pants came down, revealing his underwear. Valen shook with helplessness and fear, trying to control his warbled crying. Nick pinched his boxers in both hands and pulled them down, all the way down, around his feet, leaving him completely exposed from the tips of his fingers all the way down to his shackled ankles.

Lex looked away, face twisted in a grimace. *Stop him, please please please stop him, please don't let him* –

Nick kept his eyes fully on Valen's quivering, vulnerable form. Valen's terrified gaze watched his hands, expecting them to come over and start fondling him at any moment.

But no. He was granted at least this one mercy for now, that Nick was done touching him. The human walked over to his workbench and picked up his camera, opening to make sure it had film inside before coming over and starting to snap photos. Adding more eyes to violate his privacy, his dignity, so his humiliation was potentially unending, so pictures could be shown to anyone and everyone forever after.

He thought of his husband somehow finding the pictures. The thought made him sick to his stomach.

Lex was looking at him again, staring, taking him in, clearly making some sort of judgment.

What are you thinking? There were more clicks of the camera shutter in the background.

Lex?

Valen's keen hearing picked up the sound of Ari's medical boot thumping back towards them long before the humans did. Then he heard her voice: "The fuck? I interrupt your boudoir photography session?" At least Ari recognized the absurdity of the situation. *Ari, please, you know this isn't right.*

But Ari was looking at Valen with newly renewed hatred on her face. *Fuck. FUCK. What happened upstairs?*

"It's strictly for research purposes," said Nick's voice behind him.

Sure, I'm sure you'll be spending a lot of time researching how erect these photos can make your dick. You're all the same.

"Well, when you're done *researching*, I managed to get ahold of Patrick."

Shit, who's Patrick? They must have mentioned it earlier, but he'd been in and out of paying attention, anxiety overwhelming his attention span.

Lex seemed happy about the news, though. "Oh? Okay! What did you find out?"

Something good, I hope. "Patrick told me we need to let him go right now."

Ari sighed as she came downstairs, leaning on the railing. "Yeah, nothing about this guy in particular, but he recognized the family name Kithrara. They're the ones who own and operate the blood farms."

No. *No.* They'd looked up his surname. He hadn't been able to change his last name yet, just because they weren't actually *divorced*, because the entire Kithrara family refused to acknowledge that they were basically divorced already on every level except legal and were still doing everything in their power to try and strongarm Valen into coming back.

Even now, long after he'd escaped them, the Kithrara family somehow managed to continue ruining his life.

Valen had never behaved properly – neither as a vampire, nor as a woman. His parents had thought it would fix his "attitude" by marrying him to the oldest son of the Kithrara family – the nasty fucks of a family who owned and operated the blood farms.

It'll toughen you up, they'd said. *It'll show you how the world really works. You're in for a rude awakening.*

You need a reality check, they'd said. *And besides, the Kithrara family is eager to find a bride for him, since you know they're desperate for an heir. He thinks you're pretty. He is handsome and powerful. You could do a lot worse. This might be your only chance to marry into nobility.*

He had no way to communicate that he hated the blood farms as much as they did, the disgust and anger he felt towards the Kithrara family. They had no way to know. They just knew he was one of them.

"Oh," said Lex, her voice heavy. *No! Lex, please!* Tears streamed down his cheeks, dripping off the muzzle. This was the final nail in his coffin. This was all they needed to confirm their off-base speculation from earlier. They had no reason to be suspicious, to go against all evidence and conclude he was trustworthy, no reason at all to assume he was anything other than the worst among his kind, the worst monster among a monstrous race.

And if they thought *that* ... who knew what they would do to him.

"Do whatever you want to him, then," Lex said, her voice flat and emotionless. "I don't care."

Valen's terrified gaze swung to Lex, in Ari's arms, both of them looking disappointed and betrayed.

Please. I'm not a murderer. I'm like you. I'm a friend. Please. I cried when my cat died.

Nick stepped into his field of vision, blocking the view of the two women. "There you have it, then. Asked and answered. No need to trouble your conscience over it." He was smiling, too wide, too happy about this. "Thank you, Lex and Ari, for your service."

Valen thrashed and cried. It was all he could do.

"Right ... " said Ari. "Just hurry up and finish what you're doing so we can leave."

Don't leave me here with him.

Lex came over to the cardboard box of things she'd taken from the house, a haunted look in her eyes. She uncorked the bottle of fake blood and poured it down the sink.

6

— • —

The muzzle was never coming off.

The magnitude of that reality was starting to set in. This stupid thing was going to be on his face, in his mouth, until eventually one of these vampire hunters ended his pathetic existence. He would never get the chance to explain himself. He would never, ever get the chance to be truly understood, by anyone.

The Director had said it should be safe enough to leave him in the coffin unattended, or so Nick had told him before shutting him inside and going back upstairs, turning off the lights and locking the door behind him. Leaving Valen completely alone, in the dark, locked in place. As though he were a toy they could just put back in the toybox when they were done with him.

He wanted to *scream*. It felt like he was suffocating in here, unable to move any part of his body more than a few inches, locked in restraints that would have been excessive even for a vampire far stronger than him. And he knew with a sinking heart that this was going to be his new existence, every day and every night for as long as his captors saw fit to keep him around, and his only reprieve would be to be taken out to be tortured, and then locked back inside as soon as they were done.

If he'd known he was risking *this*, he'd have never even dared come here.

The room seemed so big and empty now, with nobody else here. Just him, in his locked box, shoved in the corner. He sobbed, trying to kick his legs, his desperate wailing and the chains jingling filling the empty room.

Never even in the darkest periods of his life had he reached such depths of despair before now. The Kithrara estate, the hub of cruelty and violence that fed most vampires in the country, had used to be the place he went to in his worst dreams. His most hated foe, his husband, was there, the crying of the human captives in the basement was there, the sadistic fucking human catchers were there occasionally. And yet now all he could think of was how much he would give just to be back there. He should never have left. He should have just locked himself in the master bedroom, never to come out. Sure, he had to act like a woman and put up with his horrible husband and pretend it didn't bother him to see humans tortured and killed, but at least it wasn't *this*. At least he could *talk*. At least he could *move*.

This is what I get for trying to make things better. It was the only thought he had to occupy himself throughout the whole night.

His parents had been right. He'd been in for a rude awakening.

***

The only comfort Valen could find in this terrifying new hell was that his tormenter was not allowed to open the coffin without someone else there.

The way Nick leered at him, made comments here and there. It made his skin crawl. He had a very, very bad feeling about what would happen if he were alone with Nick. If there was someone else there, Nick at least had to rein it in a little bit. Valen had already picked up on the fact that Nick was very aware of how to hide the parts of himself that the other hunters would disapprove of, and that he had to balance how they saw him by curating what he let slip. That he had to behave himself in public.

Priscus had been sort of the same way. A lot of men were.

Valen lay there in the coffin crying, wondering how long this was going to last. Surely he would find a way to escape eventually, right? He was being held here

with silver, but all he'd need to do would be to get the muzzle off. If there were two humans, he could just have one attack the other. Maybe he could –

He froze as he heard the front door open and footsteps approaching. *No.* That couldn't be right, could it? The hunters had cleared out to go on patrol, and Nick had said he would return in the morning. Nick didn't come into the base alone.

He wasn't allowed to.

... which didn't mean he *wouldn't*, Valen realized with a sinking heart.

The light flipped on. Valen's eyes contracted to pinpoints and he sweated, staring at the ceiling, too afraid to look.

He looked.

Nick was at the top of the stairs, leering at him. "Hello, parasite," he said. It was *so* unlike the way he'd talked earlier in the day, in front of everyone else.

Valen stared at him with watery eyes, unable to respond.

Nick came down the stairs, shutting the door behind him. He drew near like a circling shark. Valen's heart pounded, eyes following him. He was already hyperventilating.

He's not allowed to open the cage when nobody else is here. He can't hurt you. He can't open the cage.

Nick walked to the forge in the room and lighted it, setting some silver in it. He then sat in the chair across from the cage.

"Hello," he said. "I bet you're wondering what I'm doing here, because I can't open the coffin when I'm alone."

You can't. Please, please, you can't, you're not allowed, you're not allowed –

"Well, guess what? Nobody can tell me what I can or can't do." He held up a silver key.

Valen thrashed as far as the chains would allow, giving out muffled screams. This *couldn't* be happening. He'd already been having anxious fits about what sorts of experiments were going to be done on him, what kind of anti-vampire weapons were going to be tested on him, but *this*? Clearly this was not for an *experiment*. Somehow that made it way worse.

Nick knelt down and unlocked the coffin, leaving the lid propped open. Valen lay there paralyzed with terror, still held down by multiple layers of silver chains.

"You want out? You want to go home?" Nick said.

Valen nodded vigorously.

"Oh, sorry about that," Nick said. He held up his keyring, shaking it with a jingle. "Well, here, why don't you unlock yourself and be on your way, then." He dropped the keyring onto Valen's bare chest. Being that most of the keys were for locks to a fortress of anti-vampire activity, most of them were made of silver. It *burned*. Valen writhed, trying to shake them off, crying.

Nick laughed. "Come on, you're going to have to take a *lot* worse than that. You're already breaking down? I expected more fight out of you."

Valen finally managed to get the keys to slide off his body, clattering down to the cement. His lip wobbled.

Nick planted his boot on Valen's chest, right over the burn mark. Valen winced. "Because you monsters are *so* full of yourselves. You know? There's no reason for you to be submissive and scared. Come on. Be angry at me. Hate me. Try to kill me. I want to see the fire in your eyes, so I can snuff it out."

Valen turned his head away, breaking eye contact, chest heaving and tears rolling down his face.

"*Look at me when I'm talking to you.*"

Valen did so. Nick had a crazed look on his face. "I wish I could let you talk. I would make you recount all your sins, all the ways you're beneath me. I would make you write poems about your monstrosity, about how you deserve to be debased, how superior I am to you. I'd make you call me master and beg for your life. I'd make you beg so, so much. That's the only thing vampires will ever be good for, crushing under my heel." He ground his boot into Valen's burn, and Valen squirmed afresh.

"Now you know what it's like," Nick said. "To be far from home. Scared, alone, helpless. At the mercy of someone who doesn't give a fuck about your feelings.

45

Your humanity. That's what every human taken by vampires feels. That's what I felt."

That shouldn't have happened to you. We can talk about it like civilized individuals. We can –

Nick went to the furnace and came over with a glowing cup of molten silver. Valen gave a terrified cry and wriggled once again.

"And that's *all* you're going to feel for the rest of your miserable life, you fucking leech."

Valen screamed as the silver was poured onto his chest, dribbling down his ribs with a sickening sizzle.

Nick unlocked the three large chains keeping him secured to the coffin, which freed his limbs enough that he could squirm better, but his arms and ankles were still locked together. He seized Valen by the hair and dragged him out of the coffin, prompting fresh screams as the silver that had pooled on Valen's stomach trailed down over his belly button and down near his crotch.

Nick threw him onto the desk, then Valen let out a terrified gasp as Nick leaned over him, pressing him into the desk, crotch-to-ass and chest-to-back. His brain was so frozen in terror he could hardly register what was happening.

"Nothing for you to do except take it," he whispered into Valen's ear. "Just where you should be."

Valen tried to push Nick off, but the molten silver was making everything throb with pain and it just *hurt* and he was so *scared*.

Nick snapped the chains into a silver loop nearby, immobilizing Valen. Valen put his face on the desk, breathing shakily.

"You know, it's interesting what vampires think of humans," Nick said. He stepped back and let fresh, cold air hit Valen's bare skin. Valen gasped, shaking with relief to at least be free of that contact for another moment. "We're not quite animals to you, but we're certainly not people. When I was raped by the group holding me, some of them called it bestiality. Some of them compared it to

fucking a dog. Can you imagine that? They thought it was weird and taboo, but because I was like a dog, not because I was a person who didn't consent."

Valen squeezed his eyes shut, tugging on the chains. Dread built in his stomach.

"Can you imagine someone whose job it was to go out and kidnap innocent humans to be tortured and brainwashed every night, already the worst of the worst among vampires, and they're stepping outside of even *their* comfort zone to do something so wrong and unnatural that some of them think it's taboo?"

Valen was familiar with those people, the ones who collected those who ended up at the blood farms. They truly were the worst of the worst. Their empathy had been eroded away; it had to be, to do that job. To think of what they would do to a helpless human they'd kept for fun. It was almost enough to make Valen feel bad for Nick. *Almost*, because nothing could quite shake the utter terror he was experiencing right now.

"You're going to feel everything they did to me and more. You're mine from now on, understand? I can do anything I want to you. Anything. I'll do experiments on you like I'm supposed to, and then I'll come back when everyone else is gone and do whatever sick, depraved, fucking inexcusable thing I want to you, because you're nothing and I'm everything. Fucking understand?"

What does he want? Valen nodded, hoping that would maybe at least earn him *something*.

Nick slapped his ass. He *slapped Valen's ass. Hello??*

"You'd be kind of hot, if you didn't do all that shit to your body, you know. You look like a faggot. Are you married? Do you want to call your faggot husband?"

Valen nodded shakily. He was under no illusion it mattered if he said yes or no, but surely nothing *worse* would happen by admitting that, right? Even Priscus was better than this.

Nick sat down at the desk, picked up the phone, and held it against Valen's ear. "Go ahead. Call him." Valen trembled.

Nick guided his hand to the number pad. "Go on. Call him. Dial 9 first for an outside line."

With one shaking, cuffed hand, Valen dialed in the number. The phone rang. A servant answered. "You've reached the Kithrara estate."

Valen exploded into hysterical sobs.

"Hello?" the servant said. Valen recognized the voice. Cora, that was her name. She hated answering the phone, Valen remembered. He'd been the only one to ask the servants which chores they'd preferred to be assigned to.

He couldn't say anything, of course. He was muzzled. But Valen made as many noises as he could, something, *anything*. Cora gave a few more lost *hello?*s, after which she sighed and hung up.

"Oh, looks like they didn't get the message," Nick said in mock sympathy. He hung up the phone. "I guess you'll just have to stay here with me for a while. Don't worry, I'll take good care of you."

He climbed onto the desk above Valen, once again pressing him against it. Valen's heart sped up. He felt dizzy. This couldn't be happening.

Nick slid Valen's pants down. Valen started wiggling again at that. He had to do *something*.

Nick slid his own pants down. *Come on. Come ON. Why? Why this? Out of all the fucking things.*

Valen hid his face in the desk, wetting it with his tears, as he felt Nick feeling him around back there. Suddenly, there was an explosive, burning pain around his thighs. He was too scared to look back and see what it was.

"You don't like that?"

Valen sobbed as loud as he could, shaking his head.

"Good. You're here for *me*. You belong to *me*. I can use you for whatever I want. I have the right to do that. Let's get that established right away so you don't forget it."

Valen felt the distinct sensation of a penis poking into him. That, he'd done before. He would rather that than be burned, as horrible as it was.

His eyes widened and he raised his head as he realized it was *not* poking the entrance to his vagina.

He'd never done *that*. Priscus's goal had been to have children, so of course he wouldn't stick it anywhere else.

It pushed in without any further preparation or warning. Valen cried softly and kicked his legs as far as he could, which wasn't very far.

"Shh," Nick said, hands planted on either side of Valen, pressing down onto him. "You know how to take it, don't you?"

It *hurt*. It didn't hurt as bad as the burning, but it had a unique sense of utter *wrongness* to it that he couldn't quite describe. Taboo, as Nick had said, perhaps.

Take it out, please take it out.

Nick withdrew slightly, then slammed back in full force. Valen let out another muffled scream.

"Don't you want to be a man?" Nick said wickedly. "Gay men take it up the ass, don't you know?"

Valen squirmed as Nick continued to pump. He'd *never* been so eager for someone else to finish so it could be over, and that was saying a lot considering that'd been basically Valen's entire sex life until that point.

Valen could feel Nick getting more excited when Valen let out any noises of fear or pain, which added a whole new level of violation to it. It was over in a normal amount of time, but *God* did it feel long. Valen panted when Nick finally pulled out, relieved and humiliated in equal measure.

Nick's hands tangled in his hair and pulled his head back. "I hope that drives the point home. You belong to me. You're here to please *me*. In whatever way I see fit. Just like vampires do to their humans. If I want to burn you, I'll burn you. If I want to strangle you, I'll strangle you. If I want to saw your limbs off, I will. If I want to rape you, I will. If I want to keep you captive for years and years as my personal property, breaking your mind, I will. I may have to hide it so the others don't see the marks, but I'll figure out a way." He spit in Valen's face.

Valen couldn't even muster up the wherewithal to struggle any more as Nick unlatched the chains and dragged him by the hair back into the coffin, throwing him in and locking the lid.

Nick walked up the stairs and turned the light off. He turned back one final time with a wicked gleam in his eye. "See you tomorrow. I'm sure you won't tell anyone about our little visit, right?"

He shut the door, plunging Valen into darkness once again.

Valen lay there in the dark, crying. It *hurt*. The burns hurt, his ass hurt. The cruel words hurt too, more than Valen wanted to admit.

This was going to be a long, long ... however long he was going to be here.

7

Nick broke the rule about not opening the coffin alone all the time. During the day, another hunter would supervise, with some disapproval plastered on their face as Nick hurt Valen over and over again, but not enough disapproval to intervene. But at night, when everyone else was gone, Nick would sneak back in and start doing things he *knew* the other hunters would find bad enough to stop him, dropping the pretense of research entirely for acts that had no justifiable purpose other than his own sadistic pleasure. To carry out whatever brutal torture he'd obviously fantasized about enacting upon his previous captors for years and years.

Because Nick made it very clear he was doing this because vampires had ruined his life, hurt him in unimaginable ways, and that gave him the right to hurt others the same way, in his mind.

The fact that he was careful not to show that in front of the other hunters gave Valen hope that maybe, if they found out about it, someone would rescue him. But Valen had no way to tattle on him for breaking the rules, and none of them cared enough about his well-being to be suspicious enough to figure it out. Every time Nick came down and enacted whatever sadistic fantasies he'd been fermenting, he always showed up the next day acting like nothing had happened.

Valen tried to cry out any time he heard footsteps upstairs, an indication there was someone, *anyone* upstairs who might have pity on him. *Please help me, someone, anyone, please please please make it stop.*

He couldn't believe he'd thrown away his life trying to help these miserable, hateful creatures. He couldn't believe he'd ever felt bad for them. He couldn't believe it had upset him so much to see them mistreated.

No, that was the pessimism talking. There was nothing wrong with *him*. But damn was it hard to remember so, to keep together any scraps of empathy. He'd once been positively overwhelmed by his empathy. There had been times when he'd cried just from the weight of living in such a cruel, monstrous society that he had no way to fix. Maybe that was why the humans here became vampire hunters. Maybe that was why they behaved the way they did.

The rotating cast of hunters who came to assist Nick started getting smaller, fewer and fewer regular faces. Lex and Ari were there quite a lot in the early days, but after a few weeks he didn't see them again. The last time was when Lex started crying and simply walked out, and that was the last he saw of either.

Probably because they felt guilty. Which they should.

A few hunters walked out in a self-righteous huff, saying Nick was sick, that this was wrong and they refused to watch or participate. They always seemed so proud of themselves for making the right decision, for being a conscientious objector. Maybe it made them feel better, but the pain still hurt Valen even when they couldn't see it. None of them did anything meaningful to actually stop it.

He could tell they justified it to themselves, comforted themselves with the idea that he deserved it, that he was a monster. Valen would have thought that if their entire moral posture depended upon that fact, they would have spent more time and effort verifying it.

They had, he supposed, spent more time than could be expected of them already. Many humans wouldn't have even bothered to look up his name. They would have just assumed the worst and moved on.

He watched his research notes get thrown away eventually. It bothered him less than he thought it would have. His mission of shutting down the blood farms seemed so far away, barely a distant memory. He couldn't care about it anymore.

He'd been reduced to an animal with no room for any goals or emotions more complex than the desire to just not feel this pain anymore.

He lost weight. They didn't feed him, so of course he lost weight. Vampires couldn't die from starvation, only get weaker and weaker, so there was no reason to feed him. He hadn't been this hungry since he'd first moved into the Kithrara estate, and they'd tried to force him to feed directly from a human, and he'd gone on hunger strike until they gave up and let him have blood packets.

Maybe this was how the humans had felt, watching Valen self-righteously refuse to feed from them, but not releasing them. The special agony and helplessness of seeing someone else understand and disapprove of a predicament, but not caring *quite* enough to take the drastic, disruptive action that would be required to fix the situation. He endlessly reminded himself that there would have been consequences for releasing the household's humans, that he'd had a lot of things to consider, that he couldn't be blamed for putting himself first, but it all felt hollow now that he was on the other side of it.

In addition to wasting away, Valen also got to watch the effects of his heard-earned testosterone reverse now that he could no longer do regular injections, which was a special kind of torture Nick didn't even know he was inflicting. Not that things like fat distribution and muscle definition mattered much when you had no fat or muscle to speak of.

The ones he hated the most were Lex and Ari, the ones who'd put him in this situation in the first place, who'd made assumptions and hadn't given him a chance, who'd told him it would be all right. And yet they were the ones that when he heard their voices, he tried the hardest to beg for their help, to get their attention. They were the ones he missed, the ones he silently pleaded with not to leave him alone. When they were around, he started to think that maybe it *would* be okay, that they'd been telling the truth after all, if he could just make them listen.

That was the worst part, knowing that he might be able to save himself if he could make them *understand*, if he could somehow communicate, the one thing

they had an incentive to prevent him from doing at any cost. The only thing standing between him and possible freedom was this muzzle, a few pathetic inches of metal and leather that seemed so simple and yet so impossible to get around. If they even just let his hands be free on occasion, he could write, or try sign language, or just fucking *gesture*.

Something, anything. But they never gave him an inch.

The muzzle never came off.

***

He could hear Nick talking to Lex and Ari upstairs, trying to convince them to come down.

It never worked. Those two never came down anymore. The last time they had, Lex had made a big show of making sure Nick called Valen a *he*. And then left without helping Valen any other way.

He hated Lex. He wanted to strangle her and shout in her face, *Why do you think I fucking care about pronouns when I'm being tortured? Does this make you feel better? It doesn't make me feel better. Are you done patting yourself on the back about how righteous you are? Are you done taking a moral stand and leaving me to suffer here?*

How is it you care about gender, but not someone's basic life and safety?

He hated Lex, and he hated himself for fantasizing about her coming downstairs, gently unlocking him, cooing to him that she was sorry and she would help him. About her telling her partner to gently carry him upstairs and take care of him.

"How was your hunt?" Nick's voice said upstairs. He always talked to the other humans so differently than how he talked to Valen. It was so jarring to hear.

"Fine," Ari said gruffly. "Blew the fucker's head off."

Valen squeezed his eyes shut and tried not to cry. It hadn't even started yet, he couldn't cry *already*. But he knew in his heart that's what Lex and Ari *would* do, realistically. They'd call him a fucker and blow his head off.

"I was actually going to test that next, you know," Nick said. He always sounded just a little too excited, and not for the science. He was a horrible scientist. Valen had enough training in the sciences to see that. It just added insult to injury that most of the data he was generating from Valen's suffering wasn't even sound. "What percentage of its brain a vampire can have removed and still be functional. How effective a headshot has to be – "

"We get it," Ari said bluntly. "Go away."

Nick's footsteps came down the stairs. Maybe Valen would get lucky today. Maybe this would be one of the days where Nick couldn't get anyone to come downstairs and supervise his experiments. On those days, Valen would only be hurt when Nick could get away with breaking the rules and opening the coffin alone.

Valen had used to think he could maybe use that alone time to try and escape – it was foolish to be around a vampire alone. But now he hated those times more than anything, his body far too weak to even think about escape, and left to Nick's endlessly cruel whims alone.

Nick sneered at him as he came past. "Don't get too comfortable, leech," he muttered, voice dripping with venom.

Valen's luck didn't hold out. Cyril came down that day, his least favorite hunter just behind Nick. He leered over Valen's cage with that same utterly deranged look he always had on his face.

In the early days of this horrorshow, Valen would squirm and thrash and growl and do whatever he could to make things as hard as possible for his captors. He didn't have the energy for that anymore. He allowed himself to be pitifully dragged out of the coffin.

Nick strapped him into a reclining chair and then swept the bar, slamming Valen out into a lying-down position. Given the earlier conversation in tandem

with the circular saw out on the desk that'd had its safety guard removed, Valen had a horrible guess about what was about to happen to him.

"You get to be *so* useful today," Nick said. He laid out a metal bowl and a scale on the workbench next to Valen. Valen's eyes bounced around to follow his motions. "It's common for hunters to immobilize vampires with headshots, so when you tell us *exactly* how much of a vampire's brain needs to be blown off, you're going to help us kill a lot more of you fuckers." He pulled on a face shield and a heavy apron. "The brain itself actually doesn't have any pain receptors, so you should consider yourself lucky, you know."

Valen didn't *feel* very lucky as the circular saw whirred to life, the metal teeth becoming a blur.

Cyril secured another strap around Valen's head to keep him down. Despite the army of restraints keeping Valen in place, he squirmed with all his might as Nick approached.

Nick moved behind Valen, out of sight, and the saw was getting louder and louder and oh God, *it's so much worse now that he can't see.*

He felt the sharp explosion of pain on his scalp, his own sounds of panic and terror drowned out by the sound of the saw. Despite Nick's claim, it *did* hurt, although Valen was so numb to pain at this point that all he could think was, *This isn't so bad.*

His eyes wheeled around the ceiling as he felt more and more of his skull snapping off. Then the whirring of the saw died down and – there was a sickening suction sound, and a wet thunk onto the floor, and yep, there was part of Valen's head on the floor, *don't look at it, don't look at it* –

Valen might have thrown up if he'd had anything in his stomach. Nick's hand moved in and out of his field of vision, taking tools from the table. He could certainly feel *something* as Nick worked unseen behind him, but it was hard to describe what, exactly.

Cyril had a look of grim fascination on his face. "Fuck, dude. That's gnarly."

Valen's breathing picked up as Nick's bloodied, be-gloved hand came back into view with a piece of brain on a spoon. Apparently it wasn't the part of Valen's brain responsible for him spiraling, because he was doing that pretty successfully.

"Hold still, now," Nick said, making notes of the weights on the scale. "Or you'll ruin it and we'll have to do another replicate."

8

— • —

Nick was talking to hunters, trying to convince them to come down. That wasn't good. That meant the coffin would be opened, and when the coffin was open, Valen was in danger.

As much as he'd initially hated being locked in the coffin, it was now the closest to safe he ever felt. Usually Nick needed him to be outside the coffin to do anything to him. These days he was always in pain, but newer, more intense, fresher pain awaited him outside the coffin.

And it wasn't like he had the strength to move around under his own power much these days anyway. Restraints barely did anything. If you left him free on the bare cement with all the doors to the house unlocked, he doubted he would be able to even make it up the stairs to mount an escape.

The only restraint that truly mattered anymore was the one that never came off. The muzzle, which kept him from using the hypnotic powers of persuasion, the one thing that he could potentially use to ever gain any leverage again.

Nick had told him he was going to replace Valen soon. That he wasn't keeping up with his experiments anymore. He said it accusingly, as though Valen should feel guilty for not being able to close up all his wounds overnight anymore.

Maybe I could if you fucking fed me.

It'd been on his mind a lot because he was anxious about how Nick was going to dispose of him. Maybe he would just kill him, which would be all right, he supposed, but maybe he would just keep him in the coffin and toss him in a

storage room somewhere in case he wanted him again. Maybe the coffin would really live up to its name and he would bury Valen.

That was probably the worst one Valen could imagine. As long as whatever Nick did wasn't worse than being buried alive, left to suffocate in the dirt for all eternity, he felt like he could handle it.

He was too tired to be *that* anxious about it. Being anxious about it had never saved him before.

He turned his head, looking hazily at the furnace in the room. The silver Nick had put in it earlier was almost molten. Valen knew what he was going to do with it, and he wasn't looking forward to it. That was probably why he was trying to recruit some hunters to supervise him.

Although he'd been complaining that Valen was so dirty that he couldn't measure the width and length of his injuries, which was the entire point of his current experiment: to see the effects of silver on the pace at which his wounds healed.

Valen was also a scientist, and a better one than Nick at that. He knew bad experimental design when he saw it. He would have been insulted that Nick was torturing him just to get data that was nigh on unusable, if he hadn't been so preoccupied with the throbbing ache of pain in every cell in his body.

He tried to squirm, just like he had every day for the past few months, and just like every time before, he was restrained and couldn't find any position that minimized his discomfort. He cried out in frustration. It was almost worse when Nick wasn't there. At least he had something to distract him, even if it was just watching Nick prepare the next torture.

There were multiple sets of footsteps on the stairs. No, no, no. That wasn't good. He'd been hoping Nick wouldn't be able to get anyone to come down. He would just open the coffin at night when he knew nobody would catch him anyway, but it would at least buy Valen a few hours.

Lex and Ari came down the stairs behind Nick. That was different. He hadn't seen them in a long time. They ignited a set of strange feelings inside him. He

hated them, he was scared of them, he yearned for them to help him. He found his entire body shaking.

Lex looked at him, disgust plastered on her face, and she turned away, a hand on her mouth.

Please don't look at me like that, please, please.

"Thank you so much," said Nick with relief. "I really cannot continue anything until he's been cleaned up. It's interfering with measurements. Here, if you would be so kind as to unlock the cage and bring him over here."

His heart sank. Of course they were going to open the coffin. It'd been foolish to hope otherwise. Well, he knew what they had planned. As long as they didn't do anything worse than what they were going to do with the silver, he felt like he could handle it. Silver wasn't even the worst pain; that had to be the device that mimicked the feel of the sun, which Nick called his Sun Gun. Valen shuddered to think what the actual sun would be like. As long as they didn't do anything as bad as the sun, he felt like he could handle it.

Ari took the key to the coffin from Nick and knelt down, unlocking his cage. "There, just position him right on there, if you please, this won't take very long at all," said Nick's voice behind her.

"All right," said Ari, and the lid came up.

Please, Ari. Please. You don't have to rescue me. You don't have to be kind to me. Please just be a little less cruel. That's all I need. Please. Just a little less.

She lifted him up by the metal collar around his neck. Not a good start. *Please, Ari, please please please. Lex, please. Remember? Remember when you thought I might be good? Remember when you thought it wasn't necessary to torture me? Remember when it made you uncomfortable?*

Ari was looking at him. It was terrifying when any of them looked at him, but Ari's face was always so harsh and judgmental. Like she wouldn't approve of you no matter what you did. He cringed, trying to curl in on himself to protect himself from whatever was coming, feet barely brushing against the floor.

"All right," said Ari, and the world whirled around as she lifted him up, hefting him over her shoulder.

This was different. Panic tightened in his stomach. Ari was carrying him up the stairs. This was different. He never left the basement. Different could be good, or it could be bad. The worst thing he could think of was they would leave him in the sun. As long as Ari didn't do anything worse than that, he felt like he could handle it.

"Um," said Nick. "Ari, where are you – "

"I'm taking him to the bathroom," Ari snapped. "Because I can tell it would upset Lex if you did it like that."

The bathroom? Valen wondered vaguely. If he didn't know better, he would guess they were going to have him take a shower. What else could they do in the bathroom? More drowning, maybe? But the basement had a sink, which Nick had used for that before.

Valen's field of view was taken up by Lex's excited, kind-looking face. He didn't trust it. He didn't trust that face ever since the words *It's gonna be all right* came out of that mouth to kick off his months of captivity and torture.

Nick disappeared from Valen's periphery as he presumably blocked the door, because Ari stopped in her tracks. "Hold on. I insist we do it in the basement."

"Nick."

"Y-yes?"

Ari lifted one foot up slightly. "Do you see this foot?"

"Y ... yes?"

"I just got it out of a boot. But I *will* break it off in your ass if I have to. Get out of the way."

Valen wanted so, so badly for Ari not to be angry at him. She talked to everyone like that when they did anything she disliked even a little. He was so scared of doing something that would invoke her ire. He was terrified at the prospect of her easily crossing the line into making good on those threats ... especially when she was carrying him.

Nick reappeared in Valen's vision as he stepped to the side. Valen looked down, lip wobbling, trying to keep his eyes on the steps as Ari carried him up, but he couldn't keep his eyes from flickering up to Lex. *Please, Lex. Even if it's a lie, tell me it's going to be okay. I need to hear it. I need to believe it for just a fucking moment.*

Lex dashed ahead, and the light dimmed. Lex had closed the blinds in the living room. His gut twisted with agonized hope. Did he dare let himself expect that maybe this wouldn't hurt?

Ari pivoted to go up a second set of stairs, giving Valen a full view of the living room. There were four hunters sitting around, looking at the group coming up from the basement in a confused way. Electric terror surged through him at the thought of being at the mercy of a group of seven hunters at once, most of whom were men. He knew the kinds of things men liked to do to helpless captives.

"Don't worry about it," Ari huffed, and she carried him up, away from those four new sets of eyes.

This was too much. He'd never been upstairs before. He didn't know what was up there. It could be anything. It could be even more hunters. It could be some worse form of torture he couldn't even imagine.

"Shh," said Lex.

Of course, Valen thought. *As long as my suffering isn't making you uncomfortable, then it's fine. If I cry out, then you tell me to be quiet instead of helping me.*

Valen had already forgotten they were going to the bathroom. He'd been too busy worrying about the terrifying unknown that was the upstairs of the house, but then he heard water running.

Ari pounded on the door. "Yo!"

"Geez, what?" said a voice from behind it.

"Get out. We need to use the bathroom."

The faucet squeaked off, the sound of towels ruffling, the sound of the door opening. Valen was stuck facing where Lex was on the stairs. "Geez, fine," said a man's voice from inside the bathroom.

Nick appeared on the stairs behind Lex. Neither of the women could see him, only Valen, and he was giving him a death glare. He vanished as Valen was carried away from the stairs and into the bathroom. He heard Nick start to deliver a plea for them to make it quick, before he was cut off by the door closing and locking.

Despite the situation, Valen found himself smug about that. Just a little. He would take whatever victories he could get.

He snapped back to reality and the absolute terror that accompanied it as Ari set him down on the toilet. She turned her back on him and started running the water in the shower. "Go ahead, Lex. Since I can tell you want to."

Oh, *that* didn't sound good. Want what? Want to do what to him? Based on their interactions at the start of his captivity, he thought these two might be among the less hateful vampire hunters, but who knows what could have changed in the intervening months.

He froze as Lex leaned in, extending a hand to put it on his knee. He tried to lean away, so, so scared of what those hands could do to him in his weakened and helpless state.

"Shh," she said. "Hey, I'm not going to hurt you. Do you want to take a shower?"

A shower? He had a list of things he wanted a mile long, and a shower was pretty far down on the list. It *was* still on the list, though. It also seemed dangerous to admit he wanted anything. Typically when he nodded in response to that question, Nick simply laughed and took said thing away from him.

She took his elbow. "Can you stand up for me?"

Could he? That was a good question. He didn't want to try. Pretty much every movement irritated some injury he had, either internal or external. Lex reached a second arm around his back, giving him a gentle push. *I guess we'll find out ...*

His knees knocked as he fully supported his own weight for the first time in what felt like decades. It had always been shackles, or cages, or gurneys, or leashes that bore his weight.

It was pathetic how far he'd fallen, that his goals were now to overcome the hollow ache of starvation to muster up the strength to stand. But the sense of triumph it gave him was undeniable, even with a human helping him, even when he was still muzzled and cuffed. *I did it. I'm standing up.*

He turned his head and saw a *ghastly* creature, a monster with sunken red eyes, covered in blood and grime and dirt, with open wounds and oozing sores and bones visible beneath its skin.

He knew on some level it was the mirror. Vampires had reflections in mirrors that weren't backed with silver. It was himself he was looking at. But his brain just refused to register that. It was too horrific. The visage was so horrifying that for a brief moment Valen thought, *I'm glad that creature is muzzled so it can't bite me.*

He collapsed, no longer able to carry out the Herculean feat of supporting himself. The hands guided him to leaning on the counter. "All right, you're okay. Just relax."

Relax? He wanted to throw up, and probably would have if his aching, hollow stomach had digested anything besides its own lining in the past few months.

"You don't have to talk to him like he's a puppy, Lex. He's still a serial killer, he doesn't really deserve what we're doing, so – "

"Wh – " Lex sputtered. "You're the one who brought him upstairs!"

"Only because you made me!"

They're arguing. They're arguing. *About* me. *Please, please don't argue.* They would take it out on him, for sure. He squeezed his eyes shut, trying to be nonthreatening, unobtrusive, not an issue.

He startled as the hand shifted to his shoulder, eyes snapping open. Lex's kind face was looking into his eyes. "Do you want to take your underwear off?"

The water in the shower was running. He kept drifting in and out, forgetting that they were apparently trying to give him a shower. That's why they wanted to take his underwear off. Not for anything nefarious.

He wanted to trust that kind face so badly he could cry. But the echoes of the heartless *It's gonna be all right* she'd used to subdue him earlier racked his body. He shuddered uncontrollably.

He was embarrassed. He'd never been a proud man, but he'd also never been denied the most basic rights and dignity before. He didn't want to be naked in front of them – at least, not like this. Not baring his aching, punished flesh to their hands while he was helpless and vulnerable, for them to do whatever they saw fit to him.

"You don't have to. But I'll clean them for you if you want."

They're just going to give you a shower. They're going to give you a shower. It took him a second to figure out how to even take his underwear off with his hands cuffed in front of him, but he was able to manage by sliding it down a bit at a time on alternating sides.

They dropped to his ankles. There. He trembled even more, unsure of if he'd made the right decision. But did it really matter? They would do whatever they were going to do to him regardless.

"All right, you're doing great," said Lex, and she knelt. "Ari, do you have a handcuff key?"

Ari took out a keyring and handed it to her. She unlocked the manacles around his ankles, then stood, supporting him by the elbow again. "All right."

She helped him step out of the ankle cuffs and underwear, leaving him completely nude except for the handcuffs, the collar, and the muzzle. It was hard to keep his balance, even with her there at his elbow. Her eyes swept up and down him afresh, prompted by the removal of his last shred of clothing. He also acutely felt Ari's eyes on him. His face grew hot, flush with humiliation and fear. They were assessing him, taking in every inch of him. Deciding what to do. *Please at least be gentle. Please at least don't make it hurt as much as you can.*

Ari whispered to Lex, but Valen's keen hearing of course picked it up. "Should we just kill him?"

Valen felt himself hiccupping from fear. There was nowhere he could go. He was trapped between them.

"No!" said Lex.

"Are you saying that because you're thinking of his best interests, or your own?"

She looked at Valen. He looked away, lowering his head. He couldn't bring himself to make eye contact. He couldn't look at her.

"Well ... " said Lex. "I mean, we could ask him."

What? No, no, no. He couldn't make a decision. He hadn't made a decision in months. He didn't have the capability to do so anymore. Even just deciding to take his underwear off had been too much for him. They were *looking* at him. They wanted him to tell them what to do. It was too much, too much.

"Do you want us to kill you?" Lex said softly. "We'll make it painless. If you want it ... to just end."

Valen had thought about this quite a lot over the course of his captivity here. He'd never wanted to die before. And at first he'd been thinking that wanting to die was a selfish decision. He might be the only vampire – the only *person* – on the planet with both the motivation and ability to try and shut down the blood farms in a nonviolent way, with a blood substitute. He'd been lucky enough to get formal training in the sciences, to have connections in the blood processing facilities, to marry into nobility where he had access to money. It was possible no one else could do it. He should try at any cost, for the world.

But ...

He did want it to end. He really did. He hadn't realized how badly he wanted that until just now, when an end of any sort was actually in sight.

Maybe he could be a little selfish. And what if he said no? What would he be committing himself to? Would he ever get this opportunity again?

Lip quivering, he nodded, tears rolling down his cheeks.

Ari sighed heavily, as though she hadn't expected him to say yes. "Shit. Okay. All right."

Panic set in as Lex's gentle hands turned him around to face Ari, who was pulling a wooden stake out of somewhere.

"It'll be fast," said Lex. "Then the pain will all be over."

Wait, he thought. *Wait, wait, oh God, what did I just do?* The wooden stake came to rest over his heart. Ari looked like she was about to say something before the killing blow. The fear washing over him at this – being helpless under a hunter's killing weapon – was too much, and he tried to get away, tried to step back, tried to beg for mercy.

Lex's hand came around his back, trapping him, stopping him in his tracks. He kept his hands up, chest heaving, terrified and torn. "Did you ... change your mind?"

He nodded vigorously, quivering.

Ari sighed, slipping the stake back into her belt. "Okay, then. Let's just forget that and wash you off."

W-wait, wait wait wait. Now he was scared in the opposite direction, that now he'd just committed himself to living through whatever hell was coming next. He'd probably be tortured for years and years and be unable to think of anything other than this one opportunity he'd had to escape it. But he had no way to communicate anything more complex than *yes* or *no.*

"How's that?"

He flinched as he came back to reality and realized Lex had his wrist in her gentle hand, holding it under the stream of water. To test the temperature, he realized.

"Too hot? Too cold?"

He shook his head.

"Up you get, then."

Even with Lex helping him keep his balance, he banged his foot on the rim of the tub. The world tumbled over as he fell into the stream of water. Lex's hands pulled him right side up.

"How about a bath, then," said Ari behind her. They were really going to just ignore the situation and pretend like they hadn't been about to kill him. Okay.

Lex guided him into a sitting position. He folded his legs meekly, watching as Lex plugged the tub and set it to fill. "Jesus Christ, Ari, he can barely stand."

Don't draw attention to it. Please don't draw attention to how easy it is to hurt me.

Nick's voice was at the door. "Is everything quite all right in there?"

Valen turned away. *Please don't let him in. Please just give me a break from him.*

"Yeah," said Ari.

"How much longer are you going to be? I have timepoints that, ideally – "

"Don't come in, we're having gay sex."

Valen's head was swimming. That was a joke, right? To keep Nick out of the bathroom? It didn't make any sense. He was pretty sure he'd have seen it if there was any gay sex happening ... then again, he'd never had gay sex and didn't really know what it was supposed to look like, so maybe he just hadn't noticed?

The lukewarm water rose around him. "There we go," said Lex. "Does that feel good?" He silently brought his cuffed hands to rest on the bathtub rim. *It doesn't feel bad, at least.*

"Here," said Lex, laying the bar of soap next to them. "You can do it yourself, if you want."

No, no. Please don't ask me to do something. He remembered soap, a relic from a time when he was a person instead of a gaunt, broken creature whose only purpose was to be tormented for others' benefit. She'd given him a task. He had to try.

It slipped out of his hand on the first try.

I can't do anything to help myself. Not even this.

"Okay, that's okay," said Lex. "You're doing great."

I'm obviously not. I'm obviously doing very, very bad.

She brought Ari's keys around again, and tugged his wrists forward.

Was he dreaming? Did Lex intend to unlock his wrists? The ankles were one thing, but the *wrists?* Chained wrists was the bare minimum security needed to stop him from trying to take the muzzle off.

"Be careful," said Ari in a warning tone, obviously thinking the same thing.

"Come on," said Lex, "he's clearly not in any state to do much of anything."

Stop drawing attention to it, please, please.

The handcuffs slipped off. His hands were free.

Did he dare hope maybe the muzzle would come off too? It seemed such an impossibly lofty goal, but so had the handcuffs coming off. He cautiously brought his hands up towards the muzzle. *Maybe, maybe, maybe...*

"No," said Lex softly. "I'm sorry, that has to stay on."

He let out a pitiful whine like a dog. He pretended not to hear her, shaking hands brushing against the grate over his face.

Lex gently grabbed his wrists and lowered his hands down into the soap and water. "I'm sorry. That has to stay on. I'm sorry." She twisted to look at Ari. "Are you sure we can't take the muzzle off?"

Why did I ever dare to hope it might come off? Why are you daring to hope?

Ari sighed and sat on the toilet. "Lex, you know he could just open his mouth and tell us to kill each other, and we'd have to do it."

The worst part was, Valen could not even tell himself it was unfair to have the muzzle on anymore. He *might* tell them to just kill each other. He wasn't proud of it, he never would have thought himself capable of such cruelty towards humans, but he knew in his heart he would probably take whatever scraps of opportunity fate afforded him at this point. The muzzle was going to stay on.

"He ... he might not. He might not want to do that."

"If he didn't before, he certainly does now."

Valen didn't make eye contact. He couldn't. Lex clearly wanted him to. He just stared into the bathwater.

"Okay," said Lex, getting up. "All right, let's clean you up, then."

There was a detachable showerhead, so Lex removed it and snaked it down over his head, unplugging the drain and letting the water wash over him for a few minutes, the murky residue swirling down the drain.

It felt ... nice. A little bit. The water was at a good temperature. The water pressure was gentle. He did his best with the bar of soap, uncoordinated hands rubbing it along his body.

When the water started to run clear, Lex plugged the tub again. "There you go. You're already looking a little bit better."

Lex got up and went across the room. He sat there staring into the water, tracking the bubbles. *Maybe ... Maybe ...*

Ari saw his hands going for the muzzle. "No. Don't try it."

He didn't dare push Ari's patience. He obediently removed his hands.

He flinched as Ari reached over, but it was just to turn off the water. The tub was full. In the newly fallen silence, he heard Lex at the sink, wiping off the manacles.

Maybe that would be nice, or at least a little less unpleasant than before.

She came back over to the tub, kneeling. *Don't leave, Lex, please don't leave me ever again.*

"Do you want me to help rub the soap on your back and stuff?"

He wanted that so very badly. To feel a gentle touch, from her of all people. Maybe he would regret it, maybe it would hurt. He nodded, committing himself to it.

She lathered some suds onto her hands, then moved behind him. He didn't see the touch coming, so he jumped when it happened. But she rubbed his skin gently.

"There we go," she cooed. "It feels nice, right?"

It did. It felt so nice he wanted to cry. Her touch was gentle even over his open wounds. She lifted the metal collar to wash his irritated skin underneath it.

"Close your eyes for me." He hadn't even been listening, but his eyes snapped shut instantly. Something cold oozed out onto his head, and he had to rein in his imagination to realize it was shampoo.

She ran her fingers through his hair. Since his eyes were closed, he could imagine better circumstances, that they were lovers, safe at home on the couch, and she was running her fingers through his hair affectionately, instead of this hell he found himself in.

She loosened the muzzle. He *did* start crying then, from the relief. It wasn't *off*, but it wasn't as tight. It was the bare minimum of comfort that he'd been denied for months, that he'd started to think maybe he somehow didn't deserve for how systemic its denial had been.

"Sorry," she said. "I'm sorry we can't take it off. You know you have to keep it on."

You just had to remind me one more time.

"All right, let's rinse you off." Lex stood and retrieved the showerhead again, setting it to a gentle stream. He leaned into it, savoring it, knowing the end was coming, thinking this might be the last pleasant sensation he would experience in his life.

The faucet squeaked as she turned it off. She looked down at him appraisingly, the same as she'd done before. He quivered anew under the examination.

"Okay," said Lex. "You did so good. Now, let's just get you dried off, and then we'll go back downstairs, okay?"

Back downstairs. Back to Nick, and the basement, and the coffin. Back to sanctioned torture during the day and under the table sadism by night.

He grabbed the fabric of Lex's pants, sobbing into her knees. *Please, please, please, please, please, please. I don't know what you could do, but* please *do something. Anything but back there.*

"Oh," said Lex. "Oh, shhh, shhh, it's okay, it'll be okay ... "

Again. She was doing it to him *again.* She *knew* it wasn't going to be okay. She had to. But she didn't want to see him upset. She didn't want to *see* him upset. If she didn't see it, it wouldn't bother her, if she didn't think about it.

She probably thought that made her compassionate.

"Alex," Ari snapped.

Ari was irritated. But she was looking at Lex, not at Valen. "Don't," she said.

"What?"

Ari sighed and squatted, eyes drilling into Valen. The suddenness of her being level with him was startling, and he couldn't suppress the pathetic sound that escaped his lips.

"Hey," said Ari. "It's not okay. I know it's not okay. I know it's not all right for you right now. It's actually pretty fucked up right now. But me and Lex are going to see if we can make things a little better, okay?"

His grip on Lex tightened. *What is that supposed to mean? How can you make torture* a little better? *What the fuck are you thinking?* Despite his wild thoughts … it *did* comfort him a little to hear someone else acknowledge his situation was abhorrent. Ari had been the first person to say *to* him that what was happening to him was unacceptable, rather than just telling Nick off as though Valen weren't in the room.

"All you have to do is hang in there just a bit longer. Can you do that for me?"

Do I have a choice? He'd already told them not to kill him. He kept his grip on Lex's legs, but managed a nod.

"Great." She tossed a towel on top of his head. "Dry yourself off, then."

Lex helped him sit up on the lip of the tub and lent a hand to towel him off. Ari found a blow-dryer under the sink, and Lex used it to dry off his hair and the skin under the muzzle and the collar.

"All right," said Ari, holding both pairs of cuffs. "Sorry, but it's time these go back on. We can't hide in the bathroom forever."

He almost freaked out. This was the best taste of freedom and kindness he'd had in so long. Putting the cuffs on almost felt like that was making it go away.

But he had no choice. And maybe, just maybe, it would be bearable if Ari and Lex could *make things a little better*. He held his wrists out. Ari fastened the restraints on, then knelt and did the same for his ankles.

"Do you want me to carry you back down, or can you walk yourself?"

Ari was clearly overestimating his capability to walk. But maybe it was nice of her to give him the chance to try, if he wanted it. He didn't. He remained silent.

"I'll take that as a vote for carrying." She leaned him onto her shoulder again, picking him up and steadying him with a hand across the back of the legs.

Back downstairs. He fought off the rising wave of nausea and anxiety with each step as they descended. He could hear Nick humming, hear the rustle of ashes in the furnace. Nick still intended to carry on his experiment.

Please, Ari, please, you can start making things better right now. Please?

"Ah, there you are," said Nick as they came downstairs. "Thank you so much, just what I needed ... While you're here, while we have him out, I could, perhaps, just very quickly get data from this timepoint – "

He pulled a stone cup of glowing hot molten silver out of the furnace, holding it at a distance. "I'm testing the effects of silver on wound healing, you see – "

He said it like it was the most natural thing in the world, his desire to pour molten silver into Valen's open wounds. *What effect do you fucking think silver has on wound healing? Hey, jackass, it slows it down. By a lot. Anyone could have told you that. You don't need a p-value of 0.05 to prove it.*

His thoughts could be snarky, because he didn't voice them. He wasn't nearly that brave in actuality. The pit in his stomach felt heavy. He squirmed. *Ari, please, fuck ... Come on ... Did you mean it?*

Ari turned him around, removing the view of Nick and the threatening metal. He felt himself being dumped back in the coffin, and the lid slammed closed. Without any of the extra restraints that kept him immobile inside of it.

"Ariana, I need – I need him outside of it to – "

"Sure thing." Ari held the key to the coffin out like she was going to hand it to him, then yanked her hand back and put it in her own pocket. "But, you know, I

just remembered there's somewhere I gotta be real fast, so maybe I'll come back later and help you with that."

Ari turned and hustled Lex up the stairs before Nick could protest further. She maintained eye contact as she shut the door.

Valen felt hope in his chest. Just a flicker. It wasn't a rescue, but it was *something*.

9

Valen had been given an opportunity, one he could not afford to waste. His hands were cuffed in front of him, and not secured to the inside of the coffin, and then he'd been left alone when everyone went home.

He *had* to get the muzzle off. If he couldn't get it off tonight, he would never be able to, he was sure.

He'd been trying for *hours*. He'd never gotten a good look at whatever mechanism kept the muzzle on, but he'd been desperately clawing at it ever since Nick had locked the basement door. In a time when he'd been stronger, he would have been able to tear through the leather like it was nothing.

He needed to have one hand on either side of his head to be able to open it. That much was clear from the start. But his wrists were locked together, with just about an inch between them, unable to do anything but move together to one side or the other.

If he could get his head down by the other end of the coffin, maybe he could catch it on the cuffs that usually kept his feet locked in place and tear it. He tried desperately to fold his body in the narrow space to do so, but only succeeded in rolling from prone to supine a couple of times.

The open wounds from earlier still hurt. He'd been pushing through the pain, but it was starting to get to him as he tried to move around.

This stupid experiment Nick was running, if it could even be called that. He made all sorts of cuts on Valen's body, then started pouring molten silver into half of them. To see if or how much it impeded the healing process. And when

inevitably the punished wounds closed more slowly, he would report that his results were silver impaired wound healing. Which was probably true, but also not what this piss poor experiment was showing. It was showing that *molten* silver impaired wound healing, and it couldn't be ruled out that the extreme temperature burning him had been what'd done it. No, a much more appropriate experimental control would have been to pour a metal that was molten, but not otherwise harmful to him, in the non-silvered wounds. Aluminum, or iron – *Why are you thinking about this why are you thinking about this why are you thinking about this why are you thinking about this –*

The vigor of his movements gradually started to die down the longer he went without any success. His heart sank, desperation returning as he started to realize the answer to this *now or never* challenge was probably going to be *never*.

He lay facedown in the coffin, letting his head drop onto the metal bars.

The front door opened upstairs. This was what Valen had hoped he could free himself to avoid: Nick's after-dark visit.

He let himself shake with fear as he heard Nick's footsteps approach the basement, the keys jingling. Suppressing it never helped. Why bother?

The door creaked open. Valen tilted his head to look up, where Nick was menacing him from the top of the stairs.

They just looked at each other for a moment.

"That dyke cunt took the key, but don't think that'll save you." Nick started down the stairs. "There are still plenty of things I can do to you through the bars."

Valen pressed himself into the corner, as far away from Nick as he could get, growling.

"Got a little fight in you today, huh? That'll be nice." He stopped at the bottom of the stairs, his boots taking up Valen's whole field of view. "It's so much better when you don't just lie there and take it. When you struggle and cry. I love knowing how much it hurts. I love hurting you."

He turned around and lit the furnace, dropping the solidified silver back into it. He then took a seat and stared at Valen, grinning wickedly. "Oh, and by the

way, I forgot to congratulate you. You've been here for six months now, which is how long I was held by vampires before escaping."

Valen wanted to offer sympathy, to tell him that such a thing never should have happened to him, to anyone, but even if he could have, it would have turned rotten in his mouth. He hated Nick. He didn't care if bad things happened to Nick, even a past version of Nick that was completely innocent.

"I've already told you a lot about them, huh? About how they hurt me?"

The metal in the furnace sizzled.

"Of course, you're intimately acquainted with some of the things they did to me, having experienced it yourself now." He leaned over. "How does it feel?"

It feels bad. The fuck do you want me to say?

Nick opened his mouth to continue, then his ears pricked up. Valen heard it too: the crunch of car tires on the gravel outside.

"Shit," said Nick, and he scrambled up to extinguish the furnace, tromping up the stairs.

The front door opened again. "Hello? Who's home?" A woman's voice. Lex's voice. And Ari could be heard behind her, with her usual sardonic comments.

Lex and Ari were here.

10

— • —

He heard their voices arguing – Ari's terrifying, angry rebuttals to Nick's timid statements. It made Valen sick to hear Nick talking like that. His demeanor always changed completely when he was alone and could bully Valen without anyone to see his true wickedness.

He couldn't make out the words, but Ari sounded angry. She always sounded angry, but especially now.

The basement light flickered on, accompanied by the door opening. Valen rolled, craning his neck to look up at Lex descending the stairs. Ari was behind her. Nick did not appear to also be coming down. Thank God.

Help me, please, please, Lex, please help me. He let out a strangulated wail, sticking his hands through the bars. He could only get them as far out as the chain on the handcuffs would let him, but he got them mostly out.

"All right," said Lex. "Don't worry, we're going to help you."

Yes. Yes yes yes yes. Please. Even if it's just something small. A few drops of blood. Bandages. A hug. Anything. Please.

When she reached the bottom of the stairs, she took one of the bony hands offered through the cage with her own. She was shockingly warm, like a cozy blanket or a refreshing bath. He almost cried on the spot. He would never be able to bring himself to let go of her.

Ari huffed, coming down behind her. "All right, listen, Dracula. I'm not Lex. I'm not gonna bullshit you about how it's all gonna be okay, but we know this is fucked up and we're here and we're trying to figure out how to fix it."

78

Relief washed through him. *Oh my God. Maybe, maybe, maybe this daymare is finally over.*

"I'm sorry," said Lex. "I'm sorry we let this happen. This wasn't at all what we were imagining when we brought you here."

I forgive you, I forgive you, please, please just get me out of here, I'll do anything.

Ari knelt and unlocked the coffin. Lex's hands got further away as Ari opened the cage. This perturbed Valen in a vague, uncomprehending way. He wanted Lex's hands to be close, and they were getting further away. He stretched his arms out, not wanting to let go.

Lex had a bemused look on her face. Ari's hand appeared next to him. "All right, come on, buddy."

No, I can't let go, I can't let go of Lex, she's going to help me, she's going to get me out of here.

"How about you take my hand? Can you do that?"

Maybe if I can grab Ari quick enough, it'll be okay to let go of Lex. He just didn't want to end up holding neither of them, because then he would be without a lifeline.

He snatched Ari's hand and clung to her.

"All right, easy now, just relax." Relax. *Relax.* There was a time when Valen would have been insulted by the suggestion, but even now he could hear the ridiculousness of the request.

She hefted him up – not by the metal collar Nick always used, but by under the arms, moving him into a sitting position and then helping him stand. Her hands were strong and steady, comforting, warm. He suddenly *did* feel like, maybe, just maybe, he *could* relax a little.

Maybe a little.

They helped him step out of the coffin. Anxiety flooded his system at this, this Pavlovian signal that there were no longer bars between him and someone who wanted to hurt him. But this was Lex and Ari. Lex and Ari were here, and they were going to help him.

"God," said Lex, her eyes sweeping up and down his body once more. "I still can't believe this. I can't believe *any* creature could go through all this and not die."

Please. Please don't. I know, I know I can take it all and not die, but it still hurts. I still feel pain. I'm still a person.

"We're not going to hurt you," Lex soothed. "Just relax."

They're not going to hurt you. They aren't going to hurt you. Relax. Relax. Relax.

Ari pulled a chair out from Nick's desk and turned it around. "Here, go ahead and sit down."

A chair. They wanted him to sit on a chair, like he was a person and not a piece of meat to be hung from the ceiling and beaten and burned and cut and shattered and violated in every cruel way the imagination could generate. *Relax. Relax.* He sat down.

"Hmph," said Ari. "The fucking furnace is still warm. Just getting his notebook, my ass." Tears welled in his eyes. Finally, *finally* someone was seeing through Nick's bullshit. "I'm not leaving him alone where Nick can get to him again."

That almost felt like too much to hope for, to ask for. The tears brimmed over and fell down his cheeks. *Thank you, thank you thank you thank you.* Even if they never fed him, if they just kept him locked up but stopped others from hurting him, he would be grateful.

Ari leaned forwards, eyeing him critically. Valen could only assume Lex had barely managed to convince her to come let her help him, and that terrified him. One wrong move and she would surely call for him to go back in the box.

Ari sighed. "Okay, listen, Dracula, I'm kind of at a loss here. You know we can't just let you go, and you know we can't just take the muzzle off, even if you promise nicely that you won't use persuasion."

That was what he wanted, ideally, but he knew it'd been too much to hope for.

"We talked to the director, and he said he's not going to make Nick stop."

THEN WHAT'S THE FUCKING POINT?

80

"You already said you don't want us to kill you, and we can't just take you to our house, but we can't just leave you here either. So. You gotta work with us here."

Valen fidgeted. This wasn't quite the rescue he'd been hoping for. What did they want *him* to do?

Lex sighed. "Hey, Ari, we both agree that thing Nick said about not letting him write was bullshit, right? Like, that was definitely something he made up so Valen couldn't communicate with us?"

Ari gave a disgusted sigh. "Yeah. For sure. He either made that up, or exaggerated it. I never seen any vampire use persuasion through writing."

"Yeah ... another excuse. I'm not buying it anymore."

Ari tore a piece of paper out of the notebook in front of her. "Here, get a pencil out of that cup, would you?"

Holy shit. *Holy shit.* Was this really happening? They were going to give him a piece of paper and a pencil, and read what he wrote.

This was monumental because, while Nick was full of a *lot* of bullshit, and lied about a *lot* of things to get away with his sadism ... the bit about persuasion being possible through any method of communication had been true.

Valen could do persuasion through writing. He wasn't *good* at it, but he'd done it before, when he'd first been learning the skill. Unlike eye contact persuasion, it was a tool he had in his arsenal.

Panic and dreadful hope clawed its way up through Valen's skin, curling around his brain and sinking its teeth in there. His heart beat wildly as he watched Lex hand a pencil to Ari. This wasn't the way he wanted it to happen. This wasn't what he wanted. But the desperation burned inside him like a wounded animal, telling him it was what he *needed.*

Ari bent forward and unlocked the handcuffs. Valen ground his jaw anxiously, eyes wheeling around, trying to calm the turmoil of emotions inside of him. This was the scrap of opportunity that he'd needed. They were giving him an inch, and he was going to take a mile.

"Here," said Ari, barely audible over the blood roaring in his ears. She set the pencil on the table in front of him, sliding the paper over. "It's been so long, I imagine you have a lot to say."

He didn't want to, he didn't want to have to do this. He *wanted* Lex and Ari to help him willingly. But he couldn't depend on trusting them to take care of him. That'd already gone so, so wrong.

When he didn't move, Lex folded the pencil into his hand, guiding him by the wrist. "It's okay. Just go ahead and write something. Any ideas you have for us, maybe? What we can do to help?"

He had no idea the full extent of what they were actually willing to do. Maybe they were only willing to stick their necks out just slightly for him – enough to give him a bath, or comfort him in secret, but he needed more than that. It didn't matter what they wanted to do. He needed what *he* needed. He needed to *know* it was going to be okay, not just hope that it would be so, not just be offered scraps and glimpses of being okay.

He fumbled with the pencil, his hands struggling to produce dexterity that hadn't been demanded of him in months. He'd used to be able to scribble out notes and diagrams in a blur. He dropped the pencil, and it rolled away from him.

He let out a whine. He had to do this right, do it perfectly on the first try. Because if they realized what he was about to do, that was it. The only people who'd shown any scrap of interest in helping him for months would realize they'd be better off leaving him here.

"It's okay," said Lex gently, replacing the pencil within his reach. "Take your time."

Waves of anxiety crashed over him. He had to do this, he had to do it, right? He might not ever get this opportunity again. But what if he didn't do it right, what if it didn't work and he made them angry? His head was swimming in panic and desperation, and he was almost nauseous at the idea that he might ruin his one chance to escape this hell he'd been trapped in by making the wrong decision.

"It's okay," said Lex. "I promise it's okay. Here." She held the pencil steady for him until he was able to notch it between his fingers, then lowered his hand down until the tip was on the paper.

Ari suddenly got antsy and stood. "Just in case," she said, pointedly looking away. "Just in case it *wasn't* bullshit, just in case writing persuasion *is* a thing, I'm going to stand over here and not read what he writes."

That might be a problem. He occupied himself with trying to write his name, warming his hand up to the motions of writing again, stretching the disused muscles. Buying more time. Ari wouldn't be reading what he wrote, so he had to make Lex do something that would also occupy Ari long enough for him to get the muzzle off.

He had to make Lex attack Ari.

He felt Lex's soft, warm hands on his arm, gentle encouragement. "Why don't you start writing out the alphabet," she said. "To warm yourself up. It's been a long time, and you're out of practice."

Oh God. Lex was being so kind. He hated this. He hated that he had to hijack the only people who'd shown him any kindness at all for months. But his only other option was to sit there and hope they took care of him. He couldn't. He *couldn't*. He needed to *know* it was going to be okay, not just hope. He needed to *make* it okay. This was the first time he could actually *do* something, and he had to *do* it. It felt like he was going to explode if he didn't.

He started to scratch out the alphabet, hand shaking now from more than just exertion.

"There we go," said Lex, putting a hand on his back. "You're doing great. When you're ready, try to write something for us."

This was it. He had to do it. He had to do it correctly, he had to do it quickly.

He had to use persuasion, go all the way back to those lessons on how to use the cruel, hated ability. He had to make Lex do his bidding with his own force of will. He had to be bigger, he had to be meaner, he had to be more of a presence, he had to be the most important person in the room, in the country, on the planet.

He had to project himself, vibrate the very air around him with his own demands and entitlement.

He had to care more about his own selfish desires than Lex's wellbeing. That was what it took to use persuasion.

"What have you got for us?" said Lex. "Any ideas?"

It was like flexing a muscle he hadn't used in a long time. He concentrated, feeling the power bubble up inside of him, pounding against his mind to be let out, to rush away and ensnare some hapless mortal. Darkness filled his heart, pooling like an inky, tumultuous ocean.

The pencil made shaky letters on the paper.

A

T

T

A

"Attack?" Lex guessed.

C

K

"Who?"

"Jesus, let him finish," said Ari's voice, the woman herself out of sight.

Fear and doubt and guilt and turmoil bubbled up inside him. He didn't want to do this. But he had to, he had to get out of here. He had to do it right – the persuasion would only be active for the few seconds after Valen wrote it and imbued it with the power, so if she somehow looked away or failed to get the message right away, he was in deep shit.

I'm sorry. He tried to suppress the tears, the haunted memories from when the Kithrara family had insisted he needed to learn how to use persuasion; it was gauche for anyone in nobility to not have complete mastery over it. The screams and crying and begging from the terrified test human, the clear evidence of how bad it felt. The reprimands from his husband, his father-in-law, his mother-in-law,

increasing in severity and violence each time he protested that he didn't need to, didn't want to.

Don't think about it.

A

R

Valen could see it work, the instant it kicked in. Lex was smart. He didn't even need to finish writing it out. Her face went from concentrated fascination, to panic, then to blank, hypnotized.

Lex straightened up and took her hunting knife out of her sheath.

"What's he saying?" Ari whirled around as Lex approached. "Shit!"

Valen averted his gaze as the two started to scuffle. His hands, in this rare opportunity of being free, desperately scrabbled at the muzzle, trying to find the buckle or lock or clip, fastener or whatever accursed thing had kept this on him for so long.

"Lex! Fuck! *Fuck!*"

He caught it, finally, and tore at it with desperate hands, afraid for one terrifying minute that he wouldn't have the hand strength to open it. But it came open and slid off. He'd never felt any sensation quite like the one when the bit slid out of his mouth, freeing his tongue.

"Stop! Fuck! Lex!"

It took him a moment to register that he was free, actually free, he could speak, he wasn't locked up. At all.

He could speak.

"Be still!" He croaked the command out, startled by how hoarse it sounded.

They did so, the awful, heartbreaking sound of their fight ceasing. He quivered in the silence, feeling the control of the situation drop directly into his lap. It felt ... gut-wrenching, in a different way. The roaring panic didn't subside. "Turn and face me."

They did, like puppets. They waited for the next command. Still, silent, eyes blank. Obedient. Their personalities vanishing instantly. He'd never felt so alone.

He could have anything he wanted from them, except for the one thing he really wanted, which was just to be their friend. He finally had a route to safety, and he'd never imagined it would give him such an ache in his chest.

The desperation clawed inside his heart again, an antsy, demanding beast. It didn't matter. Nothing mattered now, except getting out of here. Getting safe.

Safe.

He flicked the hated muzzle away from himself, onto the floor. "D-destroy this."

Apparently Lex thought the furnace was the most effective way to fulfill that command, because she walked over and lit it. Ari apparently decided it was her job to pick the muzzle up off the floor and toss it in.

Yes. Yes. It's gone. Gone. I won't ever have to wear it again. It's gone. Yes. It felt like something heavy had been physically lifted off his shoulders. "You will – you will remove the manacles from my ankles." He could barely walk, so it wasn't like it would do much – but it would make him feel a lot better to have them gone.

Ari knelt and unlocked them obediently.

He caught her scent as she came near, her neck so close.

He was *so* hungry. He'd never been this hungry, ever. It was some effort to stop himself from leaning forward and snapping clean through Ari's jugular right on the spot, with the scent of her flesh and blood so close to him.

But he couldn't. He couldn't do *that*. He'd never fed directly from a human. He'd never be able to live with himself if he did that. That was worse than using persuasion, somehow, in his mind. The ultimate stripping of bodily autonomy. The horrible, sickening thought occurred to him that if he'd just been docile and cooperative ... maybe they would have fed him willingly.

That didn't matter now. He'd already messed that chance up. He turned away from Ari. *Don't think about it.*

His eyes fell on one of Nick's notebooks on the table, one he'd had to watch Nick so lovingly arrange photographs into, like a scrapbook full of fond memories. "You will – will – you will destr-destroy this as well."

He startled when Lex reached into his field of vision to snatch it up, tossing it into the fire to obey his command as quickly as possible. It didn't really do much, but it did make him feel better having all those horrible pictures gone.

It did make him feel better ... but that book couldn't hurt him. There were plenty of things in the room that *could* hurt him, which he'd fantasized about smashing to pieces plenty of times.

He clamped one hand on the back of the chair, steadying himself to stand. His eyes swept the room, hunting. He pointed to the device that mimicked the sun's rays, the worst pain he'd ever felt. "Destroy this."

Ari walked over and smashed the bulb, throwing the thing onto the floor and breaking it into pieces.

This ignited something inside Valen, the feeling of power and safety and command, now that all he had to do was point and the things that had hurt him would be destroyed. He went around the room, pulling up his laundry list of his most hated objects, reliving a tour of his worst memories in this room, pulling things off of shelves and delivering them into the hands of his obedient thralls, who made quick work of them.

The furnace started to fill up, mountains of melting metal and fabric and paper. Valen got ahold of himself. It'd made him feel better, but he was still standing helpless in the basement. *This is pointless. Focus on getting out of here, on something useful.*

The only restraint that was still on him was the collar. The shackles and the coffin had been vanquished. He just needed this off, and he would truly be a free man. He curled his hands up around the metal collar. "You will – you will remove this."

Lex stared at him blankly, making no move to obey.

No, no ... Lex didn't know where the key was, or how to get it off. He turned to Ari and barked out, "Take this off."

Same reaction. Neither of them knew where the key was. He would not be able to get this off until ... until something.

"F-fuck," he stammered. "F-fine! Des-destroy ... " There wasn't anything left, was there? He looked at the coffin. He wanted the coffin destroyed so badly, but that would take a long time, and he had to get out of here. Get safe.

The two humans had driven here, they must have. He could just compel them to take him back to his house – although it'd been six months, was the house still safe for him?

What time was it? Would they have time to get there before the sun came up?

Where *else* would he go?

He had horrible visions of the persuasion wearing off, or him being unable to use it for one reason or another, and Ari and Lex ambushing him. It made him sick.

One of them would be easier to manage.

The coffin wouldn't be nearly as bad for a human as it was for him. In the morning, when people showed up, they would let Ari out. And it *was* going to be Ari. She was far too scary for Valen to feel in control of wrangling in his weakened state, the only thing standing between her steel-toed boots and smashing into his face his grip on hypnotizing her.

"You." He pointed at Ari. "Go – go, you will go lie down in there. And you, you will lock her in there."

Ari set the key to the coffin on the table, then went and lay down inside. Valen thought she ought to be crying and panicking, like he had. Like he wanted to do.

Lex locked Ari inside. He could tell she wanted to be upset, he could see the despair and panic tugging at the corners of her impassive face, struggling to break free.

She turned away from Ari and faced Valen. Abandoned her lover in a cage, to face him, a creature she hated, a perversion of everything that was good in the world.

He tried to harden his heart. "You will help me up the stairs."

Up the stairs they went. It was stupidly slow, but Valen didn't want to fall. It felt like his bones were made out of styrofoam, like they would snap if they were forced to bear any weight or stress.

He clung to her at the top of the stairs, already exhausted, physically and emotionally. He desperately wished that he was clinging to her as she offered support of her own accord, soothing him again. That he was safe in her arms because she cared about him, and not because he was forcing her to. She was stone-faced.

The van was outside. No other car. Maybe Nick was gone. *Please, please, please be gone.*

"You will – you will take me outside." With horror, he found that talking was getting harder. His raspy, unused voice box was starting to fray and give out from all the sudden exertion. His one weapon. He had to make it count before his voice failed him. He suddenly wished he hadn't spent all that time ransacking the workshop.

"You will o-open the door to your van." *Fuck*, he could feel his voice was about to give out. He lowered his voice, rasping it out slowly, desperate to just make one last command stick before he could rest his voice for a while. "And – help me – inside – and then – drive me – to – the place where – you found me."

He leaned over, on the verge of collapse, chest heaving. Lex supported him and walked up to her van, opening the door and helping him step up into the cab.

She walked around, hauling herself up and settling into the driver's seat.

With heaving breaths, Valen snapped the seatbelt into place. He had never used a seatbelt. He'd never needed one before now.

The car started. The scene in front of the van went from the washed-out gray of Valen's night vision to the color of full light as the headlights came on. The hunter's compound started to back away as the car rolled off. And they drove into the night.

11

— • —

The ride there was long and awkward.

Valen wanted to say something, to explain himself, to mount the defense he'd had locked inside ever since this whole daymare started.

But he needed to save his voice. He was terrified of the possibility of wearing out his newly returned defense mechanism, terrified that if he talked too much his frayed vocal cords would give out and he would no longer be able to use persuasion.

He was starving, unable to help himself, unable to even walk on his own, deep in human territory, and angry vampire hunters would be after him for vengeance. He was keenly aware of how vulnerable he was, of what a razor's edge he was on. If he couldn't use persuasion, it was over for him.

Still, he should say ... something, at least. If not for his own satisfaction, then to reassure Lex he wasn't the monster she thought he was.

"For the record," he croaked, "I never killed anyone." This was true, unless you counted the lizard he'd had when he was fifteen that'd died because his parents let him buy it without knowing how to take care of it.

She said nothing. It wasn't like she couldn't; he hadn't commanded her not to talk, and although it might be an uphill battle, she could definitely do it if she wanted badly enough.

He could tell she was not more at ease. *You wouldn't believe me even if I tried to say more. If I told you I won't hurt you, if I told you what I was here for originally,*

you wouldn't believe me. You have no reason to. Just like Valen hadn't had any reason to believe her when she'd said he would be okay, which he hadn't been.

The dark road whizzed by them, the needle of the speedometer resting perfectly at the speed limit. Valen cradled his head against the window, watching the painted lines fly past. He was glad Ari wasn't here. There was only room in the cab for two people, and having Ari in the cargo space back there,   trying to maintain control over both of them at once for hours, would have been nerve-wracking. He wasn't that good at persuasion, and doing it on multiple people made it even harder.

He turned on the radio. The emergency broadcast signal came out, squealing and beeping. " – issued for Marsh County. Residents are advised to stay indoors until sunrise. This is not a test. A V alert has been issued for Marsh County. Residents are advised to stay indoors until sunrise. This is not a test. A V alert has been issued for Marsh County. Residents are advised to stay indoors until sunrise."

A V alert, of course, meant that a vampire had been spotted. As though he were a weather phenomenon everyone had to take cover from. This was probably for him, right?

With shaking hands, he turned the radio off.

He wasn't sure what time it'd been when they'd left the compound, but it became obvious soon enough that they would not make it back to his house before sunrise. He whimpered as the sky started to lighten, clouds streaking beautiful orange and pink.

If they could pull over –

No, if there was a rest stop –

Maybe he could –

What if –

Moaning in terror, Valen undid his seatbelt and clambered over the center console, into the cargo space in the back of the van. He curled up behind Lex's seat, tucked against the wall, out of reach of the window. The same place he'd

91

been set the first time he'd been in the back of the van, in the coffin, being ferried to his place of torment.

He tucked his knees against his chest, pressing his face into them, rocking slightly.

He stayed that way for the rest of the ride. He occasionally looked up to check the progress of the sunlight. There were a few stray patches on the floor of the cargo space here and there, easily avoided, nothing compared to the cab. Lex snapped down the visor that blocked the sun from her eyes, saying nothing.

Finally, they slowed down, with the sound of tires on gravel. Then stopped. Silence.

Choking, Valen peered up, trying to get a glimpse of the outside. He shrieked as an unexpected stray sunbeam reflected off the rear-view mirror into his eye, pain exploding in his head. He dropped back down, both hands clamped over his left eye. The pain was indescribable. It rocked him down to his very core, grating on his bones, unraveling his DNA. Even if Nick had gouged his eye out and then poured molten silver directly into his eye socket, it wouldn't even be a fraction of this pain. It blotted out all intelligent thought.

Gradually, the pain started to fade in intensity. "You will – " He whimpered, curling more tightly in on himself. "You will go – go inside – into the house and – and you will – go into – the closet – and find – and bring to me my cloak – and boots – and – enough to cover myself."

The door opened and the van rocked as her weight left it. Valen panted in acute terror. That had been just one ray of sunshine, for the briefest second. He couldn't *imagine* what it would feel like to have his unclothed body in the sun for any amount of time.

He waited and waited, terrified that Lex had somehow managed to ward off the persuasion and was just going to leave him there to face the sun.

But no. Her boots sounded outside eventually. The back doors were thrown open, and he started, shuffling back, horrified that maybe the sun would reach him.

It didn't, mercifully. Lex stepped up and came to him. She had a bundle of black clothes in her arms, which she deposited next to him.

He unfolded them with shaking hands. Clothes, his clothes, his clothes from when he was a person and not a piece of meat. He slid the pants on first, one hand on Lex for balance. They were far too loose on him now, but they would do. The boots came on next, precious coverage for his feet, which hadn't touched anything but the bare concrete floor for months. He had trouble lacing them up with his uncoordinated hands, every motion aggravating his wounds and his broken bones, and now this new problem he had of being blind in one eye.

A t-shirt, something to finally, finally, finally cover his chest.

He pulled the cloak over himself, keeping an iron grip on Lex's arm. "You will – you will escort me into the house."

Lex helped him down and supported him as they walked across the grass. He kept his petrified gaze on the ground, on the vision of his boots moving in and out of the dreaded sunlight, afraid to look up, afraid to get a repeat of what had just happened, his left eye still burning.

His boots touched the familiar wood of the porch of his temporary house, then walked him into the shade. He almost wept with relief.

As soon as they were inside, Valen shut the front door, then finally let himself look up.

His house. It was still here. The broken kitchen window had been boarded up – by who? A neighbor? The lights were all off – the electricity must have been shut off long ago when no one had been paying the bills. He was too afraid to look out the window, but it would be a miracle if his car was still there.

"Close all the blinds."

Lex walked around the first floor and shuttered all the windows.

He'd done it. He was here. He was safe.

Now what?

His roaring, angry stomach demanded his attention first. He needed to feed. Everything would be easier if he could feed. He could get some strength back, he could heal faster.

He stumbled into the kitchen, where Lex waited obediently by the broken window, having pointlessly lowered the blinds over the plywood. He ignored her and opened the fridge.

The light did not come on. The fridge was room temperature. Of course. It probably had been for months.

Valen put a hand over his mouth, sick at the rotting smell released when he opened the door and broke the seal. All the bottles of artificial blood had congealed into a dark sludge, rings rimming the insides to mark when they had been fuller. Most had mold blossoming in them.

He wasn't sure why he hadn't realized that the blood would, of course, be inedible by now. Vampires were predators, not scavengers. They drank *fresh* blood. This wouldn't do anything for him.

Maybe I can –

Maybe if there's –

What if I –

He stumbled out of the kitchen, barking a command for Lex to follow him and help him down the stairs into the basement. Into his workshop.

He let out a screech as something moved, a blur of motion across his workbench and down to the floor. A ringed tail disappeared into the crawlspace … a raccoon. A raccoon had made its home here in his absence. He couldn't even find it in himself to be interested in the animal like he would have been in any other circumstances.

The light wouldn't come on, so Lex surely couldn't see very well with only the light coming from the very small window up at ground level, but Valen could still see all right.

His equipment was mostly still there. Some of it had been knocked over, apparently by his raccoon lodger. He braced himself against the workbench, clumsy hands swiping glassware off of it to shatter on the floor.

Were his supplies all still here? He lit the Bunsen burner, setting a glass flask above it. He went to pour a glucose solution into it, only to find it'd all evaporated, a crystalline crust on the bottom of the jar. Frantic, he looked around the workbench. A few jars had been knocked over, shattered, their contents scattered. Some of them were missing entirely – Lex and Ari had taken them, he realized suddenly; they had collected things from his workstation and taken them as evidence of his activities.

He lowered his head down onto the counter, crying. He couldn't make more. He didn't have even half of the things he needed to do so. And even if he could, it would take a long time, too long for him to stay and wait for it to brew. The hunters knew where his house was. And even if he could have waited, he knew, deep down, that it wouldn't be enough. The artificial blood had, at best, tided him over between real feedings. He still needed real human blood even with the most developed version of his product, and it'd been six months. He needed to eat.

He pushed the glassware rig off the bench as he got up, smashing more glass across the floor, his boots crunching over them with each wobbly step. He snarled at Lex to help him up the stairs, and she did so.

She stood by the basement door, watching him as he went back into the kitchen. He opened the fridge, groping in it, knocking over bottles which tumbled to the floor and shattered, spilling sludge and mold and glass shards all over the floor.

His chest heaved in desperation. He took a bottle, examined it, saw the black and green blooms of mold. Threw it on the ground, adding it to the mess, took another. Saw the deep, sickly color of the congealed blood that had never even been blood, an insufficient imitation even on its best days.

He staggered backwards, catching himself on the fridge door, and bottoms-upped the bottle into his mouth.

It tasted like dead meat and rot. He spat it out immediately, the remnants of the concoction spilling down his front. He let it fall to the floor, cracking and rolling away under the sink.

He knelt, the growing layer of blood and glass underneath him painting his knees, and he reached further back into the fridge, knocking aside obviously tainted bottles, seized by some mad hope that somehow there would be something edible if he just looked hard enough.

The last bottle slipped out of his hand. The dark desperation clawed at him again, the animal that had driven him to use persuasion, the thrumming, pounding fear and anger and hopelessness.

From his kneeling position, he raised his head to see Lex still standing idly in the doorway.

He scrambled to his feet, his front and hands and knees all slick with tainted blood. "Kn- kneel down."

Lex did so. He could see the twinges of fear on her face, the panic pinned into place and unable to be released. She knew what was coming. She saw the monster he was.

He collapsed in front of Lex, blood-soaked thighs laced in her own, talons grabbing her shoulders. He'd never fed from a human before, but he'd seen others do it. It was awkward, a trick to get the right position. He lowered his head down into the crook of her neck. He felt her body trembling, fear racking her body even under the spell keeping her still. He started to cry there, shaking along with her.

I'm sorry. I'm sorry.

He pressed his lips gently to her neck, a hand threading through her hair and pulling her head to the side. Tears slid down his cheeks as he planted a gentle kiss there. This wasn't how he wanted touching her to go, not at all.

He knew there was no going back once he did this. But he didn't care. He couldn't. All that mattered was his own animalistic hunger, and the sweet scent of the human who would satiate it.

You did this. You drove me to this desperation. What was it you always comforted yourself with ... You deserve it.

He bit down, his mouth filling first with the salty taste of skin, then the sweet, warm, *heavenly* taste of blood, real human blood, fresh from the source. The feeling of his fangs in her neck was intoxicating, drawing out the stream of life, feeling the warm, sticky substance leaking out under his teeth. He had *never* tasted anything this delicious, never in his decades of life. He wanted to drown in it.

He lapped at it ravenously, drawing out more, going in for a second bite, tearing more of the skin. He needed more, more, *more*. It would never be enough, it would never fill the bottomless hole in his stomach, in his blackened heart.

Lex trembled in his hands. "You're – " she choked out, her voice so, so small. "You're going to kill me."

He was drunk on this feeling, the power, the hot gore in his mouth. He grabbed her more tightly, held her more closely. Her skin was starting to feel colder, her movements weaker.

He broke off. Not because he'd heard Lex. But because he suddenly felt so wrong. Physically.

He'd gorged himself. He hadn't eaten in months, and he'd just gorged himself like a mosquito or a fat tick. Except his body wasn't designed to take in that much food at once and hold it. Quite the opposite, in fact.

He felt sick. Vomiting was a strange and rare sensation for most vampires, and Valen was no exception. He could feel it coming, though, his body reacting violently to the sudden dump of mass into his stomach.

He'd gotten carried away, he'd binged. His abused, starved body no longer knew how to handle this much food at once.

Valen turned and staggered into the kitchen, aiming for the sink, but he collapsed midway there, onto his hands and knees, and retched. All the precious

blood he'd just swallowed came back up, spattering onto the floor, dribbling down his already saturated chin.

He heaved until his stomach had turned itself inside out to empty itself. Panting, he knelt there, feeling the strength once again sapping from his limbs, the euphoria of feeding wearing off.

His blurry vision focused in on where he was, kneeling in a thick pool of blood spreading across the kitchen floor, the artificial blood and the human blood he'd just vomited up and the glass shards from the shattered bottles slicing his knees and adding his own dark blood to the pool. Blood, blood, blood. This is what he was, a creature of blood and pain and suffering.

He was born and bred to cause suffering and death. It was in his bones.

Why did it matter how hard he tried to be otherwise, when this was the outcome either way?

Maybe he should just embrace it. Maybe he should just be fine with being a creature of blood.

He shakily got to his feet, bracing himself on a chair, trying futilely to wipe the blood from his face. Lex was now on her hands and knees as well, looking pale and weak and dizzy. He walked past her to the phone on the wall.

He took it from its cradle with shaking hands, leaving bloody fingerprints on the buttons as he dialed.

It rang and rang. It was morning, after all. Everyone would probably be getting ready to go to sleep.

Finally, someone picked up. "You've reached the Kithrara estate."

"Hello," said Valen, trying to stay dignified, but his voice cracked instantly. "Is Priscus there? Can I talk to him?"

There was a stunned pause. "M-mistress Kithrara," said the voice. "It has been so long – "

"I want to talk to my husband."

"Yes, yes, of course. One moment."

He was put on hold. He leaned down and put his forehead to the wall, face taut with anguish.

"My sweet?" said a man's voice from the receiver. It sent a shiver up Valen's spine.

"Priscus," he said, voice warbling. "Please come get me."

There was a long pause. Then: "My little turtledove, where are you? It's been so long."

He hid his face in his hand, sobbing. "Priscus, please, please, *please*. Please come rescue me. I'll be the mistress of the house, I'll bear your heir, I won't demand to drink from bottles like a commoner. I won't complain. I even – I even have – " He cast a glance at Lex, then hid his face again. "I even have my own – my own human we can – to add to yours. Please, please just come get me. I'll do anything. *Please.*"

Utterly exhausted from his begging, voice starting to give out, he panted.

"This is an improvement," the voice purred. "Of course I'll come get you. Where are you?"

"I'm – I'm in human territory."

"Why ... are you there?"

"I can – it's – forget about it, it doesn't matter now. Just – just please, please come – "

"You have been very disobedient," said Priscus sternly. "And I will have to discipline you, so you don't wander off again."

He swallowed. "Yes – yes, sir."

"I will come get you at nightfall."

Panic lanced through Valen. "I won't last until nightfall. The vampire hunters know where I am, they're coming, they're going to find me. *Please*, Priscus, please save me, I'll do anything, *anything.*"

His voice cracked, giving out from the force of his begging. Mortified, he swallowed.

"Very well," said Priscus slowly. "Tell me where you are, and I'll get to you as soon as is feasible."

He moved his lips, trying to force words out of his mouth. He finally managed to rasp out, "One minute."

He didn't remember the address anymore. If Lex hadn't remembered how to get there, he wouldn't have been able to give her instructions. But he had it written down somewhere.

He set the phone down on the table, moving towards the stairs. He had some papers in the bedroom ... if they were still there.

As soon as he crossed in front of the window, it exploded outwards with a huge *BANG*, glass shards tearing through the blinds. Valen threw himself to the ground, covering his head.

He heard something banging open, the sound of plywood breaking behind him. He scrambled backwards, unable to muster up the strength to jump to his feet despite the terror coursing through him.

A second *bang* quickly followed the first, and this time Valen realized what it was: gunshots.

They found me. They got to me already. He'd thought surely he'd have more time than *this.*

"Yoohoo," said Nick's voice from outside, and his silhouette appeared at the window. "You didn't think we were done, did you?"

More sounds from behind him. He was paralyzed with shock and fear at how fast it had happened, how quickly they'd followed him and how fast they'd appeared. Footsteps rapidly approached from behind him—a third human to seal his doom—but all he could focus on was the terrifying visage of Nick clambering in through the window, a revolver in his hand.

"S-stop!" he choked out, trying to take command of the situation again.

It was too much. He couldn't keep up persuasion over three people at once. He wasn't good enough at it. He'd already been stretching himself with two. The

command rolled harmlessly off Nick as the human grinned wickedly, and that's when the force from behind him barreled into him.

Something slammed him into the ground, a full body press, cracking bones and knocking the wind out of him. He opened his mouth to try again, but a hand clapped over his lips.

"You're dead, fucker," Ari's voice snarled from on top of him. "You're so fucking dead."

Valen yanked his head back just enough to get some leverage and sunk his teeth into the meat of Ari's hand, more blood exploding into his mouth, feeling the tissue and bones crunch beneath his jaws.

His bite was pathetically underpowered. There'd been a time when he might have been able to just bite clean through Ari's hand. Even still, Ari yowled in pain.

But she didn't let go. That ... wasn't what he'd expected. He'd expected her to yank her hand back as a reflex, giving him an opening. If anything, she seemed to lean into the pain.

"Give her *back*!" Ari growled, Valen's teeth sinking deeper into her flesh, forcing his jaw closed as much as he could get it.

"Ari ... " said a weak voice.

There was a silence as Ari presumably saw Lex, limp on the floor. Saw what Valen had done. He swallowed the mouthful of blood he had.

The room tumbled over as Ari rolled him onto his front, still keeping her bleeding hand wedged in his mouth. Her face was full of frightening anger. He'd never seen any human this angry before.

She planted a boot on his chest. He uselessly grabbed her ankle with his hands.

She reached into her pocket and withdrew a wooden stake. "I'm not asking this time."

"Wait!" said Nick's voice. "Don't kill it!"

"Fuck off!" said Ari, but Nick's hands had appeared and tentatively blocked her from plunging the wooden stake into Valen's heart. "I'm killing this monster!"

"Just let me – you've already – !"

"Fine!" Ari snapped, tossing the stake aside. "Just hurry the fuck up!"

Nick grinned evilly and withdrew another muzzle.

Electric, full-body fear surged through Valen instantly. *Not again. Not again. NO.*

Ari removed her hand, and the muzzle went in and on, too fast for him to put up a struggle.

It *burned*. Why did it *burn*? He waited a moment for it to subside, then when it didn't, realized with horror why: the muzzle was made of bare silver, nothing between it and his skin.

He thrashed and screamed and kicked out to the full limits of his destroyed body, desperately trying to keep his hands free so he could remove the burning metal that had been forced into his mouth, onto his tongue, around his jaw.

Ari turned her back on him, kneeling and helping Lex instead.

Valen howled as best as he could, crying out for mercy, unable to fight off the silver chains that Nick had wrapped around his wrists, cinching them together. The chains burned too.

"Come help me," Ari snapped at Nick.

"What about – "

"Just toss him in the basement and lock the door for now."

Valen watched Nick through his one good eye, blurred with tears, as he kicked the basement door open and dragged Valen over by the ankles.

"Good night, you piece of shit," said Nick, and threw him down. Back into hell.

12

— • —

He'd really done it now. He hadn't thought things could get worse for him, but obviously they could, and they would.

He'd never imagined he could ever miss the muzzle and manacles he'd had on before, but they'd been a luxury he hadn't appreciated and he would give anything to have them back. They were padded and coated. They hadn't burned.

This was *so* much worse. Valen was no stranger to the burns from silver at this point. But more than the physical pain, it was psychological. The last muzzle had been on for *six months* and never came off. Was this one going to be on even longer?

He already couldn't bear it, the burning in his mouth and on the entire lower half of his face on top of the clawing hunger and throbbing aches and stinging open wounds and destroyed eye and snapped bones and the utter, complete humiliation and hopelessness. The mouthful of blood he'd managed to swallow and keep down from biting Ari's hand had been the only reward from this whole affair, the only comfort he'd had in ages, besides a single bath.

He was being punished. A warning that things could, somehow, always get worse for him if he didn't behave, didn't submit. All his will to fight drained from him. He hadn't realized he could make it worse for himself.

He'd made it *so* much worse for himself. He'd had one chance, and he'd acted monstrous. There had been ... circumstances that had driven him to it, but he doubted they would care. All they'd be able to see would be what he did to Lex,

the blood and gore he'd painted himself and her and the room with. Like a rabid dog that'd bitten a kind person trying to feed him.

He rolled over from where he'd landed when tossed down the stairs, entire body throbbing. On top of the – well, the everything – he'd also landed in the shards of broken glass from his workstation, some of which were now lodged in his torn shirt. He hissed with pain and stopped moving.

Lex ... He hoped she was okay, both for his own sake and for hers. He could have killed her if not for his own body punishing him for his gluttony. He would have drained her dry. He might, still, have killed her, he couldn't know ... He hadn't even licked the wound closed.

Vampire saliva had a special property that meant it could be used to close wounds and stop bleeding. He'd been too busy thinking about himself to realize Lex could have used that.

He stared at the ceiling, hot tears rolling down his cheeks and onto his ears. He hadn't even done anything before, and they'd tortured him so savagely. How much worse was it going to be now that he'd actually done something? Brutally attacked Lex? Fed off her with no regard for her well-being? Used persuasion on them both? Proven himself to be the monster they saw him as?

They were going to flay him alive.

What was he supposed to *do*? If it didn't make any difference whether he tried to be good or let himself be selfish? None of *them* would ever have to go without eating for six months.

He bet none of *them* would have lasted five minutes before giving in to the hunger and tearing into someone.

It didn't matter. They didn't have to think about that. They could just be scared of him. As though humans couldn't be dangerous. As though humans couldn't be pushed to desperation by hunger and pain.

Nick was going to take him back, and this time no one would save him. No one would even care.

He'd gotten a call through to Priscus. He hadn't been able to deliver the address, but maybe Priscus could somehow track his location ... somehow. Valen wasn't really sure how phones worked. He'd always been a biology person.

Valen tried to curl in on himself, sobbing. *That* was his best-case scenario. Maybe, if he was lucky, Priscus would come save him, and he wouldn't have to go back to being Nick's pincushion, and instead he would just live out the rest of his life being raped and used as breeding stock by the *second* worst man he knew.

The stairs creaked. Valen tried to stifle his noises. He craned his neck, turned his head upwards to see up the steps. Nick was standing there, looking down at him.

Valen started crying again, a warbling, pathetic sound. He tried to roll over, the glass shards tinkling against the cement.

Nick's feet stopped right next to his face. Valen's eyes bounced up and down him.

"How's the bare silver treating you?"

How do you fucking think? He scrunched his face up and averted his eyes.

Nick squatted down, seizing the metal collar around his neck and yanking him up slightly. "Normally I have to be alone to hurt you so pointlessly. Everyone else says it's going too far to do things like this in front of them."

Valen whimpered and tried to pull away as Nick slid his finger under the muzzle, on the broiled skin underneath it. "But maybe now they won't care so much when they see what you did to Lex. Their innocent, kind, warm friend Lex."

Nick's hand trailed down Valen's shirt and pulled a shard of glass out of him. "Mmm ... it's too bad you can't open your mouth. Maybe I'll figure out a way to cut out your tongue. I would love to make you eat glass. There's just *so* many things we could do with that pretty little mouth of yours."

Valen was now operating under the horrible state of affairs that he could make things worse for himself if he tried to fight back. He lay catatonic, eyes glazed over, limp in Nick's hands.

"*Look* at you. You monsters think you're gods, but you're nothing. That's what the vampire who tortured me said ... that he was a god, and I was nothing. But look at you."

Nick spit in Valen's face. "*You're* nothing. Humans can't even *reach* this state. We have the dignity to pass quietly on when our bodies are this broken. But you hang on, getting weaker and weaker with no one to leech off of. You're a parasite, nothing more."

Valen didn't respond, chest heaving in ragged breaths. Nick hefted the collar up so Valen's ear was right by his lips, so he could whisper. "I'm going to take you back, and we're going to have some more fun together. It'll be worse this time. First, I'll open you up and put silver inside you, so I can see you writhe in agony when I sew you back up. And after that – "

Valen's vision tumbled as Nick suddenly let go of him, dropping him to the floor. He saw Nick's shins as the man backed away.

"What the fuck is wrong with you?" said Ari's voice, accompanied by the creak of a second person on the stairs.

"Ari," said Nick. "I was just – I was just – I was making sure he was secure – "

"Come up here."

Nick cast one last burning glare at Valen and disappeared out of sight. The door slammed at the top, muffling their voices. He could hear them arguing, but couldn't make out the words.

Ari. He hadn't even thought of her. Ari was going to kill him, or something worse. Lex obviously wouldn't have any pity for him anymore, so Ari wouldn't have any reason to care whether he was tortured or not. She would probably be worse than Nick now.

She came back a while later, with some supplies gathered in her arms. She was alone. Small mercies.

She dropped the stuff on the ground. "All right, listen. Listen *carefully*."

Valen struggled to sit upright, pain raking over every inch of him.

"Stay still," she hissed, and Valen fell still instantly. He so badly wanted to do everything she wanted exactly as she wanted. Maybe, maybe if he was perfect, if he was docile and submissive and showed he wasn't a threat, her volcanic anger at what he'd done could be quelled just a little. He couldn't even tell her he was sorry for it.

"You get *one* chance," said Ari, holding up a finger for emphasis. "*One.* One chance to get that shit on you swapped out for something that doesn't burn. Don't *fucking* move," she snarled again, when Valen had started to desperately position himself in anticipation of the burning metal being removed.

Holy shit, please, please, mercy, Ari, mercy. He hadn't even considered this possibility, that it could come off immediately, and by Ari, of all people. He so, *so* badly wanted to do *exactly* what she wanted him to.

He also knew that this meant Lex was alive, because if she'd been dead, Ari would be treating him very differently.

He fell still, trying to be as still as possible, still as a statue. Ari huffed angrily, looking like she wanted to punch him instead of whatever she was apparently about to do. "I'm going to take those off, and put on something that doesn't burn, and if you move a muscle, or open your mouth, or look at me funny, or if your lip twitches, or I can see you're *thinking* about trying some shit, they're going back on. If you want them to not burn, you will sit still."

He stayed frozen.

"Nod if you understand."

He nodded vigorously.

Ari knelt down, huffing. She got out the handcuff key and unlocked the chains around his wrists. The burning stopped as they dropped off. *Thank you, thank you, thank you, thank you, I don't deserve this mercy from you.*

She bent her right hand, the one swathed in bandages, painfully. "Jesus fuck, you really did a number on my hand there."

Valen flinched, trembling, trying to suppress it, hoping it didn't count as moving.

"And you fucking stink. Jesus, dude, you smell like death." Ari opened a first aid kit and took out some kind of ointment. "Hold your hands out."

He did so, palm up, talons shaking with anxiety. Ari squeezed something from the tube into it. Burn ointment, he saw. "Rub this on your wrists."

A sob squeaked out as he did so, confused and overwhelmed. This was a good sign, right? Ari was mad at him, but she was helping him. That was good, right?

"All right, wrists together." Ari wrapped a clean cloth around his wrists, covering most of his hands and up into his forearms. She then wrapped the silver chain back around his wrists, on top of the cloth, and locked it.

"All right," said Ari, and she took out a balled-up sock. "This is clean, unless you keep dirty socks in your dresser for some reason." She came over and ran one hand over the wire muzzle, resting near his jaw.

"I'm serious," she snarled. "I don't have the fucking patience to figure out some other way to do this. If you open your mouth, I'm popping you before you can say anything, and the silver one is going right back on."

He didn't move. He wanted to nod, cry, hug her knees, back away from her, something. He vibrated, eyes staring straight ahead.

She removed the muzzle, burning sensation fading. He suppressed the sigh of relief, trying not to breathe. *I can be good. I can be good, I promise. See? I can be good. I don't need punishment.*

She held the balled up sock to his mouth. He shook, but did nothing else. She was obviously trying to put it in his mouth, but she'd also told him not to open his mouth, and he was terrified to misinterpret her directions.

"Open your mouth," she said.

Was this a test? No, that couldn't be right. She was just bad at giving directions. He cautiously, so slowly, opened his mouth, and the sock was stuffed in immediately.

It was followed by a cloth that went over the sock, wrapping around his head and being tied there. It scratched at the burns on his face a little, but it was so, *so* much better than it'd been before.

"Fucking hell," said Ari, looking down at the glass in his torso. "You're more open wounds than skin at this point."

He quivered.

Ari sighed and sat down in front of him, pulling tweezers out of the first aid kit. "Lie down."

Valen instantly went down to the concrete.

"No, no, on your back."

He rolled from his side onto his back, faceup. Ari made a face and started picking the glass out of him.

"Fucking hell," she muttered, taking out bigger shards with her hands, then using the tweezers on the smaller ones. She still sounded mad, as though Valen had hurt himself through his own carelessness and not being literally thrown down the stairs.

He started to calm down a little, letting Ari take care of him. The rhythmic feeling of the glass being removed was almost soothing, in a weird way.

She removed the last of it, dabbing a clean cloth over his torso to wipe some of the blood away, softening her motions when he whined at her pressing too hard. She finished up by rubbing some numbing ointment on some of the bigger wounds he had. Which ... actually didn't work, because vampires were immune to poison and therefore a lot of things like anesthesia as well, but he was touched by the gesture.

Lex was definitely alive if Ari was willing to extend such mercies to him.

Ari stood, grabbing the muzzle. "All right, big guy, I'll be back down later, I'm sure."

Valen watched her walk up the stairs and close the basement door through vision blurry with tears. This was good, right? Lex was alive, Ari was helping him instead of punishing him, she'd yelled at Nick.

But he could not suppress the burning, overwhelming pit of anxiety in his stomach. He'd attacked Lex. He felt so guilty and ashamed of himself, and he knew their opinion of him would forever be even lower. He was so *fucking* scared

of what was coming. He was sure the bare silver muzzle had only been a start. Even if Ari had, for some bizarre reason, taken it off instead of just torturing him more, that certainly couldn't last.

He nervously ground his teeth on the cloth in his mouth. This was an improvement for sure. If he hadn't been starved and emaciated, he probably could have managed to tear through it somehow, but he dared not even try now. He had to be perfectly submissive and docile, to show he was sorry, to try and take a shot at convincing them he wasn't a monster no matter how slim the odds were.

He lay there trembling on the ground, afraid to roll over or move at all for fear of picking up more glass shards and undoing all of Ari's hard work.

After a while of this, he started to hear bumps and talking upstairs. His ears pricked to try and figure out what they were doing.

Were they ... moving furniture?

He heard the distinct sound of his closet opening, the rustling of fabric.

Were they ... stealing his things? He couldn't possibly imagine what they could want them for.

Ari came down a few minutes later with a crate in her hands. Her boots crunched over glass as she ignored Valen, walking to the bench and starting to rifle through the supplies there.

Valen watched her vacantly, unable to make sense of what she was doing.

She paused, glancing down at him. "Hey, which of this stuff is the most important?"

He didn't answer.

"Like, which ones can you not do stuff without?" She moved her hand around the bench. "Hotter? Colder?"

Was she messing with him? What could she want those things for? To take them so he couldn't use the workstation anymore? To give them to Nick for his own lab? Then why wouldn't Nick come take them himself? Had they made Nick leave? Did he dare hope for that? He let his head thunk back onto the floor, trying not to cry.

"Hmmmph, fine," said Ari, taking a seemingly random selection of things from the workstation, and walking back up the stairs.

There continued to be curses and sounds from upstairs that sounded like them moving things. Then the two women appeared on the stairs.

Lex – his heart lifted a little seeing her. She looked okay. Mostly. She was up and walking around. Maybe he hadn't fucked things up beyond repair. The fact that Nick was nowhere in sight made him a bit more hopeful too.

His attention snapped to Ari, who was leaning down to lift him. "All right, let's go, buddy, time to leave."

Leave? No, no, no, no. Back to the hunter's compound, back to Nick? *No, I can't go back, please, please, PLEASE. Please have mercy. I know I don't deserve it anymore, but please, please have pity on me.*

"Do you want to walk up on your own? I don't think we need to chain your ankles."

He didn't think he *could* walk, both from the pain and starvation and from the sheer terror he was now experiencing, thinking about going back.

"Come on," said Lex. "It's gonna be okay. Come on up here."

"It's gonna be all right, easy, now, shh, shh," she'd soothed, and then left him in hell for six months. Why was she doing this? Did she enjoy lying to him?

But he had no choice – Ari's hands were around him, half pushing, half supporting him. He mounted the stairs with considerable effort.

"You're doing great," said Lex. She was getting closer and closer. He was about to come face to face with the evidence of his own wrongdoing, the signs that would be undeniable to everyone around him that he couldn't be trusted, that he was vicious and savage, that he had no regard for human life.

He couldn't look into her face. He got one glimpse of the bandages around her neck and kept his eyes on the floor, trying to suppress his nerves and the guilty and terrified crying.

"It's okay," said Lex. "Don't worry, I'm not mad at you. I understand you were hungry."

What? That didn't sound right. He allowed himself to relax just a little, though. He knew it wasn't true; it was far too much to expect Lex to understand and not be angry at him, but it was nice to let himself believe it for a while.

He let them shuffle him forward, but panic lanced through him as he saw they were taking him to the porch, and he saw the sunbeam there. He knew what it felt like now, and he could think of nothing he'd like less than to be dragged bodily into direct sunlight. *Fuck* being submissive and cooperative, not if it meant he'd have to go in the *sun.*

He planted one foot on either side of the doorframe and locked his knees, making hysterical noises.

"Jesus – fuck – " said Ari, wrestling with him. "Lex, go get that cloak, will ya?"

Lex strode out into the sunshine effortlessly, a goddess, a devil that could walk into fire and be fine. She came back with his cloak.

"All right," said Ari, and the world disappeared as she pulled it over him. "There, see, no reason to freak out."

He felt himself being carried out and down the stairs, under the hot sun, just as they had before. He whimpered. This was too much. It was all too much.

He was thunked onto the metal surface of the cargo van, and pushed out of the sunlight, mercifully, before the cloak was removed.

He was baffled by what he saw. They'd put what seemed like most of his belongings in here, down to his toiletries from the bathroom. His eyes roved around until he saw –

The coffin was there, underneath his folded-up bath towels. Lurking like a crocodile waiting to swallow him up. He couldn't suppress the embarrassing sounds that bubbled up inside of him at the sight of it.

"We're not going to put you in there," said Lex. "I promise. You're not going back in there."

That was something, right? Lex was probably lying, of course, but it might be better than being told he *was* going to go in there. He snapped back into his body and became aware of the fact that he'd hugged close to Ari's knees in fear.

112

She gently kept him at arm's length and squatted. "Hey, look at me. I'm not bullshitting you, we're gonna help you, okay?"

Really? He felt like his throat was closing up. If they were *both* saying that, maybe it was true? Did he dare hope that? His muddled brain was swimming in anxiety and guilt and his own overactive imagination.

She gently took his hands, pulling them forward onto the cloak. "You can pull this on over yourself if any sunlight starts to get in through the window. Or even if you just feel like it's all a little too much and want to hide. You're allowed to do that, okay?"

It was all already a little too much.

"All right, you got this, buddy. We're going to the hospital first, and then you're coming back to our house." She gave him a final pat on the shoulder, then clambered down and out.

The words finally sank in, just a little. Maybe he could let himself believe he was safe for a while. Maybe that would be okay. It might hurt more later if it turned out to be untrue, but for now, it worked like numbing cream.

He didn't feel quite as much despair this time as they shut the door to the van, locking him inside for their journey.

13

— • —

Lex and Ari were going to take him out into the middle of nowhere, dig a big, huge, deep hole, dump him and all his stuff into it, and bury him and all evidence that he'd ever been in human territory.

That was the only explanation his feverish, aching mind could come up with for the situation as he sat there stewing, waiting for the two humans to come back from the hospital. He really, really hoped they at least had the decency to kill him first. He didn't want to die, but he wanted to be buried alive even less. But the chances of such mercy were slim, because they hated him so much, found him so odious that they needed to just purge everything about him from the surface of the earth, to erase his mark on it.

The alternative was, what? They ... were moving him into an apartment some-where, or something? Relocating him, like he was a raccoon they'd trapped in their yard and were now taking to dump in the woods? That seemed even less likely.

As long as whatever they did wasn't as bad as burying him alive, he thought he could handle it.

Ari had, astonishingly, expressed interest in his scientific equipment. Maybe they were going to keep him somewhere and have him work on something? Did he dare hope they were interested in his own project?

Maybe they were just going to sell all his possessions for some spare cash before dumping him back on Nick's doorstep?

They'd told him they were going back to their house, though. What was waiting for him there? He shuddered to think about it. It could be anything. His imagination was good at running wild. A mental roulette wheel spun in his head to see what terror *this* new day would bring.

He just couldn't imagine going back to his old life, the one where he was a person who ate every day and wore clothes and had conversations with people and had enough energy to stand and didn't have his wrists and jaws locked together all day every day and didn't sleep in a metal box whose terrifying grip was the only thing standing between him and the most pain he'd ever been in getting worse. His brain just refused to consider it as a possibility. It seemed too far-fetched. Too dangerous to expect. Because if he had *hope* and *expectations*, then he could be disappointed, and he didn't think he could take the crushing weight that would put on him, to hope that he could get out of here and then find out it wasn't true. It would break him once and for all.

He could hear their voices outside the van. They were muffled, but he could tell they were talking about him. *Even if he's not evil, he's still dangerous* was a sentence he caught. He would take it, he would take dangerous over evil. *Potentially not evil* was still a step up from where he'd been before.

A knuckle rapped on the window. "Hey, we're back. I'm opening the door."

The doors opened, and when Valen felt the gentle warmth on his boot that indicated the sun was shining on it, he drew it further into himself, curling up under his cloak.

"There he is," said Ari. "Didn't move an inch, just like we asked him to. Thanks for sitting so pretty."

What was the alternative? Trying to get out into the sun? Scaring passersby? Sitting ugly?

Valen had been lying under his cloak in the back of the van while Lex and Ari went into the hospital. He knew that the doors were locked, and that realistically no one would discover him if he didn't move around too much, but it was still nerve-wracking. He occasionally heard human voices outside walking by, and he

could only imagine the terrified expressions on their faces if they saw him, and how they'd run off to try and find a phone to call the police, who'd call the vampire hunters.

"We're about halfway there," said Lex. "Maybe it'll be dark by the time we get home. Wouldn't that be nice?"

It would be nice. A lot of the things they'd been saying would be nice, if he could let himself believe them, if he could hear them over the crashing waves of his anxiety.

"Everything okay?" said Ari's voice. "At least, relatively speaking?"

He cautiously pulled the cloak down and off himself, so he could look at Ari. She was giving him a hesitant thumbs-up.

At least relatively speaking, am I okay? He was shocked to find the answer was yes. He still had a boatload of injuries, he was still starving, he was still scared out of his mind. But nothing was actively hurting him, and no one was planning to actively hurt him, as far as he knew. Well, except one thing ...

The cloth underneath the silver chain on his wrists had slid down a little, and a small section of it would graze his skin occasionally, burning him.

"Anything you want us to do before we drive off again?" said Ari, still holding her thumb up in the air.

He swallowed and held his wrist up so they could see the burns that had started to form there. "Oooh, poor little guy, let me fix that," said Lex. She came over and pulled the cloth up, her impervious, iron hands unharmed by the silver. There might have been a time when he would have been insulted by the patronization, uncomfortable with the babying and the infantilization triggering his dysphoria, but he would take it, he would take any kindness he was offered no matter the flavor.

Ari was giving her a death glare, though. "All right, all good? We're getting there, but it's still a while to go. Thumbs-up if it's all good."

He gave a shaky thumbs-up.

"All right," said Ari. "See you in a bit." She shut the doors.

***

When their journey was almost over, Lex and Ari stopped at a restaurant of some kind, one where they didn't even get out of the car and instead talked to another human through a crackly, low-fidelity speaker. They then drove forward a little bit and got their food handed to them through the car window.

Valen was fascinated by this whole process, which was something he'd never heard of, but he was far too scared that one of the food-slinging humans would see him to peek his head out to watch.

Their food smelled disgusting, but he desperately wished he could eat it. The one mouthful of blood he'd drank had barely done anything besides remind him what it felt like to eat, to wake up his body's appetite, to give his stomach false hope that it might be filled.

He let his head lean against whatever object was closest to him, which happened to be an end table. He let himself hope, just a little bit. It was dangerous, but so hard to resist.

Finally, they pulled over for what seemed to be the last time. Ari turned the car off. Both humans were just quiet for a moment.

"I'm fucking exhausted," said Ari.

"Me too," whined Lex.

Valen would have added that he was also exhausted, if he could.

"We'll unload all this junk in the morning," said Ari. "Christ. That should be fine, right?"

"I think so. I'm so tired I can barely think."

Valen assumed that he was included in "all this junk" and settled in for a long night of even more sitting in the back of the cargo space. At least it would be dark and he wouldn't have to worry about the sun. The van dipped as both humans

got out, slamming their doors. Valen curled up, closing his eyes. *Maybe in the morning, something will happen. Maybe it'll be okay.*

He startled as the doors in front of him opened, letting in the light that was still there despite Lex's optimism about it getting dark out.

"How about it?" said Ari.

Oh, I guess they're taking me inside after all. He started to think he might have preferred getting some sleep before facing whatever the humans had planned for him in their lair.

"Lex, go make sure the neighbors aren't watching, would ya?"

Nobody to see him, nobody to know he was there. Not that any of them would help him, he was sure.

Lex walked off, and Ari sat down on the bed of the van, next to Valen. Valen had been too scared to pay much attention, but she really did look exhausted.

He felt scared at that. Because *he* was the reason she was tired, and surely that would not improve her temper. *I'm sorry, Ari. Thank you for offering me even a little kindness despite the trouble I've caused you. Please, I know it's too much to ask, I know I don't deserve it, but please, if you just – if you just don't do what Nick did, I think I could handle that.*

Before he'd realized he was doing it, he tugged on Ari's sleeve, reaching out for comfort, connection, acknowledgement, *something* to reassure him it was going to be okay.

Ari turned back to look at him, at his hand, then at his face. And she smiled. She honest-to-God smiled. Valen had yet to see her smile. It was scary and comforting.

"We're at our house," said Ari. "Nick isn't here, and he doesn't know where we live."

Thank you, Ari, thank you.

"All right," said Lex, returning. "Ella isn't home, Delores wasn't answering the door so I assume she's asleep, and I told Abraham we're moving some stuff and it sounded like he was preoccupied with something, so I think we'll be okay."

"Great." Ari gently pulled the garment on Valen's lap. "Get your cloak."

Oh God, that could only mean they were going to take him out in the sun. He immediately pulled it up over himself, trying to stifle his terrified crying. Ever since he'd gotten hit by the sun that one time, he couldn't stop thinking about how painful the sun was.

"No need to get worked up," said Ari softly. "All right, come on, buddy." Her strong arms lifted him. It was oddly comforting.

"You'll like it here," said Lex, shutting the van. "It'll be nice." *I would love that, I would love to like it here, thank you, Lex, please, please be telling the truth.* His crying was frankly embarrassing, but the anxiety was mounting as they got closer and closer to his next prison and him finding out what new direction things would go in.

The sound of their feet on steps, the sound of a door opening and closing. He felt himself being stood upright and the cloak being removed.

The living room was cozy and cluttered. The shades were all drawn. It felt the same as the first time he'd been in Nick's basement, the start of his next chapter of torture, but nothing in the room looked like it could hurt him too much. *Maybe this is okay. Maybe this is okay.*

"Oh, shh, shh, shh," said Ari, and Valen's attention snapped to her as she came at his cheek with a napkin. "All right. No need for that."

She wiped the tears he'd spilled down his face with surprising tenderness.

"We're home now," said Lex.

Ari sighed. "Listen, Lex and I are tired as *fuck*, and we're not in any state to be making decisions, especially not ones that affect your wellbeing. So, how does it sound that you just lie down on the couch for a bit while we get some sleep?"

That sounded okay, right? They were going to let him sleep on a *couch*. That sounded incredible. He would get to lie down on something soft. *Soft.* He missed lying on something soft so bad. He hadn't realized how much until she'd said that. Was there a catch? Or was that just the most convenient place to put him?

"Is that okay?" said Lex. Why did she sound *guilty*? "I know you're, well ... " She looked him up and down.

119

I'm what? I'm a monster and don't deserve the couch? I know I don't deserve it after what I did to you, but if you would let me have it anyway I would be so, so grateful.

"I'll go get the liner for the couch," said Ari.

Dirty, Lex had been going to say *dirty*. Valen's head was swimming with such fear and pain that he could hardly think properly. He just automatically assumed the worst, trying to mentally prepare himself for when this unexpected kindness was inevitably withdrawn.

Ari came over with a huge plastic sheet and tossed it over the couch. Lex assisted, getting a clean trash bag from the kitchen and wrapping a pillow in it.

"There," said Lex. "How does this sound for now?"

He was afraid to answer. He hadn't expected to be offered anything nice after attacking Lex, and he was afraid to get it taken away if he misbehaved, if he did anything even slightly wrong. He felt Ari's hand come down on his shoulder, pushing him down onto the couch, which crinkled with the addition of the plastic.

"Is that comfortable?" said Lex. This was the most comfortable he'd been in months. *Soft, soft,* it was so soft. He tried not to cry.

"Hello?" said Ari, waving a hand in front of his face. "Yes, no?"

He couldn't say thank you. He should say thank you, so they knew he liked it, so they wouldn't take it away. Or would letting them know he liked it give them leverage over him, to threaten to take it away? Eventually, he settled for nodding.

"Okay. Listen, now, okay?" said Ari. "You don't need to try and escape. We're not going to hurt you, and tomorrow we're going to figure out a way to feed you."

Feed me, they're going to feed me. He choked up. They were going to feed him. It was too much, too much to ask for or to hope for. His brain refused to register it as a possibility, to protect itself from the disappointment. Maybe they were lying to him again. *I guess I'll find out.*

"First thing in the morning," said Lex. "We'll figure out some way to let you talk that'll be safe for all of us."

He couldn't even wish that they would just trust him anymore. He'd blown that chance already. He couldn't be trusted. He was just glad they were doing any of this, giving him even this chance instead of just tossing him back into hell.

"It'd be a bad idea to try and get out anyway," said Ari. "You know you won't make it on your own outside in this state."

I know. I know, I know I'm helpless and weak, I know I'll never make it. Please stop reminding me how easy it is to hurt me. I'm not going to try and run away.

"Here, lie down," said Lex, patting the pillow.

Lex helped him swing his legs over, so he was lying down on the couch. While Valen was concentrating on the feeling of her hands on his ankles, he saw Ari approaching with a cloth.

His heart sank as she tied it around his ankles. "Just as a precaution," she said. "It'll come off first thing in the morning."

He hid his face in the pillow, ashamed, guilty. The humans had driven him to attack, but his attacking had driven them to this, to having to take precautions for their own safety, to handle him with gloves. He should be grateful that they trusted him to be in the house at all while they slept.

"Okay," said Lex. "Will you be okay if we leave to go to sleep?"

He was so scared of them that he wanted them to just leave him the fuck alone, but somehow he was also so desperate for them to stay and comfort him.

Just nod, just nod so we can all go the fuck to sleep and feel less like shit than we already do.

He managed a nod.

"Okay," said Lex. "Good night."

She flipped the light switch on the way out, plunging the room into darkness. He kept his eyes on the door into the living room, watching their shadows moving around, listening to their murmurs, until eventually that room was also cleared out and the lights turned off.

He lay there, hearing the rasp of the crickets outside, signaling the safe arrival of night. It was night. He was okay. *We're home now*, Lex had said. Maybe this was okay.

14

— · —

Valen slept like shit. Not because he was tied up, or because he was still covered in blood, or the unfamiliar environment, or anything like that. It was because for the first time in months, he was trying to sleep out in the open.

Being locked in the coffin was hateful, frustrating, maddening safety. Bad things happened to him when the coffin was opened and he was hauled out, and the bad things mostly stopped when he was shut back inside. Being out in the open was danger. Being cramped in a tiny space was safety.

The open air seemed to press in on him. Every time he managed to start sinking into sleep, he'd jerk awake. He almost cried when he heard Lex and Ari waking up and moving around. He was still so, so tired, and now he wasn't sure he would ever be able to sleep comfortably again, if the only way he could fall asleep was shut inside a torture device he would give anything not to go back into.

He heard Lex's and Ari's voices in the kitchen, talking gently and sleepily to each other as they prepared their human food and beverages. He squeezed his eyes shut, yearning burgeoning in his chest. How long he'd fantasized about something like that, to live with someone who actually cared about you, the real you, who loved you holistically and unconditionally, to have soft evenings together and comfortable daytime sleeps, to wake up in bathrobes and slippers and give each other tender touches as you go about activities without any urgency, only contentedness.

"Did you sleep okay?"

His eyes snapped open to see Lex standing in the doorway, in an oversized T-shirt and pajama pants, a cup of coffee in her hand.

No, he really hadn't. But it wasn't like there was anything she could do about it. He averted his eyes.

"Ari has something we're going to try, okay?" Lex took a sip of her coffee. "I think this'll solve our problem."

Our problem? The problem of what, having a vampire in the house? He truly had no idea what their agenda for bringing him here was.

"Just sit tight for a minute, and we'll come get you."

True to their word, they came back a few moments later. Ari gestured for him to sit up, and he pivoted on the couch as best as he could. Ari knelt down and untied the restraint around his ankles. "Okay," she said, tossing it to the side. "Let me see your wrists."

He held them out, and Ari unlocked them, unwinding the silver chain to its full length. He resisted the urge to flinch back as the serpentine length of metal whipped around.

"All right, keep them together just like that," she said, re-wrapping the cloth on his wrists. "Good boy."

He flushed deeply, embarrassed, flooded with complicated and humiliating emotions.

She wrapped a portion of the chain back around his wrists, just one turn, and took out a lock and fastened them together, leaving a long length like a leash.

He didn't like that.

Ari kept the lead in her hand. "All right, Lex is going to help you walk. Don't panic."

Lex helped him to his feet, and Ari walked him forward, hands first, through the living room, into the dining room, through the kitchen and towards the back door.

He did *not* like that. He wasn't sure how much time had passed, but surely morning must be coming soon. He stopped walking as Ari reached the back door,

turning the knob. Despite Ari's command, he found terror bubbling up inside him again.

"Come on," said Ari, tugging at the chain on his wrists.

"It's all right," said Lex, giving him a gentle push from behind.

He took a few shaky steps forward. Ari opened the door and helped him step down onto the back porch, and then out into the yard.

The grass was soft under his boots. His terror only increased the further out into the yard they went.

They stopped dead center. No cover nearby, only the hedges off in the way of the neighbor's view. His limbs locked up.

Ari withdrew a stake. *Oh, they're just going to kill me. Easy enough.*

He squeezed his eyes shut, flinching backwards, and heard the sound of a hammer pounding. He slowly opened his eyes to see Ari hammering the stake into the ground, through a link in the chain. Essentially chaining him to the ground like a dog outside next to its doghouse. There was no way he'd have the strength to pull himself free in his starved, weakened state.

Absolute unbridled terror flooded through him. They'd chained him to the ground, outside, just before sunrise.

Didn't you say you were going to help me? Didn't you keep saying over and over that it was okay? Didn't you tell me you were going to be gentle? Didn't you give me hope that the pain would finally stop?

Was it just more fucking lies to placate him long enough for them to do what they wanted to him? More worthless reassurances to make him docile and cooperative?

"Woah, hey, hey," said Ari, and he suddenly realized the both of them had been talking the past ten seconds or so while he'd gone for a little field trip outside his own head. He felt their hands on him, steadying him, but his head still spun.

Why are you doing this, why are you chaining me outside, please, please don't leave me here when the sun comes up, please PLEASE PLEASE –

"Shh," said Lex. "It's okay, it's okay, I promise it's okay."

"This is going to be good," said Ari. "This is a safety precaution, but you're going to get to talk."

An embarrassing, desperate whine squeaked out of him.

"All right, here's how this is going to work," said Ari, crossing her arms. "We're going to take the gag out, and you and Lex are going to talk. Just talk. You *will not* use persuasion."

He nodded tearfully, shaking. *Please, please, I'll behave, please don't leave me in the sun.*

"But you know for our own safety, we can't just ask you nicely not to use persuasion. So we have precautions. *I* am going to stand in the house and watch from the kitchen window." Ari pointed to the lock that was keeping Valen's wrists together and chained to the ground. "I know the combination to that lock, and Lex doesn't. So there's no way you can force her to unlock you. And if you somehow manage to incapacitate her, or get us to kill each other or something, your only reward will be being locked outside when the sun comes up in an hour with no one to bring you inside. Got it?"

Valen's head swam, trying to make sense of her words. All he could think about was how badly the sun hurt him. He shook his head desperately, tears flowing down his cheeks. *Please don't leave me in the sun, please, please.*

"You must understand that we have to do something to prevent a repeat of what happened last time," said Lex. "Okay?"

He tried to steady his breathing and nodded.

"Great," said Ari, and she walked all the way across the yard, into the back door, and appeared menacingly at the kitchen window. Valen knelt, no longer able to take the pressure of staying on his feet, his legs shaking from fear and exertion. Lex leaned over him, gentle hands brushing against the cloth gag. "I want to take this off now. I don't want to keep you restrained unless we have to. I'm not going to hurt you. Do you understand?"

He nodded.

"Do you believe me?"

Do I believe that you don't like keeping me restrained? No, no human would prefer to have a vampire free around them. That's ridiculous. But clearly she wanted a yes, so he nodded.

She looked at him doubtfully. "Are you just saying what you think I want to hear?"

She'd seen right through him. He truly had nowhere to hide, unable to even placate his captors with meaningless agreements. What did they *want* from him? He nodded tearfully.

"Okay. Don't do that. I need to know what you're thinking to make this easier on both of us. Okay? I promise I won't get mad. Now, do you understand?"

Make what *easier on both of us??* He nodded.

"Do you believe me?"

Dare he tell the truth? Would she get mad if he tried to lie again? He gave up and shook his head.

"Okay. That's okay. Thank you for telling me. I don't know how to convince you, but it's true. I want us to talk. Just talk. I'm going to take the gag out, and we're going to talk. Ari already explained to you. Okay?"

He tried to suppress his trembling.

"Are you ready?"

This was it. She was going to take it off, she was going to take it off if, by some miracle, she didn't come to her senses in the next five seconds.

Lex undid the knot at the back of his head, her chest taking up his whole field of vision. His face burned, and he looked away.

The cloth slipped out, and she folded it neatly and put it in her pocket. "There. How's that?"

All the words that had been in a traffic jam waiting to get out of him suddenly failed to materialize. His tongue still hurt from being burnt by the silver muzzle, his voice box was still scratchy and worn-out from atrophy and then sudden exertion, his brain still frozen in anxiety.

His mouth was free again, his mouth was free, this time on purpose, he could talk, he should talk, he needed to talk –

"Maybe we can start by – "

"Please don't leave me in the sun." Valen suddenly found it in him to speak, voice scratchy and dry. "Please, please don't leave me out here in the sun – "

"Woah, hey, hey, hey," said Lex. "Don't misunderstand. We're taking you back in before sunrise. The only reason we wouldn't is because we were dead or something. It was just – it's just to make sure you have some incentive to not try to kill us."

"I won't," said Valen, voice cracking uncontrollably. "I won't, I'm sorry, I'm sorry, I'm so sorry I attacked you. I'm so sorry, Lex, I'm sorry, I'm so sorry."

"Shh," said Lex, putting a hand on his cheek, and for once being shushed made him feel better instead of worse. "It's okay. Like I said, I know you're hungry." She put her other hand on his chained wrists, on his lap. "I think maybe we got off on the wrong foot. Let me introduce myself. I'm Alexis, but you can call me Lex."

His shoulder shook with suppressed tremors. "My – I'm – my name – name is – Valen."

She squeezed his hand. "It's nice to finally meet you." She gestured towards the window, where Ari was still standing like an armed guard. "That's my girlfriend, Ari. She can be kind of scary sometimes, but that's just because she cares, even if she pretends she doesn't."

Ari's eyes drilled into him, a silent warning.

"Now, let me ask you something, Valen," she said sweetly. "And it's okay to tell me the truth even if it sounds bad. I promise I won"t get mad at you."

Why did you bite me even though you knew it was wrong? Do you want to die now or later? How do you want to be punished?

"Why did you come here, into human territory? What were you doing?" *She's not going to believe me, there's no way any human would believe this. If I don't answer right, she's going to leave me in the sun. She said to tell the truth and she won't get mad. Of course she would say that.*

128

It sounded so stupid now. Tears flooded his eyes as he started to stammer. "There's – a mushroom – mushrooms are – more closely related to – than to – plants – and – the – fiber – orange – because it – it – it's similar to – to hemoglobin – "

His disused voice cracked and gave out. He hung his head, gasping in huge, panicked breaths. He needed to explain himself, he needed to make her see, he needed to give her the answers she wanted *right now*.

Lex's hand caressed his jaw gently, tilting his chin back up to make eye contact with her. She was smiling patiently. "Take your time."

His feelings were a fucking train wreck; somehow he was angry with Lex, and considered himself unworthy of her kindness, and disbelieving that it was genuine kindness, and scared of what she was going to do. He hated her and loved her. She already believed him, but there was no way she would believe him, but it didn't matter if she believed him.

He tried again, getting over the hump with his brittle voice. "Please don't give me back to Nick. Please, please don't give me back to Nick. Please don't let him have me."

"I won't," she said, giving his hand another squeeze. "You're done with Nick. You're not ever going to see him again if I can help it."

He shuddered, hiccuping. "I was – I was – I was trying to – to ... " He swallowed. "I know you won't believe me, but please, please believe me, I wasn't ever trying to hurt anyone. I was here because I was trying to – to make – to make blood substitute."

There. He'd said it. It sounded so, so stupid now, even worse since he was doing such a bad job of explaining it. The goal had been just a distant memory until now. He'd been so foolish to risk himself for it.

"Because you were hoping to be able to drink something other than real human blood?"

He nodded.

"Why?"

"*Why?*" he choked. "Be-because – the blood – the farms – it's – " His thoughts were going far, far too fast for his hoarse voice to keep up with.

"Because you didn't want to hurt anyone?"

"Yes," he exploded, and he slumped over, weeping violently. "That's all I ever wanted. Please, please, *please* – "

"I believe you," she said. "Hey, look at me."

He did so.

"I believe you." Her smile faded. "I'm ... I'm sorry I let this happen. I'm sorry I let Nick do this to you. I'm ... I'm sorry I did this to you. I'm sorry I didn't give you a chance."

She was apologizing to *him*? He felt light-headed all of a sudden, unsure of how to process this. The wild hurricane of emotions inside of him didn't slow down, but he tried to file that one away.

Lex is sorry her actions led to me getting hurt.

"I'm sorry I bit you," he said. He was still covered in her blood, in the evidence of his shameful behavior. "I'm sorry that I bit you."

She raised her shoulders, sighing. "I ... kind of deserved it."

"No!" said Valen. "Nobody – nobody deserves that! Everyone d-deserves to feel – to feel safe and in – in control of what's happening to them – to their own body." His voice gave out again, leaving him shaking and coughing.

Lex's grip on him tightened. "Thank you," she said, and he looked up to see that *she* was crying now. "Thank you for holding onto that all this time. Thank you for not letting us beat that out of you."

Thank you. Someone had said *thank you.* Someone was telling him that this thing inside of him, this thing that said all life had value and he needed to minimize his harm in the world, that kindness was important and not a weakness and was owed to everyone around him – the thing that every single vampire in his life had told him was silly and juvenile and needed to be grown out of. She was telling him that this was *valuable*, a treasure to be held onto against the battering waves of life's cruelty. That he'd done her a favor by holding onto it, kicking and

screaming against life's savageness trying to destroy it, that he'd worked so hard to try and remain kind when kindness had been denied to him over and over.

He hadn't thought anyone would ever notice or care. He hadn't expected anyone to ever do anything other than tell him it was silly, that there was no room for it in this serious world. He'd thought it'd been pointless, a losing battle no one would ever appreciate him fighting, a pointless mission to stay kind when battering waves of endless cruelty made it so tempting to just let go and become cruel himself. He hadn't known why he'd been trying so hard until now. It was self-preservation. It was a core part of who he was. He wouldn't be Valen anymore if he let the world take that away from him. And now someone was finally seeing that, seeing him, the real him, and telling him it was good and precious and worth fighting for, instead of a weakness to be purged.

He burst into tears.

Her warm hands were on his skin again. "Do you want a hug?"

"Y-yes," he warbled.

She wrapped her arms around his shoulders, drawing him in. Planting his face right in the crook of her neck, his ear right by the bandage hiding the damage he'd done. Overwhelming him with her kindness, with the tantalizing, tortuous scent of her blood, right there yet again.

He tentatively opened his mouth. His lips found the hem of Lex's shirt. He ground his teeth on it, sucking.

"Are you ready to go back inside now?"

He sobbed pitifully as she pulled back from him. "Yes."

"Okay. We'll just have Ari come over here, and we'll get you all taken care of."

The sun rose a while later, onto a stake securing an empty chain to an empty lawn, starting a new day.

15

— • —

Valen's boots clattered on the kitchen floor as Lex helped him step up and back into the kitchen. Ari shut and locked the back door, then walked over to the kitchen window to shut the curtains as the sky started to streak pink with the sunrise.

"Okay," said Ari, giving a tentative thumbs-up. "We're good? We're cool?"

Lex gave a thumbs-up back. Valen let out a choked sob. What was he supposed to say? He also gave a thumbs-up.

"It's all right," said Lex. "Things are going to get better for you now. We're going to help you. Things are only going to get better."

This felt wrong, incongruous with his actions. He'd kidnapped and attacked Lex, and he was being rewarded for it. It scared him. He wasn't sure whether to trust it.

Especially Ari. God, he wanted so badly for her to not be angry at him. She was so scary, and he wanted her to like him so, so badly.

"Ari," said Lex, taking Valen's wrist and drawing him forward. "Let me introduce you to Valen. He was here in human territory because ... he was gathering ... mushrooms?" She glanced at him out of the corner of her eye, then continued, "That he was using to try and make artificial blood."

"Mushrooms are more closely related to animals than to plants," Valen mumbled, nerves completely shot.

"Ah, right ... " said Ari. She rubbed the back of her head. "Well, I ... Well, if that's true ... I mean ... I'm glad you weren't here for anything nefarious." Valen

132

could tell she still did not quite believe him, but she seemed less suspicious, at least. They were standing here, having a conversation, and he didn't have the muzzle on, and he wasn't doing anything to hurt either of them, and she could see he could behave. This was good, this was progress.

"I-I'm sorry I locked you in a cage," Valen blurted out.

"Hgn?" Ari gave him a befuddled look.

Valen's knees locked up. Had his apology been insufficient? Had Ari somehow forgotten, and he'd reminded her of something to be mad at him for?

"I mean ... " said Ari, averting her eyes. "That was just kind of fair play. Y'know." She cleared her throat. "Well, I – Given what all happened, I would say ... Well, listen, dude, I ... Sorry about ... all that." She looked ashamed. "I owe you one, so – so if there's anything you need, you just let me know."

Was this real? Were they really going to help him? Dare he let himself believe it?

"Let's get you taken care of," said Lex. "What would you like to do first? We can get you cleaned up – "

"F-feed," he said instantly. "Pl-please allow me to feed. I'm so – so – I'm so hungry, *please*."

They both looked surprised. Dread lanced through him. Maybe that'd been too presumptuous to ask for, even though earlier they'd clearly said feeding him was on the table. He realized with horror that if he was going to feed, it would be from Ari, since Lex was obviously out of the question ... So, essentially, he'd just demanded that Ari let him feed from her. That was the *last* thing he wanted to say to someone who was always grumpy and skeptical of his intentions, and he was *so* scared of her and he wanted her to like him *so* badly, he wanted to be the kind of person she would carry and protect in her strong-looking arms, he wanted her to call him a good boy again –

"Eager, huh," said Ari, turning back to the fridge.

Oh *God*, that'd definitely been too much to ask. He'd just gotten back his ability to communicate, and the first thing he'd done was make an outlandish

demand. Why had he thought that would be okay to ask? He really did need to feed every day for his health, but he didn't need it to *live*, so eating was probably a luxury for him from their point of view. They hadn't said *how often* they would feed him, maybe they'd meant they would feed him after he'd earned it, or not every day, or down the road, or –

Ari bent over into the fridge, behind the door. Valen twisted his hands in the hem of his shirt. There was no reason why they couldn't start feeding him today, right? That wasn't unreasonable to hope for, right? There was no reason why they would be mad at him for asking that, right? They'd said they would.

They'd *said* they would; it didn't mean they were *going* to.

They'd said they *would*, so why would he ask for it? Why would he push them when he was clearly already on the precipice of falling back into being viewed as a dangerous predator?

Would they take this to mean he couldn't think of anything besides blood? Would they put the muzzle back on? Would they give up on him and take him back to Nick? This was their blood—their *bodies*—why had he dared to ask for it? Why couldn't he have just waited until they offered? Were they going to put the muzzle back on? Would they think he was dangerous? Would they think he was an animal who could only think of blood? Would they put the muzzle back on?

He wasn't helpless anymore, though. He could use persuasion if he needed to, although he really, really didn't want to, given how badly it'd gone last time.

"Hello?" said Ari, waving her hand in front of his face. "Earth to Dracula."

He snapped back into his body. Ari stood in front of him with a sealed medical bag of some kind –

Blood, a pint of blood.

"Like I was trying to say," said Ari with a grin. "Today's your lucky day, my man, cuz it turns out if you're at a hospital to get stitches, all you need to do is flirt with the nurse a little bit, tell her you're vampire hunters, and fudge the

explanation for what you're going to use it for, and they'll just give you some blood."

"G-give it to me!" Valen snapped, and then drew back again, hand over his mouth, convinced that at any moment the desperation leaking into his actions would convince them to give up on this whole venture of seeing him as a person and giving him a chance.

"Hold on a second," said Ari, drawing it back. *Here it comes. They're going to make me earn it, they're going to make me humiliate myself somehow like Nick did, make me debase myself for it.* He couldn't peel his eyes away from the turgid sack, saliva pooling in his mouth. He would do whatever they asked, he knew he would, he was desperate. He was *desperate.*

He once again wrestled with the urge to just use persuasion to take it. But he *couldn't.* He was trapped in their house, during the day, that would only make everything worse for him, to prove he couldn't be trusted. But ... he wanted it *so* badly.

Lex's hand was on his back, rubbing it comfortingly. "Didn't you throw up ... before?"

When you almost killed me? Valen's eyes rolled from Ari to Lex in terror. *I did, yes, I fed from you and almost killed you and then just vomited it all back up, wasting your blood, I'm sorry, I'm sorry.*

"So, how much of this do you think your stomach can handle?" said Ari. "Decide beforehand, so you don't get carried away."

"For a human who was breaking a fast, we would probably give them crackers or something," said Lex. "Something light, so they don't get sick. You know?"

"Do you want just a little bit, and we can wait a bit to give you more?" said Ari. "Or, maybe, I don't know, we can thin it out with water or something?"

That made sense. Valen tried to steady his pounding heart. This was so stressful. He felt like if he made the slightest mistake, or showed too much interest, or not enough, this would all evaporate and be replaced by more chains. But that made sense, they were being sensible ... His clawing, aching stomach demanded

that he answer to drink the whole thing at once. Maybe there would be no *later*, maybe there would be no returning to this precious, unexpected mana from the heavens ...

But the acrid sensation of vomiting up precious blood had been so vile that he had no desire to repeat it. "If ... if you dilute it with water," said Valen, choosing his words carefully, painstakingly, like he was in a minefield. "M-maybe half of that would be a good start. Thank you."

Ari smiled. "There we go. Let's give it a try."

She turned and put the bag on the sink. Lex fetched her a drinking glass, then came back over to help Valen stand.

Ari lowered the bag into the sink to contain any spills, then cut it open with a pair of scissors.

The second the bag was open, the scent of all that blood, right there, jammed itself into Valen's nose and up into his brain, rocketing straight into whatever dark, primal part of him was responsible for keeping him fed. It bypassed his higher brain functions, his logical thoughts, a thrumming, violent, demanding urge gripping him in an icy claw and moving his limbs on impulse.

He'd slammed into Ari in an instant, clawing past her to get the bag, knocking it over, growling over the sound of the two women shouting distantly. Red was all he could see, blood, blood, blood, he needed it now, he *needed* it, he needed it more than anything, he couldn't let them stand in the way, he needed it *now*.

His weakened body had delivered a few blows which would have once broken human bones, but Lex and Ari recovered from the surprise attack quickly. He felt his limbs being wrenched back, slamming him into the counter, arm twisted behind his back, their legs pinning his own.

Horror flooded him as he realized what had just happened, and phased back in to hear Lex and Ari's voices.

"Easy, easy!"

"Woah, woah – "

"Stop, stop – "

"I've got him."

"We've got you."

"I'm sorry!" he sobbed instantly. "I'm sorry! I'm sorry! I – I didn't mean to – I didn't mean to!"

He tried to stand back up, but a hand came into his hair, pressing him back down. He was stuck in place looking at the sink, watching what remained of the blood in the bag leaking out and down the drain. Tears filled his eyes. They'd really been going to feed him, and he hadn't been able to control himself for five seconds, and he'd attacked them and spilled the blood, wasted the opportunity. There probably wasn't any way to come back from this, even if they'd been shockingly patient with him till now.

He almost used persuasion. He had something to lose now, though. If he proved he couldn't be trusted with his mouth, the gag would be coming back, or the bit, and with it the crushing helplessness.

He *thought* about using persuasion anyway. He really did. He stood no chance at getting away now, with the sun rising outside, a full day of terrible sunlight ahead of him, but he was just so scared. And hungry.

He tried to writhe forward and lick just a little of the blood from the sink while he still had the chance, before he went back to hell. It was right there, so tantalizing. Oh, it smelled like it was AB positive too, his favorite kind. The hand in his hair tugged him back, flattening him against the counter.

"Please," he wept. "Please just let me lick the sink, I'll do anything, I'm sorry, I'm so sorry, please – please have mercy, please just let me – "

"Easy," said Ari's voice, and the legs behind him pressed into him even further, stifling his squirming. "Easy. Take it easy. Breathe. Sit still."

He tried. But the blood was *right there*, and they were certainly not going to feed him *now.*

"Lex, turn the water on."

"No," Valen cried. "Please, please, please just let me – "

Lex's manicured hand appeared to turn on the faucet, rinsing the bag and sending the remaining blood down the drain. He tried to scramble towards it again before it disappeared, but the hand keeping his arm twisted behind his back pressed down, and a second hand came and pinned his other wrist to the counter.

He *almost* used persuasion again. He wanted to. But he couldn't. That would make everything so much worse for him. He wrestled with himself bitterly. The tears spilled over as the scent of blood faded.

"This isn't going to work if you can't control yourself," growled Ari. "We're trusting you to behave in a civilized way."

"I'm sorry. I – I – I – I didn't mean to, I-I-I'm trying."

"All right," said Ari, voice just as firm as her hands. "Just stay still."

He went limp, heaving, hopeless. Things *had* been looking like they could get better. But he was truly some kind of wild animal now.

"Lex, are you hurt?"

"No, are you?"

"No."

He felt Lex's warm hand on his back again. "It's okay," she said. "See? You didn't hurt us. We're okay. You're okay."

I'm okay. It's gonna be okay. He wanted to believe it so, so badly. "I'm – I'm – I'm sorry."

"It's all right," said Lex. "Don't worry. We're going to help you."

He let out a series of half-relieved, half-anxious sobs. They still wanted to help him. Maybe he hadn't fucked it up beyond repair. Maybe he dared hope they could be patient with him. Maybe he dared hope they could see beyond what was directly in front of them and believe he had something more in his heart than the desperate, clawing violence he'd been driven to.

"We're going to help you," said Ari. "But we're going to do it in a way that *doesn't* put me and Lex at risk. Understand?"

"Yes, I understand, I understand, sir – m-ma'am."

"Because Lex lost a *lot* of blood, and if she loses more, or reopens her stitches, you could hurt her really badly."

"I – I know, I'm sorry, I d-didn't mean to – "

"We know you're hungry," said Lex, "and we know you're scared, and in pain, and we know people do things they wouldn't otherwise do when they're scared and in pain and hungry."

Valen sobbed, eyes on the counter in front of him.

"But that doesn't change the fact that you can hurt us even if you don't mean to," said Ari. "This might have been too big of a leap. We'll do baby steps."

"Th-thank you," said Valen, body wracked with tremors. "Thank you, ma'am, thank you."

"Lex, go get the muzzle."

"*No!*" Valen cried, stomach flipping, once again fighting the urge to just use persuasion and high-tail it out of there, rising sun be damned. His body instantly ratcheted back up to the maximum levels of panic. "Please, please, no! Please don't put the muzzle back on! Please, please, I'll do anything, *anything*, I'm begging you – "

"Relax," said Ari emphatically, a command. "Hey, relax. We're not going to use the bit. You'll still be able to talk. It'll just be a barrier between you and lunging at us again. We know you didn't do it on purpose, but we still need to prevent it from happening again."

"But, Ari," said Lex, dismayed, "the muzzle we have burns him."

"Go get some duct tape too."

Lex pattered away.

Valen tried to stop his enormous, shaking sobs. "I'm – I'm sorry, I really am. I won't – you don't have to feed me, I don't need blood, you don't need to put the muzzle back on. I won't eat if it means I have to put the muzzle back on."

"Sorry," said Ari. "That's not gonna fly. As long as you're one sniff of blood away from going berserk – "

The muzzle was too much. He couldn't. He *couldn't*. Valen decided to cut his losses and use persuasion while he could. "You *will –* "

Ari's hand clapped over his mouth instantly, the same one he'd bitten before when she'd done so, bandages and all. Her voice was low and menacing. "I *know* you weren't about to use persuasion, because if you *were* going to use persuasion, that would mean I would have to put the bit back in to stop you from talking, and we're *not* going to do that, so you *weren't* about to use persuasion, right?"

He let out a soft whine.

"Now I'm going to take my hand off, and we're going to go back to the way we were just talking before, right?"

"Mmm-hmm."

Lex's footsteps could be heard, and he saw her hand out of the corner of his eye, placing the muzzle on the countertop, a few feet in front of him. Tears of despair instantly brimmed over.

"Go get the chain from outside too."

Valen felt so ashamed of himself, so scared of what he'd turned into, that they felt the need to do this. Lex went out the back door and came back with the silver chain.

Valen heard duct tape ripping behind him. Lex's hand came back and took the muzzle out of his sight. More duct tape sounds. Then it came back into sight, the metal wrapped tightly in tape, not a spot showing.

"All right," said Ari. "Try not to panic. You're okay. You're safe."

You're safe. You're safe. You're safe.

Ari's hands eased up, returning him to a standing position. "There we go," she cooed. "Nice and easy, now. Turn around, please."

He did so slowly. Ari and Lex were both leaning over close to him, concern on their flushed faces.

"All right," said Lex. "You're okay."

"I'm going to attach the chain to this hook," said Ari, gently running her finger along the metal collar still attached to his neck. "We're not going to bind your

hands. We're just going to make it harder to bite and lunge, so you can stop yourself before you hurt us. Your hands will be free, and you'll still be able to talk. Then you'll get to eat."

"Please," said Valen tearfully. "I – I – I – " He wanted to eat *so* badly, but he also desperately wanted to keep the muzzle off, and he couldn't decide which he wanted more, or if he had any chance of convincing them anyway.

"Do you think you can handle that?" said Ari. "It's just as long as you can't keep yourself from lunging when you smell it. Okay? We're leaving your hands free, we're trusting you to work with us here. We know you want to feed without hurting us. Think you can handle that?"

They were still going to feed him. It was almost too much to hope for, even at the cost of having to wear the muzzle. But feed him with what? He'd wasted the blood they'd already had. He assumed maybe Ari would cut her arm or something. That seemed like way too much to hope for, especially since it had been his own mistake. And while wearing the muzzle ... what was their plan? He dare not ask.

"If you can't, it's okay to say so," said Lex. "We'll think of something else."

"I can handle it," he said, instantly worried the *something else* they might think of would be even worse. "I can – I can handle it, thank you, thank you for trusting me. I won't bite you, I won't use persuasion." His chest hitched. "Thank you for trusting me."

Lex put her hand on his shoulder. "Thank *you* for trusting *us.*"

All of them knew he didn't really have much choice, but it made him feel better nonetheless.

He tried not to flinch away as Ari clipped a carabiner onto the ring on the collar. Lex handed her the silver chain – the front end of it had been wrapped in duct tape, to prevent it from burning him in the places where his shirt might not cover him.

"Just stay still," said Ari as she clipped the carabiner through the chain. "There we go. Good boy."

Heat rushed to his face as Ari tugged the chain. "Okay, let's go into the living room." Lex helped him walk as Ari led him out. "Kneel down here, please."

She was directing him in front of the radiator. That seemed okay. Not too scary. It would be warm, and they probably wanted to use its weight to connect the chain to. If he ever managed to get his strength back, he would be able to rip the radiator from the floor with one hand, but as it stood now, it would be an effective barrier to him lunging.

Ari connected the chain to the radiator with the combination lock from earlier. "There," said Ari. "Does that feel okay?"

"Y-yes," said Valen, curling up on the floor. "Th-thank you." He could at any time unclip the carabiner and free himself. He was free. He wasn't trapped. He was okay. *I'm okay. I can get free if I want to.* But if he could sit still, they would feed him, and he wanted that so badly.

"Okay," said Lex, putting a few more loops of tape onto the parts of the muzzle that would touch his skin. "Are you ready for this now?"

"Y-yes ... No! Yes. Yes, I'm ready."

"O-okay," said Lex. "I'm going to put it on now."

Valen tried to steady his trembling as Lex approached with the horrid device. *The bit is gone. There's nothing on it to stop you from talking. Your hands are free. You can just reach up and take it off. You can just take it off. Just let her put it on. It won't hurt. Just let her put it on.*

The tape-laden metal brushed his face, sliding into place as Lex came behind him and tightened the buckle.

He freaked out, pawing the muzzle off like a dog, whimpering and throwing it to the ground. He immediately wrung his hands and started apologizing. "I – I'm sorry, I tried not to – it was – it was a reflex – I'm sorry."

"Okay, that's okay," said Lex. She gave him a reassuring touch and reached down to pick it back up. "Here, why don't you take it, and put it on when you're ready."

He eyed the proffered device warily.

"You don't have to put it on until you're ready," said Ari. "But we're not going to feed you until you have it on. Okay?"

"O-okay," said Valen. If he was going to act like a shark that went into a feeding frenzy whenever he smelled blood, it only made sense that they needed to protect themselves. They were doing their best given the situation. They were being *remarkably* patient and kind to him, more than he expected. He dared let himself believe they actually cared about his well-being, despite how thoroughly terrified he was of being restrained.

He took the device from her, and she stepped back. They both just watched him, giving him time.

He blinked back tears as he looked at the muzzle. *I'm in control, I can put it on, I can take it off, it's okay. It's okay.* He lifted it to his face with trembling hands, holding it there, fumbling with the belt with uncoordinated hands. "Can you – can you please – help me – "

Lex came over before he even finished asking, securing the buckle. "There, is that okay – "

"Let me – " Valen said, panic rising again. "Let me just-just-ust take it off again."

Lex backed away. Valen struggled to undo the buckle, then eventually got it to snap off. The muzzle fell into his lap.

"All good?" said Ari, with a thumbs-up.

"Y-yes," said Valen. "J-just let me ... just let me put it on and take it off a few times."

He did so, getting gradually better at doing and undoing the buckle. Trying to impress upon his screaming, alarmed brain that the muzzle came on and off now, it wasn't a permanent fixture, he was in control of it, he could take it on and off.

"O-okay," he said, doing it up for the last time, and folding his hands in his lap. "I think I'm ready now. I think I'm ready. P-please."

"All right," said Ari. "You stay here. Me and Lex will bring it to you. Stay *there*, just like that. If you take the chain off, our priority goes from feeding you to restraining you. Got it?"

"Yes," said Valen. "Thank you. Thank you."

He watched them go into the kitchen, opening the fridge again. Relief washed through him as he saw three more bags of blood inside. They'd been smart enough to not get just one.

Ari repeated what she'd done before, setting it in the sink and cutting it open with scissors.

Even though Valen was prepared for the impulse this time, he still instantly slammed the full length of the chain, choking himself, clawing the floorboards, shrieking and growling. The sight was apparently so ghastly that Lex and Ari looked over their shoulders in alarm. Valen did not have the presence of mind to free himself even if he'd thought it was a good idea.

Feed, feed, you need to feed. Blood, you need blood, you need to kill, you need blood. Blood's been spilled, and you need to feed.

Gradually, as he adjusted to the presence of the smell, red crept out of the edges of his vision; gasping and shaking, he came down from the monstrous urge. He'd never felt *anything* like this before: the removal of all capacity for logical thought, the overwhelming animal instinct.

They're bringing it over here. You don't need to do anything. His hands splintered the floorboards as he gripped them savagely. *Just stay still.*

Ari had a drinking glass with a straw in her hand, filled with light-red blood, presumably diluted. "All right," she said, bringing it in. "Good job, you're doing good. Back up a little bit."

He shuffled backwards, the hope of being allowed to feed washing away all the lingering shame and embarrassment he had.

Ari set the glass down on the floor next to his claw marks, within his reach, and then backed up. "All right. Go ahead. All yours. Drink it slowly, so you don't get sick."

Valen crawled forward, extending his hand to take the glass. His unsteady hand knocked it over instead, spilling the blood all over the wood floor.

He whimpered. How many times could he mess up before they ran out of patience and stopped trying? "I-I'm sorry."

"It's okay," said Lex.

He *had* to get some of that into his mouth before they quit on him. He knelt and tried to lick the blood off the floor, pressing the mesh muzzle into it. After a second, he wet his hands with the diluted liquid and tried to push it through. Anything to get it in his mouth.

"We still have the other h – No. No, no, don't do that."

"Please – " said Valen as Ari came over and gently took the chain, hauling him back, sliding him across the wooden floor. "Please – just let me – "

"You don't have to eat off the floor," said Lex. "We'll get you a new glass."

"Don't lick the floor," said Ari. "We don't do that here. We're all people. We all get treated like people. People don't make other people eat off the floor."

Valen's watery eyes remained on the circle of blood pooling on the floor. He knew they were trying to force him to have some dignity, trying to keep him from sliding further into his own degradation, but all he could think about was how much he wanted to feed, and how close he'd gotten without actually doing it yet.

He watched morosely as Lex threw towels down, absorbing the mess, while Ari went back to the kitchen and ran more water, making another glass.

She came back over, and both of them knelt in front of him. "Come here, big guy," said Ari. He tentatively crawled over, staying at arm's reach, not further.

"Give me your hands," said Ari.

He extended them out. Ari took one and used it to pull him closer, his thighs sliding across the wooden floor. Then she put the glass in his hand, using both of hers to fix both of his onto the glass.

"You got it?"

"Y-yes," he said. "B-but I'm not sure if I have the – hand strength to lift it to my mouth."

Ari smiled gently. "That's what the straw is for."

Valen tentatively lowered his head when Ari didn't remove her hands. Lex held the straw steady so he didn't have to struggle to get his lips on it, poking it through the muzzle, and he sucked.

Finally. *Finally.* Tears welled up in his eyes again. It felt good. It felt so good. Not like ripping Lex open, no, nothing could compare to giving in to the animal desire to ravage someone like that, nothing would ever fulfill such a primal desire again. But this was better, in a way. This was a gentle feeding. There was no shame, no pain, no violence. He could be happy if the future was like this. The cool, rich liquid wet his parched mouth. He could feel the cool sensation going down his throat, slowly, a trickle. Ari's hands keeping him steady rebuffed whatever desire he had to upend the glass and drink it all at once.

The refreshing sensation reached his stomach, the bare, cracked pit that had once been filled regularly. His body cried out with gratitude at its salvation.

"There we go," said Ari, as he continued to obediently sip. She removed one hand and stroked his hair. "Good boy."

He shuddered and flushed.

"I'm not sure if he likes it when you do that," said Lex.

Oh no, please stop looking at me, please stop seeing. Valen tried to hide his expression.

"See, he's embarrassed," said Lex.

Ari huffed a laugh. "Lex, that's exactly what you look like when I play with your hair and call *you* a good girl."

It was Lex's turn to blush. Under normal circumstances, Valen would have been anxious, because apparently this was a *thing* that these two shared, and there was *so* much to be worried about with the implications of that.

But he couldn't bring himself to care about anything except the heavenly, sweet, gentle flow of blood into his mouth. Maybe this was the start of good things.

16

— ◆ —

They both sat there talking to him encouragingly until he'd downed the glass, the straw slurping at the empty bottom. When he started trying to swipe the remnants out of the glass to lick his finger, they took it and refilled it.

He drank three full glasses in the end before they reached the bottom of the pint of blood. Ari suggested they wait a little while to open another one, to let his stomach settle. Valen agreed to this.

"Are you starting to feel a little better?" said Lex, squeezing his hand.

Valen flushed and looked down. He *was* feeling better. The food was already starting to help. But it was also psychological. Someone had fed him. Someone cared enough to help him. "Y-yes, thank you."

"How about a bath, then, huh?"

Valen had been so focused on his hunger he'd completely ignored how utterly filthy he was. The rotten artificial blood smelled truly disgusting. Humans' sense of smell was poor, but probably even they could smell it. "O-okay."

"Go ahead and unhook yourself."

Valen reached up and took the muzzle off, a simple act of freeing himself that had been so impossible just a few days ago. It already felt like the first bath he'd taken not that long ago was years in the past. He set the muzzle on the ground, then unclipped the chain from his collar.

As Lex helped him stand, Ari crossed her arms. "Hmph. We'll have to figure out some way to get that off you eventually. We don't have the key."

147

"O-oh," said Valen, deflating. He'd secretly been hoping they'd take the collar off soon. It was the last restraint on him, but it was locked.

"Well, we can work on it," said Ari. "Hey, do you want me to carry you up to the bathroom? Our stairs are a bit fucky." Valen looked past her to see the stairs up to the second floor: they were uneven wood, some with exposed nails, and quite steep. They were, indeed, a bit fucky.

"If – if – if you want to," said Valen, voice quiet, trying not to sound too excited. "That – that would be – appreciated, ma'am."

"All right, up you go, then." He tried to suppress his reflex to flail and grab things to stop himself from falling as Ari scooped him up, one hand on his back, the other under his thighs. He slid into her chest, arms curled up, blushing fiercely as she carried him bridal style.

Ari looked down at him and winked, and he averted his eyes quickly. "Hold on, bat boy."

Valen did not think he could get any redder, but his body kept finding more blood to send to his cheeks and ears. He could see Lex smirking in an amused way behind Ari. He worried about what it could mean … They were teasing him, that's all, surely. Not that they were angry at him, or threatening him. Just good-natured teasing.

It was the first time in his life he found he didn't mind it.

Ari carried him up the stairs. It reminded him of the first time, when she'd done it over her shoulder, with his arms still cuffed and the muzzle still on, as he'd given Lex desperate pleading eyes, hoping against hope for some compassion.

"There we are," said Ari, setting him down in front of the bathroom. "Taxi dropping you right off. Have a good time."

"I imagine you'd like some privacy," said Lex.

"We'll get you a towel and stuff, and you can take as long as you want," said Ari.

"Um – " said Valen. "I – I – I might need help getting in and out of the tub. You can – you can stay, if you want. If you want to. Please. You don't have to."

Ari quirked an eyebrow. "Eh?"

"You don't have to." Would they think he was dirty, perverted for wanting that? *He* certainly felt that way.

"Start running the water, Ari," said Lex. "I'll be back with the towel."

Their bathroom was dirtier than the one in the hunter's compound, the mirror slightly cracked, but it had a lived-in feel that was comforting, even if all the hair everywhere was kind of gross. Ari squatted next to the claw-foot bathtub and started the water, running her hand under it.

Valen clutched his hands to his chest as he caught sight of himself in the mirror again. He barely recognized himself under the burns on his face – but this was better than the first time. That was him, under the muck and despair; he could see himself there now, as though he were being excavated out.

"Hey," said Ari, and he turned to see her watching him stare at himself in the mirror. "Come here, kiddo."

Surely Valen had to be decades older than her. But he sat on the toilet next to her without complaint.

"We're gonna get you cleaned up," said Ari. "And we're gonna help you get better. There's no need to look at yourself like that."

He looked down at his lap.

"Now, do you wanna keep all your clothes on, or take a proper bath?"

"I've got a towel," Lex sang, coming back in. "Bath time, then?"

Ari closed the flow of water. "Do you want us to look away while you undress?"

"I – I think I'll fall down if I have to – I think I need help to – "

"All right, that's okay, I'll help you," said Lex.

He pulled his shirt over his head, then would have lost his balance if not for Ari's hand on his back. He let it fall to the floor, then leaned over and pulled his pants down, again only staying upright because of the two women holding him up.

He was just as emaciated as before, and just as injured, but the motions of his hands were less unsure.

"Are you sure you don't want some privacy?" said Lex.

They had already seen all of him and more, been privy to his most brutal debasement and his lowest points. The concept that his mere nudity would mean anything in front of them was laughable in his mind, but he appreciated the gesture. "I don't mind."

"Okay," said Lex. "As long as it's what you want."

It felt like navigating a minefield to talk to them. He still had no idea why they'd changed their minds, and they could change them back at any moment. Valen pulled his underwear down, then turned to step up into the bathtub. He had free use of his hands this time, but just as he'd predicted, he still banged his foot on the ledge trying to step up into it.

"I gotcha," said Ari, steadying him. She picked him up and lowered him into the water.

She let go, and he sank down into the warm water, tub luxuriously deep.

"It's nice?" said Lex.

"Yes," he said, eyes watering. "Th-thank you."

Lex shrugged. "Well, we kind of had to." *No, you really didn't. You definitely could have gotten away with leaving me in hell.* Lex produced a folded-up washcloth, sliding it onto the edge of the tub. "Here, the soap's over there. We, ah, don't have one of those nice detachable shower heads, so we'll just have to refresh the water more than once."

Part of Valen wanted her to use the washcloth with her own hands, but he knew it would be inappropriate to ask her to do that. He took the washcloth and wet it, then rubbed the soap on it.

He started washing the copious blood off his face. He'd known he was filthy, but he was still surprised by the amount of blood that came off, the speed at which the water turned rusty red. "O-oh," he said, peeling more grime off. "I – I – I'm – It must have been ghastly to – to look at me like this the whole time."

"I'll start getting your stuff out of the van," said Ari. "You'll need some new clothes." She prodded the pile of vile, blood-soaked clothes on the floor. "Um, do you think it's worth trying to save these? Can we just get rid of them?"

"If – if – I can mend the holes, if you – if it's not too much trouble to launder it – if you have a – supplies – to sew."

Ari grimaced. Had that been a mistake? Had they wanted to get rid of them? But she reached down and picked up the clothes without complaint. "Right ... I'll go throw this in the wash, then. We brought all the clothes you had in your closet and dresser."

Oh, *that* was why they'd taken stuff from his house. "Th-thank you. I – I'm grateful to – that you thought to b-bring my things."

Ari shut the door behind her, leaving Valen and Lex alone in the bathroom. Valen suddenly lost all courage to look directly at Lex, lowering his eyes to focus on rubbing the washcloth on himself, trying to pat his open wounds as gently as possible.

"Do you want me to wash your hair? Since you don't seem to be able to lift your arms above your head."

"Yes, please," he said, barely above a whisper. That sounded *incredibly* nice.

Lex squeezed some shampoo out and started to lather it onto his head. He closed his eyes, the soft touches washing over him, but disquiet growing in the pit of his stomach kept him from enjoying it completely. He was enjoying Lex's touches—a lot—and maybe that was supposed to be only something Ari had a right to. The very last thing he wanted to do was upset Ari, to make himself unwelcome here in this haven he'd dared to hope for this whole time, to make her feel like she had to be territorial. What if she walked in on this? Would she be angry Valen was receiving affection from her?

"Are you sure – is it – " He realized partway through he'd made a fatal assumption, and the pendulum of his anxious, overthinking mind swung the other way – it'd been presumptuous to assume this was affection and closeness in the way he was thinking of it. He'd just never been touched so intimately by someone he actually *wanted* it from, and it was making his brain go haywire.

But it was too late to abort the question. "Go ahead," said Lex encouragingly.

Valen swallowed. "Are you sure Ari would not object to the way you're touching me?"

Lex's hands stopped on his scalp. His anxiety skyrocketed. He'd definitely made a mistake of some sort. Oh God, they were going to kick him out, or give him back to Nick, or – or –

"Of course," said Lex, her voice tinged with amusement. "She doesn't care. Why do you think she would?"

Valen shook, sending out tiny ripples in the water. Now if he explained himself, he risked *Lex* being offended at his train of thought. He wanted so badly not to intrude on their relationship, while at the same time yearning for nothing more than that very same, impossible thing. He was here, in their house, and they were both helping him and treating him gently, and he wanted that to go on forever and forever –

He let out an overwhelmed squeak. "I – I'm not sure – I'm sorry."

"It's okay," said Lex, sounding more baffled than anything. She went back to her rhythmic motions on his scalp. "Have you ... Has no one ever washed your hair for you before? Besides that time I did it at the hunter's compound, I mean."

"N-no, no one has."

Lex patted his shoulder. "It's nice, isn't it?"

"Y-yes."

"Me and Ari do it for each other all the time."

He let out another strangulated whine. *Jesus Christ, Valen, keep it together.* How pathetic and starved was he for connection with someone he could be genuine and tender with that he immediately piled all those hopes and desires on these two hunters who had hurt him so badly?

Lex poured some water over his head to rinse the shampoo out. "Oh, um ... " she said. "Right, I needed to ask you ... I think, at your house, I heard you ... talking on the phone? I assume that was someone you wanted to come help you, right?"

Fear shot through Valen as he recalled the phone call to Priscus. He'd almost forgotten about it already. "Oh – oh, yes, yes, I – I'm sorry – I'm sorry, Alexis."

"Don't apologize," she said. "It's okay. I probably would have done the same thing. We just need to talk about it because it means someone is on the way to get you, right?"

Oh God. He'd begged Priscus to come save him. "I – I – I asked my husband to come rescue me." Was it his imagination, or did Lex look a little disappointed?

"Oh." She fidgeted. "Well, should we – should we call him again and make arrangements for him to come get you?"

"No!" Valen blurted out, then eased back. His initial response was always, *No, I don't want to go with Priscus*, but it was a very good question now. He'd called Priscus because he was at the very end of his rope, completely out of options, and he'd figured that being abused was better than being tortured ... Now that it was looking more and more like torture was off the table, though, all his hatred of Priscus was returning.

But ... did he dare pass up this opportunity to make it out of human territory? To make it back to safety, out of the reach of vampire hunters? How much did he trust that this treatment from Lex and Ari would continue? And did he trust them just because he *wanted* to believe they would continue to be kind to him?

"Really?" said Lex. "But – but you called him. Do you not want ... ?"

There weren't any good options for him right now, but he chose where he was, what he could see, a tentative peace over guaranteed misery. "My husband is – my husband is a horrible man, whom I despise. I would only – I only called him as a last resort, because I was desperate to escape torture. I would count myself lucky if I never saw his face again."

"Oh." Lex fidgeted. "Well, if that's the case ... does he know where you are? Do we need to hide you?"

Valen's heart was overwhelmed by the speed at which Lex became ride-or-die upon hearing that a hated husband was in the picture. "I was unable to give him the address before – before – those two arrived, and if he – even if he was able to

track the location based on the phone number, or some trick, it would only lead him to – to my house out deep in the country."

"Sheesh, that's a good five hour drive. Yeah, I don't know if he really has any way to find you then ... right?"

"I believe so," said Valen. "At least, I hope so."

The door cracked open, and Ari's disembodied arm came in, laying clothes on the sink. "Clothes," she said succinctly, pointing to them without sticking her head in. "There. Bye."

The arm withdrew, and they both heard the sound of furniture moving downstairs.

"So, if I can ask," said Lex. "I'm – I'm curious as to why you're married to him if you hate him so much."

Valen let his eyes fall down into the soapy water. "It was my parents' idea. I – I did not have the courage to defy them on the issue until well after we were married and it became obvious to me how truly horrible it was."

"Oh," said Lex, sounding very, very sad. She watched Valen listlessly rub the washcloth on himself for a moment before saying, "Kind of the same thing happened to me. Well, not quite that bad, but my parents tried to set me up with this family friend's son as soon as I told them I was dating Ari. They seemed to think they could convince me not to be queer if they just tried hard enough to find a man I would like better than Ari."

"They – Mine also seemed to think they could convince me – not to be transsexual – if I married a proper husband and had proper wifely d-duties. They were – were also trying to break me of my – pacifist beliefs, believing them to also be im-improper."

"I'm so sorry," said Lex, voice heavy. "Oh my God, that's awful. I'm so glad you got away from that."

"As am I." He swallowed. His voice was starting to get raspy again from using it so much, but he was finally, *finally* having a conversation with someone who could understand him even a little bit, and he didn't want it to stop. "I – I still

couldn't get him to sign the divorce paperwork I initiated, which is why I – I still have his last name. Any time he – he s-starts to consider just letting me go, h-his parents say that divorce isn't something to – to consider, and that he needs to be a proper husband to make me a proper wife."

Lex suddenly got a look of intense sadness on her face. "I'm – I'm so sorry, Valen, I feel – I feel so horrible."

"It's not your fault."

"No, I – " Her voice wobbled. "When we looked up your last name we assumed it meant you were an evil person working for the blood farms. I – I – I feel so horrible about what we did to you."

Valen would have been angry at her, at some point in the past; he still was to an extent – but he was mostly just ... too tired, and scared, and desperate for any gentleness to be angry about something that had already happened in the immutable past. "It was – Your train of logic was sound ... It was a fair assumption to make, given the circumstances."

He looked up to see that Lex was full-on crying now. "It doesn't matter, I – I'm so sorry, Valen, I'm so so sorry, I don't know if you can ever forgive me. It's our fault this all happened to you. I'm so, so, so sorry. How can I even begin making it up to you?"

He couldn't say it was all right, because it wasn't, but ... "You are already off to a good start." He smiled weakly. "This still feels – not quite real. This is – the rescue I'd been hoping for. I am st-still a little afraid of waking up back in the basement."

"No!" said Lex fiercely. "Absolutely not. I won't let that happen to you. I shouldn't have let it happen in the first place."

He wanted to believe her so badly. "Thank you." He dipped his head. "I think I am quite ready for a water change."

Lex pulled the drain in the tub, watching the muddy brown water be flushed away, then plugged it back up and set the water to warm again.

"So, if – if I may ask in turn," said Valen. "How did you and Ari – become involved?"

"We were childhood best friends," said Lex, blushing and smiling, as though overwhelmed by the softness of the memory. "And we both got tired of boys breaking my heart over and over again."

"That is – that is wonderful."

It took one more water change before he was clean to his own satisfaction, at which point Lex helped him stand and towel himself off. He felt so, so much better than he had after his last bath. There was no muzzle or cuffs to go back on, no hell downstairs to go back to after the reprieve. He would go downstairs and instead of Nick and more vampire hunters, there would be Ari, bringing in his belongings, and more blood if he plucked up the courage to ask for it.

"Here, let me put some bandages on before you get dressed," said Lex. She got out some ointment and bandages from the cabinet. He sat on the edge of the tub and tried not to shake as she rubbed ointment on his open wounds, gently wrapping them in gauze. The air was still warm and humid, the only sound the dripping of water, and Valen watched Lex's delicate hands working tenderly at his injuries. Part of him thought it'd been worth it to accumulate the injuries if it meant Lex would touch him like that.

"There we go," she cooed, securing the last bit of gauze on him. He was practically more gauze than skin at this point. "How's that feel?"

"Better. Thank you."

"Great, want to get dressed, then?"

"Yes, please."

"Geez, good thing Ari brought you a belt too," said Lex as she helped him step into his pants. "You're, like, five sizes too small for your clothes now."

Valen had no comment on that. Lex apparently interpreted this to mean he was glowering, because she apologetically said, "Well – well, we'll get you back up to a healthy weight, don't worry."

156

So they *did* intend to feed him long-term. That was a relief. He didn't worry about where the blood would come from. They seemed like they were really going to do this for him. Tears welled in his eyes.

"I promise," said Lex, clearly distressed, doubling down. "It'll be okay – please, I promise it'll be okay, please don't be upset."

Valen decided to save his voice, so he merely wiped the tears from his eyes.

"Can I give you another hug?" said Lex.

"Yes," said Valen instantly. Her arms came around him. This time she leaned fully into it. She was ... so warm.

"Thank you," Valen whispered.

Lex smiled. "Come on, let's go downstairs."

She went down first, in case he fell. Ari's voice could be heard from the kitchen. "Are you *really* sure there isn't anyone else there I can talk to?"

Valen peeked his head into the kitchen behind Lex. Ari was on the phone, looking agitated. His preternatural hearing let him hear the voice coming out of the speaker. "Yes, Ari, it's only me here, now."

Valen's blood turned to ice. It was Nick's voice. Ari was talking to Nick on the phone. *Why was she talking to Nick?*

"Fine," said Ari. "Whatever. Just tell everyone else we can't go on patrol tonight."

"But you were supposed to go on patrol last night, and you didn't."

"Yeah, and we already didn't do that."

"You are scheduled to – "

"I know we're *scheduled*, Nick, I'm telling you we have to be excused for now because Lex lost about seventy-five percent of the blood in her body. You were there."

Valen flushed with guilt and embarrassment, drawing back behind Lex and leaning into the wall.

"Yes," said Nick. "I'm aware. Fine. What about my research specimen?"

Valen put his knuckle in his mouth, trying not to cry out.

"Just as I told you, I killed it," said Ari. "And no, we're not catching you another one, before you ask."

Nick growled in frustration. "Fine. If you are quite done being a bitch, you can hang up now."

"You're lucky I can't kick your balls through the phone lines. Bye, scumbag." Ari slammed the phone into the cradle. "It seems like it's getting harder for Nick to hide what a piece of shit he is. He usually behaves to your face, at least."

"Ari," said Valen weakly. "Thank you for telling him I'm dead. Thank you for – for – for – for – "

"All right," Ari grunted. "No need to cry about it. Come on into the living room. I guess it's doubling as your bedroom for now."

They brought in Valen's dresser, end table, towels, all his clothes, some of his lab equipment and books, and whatever else they'd thought to grab. There really wasn't that much of it, and it *sort* of fit in the living room.

Ari arranged things and kept looking back at him for a thumbs-up or thumbs-down, but he was afraid to express any preference on anything in their home and just agreed with whatever they were doing. They helped him put some clothes and shoes in the hall closet, and hung up extra curtains and taped them to the wall to ensure absolutely no sun could get into the room.

Once that was all done, Valen was ready to feed more, so they went back into the dining room and had him repeat the exercise of loosely restraining himself. They did this a few more times over the course of the day, and each time he felt a little less afraid of the muzzle. It was still looming in his mind as a threat, but he could take it off now, so that was something.

Valen was obviously extremely tired, so they eventually offered to just let him go to sleep, which he found agreeable. They pulled the plastic off the couch and removed the cushions, and unfolded it to reveal a mattress stored inside.

Tears welled in his eyes once more as he watched Ari stretch a fitted sheet over it and Lex put pillows and blankets on it. This was a bed. A *bed*. He'd get to sleep

in a *bed*. They wanted him to sleep in a *bed*. He'd given up hope of ever having such a luxury again, of ever sleeping in anything except a metal box.

He turned around to see Lex holding a pair of soft sleep pants and an oversized t-shirt. "Do you want to borrow some pajamas? I noticed you don't have any."

"I ... " The tears spilled over. "I – Thank you, yes, thank you, I would like that so much."

Lex helped him change into them, then helped him lie down, pulling the blanket up over him. He rolled over and buried his face in the pillow, the feeling of the soft fabric over his whole body practically overwhelming.

"Everything all right?" said Ari, giving a thumbs-up.

Valen bit the pillow, immediately ripping two small holes into it, but he was too overwhelmed to care much. "Mmm-hmmm," he whined. Maybe he'd be able to sleep this time. Maybe.

"All right. Well, good night, then. Er, good day." They turned off the light and left him alone.

17

— • —

Valen still couldn't sleep. Laying there with his eyes closed to rest was vastly better than nothing, because he was so, *so* tired, but every time he felt himself sinking into blissful unawareness he jerked back awake.

It was the same reason. *I'm out in the open. I'm in danger. I'm not in the coffin. That means I'm in danger.*

Shut the fuck up. I'm not in danger. I'm in a bed. You are going to sleep in a bed like a person, and not ask to be put back in a fucking cage like an animal.

He'd been given pajamas and a pillow and clean sheets and a bath and food and safety and love and it still wasn't enough to make him comfortable enough to fall asleep. Nick was still out there, Nick's voice had come through the phone. Nick was here, and sure, Ari had been snippy with him, but she'd talked to him.

It was then that Valen suddenly realized he wouldn't feel comfortable enough to sleep until there was a border between himself and Nick.

It was a dreadful realization, a pit sinking in his stomach, but it seized him all at once. Nick wasn't that far away, he was a single phone call away, all he'd need to do to pop over would be to get the address, and he was clearly still interested in hurting Valen.

That was why he couldn't sleep. Because he *shouldn't* feel comfortable. He *should* be scared. He *was* in danger.

He heard Lex and Ari elsewhere in the house sporadically, speaking to each other softly. What had he been thinking? They were being kind to him *now*, but

they were the ones who'd dragged him into hell in the first place. He knew the kind of callous disregard they were capable of. Why *would* he feel safe with them?

Why was he just lying here?

"We're going to bed now," said Lex's voice behind him, and he flinched at the sudden intrusion. "Is everything okay? Are you good to keep lying down until morning?"

He kept his back turned, ignoring her, body tense, trying not to cry.

"I'll take that as a yes, then. Good night."

The rest of the lights in the house turned off one by one, leaving Valen alone. Stewing. Second-guessing. Overthinking.

Previously he'd been cooperative because he really had no options, but ... it was night out. And he was fed. Obviously a single day's worth of feeding, no matter how generous, wouldn't be enough to restore him to full health, but the food and rest and wounds being treated had restored some of his strength. He felt like, maybe, he could stand and walk on his own. Maybe, if he pushed himself, he could run. Slowly.

He had a chance. For the first time, he wasn't restrained, he wasn't too weak to walk, and it was night outside. *He had a chance.*

I have to get out of here.

Terror suddenly crashed over him. He *had* to get out of here. He had an opportunity, and it would be foolish not to take it. If anything bad happened now all he'd be able to think of would be this one opportunity he hadn't taken. There was nothing keeping Lex and Ari from giving him back if they changed their minds, and until now he'd dealt with that terror by trying to convince himself to trust them, but now that he had some modicum of power back, all he could think of was how little he knew them, how little sense it made *to* actually trust them, when they were the ones who'd put him here.

When he only trusted them because he wanted to. Because he had some sort of weird complex about wanting them to like him.

Fuck this. Fuck Lex and Ari. Fuck Nick. Fuck humans, fuck human territory. I have to get out of here.

He waited with his heart pounding until he was sure Lex and Ari were asleep. Silence fell over the house. He swung his feet over the side of the bed, feet gripping the wooden floor.

He took a moment to psych himself up to stand, bracing himself on the arm of the couch. He pushed himself up.

I'm doing it, I'm standing. It wasn't as hard as it had been. He could do this. He could walk on his own. He walked forward, feet padding softly on the floor. *Okay. I can do this.*

He got to the stairs. *I can do this. There's a railing.* He unsteadily mounted the fucky stairs, pausing at the top to rest, then leaning outside their bedroom door to put an ear to it.

Snoring. They were definitely asleep.

They're asleep, and I can walk on my own. I climbed the stairs. I can do it. It would be a long, long walk back to vampire territory. But fuck Priscus too. He wanted to be alone, safe at home, his *own* home, his real home back in vampire territory, where he could just lock the door and then collapse onto his own couch.

The van. Maybe he should steal their van. But where were the keys? He didn't see them around. Maybe they were in the bedroom. The thought of trying to sneak in and take the keys without waking them up was too much for his anxiety-riddled brain, which was just screaming at him to *Go! Go! Go while you can!*

He had to take *something*, though. He couldn't just leave with only ducky pajamas.

He came back into the living room, unbuttoning the sleepwear with trembling hands. He needed to change into his outfit that covered him head-to-toe, that blocked out the sun. There was no way he would be able to cover the entire distance with whatever was left of the night.

He slid open his dresser and started swathing himself in his black outfit. Shirt, pants. Binder? No, sports bra, this was no time to be restricting his breathing.

Socks, boots laced up tight, jacket, overcoat, mask, scarf, hood, then cloak overtop of it all. The house was darker through the tinted lenses of the mask, and his own heavy breathing huffed back in his face as he loped around, desperately trying to cobble together a plan to get himself safely home through the muddled anxiety of his brain.

He found his satchel in the bottom of the closet. He dumped out whatever rubbish was in it, then walked into the kitchen and opened the fridge. There was one bag of blood left. He snatched it up and put it in the satchel. He then got a plastic bag and filled it with ice, and it went inside after that. He'd need this for sure.

What else? His books. He was loath to leave them behind, but he had to. Except ...

He walked over to his books and picked up one, *The Natural History of Viruses*. He flipped it open, hand running over the title page, where a looping scrawl read:

To my dearest turtledove,

I hope this will start making you feel more at home. I want you to be comfortable here.

Love,

Priscus

Priscus always resorted to gift-giving when his shallow emotional intelligence failed to find some way to actually treat Valen as a person. He was infuriatingly good at finding the right gifts too. Viruses didn't affect vampires, but Valen still found them fascinating. He'd considered many times tearing out the page with the note at the beginning, but something had always stopped him from doing so.

He wrapped the book in a plastic bag as well and slid it into his bag.

His panicked brain was too overwhelmed to think of anything else to bring. He had food, and his one most sentimental object among the possessions he'd brought with him. Everything else could be left behind. *Go! Go while you still can!*

With a trembling hand, he opened the front door and walked out, not even closing it behind him for fear of making too much noise.

***

Humans had so many *lights* during the night. Vampires had such good night vision that they had virtually no need for artificial light of any kind outdoors, and barely even needed them inside. But human territory was lit up like a casino. Streetlights, buzzing neon signs, headlights, billboards. Valen could barely even see the stars.

He'd once had all the constellations memorized, in his studies. He'd learned how to navigate by the stars to sail – he'd never actually been sailing, though, it'd all been from a book. He thought he remembered just enough to know which direction to go in, though. If he just went north, he'd hit vampire territory eventually.

Part of him wanted to stop and interact with the humans he saw. To stop in a gas station and strike up casual conversation with the bored night shift cashier. But he knew to keep his distance. The occasional person he let get within six feet of him viewed him with suspicion and then scurried away. And why wouldn't they? He sure made an impression, dressed in all black in the dead of night, hurrying along with a jerky gait. All it'd take would be for someone to peep in his satchel and see the blood on ice to complete the picture.

He needed to hurry. This close to the border, vampire hunters patrolled at night.

Valen guessed that he walked for about four hours before the sun started to come up. It was an agonizing pace, a far cry from the enormous speed he used to be capable of, and he had to take breaks, but it was progress. He occasionally found a spot out of sight to sip from the bag of blood, not wanting to drink it all and then carry on the physical exertion and risk his still-fragile stomach rejecting the precious life-giving liquid.

He tried to stay as far away from everyone as possible, to make it less obvious what he was, paranoid that the white van would show up at any moment, the coffin springing to life from the back to swallow him up. A few good Samaritans noticed him and pulled over to offer him a ride, which he always declined feverishly while trying to keep his voice low, terrified that they would somehow be able to tell by his voice alone.

The sun did come up eventually, of course. That was so, so scary. It'd been scary even when he'd been doing it on purpose, on a route he'd traveled before, where he knew where the shade was and how to get home safely. He also ... hadn't actually known how bad the sun felt, back then. He knew now, and it made it even more terrifying. But he just had to keep going north. The daylight would make it much harder to see, even through the darkened lenses, and there would be more humans out, but he just had to keep his head down and keep going.

The sun would also make it easier to navigate than the faint stars. The sunlight was starting to streak the sky pink in the west, so he just had to keep it on his –

Wait a minute. The sun was ... rising in the west?

No. No no no no. He collapsed to his knees. He'd been going in the wrong direction this whole time, he'd been going *south*, deeper into human territory, further away from home. He hadn't been able to see the stars very well and had read them incorrectly about which way was north.

He was so, so stupid. It'd been a stupid mistake to try and make a break for it, it'd been a stupid mistake not to prepare better, it'd been a stupid mistake not to think to look for a map or atlas to bring, it'd been stupid to assume he could rely on his own sense of direction.

Stupid, stupid, stupid. He'd panicked and acted on impulse. He wasn't even confident he'd be able to make it back to Lex and Ari's at this point, if they would even still bother to try and help him after the incredibly stupid decision he'd made.

He was just so, so scared. It was so hard to think. So hard to make decisions, when it felt like there was an open pit underneath of him he could slip and fall back into, into hell.

He leaned over, hands on the ground, the lenses of his mask starting to fog up as he breathed heavily, panic rising up once again. He'd messed up so, so badly. Why hadn't he just stayed where he was? Why did he think he could try and make decisions for himself? Why hadn't he –

"Are you, okay, lady?"

It was a child's voice, from startlingly close, and he lifted his head to see a gaggle of little girls running towards him.

A playground with more children was behind them. A school. He'd wandered near a school, without even realizing it, that's how poorly he'd been keeping track of his surroundings. He'd *never* have come near a school if he'd known. There was *nothing* that would prompt humans towards violence more than if they felt you were threatening their children.

"S-stay away from me!" he yelled.

The group stopped, frozen at his tone. No, no he couldn't scare them. That would make everything so much worse.

"You fell to the ground and didn't get back up," said one of the girls. "We got scared for you. Do you want us to go get our teacher? School hasn't started yet. We're just playing."

"N-no," he said shakily, bracing himself and getting to his feet. "That – that's very kind of you, young miss, b-but I don't need help. Run along now."

"I like your costume," said another. "Your necklace is really cool."

"Tha-thank you, but I really must be going."

"Girls!" said an adult's voice, and a woman came power walking towards him. "Come on, don't bother people walking by on the street."

Valen looked at the three children like they were bombs, fighting the urge to throw them away from himself and scream about how he didn't do anything to them. He started to back away, stumbling.

"Sorry about that," said the woman with a smile. "They're just very eager to –
"

She stopped as they finally made eye contact. *Eye contact.* She could see his eyes through the mask. She could see him, she could see that his eyes were red, and make the connection as to why he'd dressed this way to cover himself.

"G-girls, come back here!" she screamed, facial expression shifting instantly.

Valen's exhausted, terrified, self-loathing brain snapped into an even higher level of panic, his body already utterly wrung out from the adrenaline to get to this point. He had no idea what to do.

As the woman bravely stepped forward and gathered the three children to herself, Valen gave in to instinct and ran, pivoted on his heel and just ran.

Some of his vampiric speed came back to power that run, the sheer fear coursing through his veins. He'd been spotted, and the hunters they would surely call wouldn't be like Lex and Ari, they wouldn't, they would be like Nick, he knew they would be like Nick. Or even worse, they would just catch him and give him back to Nick. Or somehow, something worse than Nick.

The sun was still making it hard to see as he ran blindly, so he didn't see the steep drop-off he'd just charged right over until he was in midair.

Oh.

He tumbled down headfirst, scratching through weeds and bramble, head over heels, slamming different parts of himself into the ground as he cartwheeled – head, knees, chest, back, arms –

He landed at the bottom, very definitely on his legs, both legs, which his brittle, styrofoam bones didn't like at all. He couldn't suppress the massive wail of pain as they snapped, and he finally rolled to a stop in the dusty earth.

His whole body throbbed, but especially his legs. He curled in on himself, sobbing. Because of the pain, but also because he knew instantly that this was the end. He wouldn't be able to walk like this. Some human had seen him and been scared, and they were probably going to call the vampire hunters, and he couldn't walk.

They were going to kill him. He didn't want to die, not really. It would be a relief to not be tortured again, but as long as he was still alive, there was hope things could get better. He thought of Lex and Ari. He didn't want to die before getting to experience for himself something like the love they shared. He wasn't done living.

But what he wanted didn't really matter. The hunters would find him eventually, and Lex and Ari were surely too far away if they even cared to try and save him, *again*, after he'd massively fucked up, *again*.

"You okay, darling?"

Valen's head snapped up to see two humans in a car, shockingly close to him. As he strained to see through the bright light, it registered why: he was by the shoulder of a major highway, the major highway he'd gotten scared of and taken the side road that led him past the school to avoid.

There were two humans in the car, a man and a woman. The man was in the driver's seat, leaning out the window to look at him in a concerned way.

"Y-yes," he said, but his voice cracked, and surely they could hear that he was still actively crying.

"Do you need us to take you somewhere?" said the woman.

God, it hurt so bad, the veneer of generosity and helpfulness that he knew would disappear as soon as they *realized*. Every human had approached him in a friendly way, only to change into a different animal completely as their suspicions grew. He wanted it to be real so bad, but he knew it couldn't be. He wanted it to be for him so badly, but he knew it wasn't. He knew it would break like tissue paper under the weight of what he *was*.

No, not what he was. What people like him *did*. The vampires had created this atmosphere of fear and suspicion that was hurting him so badly with their horrible behavior. None of these humans had any way to know who he was. Of course they were afraid ... but so was *he*.

"L-leave!" he yelled, persuasion flaring out from him like a whip.

The man got a blank look on his face and sat back in the seat, pulling the car back onto the road and vanishing into the distance.

Valen curled up again, head on his knees. Another person who would report him at the first opportunity. But what did it matter?

The sun crept along the road. Valen was safely swathed in the shade from the overhang he'd fallen from, so at least he had that going for him. The road itself was firmly entrenched in sunlight. He pitifully dragged himself away from it, until his back touched the sheer hillside, leaning into a shrub.

Another car slowed down to ask if he was all right, since they'd seen him fall and had turned around to make sure he didn't need help. Part of him wanted to take his chances and accept help, but it was a complete dice roll as to which of these humans could be convinced that he wasn't dangerous. He could just use persuasion to force them to help him, but ... that might make it worse when inevitably someone else intervened. They all offered, they all told him it was going to be okay, just like Lex had, but none of them would care either if he ended up back being tortured. Tissue paper with a comforting image painted on it, which would tear as soon as he tried to lean on it.

He used persuasion again to get them to leave, at a complete loss, not even wanting to risk going into the sun since he could feel some parts of his clothes had torn in the fall.

He whimpered, curling up into the shrub as best as he could. He lost track of time, but the cars stopped coming eventually.

After hearing nothing but silence for a suspiciously long time, he cautiously raised his head and saw why. The road to the east had been blockaded by a police barrier. A few police officers were standing in front of the barricade, trying to deter a crowd of rubberneckers from getting any closer.

Valen's instinct upon seeing such a scene was to see if there was any way he could help, but of course, this was for him. The problem was there was a vampire in human territory, and it wasn't safe to get close to it, and Valen couldn't very

well stop being a vampire, and he'd been *trying* to leave, so not much he could do on either front.

Someone had called, and the human authorities had noticed he wasn't moving, probably guessing because of the sunlight, so they'd just set up a blockade to keep people away. Until the vampire hunters got here, presumably.

Why couldn't he have just stayed with Lex and Ari?

He lay face down in the dirt. *Here it comes. Please, please, please. I know you have no reason to, but please. Please just come talk to me, somehow. I won't use persuasion. I promise. Please give me a chance. Please please please. I made a mistake. I made a stupid mistake. I shouldn't have to die for making a stupid mistake.*

You idiot, you'll be lucky *if dying is all you get from this whole miserable encounter. You won't be making any mistakes again, because you won't have a chance.*

The officers moved the barriers to the side, allowing a gray car entry to the blocked road. Valen whimpered in fear, pressing himself into the dirt. That must be them. He didn't have a chance. They'd had ample opportunity to prepare, so even if Valen had been at full strength, he probably wouldn't have been able to get a leg up on them. He was done for. Whatever they were planning to do, they were going to do it.

No one was going to rescue him this time. If they didn't just kill him, he'd be taken back, and Lex and Ari would see him in the cage and shake their heads and say, *Oh well, we tried to help you, I guess you really deserve it this time.*

I'm sorry, Lex, I'm sorry, Ari, I'm sorry Lex and Ari. Hey, that rhymes –

The car stopped a ways off, out of shouting distance. Of course. Because they didn't want him to use persuasion. Both doors opened, and two men got out. He couldn't recognize them from this distance. One of them balanced something on the hood of the car that looked like a hunting rifle. Valen squinted. It was hard to tell because of the harsh light, but if they'd been trying to kill him, they probably would have a crossbow with a wooden stake, but it definitely wasn't the right shape for that, not to mention this distance was too great for a crossbow.

Something puffed softly in the dirt next to him. He cast his terrified gaze down to it and saw a dart with some translucent liquid inside.

Oh no. No, no, no, no. *Please, not this.* He knew what it was. It was a device that had been tested and developed on his own body. It was as close to a tranquilizer or poison you could get for a vampire: a suspension of silver in an emulsifier, inside a dart that would deliver it straight into the bloodstream, where it would stay until his body could filter it out and pass it.

Another dart stuck into the wall behind him. "Wait," said Valen, terrified. They were too far away to talk, but they were taking aim at him, so maybe they could read his lips. He held onto that hope for a second before remembering he was wearing his mask. He put a hand up, trying to shield himself. "Please. *Please.* Please, I – I don't want to – "

The next dart stuck into his outstretched hand, piercing through his glove.

His entire body was on fire instantly, the burning sensation blossoming out from his hand and tearing through all his veins like a wildfire, pumped along by his racing, fearful heart. He'd never experienced this without being restrained before, and he found that his limbs were taking full advantage of their ability to move around. He convulsed, shrieking, rolling, and writhing. He raked his claws into the dirt over and over, grunting, foaming at the mouth like a wild animal, raising his body off the ground, hips in the air, back arching in absolute agony.

With a shaking hand, he yanked the dart out of his hand, tossing it to the side. He rolled again, thunking his head into the ground over and over until he drew blood. Something, *anything*, any way he could move his body that had any chance of making this all-consuming fire stop, pushing himself along in the dust by the balls of his feet, hands tearing at the dirt.

He was vaguely aware of the sound of tires crunching on the road. Then the sight of the tires through his blurred vision. It stopped a few feet from his head. He dragged himself forward, wailing, begging them to keep driving forward to crush his head and render him unconscious, but all that came out of his mouth was pained sounds.

"Got it," said one of their voices. Valen's eyes were at ground level, on their boots. He continued to writhe, crawling towards their feet, hoping that one of them would kick him hard enough to knock him out.

"Jesus fuck," said the other, and the boots stepped back slightly. "She's fucking rabid."

"I told you it hurts them."

"P-please," he managed to choke out. The sound of the trunk opening. Hunting gear being dropped onto the cement in front of him, ropes and silver chains and ... .and a muzzle.

Even through all this, they still intended to take him alive. He took it all back. He wanted to die so, so badly. Anything was better than this, being on fire at the feet of two hunters who wanted to hurt him even more.

Hands removing his mask, hands pinning his wrists to the ground. He squirmed under them, letting the tears flow, not holding in the sobs wracking his body. "*Please.*"

"Put her in the trunk," said the first voice. "So she's not in the sun."

He started to wail even louder as he felt the all too familiar sensation of a muzzle being slipped onto his face. He desperately pulled his hands towards his face, fighting the hands pinning him and the seizures and convulsions of his uncooperative muscles, trying to keep it off.

But it went on anyway, and then the hands were lifting him up, forcing him to stand. He flailed his legs, strong arms wrapping around his chest to immobilize him.

The man holding him pivoted, starting to feed his legs into the trunk of the car. "Fuck, tie it up first."

Valen kicked and screamed as much as he could, out of fear and pain and hopelessness.

"Settle down!"

"You dumb shit, she's having seizures, she can't just sit still."

"Knock her out, then."

The prospect was terrifying, because he had no idea where he would wake up. But he wanted it more than anything. He knew from experience it took *hours* for the silver darts to wear off. He sobbed and moaned, tilting his head to expose his neck. He knew this was the fastest way to render him unconscious, cutting his spinal cord with a knife.

Still, he shook even more as one of the men withdrew a knife and came at him with it. But the blissful unawareness of the horrible situation that followed was worth it.

18

———·———

Coming back to consciousness was like being slowly lowered into a pool of acid.

He was aware of the burning in his veins before anything else. It was ... less intense, but definitely still there. He choked back a sob before even opening his eyes, wishing desperately that he'd stayed unconscious until it'd worn off. It was at least tolerable now, though. His pain tolerance had gotten ... a lot higher over the past few months.

The next thing he became aware of was the restraints. Of course. What would he be, if he were free to move around? At least none of them burned. He felt his hands in metal handcuffs in front of him, and the muzzle, of course. It was the only thing he could think of for a second, chest puffing in and out with pathetic, scared breaths. *The muzzle comes off and on, now, it's not permanent.* He clung to the hope that it could still be true.

The next thing he became aware of was a very strange sound, a kind of chirping. And a bell tinkling, and metal wire rattling.

He was afraid to open his eyes. He was afraid of what he would find out. The worst thing he could think of was being back in Nick's basement. As long as it wasn't as bad as that, maybe he could handle it.

He opened his eyes. The light in the room was dim, but it looked like a living room. The softness underneath him was a couch. A chain connected to his collar secured him to a radiator again, which would explain why his feet weren't chained also.

The sounds had been a small gray bird sitting in a cage across the room. Valen looked at it with watery eyes. It raised its head, yellow crest on its head rising with faint interest. It peeped again.

Valen's eyes trailed down to the table nearby, upon which was a pair of bloody pliers and two long, white fangs. Valen tried to run his tongue over his teeth, but the bit from the muzzle got in the way. He could feel a dull pain where his canine teeth would have been, though. So they'd pulled his fangs out. They'd grow back, but ... that probably wasn't a good sign if it heralded how he was going to be treated wherever he was now.

He lowered his head onto the couch. Once again, at the mercy of the whims of the humans around him. And now he had to sit here, squirming with the remnants of silver in his veins.

At least there was this little bird here. That could distract him a little bit, at least. It'd been a while since he'd seen a cute bird like this. His mother had one when he'd been younger, but it'd died before he'd gotten to play with it much.

He wouldn't be allowed to play with this one, of course. Such human things weren't for him. But until they came back in and started torturing him again, he could at least look at it.

It stretched its wings out, preening itself. It then hopped around, rattling the bells and toys in its cage, calling loudly.

"Shh," said a man's voice from the other room. "Princess D, I told you our guest needs to sleep."

Valen buried his face in the couch, trying to look like he was still unconscious, desperate to delay whatever horrible thing was about to happen to him.

A man came in. He looked familiar. He got a blanket and put it over the bird's cage. "Goodnight. Shh. Quiet."

He left the room again. Valen trudged through the muck in his brain to try and remember something, a memory from a different lifetime. The cloak coming over his prison, a man commenting that it was like putting a blanket on his birdcage to make the bird go to sleep.

One of the hunters. What had been their names ... ? Bailey and Jerome. He was at Bailey and Jerome's house.

He listened vaguely to the chatter in the next room, their two familiar voices. Yes, that's who it was. They weren't horrible, as far as the hunters went. They'd taken no pleasure in hurting him and had quit early on.

"He awake yet?"

"Nah, still conked out. You get ahold of the girls, right?"

"Yeah, they're gonna come over soon."

"Good. It's a she, though."

"What?"

"The vampire. It's a she."

"No, Lex and Ari called it a he. Even Nick called it a he sometimes."

"Nah, bro, look at her."

"I looked at her and I looked at a vampire that Lex and Ari called a he."

"Bro, it's a titty vampire. She's got titties."

"So do you, fatass!"

"I'm telling you, it's a lady vampire."

"It's transsexual."

"Nah, fuck off, bro, you're pulling my leg."

"Why do you think it looks like that? It had facial hair when it got here, you remember that. It's cuz he was on shots."

"Fuck you, man, transsexual vampires ain't a thing."

"Why not?"

"Because ... because ... it's a vampire! Why would a vampire give a shit about gender?"

"You think vampires don't have gender?"

"I don't know! I don't know what goes on in their heads!"

"What, you think there's no room for anything in there besides blood?"

"I don't know! Fuck you, man."

"You dumb fuck."

There was uproarious, wheezing laughter from the other room, both of them.

Their tone was lighthearted, but Valen was deathly afraid that these two men were going to rape him. They were talking about him, his body, and he was trapped in their home. They'd shown no interest in doing so, but it was something every man who'd had him alone in a vulnerable position had done. Priscus had done it. Nick had done it. Why wouldn't they as well?

They'd mentioned *the girls*, though. Maybe that meant Lex and Ari. Maybe they were coming to help him. Maybe, maybe, maybe. Maybe it would be okay.

Valen tried to lever himself upright, but pain shot through his shattered legs as he did so. He couldn't stifle the muffled cry.

The men's voices stopped. "You hear that?" said one. Valen's chest hitched. He was already struggling not to cry.

Two pairs of footsteps. The two of them came into view. Standing upright, looming over him, looking at him with unknown intentions. He wormed backwards, but the chain connecting him to the radiator went taut and kept him from going much further.

"Hey, you're awake!" said one. "My name's Jerome, and this shithead is Bailey."

"I'd say a pleasure to meet you, but you probably hate my fucking guts," said Bailey. "Sorry about the, uh, the … " He motioned to the palm of his hand. "The dart. It was kind of all we had that was nonlethal."

Valen broke eye contact, losing his courage to look directly at them.

"And sorry for the, um … " said Jerome. "The chompers. We figured it would, uh, be best to pull them before you woke up. We put some topical ointment on your gums, but I dunno if that stuff really works on vampires."

"Were you trying to sit upright?" said Bailey. "Hey, do you want me to help you?"

He came over and grabbed Valens's upper arms, pivoting him into a sitting position. Valen cried out, letting out muffled sobs at the stabbing pain in his legs.

"Woah, hey, sorry," said Bailey. "You don't have to scream. We're not gonna hurt you."

They didn't understand. They thought he was afraid. He *was* afraid, but he was *already* in pain. And now he was stuck back at square one, being stripped of his ability to communicate by people who didn't trust him one bit.

"Your girls are on their way," said Jerome. "That'll be nice, right?"

Please, please, please, please, please, please, please, please, please, please. He let himself latch onto the hope that maybe he hadn't completely exhausted Lex and Ari's patience, that they were still willing to help him even after all his mistakes, even if it meant confronting these two men.

"Hey, hey, hey," said Bailey. "There's no need to cry, sweet thing, come on now." He felt the man's big, calloused hands on his cheek, wiping a tear off. He knew it was supposed to be comforting, but the pet name and intimate touching just sent him teetering on the edge of a panic attack.

Please, please, please, at least just let me keep my clothes on. Please at least be gentle. Please at least don't make it hurt as much as possible.

The doorbell rang, cutting through his spiral. "Finally," said Bailey. He walked out of the room, accompanied by the sound of a door opening. "Who's there? I'm not interested in anything you're selling."

"Very funny, shithead," said Ari's voice. Dreadful hope surged through him. Lex and Ari were here. Maybe, maybe, maybe, maybe, maybe. Bailey closed the door behind them as the two women came into the room. Lex rushed to sit beside him, practically body-checking Jerome out of the way.

"Valen!" she said, taking his hand. "Oh my God, oh my God, oh my God, thank you, thank you, thank you, thank you."

Valen looked up at Ari. She was probably going to be so, so mad at him. But to his shock … she just looked relieved. She came over and leaned his head into her chest, putting her arms around him. "There you are. There you are, we've got you."

"Wh – " said Lex, her eyes falling on the fangs on the table. "Did you – did you fucking *rip his teeth out*?"

"We need to submit them to prove we killed him," said Jerome. "You know that."

"Nick was probably suspicious when *you* didn't do that," said Bailey.

"We did it while he was asleep," said Jerome.

Oh, so there was some reason for it besides just pure sadism. That ... did make him feel a little better.

"Whatever," Lex scoffed. "Shh, shh, it's okay, I've got you." Her hands worked at the muzzle, unbuckling it.

"Are you sure that's safe?" said Jerome. "Like really sure?"

"Yes," said Ari.

Relief washed through him as the muzzle came off, freeing his mouth. "There we go," Lex cooed, palming his cheek gently. "There we go, there you are, sweetheart."

"I'm – I'm sorry," said Valen, instantly in tears. "I'm – I'm sorry I ran away."

"You don't have to apologize," said Lex. "Can I have the key for the cuffs?"

Jerome produced the key, but then retracted his hand before Lex could grab it. "You have some explaining to do. We nabbed him because you obviously wanted him alive."

"Right," said Lex. "I will, but – can – can we explain it after we – He really doesn't like being tied up."

"As long as you're sure he won't try anything." Jerome handed her the key.

She unlocked the wrist cuffs, dropping them to the ground, then she detached the chain from the collar on his neck. "There, is that better?"

"Th-thank you," he whispered.

Lex stroked the nape of his neck. He found his lap very interesting, hunching in over himself.

"This is Valen," said Ari. "And he hasn't committed any crimes, so it's not right to punish him."

Bailey and Jerome looked at each other. "You're ... you're sure?" said Bailey.

"Yes," said Lex. "He was here because he was gathering ingredients to make artificial blood. Valen, do you want to tell them about it?"

Valen's eyes fell on Lex's hand on his own. He was so, so scared. They were just talking with him, but it felt like his brain was broken. He'd gone through such wild swings of circumstance over the past few days. He felt like he would never feel safe ever again.

All he could expect was more pain, more brutality, more restraints, even after escape. He'd been foolish, thinking it was worth fighting to stay alive for something as unattainable and nebulous as genuine love. As though this were some children's story where friendship and love could solve all their problems. Everyone who'd ever loved him had loved an imaginary version of him that didn't actually exist, and withdrew their love as soon as they found out who he really was. Just like the scared humans had done as soon as they'd realized he was a vampire.

Priscus had been right, his parents had been right. Valen really wasn't equipped to deal with reality. It'd been childish to think he could do anything in the face of the overwhelming tidal wave of cruelty that was the real world. He'd tried, and now, even when he'd thought he might have gotten away, he was sitting here with silver prickling the inside of his veins and two broken legs, trying to make himself as small as possible in front of *four* vampire hunters.

"Please kill me," he said.

"Wh-what?" Lex gasped. "No, no, we're not going to kill you, sweetheart."

Of course. That was selfish. He wouldn't be allowed to die as long as he could still be of use to the humans. Whether it was as their plaything, their experiment, their good little pet.

"Hey, talk to me," said Lex. "What's wrong?"

What's wrong? What's wrong? Where to even begin? The tears burst out of him, and the only thing he could say to summarize the situation was:

"It hurts, it hurts, it hurts so bad and it's never going to get better."

"Hey," said Ari, and he felt her hands on his shoulders, as though pushing him back down into his body. "You're feeling really bad right now because of temporary things. Don't make any permanent decisions right now."

Lex's hand squeezed his. "All right, all right. It feels bad physically or emotionally?"

"B-both," he wailed. "Please, please have mercy on me. I – I'm sorry." He was scared because he'd slid down even further into the pit. It wasn't enough anymore for them to just not hurt him, he needed help, and he needed them to give him more blood, after he'd wasted and thrown away so much of what they'd already given him, and it seemed far too much to ask for more. They'd said it wouldn't be right to punish him, and yet being punished had been his existence for the past few months, and his brain had been completely scrambled about what he deserved or didn't deserve.

"This is weird," said Bailey. "Geez, this is weird."

"Shut up," Ari snapped. Valen felt her breath on his neck as she came in closer, hugging him. "We're still going to help you, Valen. All right? Let's unfuck this thing together. We'll help you dig yourself out."

Valen's heart stuttered, more tears flowing down his cheeks, whimpering.

"Now, what is it that hurts? Physically? What can we fix?"

"The – the – the si-silver dart is still – is still – "

"Jesus, that hasn't worn off yet?" said Jerome.

"N-no," Valen said. "Please, it hurts, please, please."

Valen worked up the courage to look up and saw that Jerome had a stunned look on his face. "I ... I didn't know it hurt that badly. I'm sorry."

"Why *wouldn't* it hurt?" Valen wailed. "Why – why – "

Lex leaned into his field of vision, tilting his head to look at her. "All right, don't get worked up. Focus on what we can do now. How can we help you?"

There was nothing they could do to make the dart work out of his system faster, or to unbreak his legs, or un-cut his tender, beaten flesh, or take away the massive gaping hole in his chest where his emotions and personhood used to be.

181

He sniffled. "I – I – Please, pl-please just – knock me unc-uncon – knock me out again."

"Really?" said Ari.

"It – it'll wear off, I think – I think it will wear off."

"Okay," said Ari, squeezing him reassuringly. "Okay, we'll do that. What do you want us to do longer-term? Where were you trying to go? You went south."

"The – the border."

"Do you want us to drive you to the border?"

Of course, it wasn't safe for them to drive him all the way into vampire territory, just to the border. But in this state, even being fed, it would take ... an agonizingly long time for his legs to heal, to be able to move around on his own. The thought of being alone in this state sent fresh waves of anxiety over him. He'd wanted to be alone before, but now the thought was terrifying. "Pl-please let me stay with you, ma'am, if – if – if you're still amenable to – to hosting me."

"Of course," said Lex. "Of course we will."

"Are you *sure* that's what you want?" said Ari. "Are you just saying that?"

"I c-can't be on my own like this," said Valen. "It – it already didn't work." The fact that they were trying to let him go now did make him feel a little better. Maybe he wasn't trapped here. His anxiety started to uncoil in his chest a little.

"All right," said Ari. "Then we'll knock you out, and when you wake up, you'll be back at home. At our house. Nice and safe."

"In the ducky pajamas?" What on *earth* had compelled him to say that?

A ghost of a smile flashed across Lex's lips. "Sure, if that's what you want."

"We did it with a knife to the neck earlier," said Bailey. "Was that okay?"

"Y-yes," he said. "That's – that's the fastest way. But – but maybe make it bigger this time? So I – so I'm out for longer. Please? If that's – if that's okay."

"Of course that's okay," said Lex. "Are you ready?"

"Wait, b-before we do that ... Can I ask something?"

"Yes, what is it?"

He flushed and looked down, feeling very embarrassed, but ... he wanted it so badly. He wanted this frivolous, forbidden thing. The thing he'd heard on his very first day of captivity, and knew he would never be able to ask for, because brutality was for him, not these small, delicate, pleasures. Not these things human bonded over, this camaraderie around shared experiences. "Can I ... can I p-please hold the bird?"

After a moment of silence, Jerome and Bailey both burst out laughing. "What, Princess D?" said Bailey. "The scream queen?"

Valen kept his eyes down, very red.

"Sure, man," said Jerome. "What the hell, sure, you can hold the bird."

Despite the aches and throbbing, screaming body and burns deep, deep down inside of him, Valen let out a gasp of delight. "Thank you."

Jerome walked over to the bird cage and slid the blanket off of it. The bird had moved to one leg with its beak buried in its wing, and it looked at the humans with half-lidded eyes, as though irritated at being woken up.

Jerome slid the cage door open and stuck his hand in, and the bird stepped up onto his fingers. "Hey, little miss, you wanna come meet someone new?"

Jerome came over. The bird's crest rose again, and it tweeted. "Hold your hand out," said Bailey, taking Valen's wrist and manually positioning his fingers. Valen's hand fell again as soon as he let go, so he replaced his supports. Jerome set his hand so it was touching Valen's. Humans' hands always felt so very warm on his own.

The bird stepped up onto Valen's finger, and everyone cheered.

19

— · —

We'll knock you out, and when you wake up, you'll be back at home. At our house. Nice and safe.

He did not wake up back at home, nice and safe. He woke up inside the coffin, in Nick's basement, and he started to writhe and whine and cry instantly.

This felt too surreal and dreamlike to be real, the coffin pressing in on him and squeezing him in a way it never had in reality, the voices from the hunters upstairs too loud, laughing at him, taunting him. He was yelling for help in a way he couldn't have before, but everyone was still ignoring him. But the anxiety shooting through his veins was very, very real.

He very well *could* wake up in the coffin, in Nick's basement. He had no way to prevent that, no reason at all to believe it wouldn't happen besides the word of the two hunters who'd put him in the coffin in the first place, and he felt so, so stupid. Why had he asked for this? To be unconscious and toted around? To avoid pain?

He would rather be in pain than helpless, he decided, but it was too late. He *was* helpless. He was in the coffin. He couldn't *move.* He was completely paralyzed, still like a corpse, and the voices of the hunters upstairs got louder, laughing at him, dismissing him, saying he deserved it, and the coffin's iron grip squeezed him, breaking bones, and –

He *finally* woke up, and found that the screaming he'd been trying to do in the dream had manifested with his real voice, his stupid, terrified yell tearing through the silence of the house.

He stopped his thrashing, clutching his hands to his chest, where his heart pounded wildly. He swallowed, panting in terror and sweating. As his eyes adjusted to the dark, he saw he was in Lex and Ari's living room, on the pullout couch, right where he'd been before his ill-fated escape attempt.

He was even in the ducky pajamas, just as promised.

He tried to slow down his breathing and heartbeat. He was safe. It was just like they'd said, they'd made good on their word. He had no reason to panic. If he kept telling himself that, maybe he'd finally start to believe it. The open air of the room seemed to press in on him, head swimming. Movement out of the corner of his eye, in the doorway, someone approaching. The smell of humans, the sound of footsteps coming towards him. And he was helpless and immobile, his throbbing, aching legs still unable to support his weight, his starved, skeletal frame barely nourished by a handful of feedings, his brittle bones ready to break over and over again.

"Get away!" he cried.

It was only after he did it that he realized he'd just used persuasion, and it'd been Lex in the doorway, probably trying to help him, but she marched away like a zombie. He released the persuasion immediately, and his sensitive ears heard her fall to her knees and let out choking breaths.

No, no, no, NO NO NO. He'd already blown it, he'd used persuasion, the one thing he needed to not do if he wanted to keep the muzzle off. He instantly exploded into tears, shaking and crying. He couldn't run away, he couldn't get away, and they were going to come and take away his ability to speak. He pulled the blanket over his head, lying down flat and biting into the pillow.

He heard Ari coming down and talking to Lex, who relayed what had just happened. *No, no, no, no.* Ari was going to come in here and be angry at him for using persuasion on Lex again, after he'd said he wouldn't, and she would put the muzzle back on. He could use persuasion on *her*, maybe, but then what? He had nowhere to run, even if he kept one of them under persuasion for a longer time and had them carry him around until he could walk.

He heard Lex go into the kitchen. *No, no, no, come back, please come back, please don't leave me alone with Ari.*

Ari darkened the door to the room. Still whimpering and sniffling, Valen peeked out from under the blanket. She looked at him with chagrin on her face.

"I'm sorry," he cried. "I'm sorry, it was an accident, please – "

"All right, take it easy." Ari came over and sat on the edge of the bed, and Valen shrunk away from her, quaking.

"I won't do it again, I swear, I won't use persuasion, I won't run away – "

He cut himself off as Ari grabbed his elbow, leveraging him into a sitting position, forcing him to sit up and make eye contact with her. "Hey," she said. "Calm down."

He sobbed.

Ari wrapped her arms around him. "Shh. I'm not going to hurt you. We're not going to hurt you."

"Please don't put the muzzle back on! Please don't!"

"Shh. Calm down. I'm not going to. Calm down. It's okay."

Lex appeared in the doorway next, holding a steaming hot mug.

"I'm sorry I used persuasion on you," Valen wept. "I'm sorry, I didn't mean to. It was an accident, please believe me. I won't do it again. Please don't put the muzzle back on, I promise I don't need it to behave, please, please."

Ari said, "It's okay. We just took you out of six months of being brutally tortured a few days ago. We understand you're scared."

Please, please, I don't know what you need to say to convince me your comforting words are true, but please say it. He took in deep, ragged breaths.

"You understand why using persuasion is an issue, though, right? You know not to use it because it feels bad for us, not just because it'll make us mad at you, right?"

Even after all this, they were *still* worried that he might not understand that they were people who disliked having their will overwritten. It was almost insulting at this point. "Yes, I understand, I promise I understand."

"Okay. Just. Just calm down."

Lex looked at him softly. "What are you afraid of? Like, what do you think is going to happen?"

What the hell is that supposed to mean? What do you think? *More of the same daymare I've been in for the past six months.* Valen grabbed his chest, hyperventilating.

"Take it easy," Ari soothed. "You're safe. How do we make you feel safe? What do you want us to do?"

"I'm not sure," Valen said. He was flailing, a drowning man desperately trying to find something buoyant to cling to, but there was nothing.

"Okay, that's okay," Lex said. She set her mug on the end table and sat on the bed, next to Valen, putting a comforting hand on his thigh over the blanket. "Is there anyone you want to call? I know you said you didn't want your husband to come get you after all, but is there anyone else you trust? Family? Friends? So you're not just stuck here with us? We want to help you however we can."

"We're not trying to hold you prisoner," Ari said. "Just to make that clear again. We know you didn't do anything wrong, and we're trying to help you get better, that's all."

Valen drew his hands to his chest, quaking, trying to see through tear-blurred eyes. The thought of being with his parents, or even worse, Priscus, like this made his stomach turn. If he could make it to them, his parents would take care of him physically, but would it be worth it? Valen had always had such a hard time enforcing his boundaries with his parents, and he often fell prey to their emotional manipulation when he was vulnerable. It was why he barely ever talked to them. And he'd *never* been more vulnerable. They'd probably just cart him off to his husband's place. And Priscus ... he shuddered at the thought. Unlike his parents, he knew Priscus would come to the border, or all the way into human territory to get him, but that would definitely be worse. "N-no, there's no one. I have no one."

"You have us," Lex said with a gentle touch on the arm. "You're not alone, I promise. I promise we're going to do whatever it takes to help you."

He closed his eyes and breathed deeply. They were trying to help him. The idea of trusting them after how they'd dragged him into hell and then left him there ... But they fought monsters every day that looked just like him and could kill them faster than it would take to clarify intentions, and they were imperfect people with their own trauma and shortcomings, could they be blamed? They clearly understood the extent to which what they'd done was wrong, and learned from their mistakes. Was that enough? Was that enough that he would be safe with them?

"Did you have a nightmare?" Ari asked. "Is that how you woke up?"

A *night*mare. He supposed they would call them that, not daymares. He nodded slowly.

"You look so tired," Lex cooed, making Valen self-conscious. "Is there anything we can do to help you sleep?"

Was it *really* okay to trust these two to help him? Maybe. It wasn't like he had many options. He wrapped his arms around himself. "I'm – I'm not sure. Be-because, um ... No, I don't think so."

"It's okay, what is it?" Lex prompted. "Is there something that will make you more comfortable?"

He couldn't suppress the embarrassing whine that came out. "The-the only time I wouldn't be hurt was when I was in the coffin, and-and now it f-feels like I'm in-in danger when I'm out in the open, so-so I don't-don't know if I'll ever be able to sleep again."

"So you feel like you can't sleep unless you're inside the coffin?" Ari asked.

Oh no, no no *no*, he couldn't answer that, he couldn't say anything that could ever be misconstrued as asking to be put back into the coffin even a little bit. "Please don't put me back inside there. I can't, I *can't* go back in there no matter what, please, please – "

Ari held up a hand, cutting him off. "All right, all right, calm down. So the point is you feel like you need to be in an enclosed space to feel safe, and that's why you can't sleep out in the open, is that it?"

He nodded shakily. It just felt so damn *hard* to decide what to do. He wasn't used to it. Nick would always just do whatever he was going to do to him no matter what Valen did, and now that he had some capacity to help himself he was deathly afraid of messing it up.

Ari clucked her tongue. "Lex, you stay here with him." She gathered her coat and keys and wallet.

"What?" Lex said. "Where are *you* going?"

"To the hardware store."

***

Ari returned quickly, with what appeared to be *lumber* in tow. She took it downstairs, and Valen nervously curled up on the couch listening to her use a variety of saws, hammers, drills, and things of that nature. When he asked Lex what she was doing, Lex checked in with Ari, but when she came back up it was only to fold in the couch "to make room in the living room," setting Valen down in the easy chair and taking the trappings on the couch downstairs.

The sound of a staple gun was next. He sank fearfully into the chair.

"All right, bat boy," Ari's voice came from downstairs. "Get ready to get your tits blown clean off."

"Ari," came Lex's exasperated reply.

Heavy, thumping movements of something being dragged upstairs. They pivoted around the corner and out of the basement, carrying a long wooden object between them.

A coffin. Not the monstrosity made out of metal bars, an honest-to-God wooden coffin. Unfinished wood, but in the right shape.

They let it thump to the floor. It sounded solid.

"How's this look?" Ari said proudly. Lex opened the lid to reveal the inside was lined with the soft trappings of a bed, complete with a cat plushie. There was a

lock on the lid – on the inside, so that whoever was lying inside controlled when it could open.

Tears pooled in his eyes. "You made that for me?"

"Yeah, man," Ari said. "Here, you wanna try it out?"

He nodded.

Lex and Ari each got one hand under him, forming a sort of swing with their arms, and hefted him from the couch and into the coffin, laying him out gently. He settled into it, crossing his arms over his chest even though there was plenty of room inside.

"How's it feel?"

"It's ... comfortable."

There was a handle attached to the lid so that he could pull it shut without having to use his legs to get up. Lex guided his hand towards it, and he pulled it shut.

"What do you think?" Ari said.

"This – this is good." It felt very, very good. Safe. Secure. Dark. Safe safe safe. "Yes, I think this is good."

"Try the lock."

Even his vampiric eyes were barely able to see in this darkness, but he saw the deadbolt on the inside. He slid it shut, and the door rattled as someone on the outside gave it a tug.

"See?" said Ari's muffled voice from outside. "Nice and secure. Now, how about you open it back up?"

Valen undid the lock and pushed the lid open, and it flopped onto the couch beside him. "You wanna try sleeping in this?" Lex asked.

"Yes," he said. *Oh my God. Maybe I might actually be able to sleep in this. Maybe I can actually sleep and not feel too tired to think.* "Y-yes, I would like to try it. Thank you."

"Good." Ari patted him on the arm. "You can open it and close it however you want, and if you start to get a little freaked out, you can just haul yourself up over the edge to get out, yeah? And if you need anything, you can just yell for us, okay?"

"Yes," he said, slowly pulling the coffin closed, making them disappear little by little. "Thank you."

He rolled over and his face brushed against the cat plushie. Slowly, his hands came up and encircled it, and he curled up around it, snuggling it to himself.

20

—·—

"I'll go check if he's awake. ... Valen, are you awake?"

"..."

"Take that as a no."

"Should we wake him up?"

"Just let him sleep."

***

"Is he awake now?"

"He'll let us know when he's awake."

"I'll just check on him."

"Keep your voice down."

"Valen, are you awake?"

***

"It's been, what, twelve hours at this point. Are we sure he's still in there?"

"Yeah he's still in there, where would he have gone?"

'Okay, I can hear him breathing."

"Yeah, Lex, keep your voice down."

***

The sleep was good. It was so, so good to his exhausted, utterly spent brain. He had some of the weirdest dreams he'd ever had. And when he woke up, he couldn't remember where he was, why he was there, what was going on, what decade it was, who he was. All he knew was that it was dark and cozy and comfortable and safe. The sleep had been that good.

He wiped drool from his mouth, finding it attached to a rather large puddle on his pillow. He felt some strange object underneath him, then found that it was his arm, limp and numb from having slept with it pinned under his body. He groggily flopped it over and started massaging it to return feeling to it.

He felt *okay*. He was very, very hungry, and a lot of his injuries still had a long way to go to heal, foremost his legs, and he still had the stupid metal collar on. But this was the best sleep he'd gotten in a long time. It didn't feel like everything was so impossible and overwhelming now. Maybe it would be okay, for real.

"I think I heard him moving around."

"Give it a rest, would you?"

Voices from outside. "I'm awake," he tried to say, but his voice was still thick, his mind half-shrouded in sleep.

Apparently the message got through, because footsteps approached. "Can I open the door?" said Lex's muffled voice.

"Yes," Valen said, groggily fumbling to undo the lock.

The door squeaked open, and Valen squinted against the light of the living room to see Lex and Ari's faces.

"Good morning!" Lex said. "How are you feeling? How did you sleep?"

Valen rubbed his face, trying to wipe away the crusts keeping his eyes glued shut. "Good morning ... How ... how long was I asleep?"

"Sixteen fucking hours," Ari said. "You just had a godly power nap, my dude."

"You deserve it," Lex said. "How are you feeling?"

"A little better," he mumbled.

"Did this thing help you sleep?" Ari said, nudging the coffin with her foot.

He nodded.

"Good. Do you wanna hang out in there a bit more, or come out onto the couch?"

"The couch sounds nice," he said timidly, still not used to making decisions.

Lex and Ari lifted him up and out, settling him onto the couch and piling up a fortress of pillows around him to make him as comfortable as possible.

"There," said Lex. "I know it probably still hurts, but how are you feeling?"

Better, was what he'd answered earlier. It was definitely true, but if he dared to get his hopes up, and be bold enough to make demands – no, requests ... "Hungry, ma'am. I-I feel a lot better, but – but I would be very grateful i-if there was more blood in the fridge, if I would be allowed to have it."

"Oh, we actually ran out of that stuff from the hospital," Ari said.

"Oh. Wh-when will you – when will getting more be feasible?"

"Oh, um," Ari said, averting her eyes. "I don't think we can really get blood that way again, it was sort of a one-time thing, special circumstances. I think if I went back to the hospital and asked for more, that'd be pushing it and they might start asking questions."

Valen tried not to cry, but it was just so hard to hear. No more feeding, then, it looked like. "All right," he said, voice wobbling. "I understand, ma'am." It was going to take so long for his legs to heal enough to walk without being fed, but he was grateful he wasn't being hurt anymore. He tried to focus on that good, at least.

"Yeah," Ari said. "And, um, Lex can't really feed you, since – since she lost all that blood recently, not sure how long it'll be before she's fully back from that. So ... "

Valen tried to suppress his anger. Hadn't they kept saying over and over again that they were going to help him get better? How were they going to claim that, but then in the same breath tell him he's going back to starving because they hit an

194

inconvenience? Hot tears pricked at his eyes, from anger and fear and resignation. He bit his tongue.

Lex seemed to notice his expression, and he crumpled in on himself, hoping they wouldn't be mad at him, or think him entitled. But surely she couldn't think this was fair, right? It wasn't unreasonable to be disappointed. He'd accepted it, even, he didn't demand they try it anyway.

After an awkward silence, Lex elbowed Ari hard enough that the taller woman exhaled sharply. "What Ari is *saying*," Lex continued, "is that since there aren't other options, *she's* going to feed you."

Valen's mood lifted instantly. "Real-really?"

"Yeah," Ari said, though clearly not looking happy about it. "Obviously it's not ideal, but I'm really the only one here with enough blood for you to drink. So. So, have at it, I guess."

Ari just stood there. Valen struggled to think of how this was going to go. She was giving him permission to feed, but she was still standing out of reach, and she knew full well that Valen wasn't able to walk. "Um," he said, easing into the topic like he might step on a landmine. "How do you want me to – "

"Not on the neck," Ari said quickly.

"R-right ... " Valen said, losing his nerve and trailing off. Ari was just so *scary*, and clearly didn't like putting herself in a position where she was so vulnerable, letting herself be hurt this way, and Valen was so, so afraid that if he messed it up somehow he would ruin everything.

"The arm would be good, I guess," Ari said.

"O-okay," Valen said.

"What?" jabbed Ari. "That not good enough for you?"

He clutched the blanket to his chest and looked up at her with wide, fearful eyes.

"Ari, you know that's not it," Lex said. "Come on. Relax."

Ari visibly untensed her shoulders. "Right. Sorry."

"You can't just tell him to feed and then stand there when you know he can't reach you."

Ari flushed, looking embarrassed and vulnerable. "Right. Sorry." She took a few steps towards Valen and held her arm out. "Well, there, g-go ahead then." She tapped the skin of her forearm. "Right about there should be good, right?"

Valen bit his lip. It felt like he was on a tightrope, trying not to fall off. It was so stressful. But ... "I-I can't, I'm sorry. Bite you. I can't."

"Sure you can," Ari said gruffly. "Gave you permission and everything."

"No, no, I – " He whimpered, sinking down into the pillows. "I-I don't mean to sound ungrateful, I really appreciate this, I-I really, really do, b-but – "

"What's the problem?"

"I don't have my fangs, a-and I don't know if I can really bite hard enough to draw blood with my blunt teeth, and – and – "

Valen could see the gears turning in Ari's head, and then her eyebrows went up in realization. "Oh. *Oh*. Shit. Fuck. Yeah, sorry." She retracted her arm. "Okay, how about this, then, I'll just make a cut on my arm for you to drink from, then when you're done, you just close it up with that super special vampire spit you got."

Relief washed through him. "Yes, th-that sounds perfect. Thank you, ma'am."

Ari withdrew her hunting knife, and Valen whimpered, trying not to look at the blade. Blades were still a bit scary for him.

Ari made a small cut on her arm, then sat on the couch next to Valen. "Bon appétit."

"Th-thank you," he wept. "I-is it really okay?"

"Yep. Now, come on, before it gets cold. Hah."

Valen leaned down and drank, primly and softly, afraid to go too hard or too fast. Ari's hand came up to stroke the nape of his neck, warm and gentle. "There you go," Ari said encouragingly. "Good boy."

He flushed beet red, but didn't stop. *Oh, please, Ari, do you know what you're doing to me when you say that?*

Her blood tasted … sweet. He knew what this was. Her blood sugar was abnormally high.

When Valen had taken enough blood that he started to feel a little fuller, and was afraid to take more, he swiped his tongue up the wound to close it. "Thank you," he said, voice thick.

"'Course," said Ari. "We can't let you starve now, can we?"

Yeah, you really could.

He should say something about the way it tasted. If Ari was developing diabetes, it could still be prevented if she knew about it. He swiped his lips and tentatively said, "Um, ma'am, have you been tested for diabetes?" His courses in school had been mostly biomedical-focused, but he'd touched on some veterinary medicine as well. That included human diseases, and diabetes could lead all the way to limb amputation if not treated.

Ari furrowed her brow. "What?"

Oh *no,* no no no, that'd been wrong, that'd been the wrong thing to say. He should have just pretended not to notice, he shouldn't have commented on the quality of Ari's *blood,* her own body that she'd offered to him as a generous gift. "I'm – I'm sorry, I shouldn't have – shouldn't have said – said that, I – "

"Are you saying you can taste diabetes in my blood?" Ari snapped. "Or something?"

"I'm sorry," he wept. "I'm sorry, I'm sorry, pl-please forgive me, I – "

Ari stomped out of the room, huffing. Valen continued to babble and shake. "Alexis, I'm sorry, I didn't mean to – I don't know why – Please, just – "

Lex put her hands firmly on his shoulders, and he immediately shut up, quivering. "Did you taste something in the – "

"Yes," he said, hot tears streaming down his cheeks. "Her blood sugar seemed high, I was just worried for her health, but I shouldn't have said that, I didn't mean to offend her, or – or make her uncomfortable, I'm – "

"Okay," she said, giving him a squeeze. "Just calm down. Calm down, you didn't do anything wrong."

"I'm sorry."

"Okay, just. Just stay there a minute."

Lex followed Ari out into the dining room, and Valen heard them talking to each other, low and irritated. His brain was locked up in terror again, too scared to follow along, to try and figure out what he'd done wrong. Everything felt a lot more manageable now that he'd gotten some sleep – but having Ari mad at him was still a terrifying prospect.

After a minute or two of heated discussion, they came back in, Ari at the front, looking ashamed. "Diabetes runs in my family," she said. "I get freaked out thinking about it. It wasn't anything you did."

"Oh." It hadn't been anything he'd done at all; he'd just accidentally stumbled upon a sensitive subject, which had blindsided her. "Okay. That's understandable. I was just – just hoping to possibly be helpful if you didn't know. Getting treatment earlier can be – "

"I know," Ari said quickly, and Valen snapped his mouth shut. *Fuck, I messed up again, of course she doesn't want me giving her medical advice, shut up, shut up, just shut up, just stop saying the wrong thing and making everything worse!*

Lex gave her a little kick in the shin. "Ow – I mean. Yeah, I know I *should* go to the doctor. Thank you for worrying about my health."

"And?" said Lex.

"And ... I hope you feel better."

"And you're ... ?"

"I'm ... hoping that you feel better?"

"You're sorry, Ari. You're sorry that you got upset with him and made him scared."

Ari rubbed the back of her head, finding her feet interesting. "Oh. Yeah. That, um, that too. You don't deserve to get scared or anything. I know I can be kind of intense sometimes."

Oh. Everything really was okay. He took a breath to steady himself. "Thank you. I understand."

198

"Now, then," said Lex, with a little clap. "We talked to Bailey and Jerome on the phone, and they're gonna come over tonight, all right? Unless you don't want them to?"

Bailey and Jerome, the two hunters who'd grabbed him from the field and given him back to Lex and Ari. The ones who'd used the wretched silver dart, and chained him up again. He had very mixed feelings about all four of these hunters, and the thought of being in the same room as all of them made him very afraid. "What are they coming over for? Ma'am? If I may ask?"

"They're going to feed you too," Ari said. "You're gonna need more than just one feeding until you're back to a healthy weight."

"Oh," said Valen, touched. No human had been kind to him, ever, before this, and now four of them were all at once. "Th-thank you. That sounds wonderful."

"They're bringing a board game too. Hope you like Monopoly."

21

—·—

Valen was able to quell his mounting anxiety for a little while by resting in the coffin with the door locked. Cozy and safe in the dark. Lex and Ari made indistinct sounds in passing outside, whispering, thinking him asleep.

They gave a soft knock to rouse him, asking him to come out and permission to lift him bodily onto the couch, which he granted. They arranged him in the mountain of pillows, throwing a blanket out over his legs. Lex crooned over him and made sure he was as cozy as possible.

It felt ... a little infantilizing, but he would take whatever comfort and softness was offered to him at this point. Maybe he could be a creature with dignity again sometime later in life.

The two other hunters came soon enough. Ari opened the door. One of the male hunters said something boisterously, which he couldn't make any sense of, but which seemed to be a joke because the other humans all laughed at it.

Valen could tell Ari was unamused even just by looking at the back of her head. "You think you're so funny. You're gonna need Jesus to save you if you don't knock that shit off."

The larger one came in first. Bailey, he remembered. "You're right. We're actually here to deliver a pizza. You want an XL or medium?" The smaller one, Jerome, came in just in time for Bailey to hook his arms around his shoulders.

"What is this, dinner and a show?" Ari shut the door.

"Nah, we're not doing standup. The show is what this is for." Bailey gestured to a large instrument case strapped to his back, which Valen realized must be a guitar.

"You think you're so goddamn funny." Ari seemed to know her job was to play the irritated straight shooter, otherwise their antics would just be annoying rather than endearing.

"You know you love us."

"Only because nobody else will."

Bailey grinned widely, then turned towards Valen. "And there's the man of the hour! You're gonna eat like a king tonight."

Valen pressed himself fearfully into the back of the couch. The hunter's tone was light, but all of a sudden, all Valen could picture was earlier when Bailey had been looking at him through the sight of a rifle.

"It is *man*, right? Jerome insisted it was man."

"You were all juiced up on T when you got here," Jerome added. "So I assumed. Sorry you haven't been able to get your juice while you've been here. It's clearly worn off by now."

Why are you worrying about getting my pronouns right? Why is that what everyone's focused on? He knew they were probably just trying to be respectful and make him feel better, but it did little to put him at ease.

Lex had done that, insist that Nick use the correct pronouns while torturing him. As though Lex thought torture was okay as long as she wasn't also being transphobic. Like his gender was more important than his basic rights.

"S-sir, with all due respect, I appre-appreciate the apology, but I worry more about having my personal structural integrity respected than my gender identity."

The four humans all looked at each other awkwardly.

"Right ... " Jerome said. "Listen. I know an *I'm sorry* isn't gonna do jack shit for something like ... this. But we really do mean it. We're sorry. That's why we're here to try and make up for it, even if it's just a little bit."

No, no, *no*, he couldn't handle this. It was as if experiencing kindness from these four was just throwing into relief how universally hated he was by everyone else. All his friends had left him, his husband and family were menaces, and now the humans, the ones he'd been trying to help, treated him like *this*.

Valen burst into tears. "You left me there, you just *left* me there, all of you. You just watched. And you're the *kind* ones. What hope do I have, on either side of the border?"

Lex came over and wrapped her arms around him. "Shh, shh, you're okay," she soothed.

He tried to scoot back to put some distance between himself and Lex, choking back a sob. "I'm not okay! I'm very much not! I'm a starved and injured vampire in a room with four vampire hunters, who helped someone torture me! I would say this is as far from okay as one can be!"

Lex withdrew, looking hurt. Ari took her elbow and pulled her away. "Give him some space, Alex."

Jerome sat down on the edge of the couch. Valen clutched the blanket to himself, tears streaming down his face. "I get it," Jerome said. "We suck. I know we suck. I'm sorry we suck. Please let us try and suck a bit less by helping you."

Valen loosened his death grip on the blanket.

"You're safe," Lex said. "I promise you're safe now."

"We realized how fucked up it was, what we did," Ari said. "And now we're trying to fix it. That's it."

"Okay," Valen said, voice wobbly. "Thank you."

"Do you want us to just feed you and leave?" Jerome said. "We were gonna, um, kind of hang out, but ... well, if it's just going to make you feel worse, we don't have to hang around."

Valen tried to control his breathing. He was trying so hard to just *listen*, but they were four *vampire hunters*. "You can go about your business. I won't – I don't mind. I'll stay out of the way. You won't even know I'm here."

"Er," said Jerome, awkwardly fiddling with one of his dreadlocks. "No, I mean, we were going to hang out here, with you, to try and make you feel better."

Got it.

She's fucking rabid.

I told you it hurts them.

Put her in the trunk.

Fuck, tie it up first.

Settle down!

Valen curled in on himself, ears involuntarily pinned to his head, lip wobbling. "I – I – I – "

"It's okay," Bailey said, sitting down and putting an arm around Valen. "Breathe, babydoll. It's okay."

I'm sorry we suck. Please let us try and suck a bit less.

Valen broke down into tears. "Why did you think it would be okay to do that to me even if I wasn't innocent? Why do you think anyone deserves that? I was in there for *six months*, locked in the coffin except to be taken out and tortured, and you didn't even give me a chance, you kidnapped me and tortured me, you didn't even *let me talk*, and – and – " His protest dissolved into wretched sobs. "Why do you think it's okay to do that to any living creature? You're *monsters*."

Bailey eased back, face dark. The humans all looked at each other awkwardly as Valen continued to bawl.

Jerome patted the blanket. "Listen ... " he said. "Like I said, saying sorry can only go so far. Trying to make it up to you can only go so far. I'm not saying it's right, or we should have let it happen. But maybe you'll be less freaked out if you understand. Most of us have lost family members to vampires. We know what happens to them. They just get taken and snatched up out of nowhere, thrown into the meat grinder. It's happened to us, and it can happen again, to anyone we care about, at any time. I don't know if you've ever been through something like that, but it ... does things to you. Makes you numb. Makes you care less about things you'd normally care about. Makes you think someone on the other side

should have a turn suffering. Makes you think maybe you should just let the unthinkable happen if it means it can stop the flow of blood."

"It's fucked," Bailey said, tears welling in his eyes. "The whole thing is just fucked. Valen, man, please, you gotta understand. The only vampires we ever meet are the ones who cross the border, and they're usually the worst of the worst. We never met anyone like you before. We're on edge all the time, knowing every night someone wants to kidnap or kill us. Obviously I'm not saying it was right, but surely you gotta understand at least a little bit, right? We're not total monsters, I promise we aren't."

"You know what vampires are capable of," Ari added. "You know how they can be dangerous. But you don't *feel* it like we do. You've never been a prey animal."

Valen had felt like a prey animal more than he cared to admit, more than he could describe. But they were right, to an extent ...

Valen squeezed his eyes shut and took in deep breaths, trying to calm himself. "Yes," he said carefully. "I understand, in theory, the reasons behind your actions."

"I'm sorry it took us so long to realize," Lex said. "I'm sorry. I'm sorry we just ignored the way you were suffering."

Valen thought about the humans at his previous home, the ones the other nobles fed on, and how he'd refused to feed on them, and then did nothing else to help them. He had even less justification. He hadn't done that out of mortal peril and desperation like they did. It'd been out of inertia and apathy and lack of initiative. Out of fear of change and radical action.

He'd thought to himself, *If I free those humans, they'll just go get more, so it wouldn't do anything*. And he'd been right, in a way, in that the problem was systemic and couldn't be resolved by an individual. But ... he'd refused to feed on them out of squeamishness, and then walked past them every day and didn't help, the same way these humans had done to him. He understood the reasoning far better than he wanted to admit.

"Okay," he said, his rabbit-quick heartbeat finally slowing down. "I understand why you did it. I do. It's just difficult to feel safe."

"We've learned our lesson," Lex said. "We're not gonna let something like that happen again, to you or to anyone."

Valen nodded. "Thank you. Thank you, ma'am."

"There, see? Everything's okay." Bailey slung his guitar around and started to pluck a few strings. "Now, time for dinner and a show!"

Valen couldn't help but smile. Bailey and Jerome were just so ... *goofy*. It felt weird. As though he hadn't expected the vampire hunters to have any personality beyond wanting to hurt him. "Excellent," he said timidly. "I'll be sure to spread the word about the excellent service at your establishment, haha!"

"Oh, he's funny," Jerome said.

"Yeah, yeah, he's funny, but he's also fucking *hungry*, I bet. Time to chow down, big guy." Bailey rolled his sleeve up. "Ari said the arm is an option, yeah?"

"Um ... " Valen shrank back. "I can't bite – You – you pulled my fangs out."

Bailey blinked. "Ah. Shit. We did."

Ari wordlessly handed over her knife.

"Right ... " Bailey said. He took the knife unhappily. Jerome looked like someone had threatened to stab him, and took a step back without a word. Valen looked at him apprehensively.

"All right, here I go," Bailey said, looking queasy. He positioned the knife over his arm, in the spot where it seemed safest. He took in a pained, hissing breath as he made a cut with the knife.

"Jesus, you big baby," Ari said.

"Ey, ey, some of us don't see blood once a month, ya know. Only when something's the matter." He sat on the edge of the bed and held his bleeding arm out to Valen. "Eat up."

"Thank you, sir," Valen said politely, and bobbed his head in a bow. He leaned forward and took Bailey's arm delicately, drinking in small, dainty sips.

"There ya go," Bailey said, ruffling Valen's hair. "Bet that feels better."

Valen finished his drink, swiping his tongue over the wound to close it, then brought his head back up, licking his lips. "It does. Thank you, sir."

Jerome was still cowering against the wall.

"You don't have to if you don't want to," Ari said. "The two of us are plenty."

"Is everything okay?" Lex said. "Like, something up?"

"Um." Jerome swallowed and drew forwards, wringing his hands. "No, I – I want to help. I want to help him get better. I do. I just ... "

"Is getting fed from too much, even if it's from an open cut?" Lex said. "Blood loss affect you?"

"Um ... " Jerome nervously shook his head. "I, no, that's not it. I – "

Valen panicked a bit, guilt and fear flooding him, as he saw the internal struggle about whether or not to feed him. "Don't feel obligated, sir, it's quite all right. I've had more than enough for today." Two feedings was definitely enough to stave off the hunger – if he wanted to get back to a healthy weight, he'd definitely get better faster with more, but this had saved him from the hunger, at least. But what was the issue? Was Jerome afraid of him? That wasn't good, *at all*. It'd seemed like things were going well, but now he started to spiral into anxiety again.

"I want to," Jerome said, sounding like he was about to cry. "I do, I'm sorry. I just can't, man. I'm sorry."

Bailey squeezed his shoulder. "You don't have to tell them, J-man."

"No, I ... Okay, yeah, I want to." Jerome sighed. He rolled up the sleeve of his hoodie, revealing a series of scars striped up his forearm. They looked old, but they were easy to see because they were raised and bumpy, and darker in color than his already-dark skin. "I just, um ... I just got some baggage about cutting myself," he said, swallowing thickly.

Lex and Ari both looked sorrowful. "Oh," Lex said softly. "Of course. Don't worry about it. Whatever you can handle. It's fine if you can't."

Valen was horrified by the reveal of this injury, but ... the humans all seemed to know what this meant, and Valen ... didn't know what could have caused an

injury like that. His imagination ran wild trying to guess. Had Jerome been forced to cut himself to feed vampires before?

"I would never force you, sir," Valen says. "I promise. I don't know ... why, or who would make you do that, but ... "

The humans all looked at him like he'd grown a second head. He shrunk back fearfully. "I'm sorry, I'm sorry if that was rude, sir, I am – I just don't understand, I – "

Jerome laughed, his thick voice breaking up the tension in the air. "Of course. Oh my God. Vampires don't scar, so of course you wouldn't know. I can't imagine they self-harm either." He ran his fingers over his forearm. "I ... did this myself. When I was younger."

"What? Why?" Valen blurted out before he could stop himself. He was *horrified* by this idea.

"It's hard to describe," Jerome said. "I was ... in a lot of emotional pain. It felt like ... I didn't deserve to *not* be in pain, in a way, that I deserved it. Or maybe it was easier to have a bigger problem. A cut on the arm is easier to treat than feeling like shit, you know? You probably wouldn't get it, but it made sense to my brain at the time."

Never in a million years would Valen have guessed a human would feel like that. He'd had thoughts like that before, but they'd been driven by guilt and disgust at himself. He'd never cut himself, but he'd starved himself often enough. But he did that because he needed to hurt others to feed; why would a *human* hate themselves enough for that? Why would they *possibly* feel guilty about existing like Valen did?

Maybe he shouldn't say this. Maybe if he told them about how he'd sometimes gone days without eating because of the shame and self-loathing, only eating when the hunger pains became too much to bear, maybe they'd say he *should* have done that, because he's a monster and hurts others when he takes care of himself.

"I ... do get it," Valen said bravely. "More than I care to admit. I ... often starved myself for similar reasons. I felt too guilty to drink. Too guilty for existing. I never cut myself, but I often had self-inflicted pain. It was ... stupid."

Jerome let out a slightly choked murmur of pity, putting a hand on Valen's shoulder. "It wasn't stupid, man, neither of us were. I mean, heck, for you, it at least made sense, right? Because you felt guilty for drinking people's blood, yeah? That's only natural."

"No, I ... I still did that to myself even when I started drinking the imported blood."

They all blinked at him. Oh, they ... they didn't know about the imported blood? But of course, how *would* they know?

"There are specialty shops on the other side of the border who import blood from overseas," he explained. "Where there's infrastructure for collecting it from paid volunteers. Places where things are kinder, where humans and vampires aren't constantly at each other's throats like we are here."

"Penpals!" Lex declared. "I told you, I fucking told you! They get it from the vampire's penpals!"

Oh, so they knew about the penpals thing. Valen smiled a little. "Yes. I've thought about trying to move there, but they're extremely stringent about immigration." It only made sense that the few vampires who'd managed to build some semblance of peace would be extremely protective of their humans. But more to the point ... "But it's entirely voluntary, so I shouldn't have felt guilty for eating back then, but ... it still lingered." He looked up at Jerome. "I wouldn't have thought humans would have any reason to feel that way. You're innocent."

Jerome gave him a sad smile. "It's so much more complicated than that. We got ... things to cope with even though we don't have to drink blood, you know? Dunno if you want me to dump all this on you, but my ...   I was depressed as fuck growing up. It's easy to fall into when things seem so hopeless. It's so hard to stay out of jail, when it feels like they're *trying* to get you in there. And my ... the first time doing it was when ...   "

He put his head in his hands, starting to cry. Bailey sat down and put his arms around him. "It's okay. You're all right."

"When my daddy found out I was gay," Jerome choked out. "And I told him I was worried about – about catching GRID, or whatever that – that gay flu going around is, that people are dying from and he said – he said maybe it would be better if I did." He broke down into full-blown sobs.

Lex and Ari came over and added themselves to the comforting hug as Jerome cried. Valen stared at him with misty eyes, absolutely blown away. For some reason, he hadn't imagined humans to be capable of such cruelty. At first, to anyone – he wouldn't have guessed they could be so cruel to him, a vampire, but to say such a thing to another human?

Why?

His worldview had started to crumble in his hands. He'd mostly been picturing humans living picturesque, ideal lives ruined only by the monstrous actions of vampires. How had he been so narcissistic to think the world revolved around him and his crimes like that? Why hadn't he thought that humans were fully-realized individuals who could invent their own bigotry against other humans?

"I'm … sorry, sir," Valen said. "That's unbelievably cruel. I'm sorry that happened to you."

Jerome sniffed and looked up at him, wiping his eyes. "Yeah," he said, voice wobbly. "But hey, I don't have to care about what he thinks anymore. Fuck him, haha. I got everyone I need right here."

"Yeah, man, yeah you do."

Jerome disentangled himself from the hug. "Well – well I don't care that my blood ain't good enough for the Red Cross – it's good enough for you, and you know blood better than they do. Come on, let's figure out some way to make this work, huh?"

The group tossed ideas around, and hemmed and hmmed for a while, before Jerome eventually agreed that it would be okay to make two pinpricks, like a bite,

rather than a cut. It took a lot longer to get the blood out, but Jerome didn't mind, and good-naturedly played with Valen's hair while he did so, which was soothing.

Valen was overfull by the time he was done. He was starting to get a bit afraid that he'd throw up again. "Thank you, sir. I feel much better now."

"Well, we ain't done yet!" Bailey jovially picked up his guitar. "Get ready!"

"R-ready for what?" Valen stammered.

"He's gonna play you a song," Lex said.

"It's supposed to make you feel better," Jerome said. "If you'd rather not, we don't have to."

Valen drew the covers further up himself. "Th-that sounds nice. That could be nice. Thank you."

"Right," Bailey said. His fingers started working at the guitar strings, plucking out a jaunty tune. "Now, I'm good on the guitar here, and Jerome's got the golden pipes, so I'm gonna let him lead, and I'll be the backup singer."

Jerome reached into his bag and pulled out a tambourine, shaking it. "And you ladies might know the words to this song, so feel free to sing along." This with a wink at Valen, which caused him to slide down into the couch.

Jerome started singing.

Oh it happened one night when the moon was bright
And full, but not as full as my heart

Lex and Ari instantly recognized the song and joined in, smiling widely and laughing. Apparently this song was ... very funny, but Valen had never heard it.

When I saw her, I knew she could tear me apart
She was pale and dead and covered in blood but hey
Nobody's perfect
And she paralyzed me with a glance
No persuasion needed
And no sooner had my lips touched hers
Than all the blood had left my body
But it was worth it in the end as the feeling fled my limbs

Valen went beet red, realizing suddenly that the song was about a human man taking a vampire lover and getting killed for it. It was undeniably a sad story, but ... it was so chipper. Was this supposed to be a joke?

Bailey knelt down next to Valen, gesturing to him grandly during a particularly intense verse.

Oh you're so big and bad it's true

But that's what I like about you

Jerome knelt on his other side, shaking the tambourine.

It's true that you could snap me in half

But baby, maybe I'm into that.

Valen tossed the covers over his head, mortified.

And if this ends with me getting all my stuff sucked out,

Well, that's sort of what I was hoping for

There was silence for a moment, no one singing, the guitar twanging. He cautiously raised his head and peeked over the blanket, only to find that everyone was looking at him and pointing.

"I'm sorry," he stuttered. "I don't know the words."

"Oh, this part is just a big growl," Bailey said.

Valen's eyes bounced around the room.

"Go on," Jerome said. "Give us your scariest growl."

Valen nervously clutched the blanket, scanning them all one last time to make sure it was really okay before letting out a tiny, strangulated noise.

They all knew Valen had a better growl in him. Hell, they'd *heard* him give better growls in the basement. But he was afraid to go too hard, to seem too threatening. Nobody pushed it. They gave a cheer.

Valen's spirits soared. He'd participated, and they were all cheering for him. He knew it was supposed to be a silly song, clearly it was supposed to be a silly song, but ... it made him feel better. Less alone. Less different from the humans, to know that he wasn't the only one who'd had lofty ideas about love between

humans and vampires, to think about a world where a human would walk up to a vampire and kiss her.

His eyes shifted over to Lex and Ari. He couldn't decide how he felt about them. But he was definitely feeling *something*.

22

— ◆ —

"All right, up you go."

Still in his pajamas, Valen tentatively stepped up onto the bathroom scale.

Ari scrutinized the numbers. "All right, seventy-three pounds! You're getting there, big guy!"

"How much did you weigh before all this?" Lex asked.

"A-about a hundred and ten pounds, I think." It was a distant memory, not being able to see his ribs, not having sunken, bruised rings around his eyes.

"That's still on the light side," Ari said. "We've gotta fatten you up."

"He's already gained ten pounds."

"Yeah, it's a wonder what three square meals a day can do to ya."

Valen wasn't used to three square meals a day. Vampires didn't *do* three square meals a day. They did one meal a day, and it usually wasn't any particular shape. He'd been positively overwhelmed by the bounty being offered to him. It was hard to get used to after so long with absolutely nothing, but it was a welcome change. "Thank you."

"Everything okay?" Ari asked, apparently noting something wrong with his response. He could never seem to answer quite correctly.

"It's just – it's just been a lot."

"Of course ... You just take it easy. You don't have to worry about anything anymore." He'd been trying to slow his racing mind down to believe that over the past few days, he really had been. It was *almost* starting to work, now that he could actually get decent sleep, which made everything less overwhelming.

The massive amount of blood he was given every day was also getting him healthy pretty quickly – his healing had sped back up to the point where his legs were already un-broken and his fangs had grown back. He still appreciated a bit of help walking, though, which he readily accepted as Ari helped him down the stairs and into the living room.

"Um ... " Ari said, eyeing the coffin. "So ... I promise it's okay ... but ... "

Valen's anxiety spiked. Oh no, they'd noticed that Valen had torn up his pillow. *Again.* Valen had lost track of how many of their bed sets he'd ruined. He drew his limbs closer to himself, face reddening.

Lex spoke before he could. "Oh. We can replace it again, don't worry."

Was she disappointed? Angry, but just hiding it? Losing her patience? It was hard to tell. He was starting to get healthy again, and less helpless, but he was still terrified of wearing out his welcome at Lex and Ari's house before he was ready to leave. Or even worse, the ever-present fear of them changing their minds and calling Nick.

Valen wrung his hands. "I'm sorry. I'm sorry I keep ruining them." He tried not to cry. "I'm trying not to, but I do it in my sleep."

"It's okay," Lex said, taking his elbow. "It's not a big deal."

He broke eye contact.

"I noticed that you grind your teeth and bite things when you're awake too."

Valen was *so* incredibly self-conscious of his mouth, his main weapon for preying on humans, whether in the form of persuasion or using his very evident fangs to bite and tear. He hated that they were paying such close attention to the way he bit and chewed things. That was one thing humans didn't really do—bite in a significant way—one thing that would remind them how bestial he really was if he wasn't careful to keep it under wraps. That he chewed on things like an animal, because he wasn't human, and maybe not a person, if they changed their minds.

"I'm sorry," he said, tears spilling over. "I'm sorry, I'm sorry, I promise I'm not – I'm not – "

"Relax," Ari said, and grounding hands appeared on his shoulders. "We're just trying to figure out how to fix whatever problem you're having."

Right. Of course. *Calm down.* It was so embarrassingly easy to send him spiraling into panic. He sniffled and wiped his cheek with the back of his hand. "It's an anxious habit. It was – chewing on the muzzle was really the only thing I could do sometimes."

That was a massive understatement. He'd never been a nervous chewer before, but practically all day every day for the past few months he'd spent gnawing at the muzzle, the damnable contraption keeping him trapped there, half in hopes of somehow getting it off and half to just soothe himself and get *some* stimulation that wasn't painful. Grinding his teeth on the metal bit that kept his tongue pressed to the floor of his mouth had been his only release at times, as he sobbed and screamed and cried hopelessly, unable to do anything else. Not to mention all the times he bit down on it because he was gritting his teeth in pain.

Lex smiled at him sadly. "It's okay that you do that. I don't think you should try and make yourself stop. Can you open your mouth for me for a minute?"

He tentatively opened his mouth, feeling extremely self-conscious with his fangs, the foremost evidence of his monstrousness, on full display. He didn't want them to see him as a predatory beast, but he also felt a strange mix of embarrassment: He wanted them to like him, and he was worried that inspecting his fangs would affect their opinion of him.

Lex leaned over and performed some inspection, the criteria of which were known only to her. After a few moments, she asked, "Do you want us to get you a chew toy?"

Valen shut his mouth. "A chew toy ... ?" Like for a dog? He hesitated – he was so, so nervous to remind them at all of his animalistic nature.

"I bet the kind they make for dogs would stand up to your chewing better. Or we could try and find a binky, or something along those lines."

But it was too tempting to pass up.

"Yes, I would like that."

***

Lex and Ari had gone back to work after a certain point. Of course they had – they were working class, it would be hugely burdensome for them to continue to miss work, and Valen was determined to be the least amount of burdensome possible, so he was happy that they went back to work.

But that did leave him at home alone for long periods during the night. He got jittery. Night was safer than the day, but only by virtue of his nature – night had historically been when Nick had taken free rein to do whatever he wanted, when the base was empty since everyone was out on patrol.

Still … it meant there was no sunlight, which was a definite plus. The patch of burned skin on his face and destroyed, shriveled eye where the sunlight had hit him had taken by far the longest out of all his injuries to heal, still being raw and painful long after the others had started to close themselves up. He had no desire whatsoever to encounter the sun a second time.

He tried to pass the time reading, which had always been his favorite go-to pastime. But pretty much every time he did, his brain started to wander off, like a dog let loose in a field. It felt like trying to grab something particularly slippery, and he would often sit there staring at one page and look up to realize that several hours had passed and he'd done nothing but read the same paragraph dozens of times without absorbing a word. The physical damage was starting to heal, but his ordeal had done more than physical damage to him. When he was alone in the house and therefore not embarrassed to do it in front of Lex and Ari, he would often cry over the loss of the activity that used to bring him the most joy. Hardly anything did anymore, and he tried to grab calmness and happiness like sand running through his fingers. It was almost embarrassing how eager he was for Lex and Ari to come home, so he'd have something to think about besides how damaged and lost he felt.

One day when Valen was lying down in the coffin, halfway between sleep and trying to read, Lex and Ari came in without him even noticing.

"Hey," Lex said gently, setting some crinkly paper bags down by him. "We got some things for you."

"Oh. Thank you." He leaned over and wordlessly examined the bags. There were several dog toys that looked like they could take some chewing, as well as chew toys for human infants. Binkies, Lex had called them. These things would *never* hold up under the force of teething vampire children.

And underneath that – books. Easy books, written for children.

He tried not to let it show how relieved he was by this collection of items. He could tell the chew toys would be a huge comfort just by looking at them, and he could have wept looking at the books – they had pictures of animals. Maybe he could get back to where he'd been before eventually, but ... baby steps.

He lifted one out, a picture book about mammals, and opened it to a page about elephants. He remembered the first time he'd learned about elephants. He'd wondered what their blood tasted like, then what they sounded like. They made noises too low in pitch for humans to hear, but could vampires hear it? No one seemed to know the answer.

His eyes drifted over the text, going slow, but taking it in. He slowly ran a hand over the picture, simple and colorful. Gentle. Easy. He grabbed one of the pacifiers and put it in his mouth, chewing it quietly.

***

Valen was still massively underweight, but after a few days, Lex started to help feed him. Ari was still visibly unhappy about being fed from, but she did it without complaint, and with Bailey and Jerome's visits he had *four* people feeding him – a virtual glut that any vampire noble would be jealous of.

Valen took a moment to reflect on the irony – in direct contrast to vampires' typical domineering habits, he hadn't even sought this out, yet he had four humans willingly and enthusiastically offering him their own fresh blood every day. That was a luxury vampire nobility could not even buy; the closest they could get would be to have four brainwashed slaves following their commands. Valen felt like a god among vampires, despite the fact that he was using toys and books made for human children and sleeping in an unpainted wooden box with a duvet stapled to the inside of it.

Regaining some of his strength went a long way to starting to ease his anxiety about being so completely helpless and at the mercy of the hunters, but he was never able to clear the anxiety entirely. He was still deep in human territory, and Nick was here, somewhere, out there.

He heard Nick on the phone once, and couldn't suppress his urge to cower. He buried himself under the covers in his coffin, shaking.

"You're okay," Lex soothed, rubbing his back through the blanket. "He's not here."

"D-does he know where you live?" That was the million dollar question. One crucial barrier between Nick and him. His befuddled brain couldn't remember the fact that they'd already told him Nick didn't.

"No," Lex said. "No, he doesn't, remember?"

Valen found this little comfort, and huddled further under his covers.

Ari finished her conversation and hung up the phone, coming back in. "Nick is still trying to rope someone else into getting a live capture. I think he's getting desperate, because he called just to tell me the bounty's gone up again."

Valen couldn't stifle the embarrassing whine.

"We're not giving you back," Ari said firmly. "We're not letting him find out you're still alive, and we're not letting anyone else take you. You say the word, and we take you straight to the border."

Valen peeked out from under the blanket. He considered it, he'd been considering it. He could walk again, he was getting steadier on his feet ... Still, the thought of being on his own again was scary.

But ...

"You were talking to him."

"Nick? Yeah, on the phone." Ari didn't seem to understand what he was trying to say.

"And at work sometimes, yeah," Lex added, as though this were helpful.

How could Valen communicate how *unsafe* that simple fact made him feel? "You were talking to him like he's a person and not a monster."

Lex and Ari looked at each other, then back at him. "He's fucked up," Ari said. "But everything he did, he had permission for."

Valen burst into tears, the entirety of his ordeal hitting him at once.

" ... Right?" Ari said.

"No," Valen wept. "No, no, a thousand times no." They didn't know, they truly didn't know, oh God, he was going to have to *tell* them. "He came back at night when the compound was empty because everyone was out on patrol. He opened the coffin when he was alone, he broke the rules all the time."

"What?" Ari growled. "What for?"

"Ari," Lex said, looking sick.

Valen just sat there and cried, trying to speak but choking on the words. Ari knelt, steadying him and supporting him in her arms. "Breathe, breathe, you're okay."

Lex handed him a tissue. He took it, but was still crying too hysterically to use it. "Let it out, baby," Ari said. "You're okay."

Valen took in great, sobbing gasps, wiping his eyes, then blowing his nose. "S-sorry."

"You're okay. Let it out."

His lip wobbled. He grabbed the stuffed cat Lex had put in the coffin, hugging it. "Nick has a shocking sadistic streak that he knows how to keep hidden."

Ari stood, palming her mouth. "All right. Fuck."

"I'm sorry," Lex said. "We didn't know."

"He did it all the time. When we were alone. He – he – he would do anything he couldn't get away with during the day under supervision. Things that – that could have no possible justification. Humiliating things, senseless torture, rape – "

"What the *fuck*," Ari said. She was turning a cartoonish shade of red with her anger. "I'm going to kill him. I'm going to fucking kill him."

"We need to tell the director," Lex said, white as a sheet. "He needs to know."

"We can't," Ari said through gritted teeth. "We can't do anything with this information without everyone finding out Valen is alive."

The director was the one who authorized Nick to torture him in the first place. Valen didn't have high hopes about how that would go even if it *didn't* put him in danger from Nick.

Valen took one of the chew toys and put it in his mouth, grinding anxiously.

"I'm going to fucking kill him. I'm going to shoot him as many times as bullets I have, and then I'm going to get more bullets and shoot him some more. They're going to be scrubbing him out of the carpet for months afterwards."

Ari's anger and tone were too much, even though they weren't directed at him. Valen pulled the blankets back over himself, shaking with fear.

"Ari, shut up. You just said we can't do anything to let anyone know Valen is alive. And getting yourself arrested isn't going to help anyone."

Ari's footsteps could be heard stomping away, then the sounds of Ari whaling on a punching bag in the next room.

He felt Lex's gentle hands on him once again. "What do you want us to do, Valen?"

Kill him. The only way I'll ever feel safe again is seeing Nick's corpse, watching him die, knowing he's not out there and can't hurt me anymore. But of course they couldn't just go murder him. It was like Lex had said. "I don't know," he admitted tearily.

Ari came back in, still breathing heavily. She had a foil package in one hand. "Take this. All of it."

Valen hesitated, then took the package. It had several small white pills inside. "What is it?"

"Emergency contraception."

Valen's panic immediately surged. "You don't think – It isn't *possible*, surely, for a human and a vampire ... ?"

"I don't know. But I'm not taking any chances. The whole pack."

"Will it even work?"

"It's hormones, so if testosterone injections work on you, then maybe."

Valen forced his vision to focus on the pills. He was probably well outside the window of time when such a medication would even be effective. But if there was any chance at all that it would work, to prevent any chance at all of him conceiving ...

He nodded grimly, then started pushing the pills through the foil.

***

"Try the bolt cutters again."

"We're not trying the fucking bolt cutters again. We already saw that didn't work."

"I don't think we're going to make any progress this way."

"We might if you give me longer than ten seconds!"

"We might have to use the saw."

"We're not using the fucking *saw*. You're going to take his damn head off."

Valen tried so, so, so hard to stay still as the two women went at the metal collar with everything they had. Ari was currently trying to pick the lock, a book with diagrams of locks and lockpicks out on the table next to Valen's head. Ari gripped

his hair with one hand to keep him steady, peering down into the lock as though she could see the pins. "Fuck me, I didn't expect this to be so hard."

Ari stood him upright. "And you're *sure* you can't break it now that you've gotten some strength back."

Valen had already tried to explain that the collar and lock both had silver on the inside, because Nick was very good at making things from silver, and therefore Valen would *never* be able to break it no matter how strong he was. But he tried again for good measure, just to demonstrate. Nothing happened, his hands trembling as he pulled with all his might. "Yes, ma'am, I'm quite sure."

Ari scowled. "All right. Lex, hold the light." Valen craned his neck, stretching upwards as far as he could to give Ari more room as she went at it with the lockpicks again.

"Maybe we can try and get the key off Nick – "

"No, I'm not doing *anything* that could clue that maniac in to the fact that we have Valen."

Valen squeezed his eyes shut, wanting to be rid of the last evidence of Nick's domination of him, the last thing binding him, more than anything. This had been *enormously* stressful for him so far, though, mostly because Ari had been on a hair-trigger with her anger the entire time. He was afraid of pissing her off even more, and tried to be as quiet as possible throughout the whole process to make up for being the center of attention.

Ari started to huff and puff angrily, motions becoming agitated. She eventually broke the lockpick and tossed it to the ground, cursing.

"All right, let's take a break," Lex said.

Ari plopped down onto the chair next to the workbench. "Fuck. I can't – I can't – I still can't believe he did that." Her temper was absolutely boiling. Her anger was exacerbating Valen's anxiety, even though it was self-directed.

She stood back up and grabbed the collar again, a bit too roughly, and he winced back, suppressing a whimper.

"Ari, stop, take a break."

"I'm *fixing* this," she snarled. "I'm getting it off, I'm fixing it. Give me the saw."

"Ari, you're scaring him."

Ari looked at him, startled, as though she hadn't realized.

Finally, the tools in her hands clattered to the floor. "I'm sorry," she said, tears welling up in her eyes. "I'm so *fucking* sorry we did this to you."

Oh. *That* was why Ari had been so intent on this. On doing this *now*, on getting the collar off *now*. He felt himself softening, and he reached out to her, but she quickly pulled him into a hug.

His ear was near her heart, and he heard it beating, and the roar of blood rushing through her veins. "F-fuck. I'm sorry, I'm *so* sorry," Ari said.

Valen thought of the humans at the Kithrara estate, the ones he didn't help, the humans he didn't want to risk himself for. They'd all think he was a monster, most humans would. He would cry like this when confronted with the evidence of his complacency in a system that committed atrocities on a massive scale, of the damage his passivity had caused. Of the good he could have done, but didn't.

What would he want to hear from one of them?

"I'm ... not going to say it's okay," Valen started. "Because it isn't. But when we make mistakes, what matters is what we do after that. And you've chosen to do everything within your power to fix things, even though it meant confronting your own feelings of shame and guilt. Looking uncomfortable truths in the eye takes courage and integrity, and for that I admire you."

Ari let out a choked sound. "Wow, okay, Aristotle."

What did *that* mean? Had Valen said the wrong thing?

Lex let out a laugh, slapping Ari on the arm lightly. "You goofball. Come on, sit down, let me try for once."

Oh. All it meant was that Ari was overwhelmed, and didn't know how to handle the situation. She sat down, wiping her nose on the back of her hand. *Thank you for trying. I know it's hard to make it right, but thank you for trying as hard as you can.*

Lex took the wheel. Valen recognized that Lex and Ari had wildly different strengths and weaknesses, and had already learned to appreciate the differences that made them stronger together, the both of them different but equally valuable people. But it would be a lie to say he wasn't significantly more relaxed now that it was Lex handling him, rather than Ari.

Her hands were much steadier, and she was calmer. She spent a minute examining the diagram of the lock with all its pins, then took the lockpicks and started fiddling with it.

The lock popped open. It was off, oh it was *off*. The feeling was unparalleled as the collar snapped off and clattered on the ground.

Lex smiled. "There, see? Nothing we can't fix."

23

— • —

There was a knock at the door.

That was bad. In the time Valen had been here, Lex and Ari hadn't had any visitors besides Jerome and Bailey.

Valen had been lying secure in his wooden box sleeping, but the knock woke him up. His stomach started to twist with anxiety. Who could it be? Not Nick, right?

Lex walked forward and opened the door.

"Ah, Alexis." That was all Valen heard. Because it was *his* voice. Why was Nick here?

Why is Nick here?

I thought he didn't know where we live!

I thought you were going to take care of me! I thought I didn't have to worry!

Valen was immediately so wild with terror, heart pounding, ratcheting up to maximum panic, that he couldn't even focus enough to hear anything that Nick was saying.

They'd betrayed him. All the comforting words had been just for show. He'd been trying so hard to convince himself to believe them, and the prickling anxiety in the back of his mind that he couldn't ignore had been *right*. They were just going to hand him right back over. His racing mind slowed down a bit as he noted Lex and Ari both sounded unhappy in this conversation with Nick, and that time was dragging on without the coffin opening, without them telling him Valen was here.

Calm down. Calm down. They weren't opening the door. They weren't giving him away. They didn't plan this. Of course they hadn't. Nick must have come over unannounced somehow. He wasn't supposed to know where they lived, but he must have found out somehow and invited himself over. He didn't seem to realize Valen was in the box.

Which meant one thing. There was one thought now blotting everything else out. His survival now depended entirely on his ability to be quiet.

The words in the conversation above him still flowed past him without comprehension. He was   far too tense and scared to follow the conversation.

Slowly, so slowly, he lifted his hands to his face and clamped them over his mouth and nose. Humans' hearing wasn't good enough to hear that, right? Nor his panicked breathing? Nor his hammering heart? Nor his sweating or tears slipping down his face?

There came the sound of things tapping on top of the coffin. His entire body stayed rigid, about to snap like a taut spring.

He ground his teeth. Humans' hearing wasn't good enough to hear that, right? It *hurt*. His teeth clicked together.

He had one of his chew toys in the coffin with him. Nick wouldn't be able to hear that, right? Surely his hearing wasn't good enough to hear fangs sinking gently into fabric, muffling the sound of his teeth?

He very, very slowly reached down and took the dog toy, bringing it up and putting it in his mouth.

He sank his fangs into it. In the microsecond after his brain had sent the signal to his nerves to shut his jaw, but before his jaw had responded and closed, he realized with electric panic that he'd grabbed one of the dog toys that had a noisemaker in it.

The toy squeaked. It was like a gunshot. Valen's heart stopped. He remained completely rigid, sweat pouring off his forehead.

"Do you have a dog?" said Nick's voice.

Valen's fingers twitched. He expected the coffin door to be ripped open at any moment. The seconds stretched on and it didn't come. The voices continued their conversation. He still couldn't make himself focus enough to actually listen to what they were talking about, eyes rolling around in terror.

Finally, finally, *finally* footsteps moved towards the front door, and he could hear Ari ushering Nick out. Valen waited in silence, wracked with full-body tremors.

"Valen, he's gone, please open the door." It was Lex's voice. Valen's hands shook almost too badly to undo the lock. The coffin flew open, and Lex pulled him up and into a hug.

"I'm sorry," he wept. "I'm sorry, I forgot that was one of the toys that had a squeaker in it. I'm sorry." He felt so *stupid*. The anxiety had just been eating a pit in his stomach, and he'd needed *something*.

"You're okay," Lex said.

"It's all right," she'd said, and then locked him in the coffin and tossed him down the stairs into hell.

"I'm going to fucking kill him." It was Ari, and she was *mad*. At first Valen was terrified that she was talking about him, until it registered that *him* meant Nick. That was good, that was one thing he had going for him. Lex and Ari were still on his side. He clung to it like a drowning man on a life preserver.

"What do we do?" Lex said. "I feel like he definitely figured it out. He definitely figured it out, right?"

He definitely did, he must have. If he'd figured out where they lived, he must have figured out Valen was here, right? He was out there, plotting, scheming, making his weapons, imagining all the horrible things he was going to do to Valen once he got his hands on him again.

"And he has another vampire. We have to do something, right?"

He has another vampire? Valen was sick at the thought of someone else being there in his place. Valen wasn't alone in this hell anymore. Nick had another victim. They had to get them out.

Which was terrifying, because Valen might have to do something to help them. If it came down to it, he couldn't *not* help them, but when it came down to it, he might not be able to make himself help them either, if it meant confronting Nick. His body would lock up, like it had just now.

Ari ground her teeth. "We have to get Valen out of here. Across the border."

Yes. Yes, please. Please. I need to get out of here. Where he can't reach me. He was in a fit enough state to be on his own now, right? Physically, at least. Yes, probably. Mentally?

Maybe.

"Can you run?" Ari asked. "Are you going to be okay on your own?"

Valen tried to control his breathing. He could, right? "Yes. I-I think so." Maybe he would have to be, because the alternative was staying here when Nick knew where they lived, and *oh God he knows where I am –*

Ari came over and wrapped her arms around him. "Good," she said softly. "I don't want anything to happen to you."

He just let himself be held, the anxiety melting slightly, here in her strong arms. His eyes started to slide closed, soothed by the sound of her beating heart. He had to resist the urge to follow her as she released him.

"Which is why you're going home at nightfall."

Valen had mixed feelings about it. Truly he would only be safe over the border ... but he was strangely loath to leave Lex and Ari.

It didn't have to be goodbye forever, he told himself. They had phones. They could call each other. It's not like he would never get to see them again. Even though they were unsafe in vampire territory, and he was unsafe in human territory, they could figure something out. If the two of them wanted to ...

With considerable effort, he wrenched his train of thought back on the tracks. Truly the only thing that could distract him from the fear of Nick was the possibility of ...

Of what ... ?

Of ... *something* with Lex and Ari.

But there would be time to think about that later, when Nick was no longer a looming, imminent threat. He nodded resolutely. "Okay."

"What about the other vampire?" Lex asked.

Right ... he couldn't leave without making sure Nick's second potential victim was safe from him. He braced himself – most vampires who came over the border were here to catch humans, so this was bound to be one of the worst of the worst among vampirekind. Maybe even one of the hunters that worked for the Kithrara blood farms, some of the nastiest people he'd ever met.

"Valen, can you hang around long enough for us to bust them out?" Ari asked. "I'm thinking we just ... go grab them and dump them in your lap, and you both go home. Nick is gonna be pissed, but I bet we can finesse this in a way that we don't get in too much trouble. We might lose our jobs, but Lex and I were thinking of quitting anyway. I'm not putting my job over my humanity. And it does come down to that, thinking about letting someone else go through that. Even a vampire that was here to catch a human."

He could do that, right? All he'd need to do would be wait, and then get delivered home and make sure this second vampire got home as well. The thought was ... well, it weighed on his conscience to know that freeing a random vampire might mean they'd just go take another shot at kidnapping someone, but what was the alternative? Kill them? Leave them?

Valen could try talking to them. Maybe they could be reasoned with, especially since their last attempt had failed. He nodded. "Yes. Thank you. Yes, we can do that."

Ari ran her fingers through her hair, huffing. "Okay. Guess we just need to figure out what we're gonna do, then."

24

Nick was meeting them at the base, so they decided Valen should stay home while they went to the hunter's base. That seemed safest, since it would keep the most distance between Nick and Valen.

That was logical. Nick was going to be at the vampire hunter's base, so it only made sense for Valen to stay home.

Alone.

Undefended.

He lay in the coffin with the door locked, sweating bullets. *They're meeting Nick at the base. He isn't going to show up here. Unless he is. I'm a coffee table, that's all. Just a coffee table. Why do they need an entire table for a single beverage? They're so strange.*

Bailey and Jerome were on patrol tonight, but they'd been filled in on the details and were planning to make a pitstop to check on Valen, just in case. They were afraid if they called off completely, that would increase the suspicion to outside parties and harm their plausible deniability that the girls were planning on snatching Nick's second research sample tonight.

Valen had been scared to be around any of the vampire hunters, but somehow it was *so* much worse now that he was alone. He put a chew toy in his mouth – one of the ones without a noisemaker, he'd made sure of that. He just had to wait.

And wait.

Suddenly he could hear the doorknob of the front door rattling. He remained frozen.

It's just Jerome and Bailey.

The front window shattered.

IT'S JUST JEROME AND BAILEY. THEY JUST FORGOT THEIR KEYS. RIGHT?

Footsteps approached. The bone-deep fear seizing him demanded he lay completely still, so he obliged. His teeth ground silently on the toy.

The lid of the coffin rattled, but the lock kept it shut.

His heart leapt in his throat. *I'm a coffee table. Just a coffee table. Don't mind me.* He kept lying completely still. *Maybe he'll just go away.*

The prongs of a crowbar stuck into the coffin, prying the lid open. The lock snapped off the wood, and the door came open.

That was what Valen finally needed for his brain to permit him to move. He flailed wildly and started shouting at the top of his lungs, what he'd needed to shout every time he'd been unable to save himself over the past six months. *"NO! STOP! STOP, PLEASE STOP! PLEASE! STOP!"*

He lay there with his arms extended, eyes squeezed shut, face screwed up. The seconds drew out. Nothing happened.

He opened his eyes.

Nick was hovering over the open coffin with the crowbar in his hand, but his face was frozen in the trademark blank expression of a human under hypnosis by persuasion. Valen had used persuasion on him without even realizing it, the adrenaline and panic had been so bad.

Of course. Valen was a fed, healthy, unrestrained vampire. He wasn't helpless anymore. He'd somehow forgotten.

Valen slowly levered himself upright, slithering out of the coffin and slinking away from Nick.

Okay, nothing was different. Valen still just had to wait. When Lex and Ari came back, they'd know what to do. They'd help him get unstuck.

And he *was* stuck. He had to make sure Nick stayed under persuasion. He couldn't do anything besides that until they got home. He whimpered. He could

definitely do that – only one human wasn't any trouble at all to control – but what if he couldn't? What if something happened and Nick got out from under him?

Calm down. Nick isn't a threat to you right now. Nick had obviously miscalculated. He must have assumed he just needed to work around Lex and Ari and that they'd kept Valen muzzled and weak. Of course he would have, most people would just assume a vampire in his position would have already killed Lex and Ari and ran if he could, especially after he'd already tried to make a break for it. And what sort of vampire would let humans pull out his fangs if he were free and able to move around?

Still. Valen huddled in the corner of the room, bristling like a scared cat. Nick was *right there.* How was he supposed to just sit there like everything was fine? His body was still wild with adrenaline and electric panic.

"You – you can't do anything to me!" Valen said. Maybe saying it aloud would make him believe it.

Nick didn't respond.

"You – Go sit on the couch."

Nick obeyed, wordlessly sitting down.

See? He's doing what you say, not the other way around. Okay. Maybe this was okay. Valen started to pace across the living room, still jittery and panicked. He went into the kitchen and picked up the phone, putting it to his ear. His leg jiggled up and down as he listened to the busy signal.

Call Lex and Ari? He might be able to get ahold of them at the hunter's base, but he might get some other hunter on the other end of the line. He wasn't sure he could handle it if that happened.

He replaced the phone and made a beeline back to Nick, deciding it was definitely worse when he couldn't see him. He looked into Nick's face. There'd been so, so many times he'd wanted to say so much to this man, but couldn't.

"You … your experimental design is horrible!" No response, of course. "Say it!"

"My experimental design is horrible," Nick said mechanically.

For some reason, that felt like a victory. He was still freaking out, but the feeling of being drunk on the power started to flow into him on top of that. "You have a small penis! Say it!"

"I have a small penis."

Really, Valen? Really? That's what you went for?

Valen normally didn't have the instinct to body-shame, but it'd been so strong for some reason. Well, Nick had started it. He was the one who'd made it personal.

He was the one who'd brought his penis into it in the first place. When there'd been absolutely no reason for it besides just because he could.

That'd been the only reason for *so much*. "You're the worst!" Valen screamed. "You're scum! You represent everything bad about humans *and* vampires!"

Nick said nothing.

"Fuck you!" Valen extended his talons towards Nick, but then picked up the pillow next to him and tore it open. "Fuck you! I never thought I could hate anyone more than my husband, but you win by a landslide! I should kill you right now! That way you could never hurt me or anyone else ever again!"

Nick said nothing.

"Give me one reason why I shouldn't."

It was rhetorical, of course. But Nick was under persuasion and had to follow commands. "It would be hard to get away with it."

Valen stared at him, then broke into manic laughter. "That *is* what you care about. Whether or not you can get away with it. Not whether or not you should. Not whether or not you have the right to. But if something bad will happen to you if you do."

Nick said nothing.

"Why do you think you have the right to act this way? Tell me!"

"Because I can."

Valen stared at him. That was really all there was to it. He just didn't have to care about anything other than his own feelings. He wanted to hurt Valen, so he did.

"But why? Why do you *want* to? Tell me!"

"Because I want to make someone else suffer the way I suffered."

The dispassionate, emotionless way he said it due to the persuasion was jarring. Valen's skin crawled.

The worst part was ... Valen knew what that felt like. To be so lost in your own suffering and fear that there wasn't any room in your head for concern about others' emotions. To want to just not be alone in your suffering. For someone to understand, even if you have to make them. For someone to *be* there with you.

To scrabble at the only thing that had any chance at all of making the suffering stop. To just not be able to care if it was wrong to make others suffer.

It was how he felt biting Lex.

It was how he felt right now.

Valen just stood there, looking at Nick and panicking and boiling with anger for a solid minute, before it finally got too much to bear and he broke down. He burst into tears, screaming, and all at once lunged at Nick.

His teeth found their mark on Nick's throat. The second time he'd bitten a human's neck.

Because of you I starved, and now because of you, I'll feast.

He didn't just open the jugular, though. His fangs sunk into Nick's windpipe, and with that, the spell of persuasion was broken, as most vampires couldn't use it to force a human to stay still while dying. Nick started to gurgle and writhe, trying to push Valen off, but Valen growled savagely and pinned Nick's wrist to the wall, keeping Nick's neck in his iron jaw.

He was strong now. All those times, Nick had overpowered him because he was starved and chained up. There was nothing standing between them now to keep Nick safe from him.

He could see Nick's face out of the corner of his eye as he felt the pulse in his mouth. Nick was panicked. Knowing how badly he'd fucked up. Knowing his end was imminent.

And the horrible thing was, Valen liked it. He *liked* knowing Nick was scared and suffering. It was horrible. It was horrible because he knew now this was how Nick felt while torturing Valen, and Valen was caught in the cycle of violence he'd been trying so hard to break.

You'll kill Nick if you don't back off right this second. You're going to kill him. You're going to be a murderer.

But something in him was broken. He didn't care. He couldn't care. This was the only way he would ever feel even a little safe again.

If you're so determined to make me a monster ... then allow me to indulge you.

He closed his jaw, crushing Nick's windpipe, and yanked his head back. There was a sickening *snap* and wet squelching sound as a huge chunk came out of the human's neck, leaving Valen with a mouthful of gore, blood soaking down his front. Nick toppled over immediately, still twitching and writhing with his last moments as his life poured out of him.

Valen swallowed, then immediately choked on the solid pieces in his mouth, his digestive system unused to taking in meat and tissue. He spat it out, blood stringing from his lips, adding to the mess painting him. It felt the same as when he'd attacked Lex. He was the same bestial, desperate animal he'd been back then.

He fell on Nick's corpse and held it up to his mouth, drinking the firehose of blood coming out of his neck. He felt disgusting. He felt monstrous. He felt alive and safe and powerful.

He heard a car pull up out front.

Reality crashed down on him. Valen dropped the corpse, pulling his hands back to his chest, coming to his senses immediately. He'd killed someone. *He'd killed a human*, and sure, it had been Nick, but *he'd killed someone in cold blood* when they couldn't fight him off.

He heard Bailey's and Jerome's voices outside.

Oh no. No no no no. It wasn't even Lex and Ari. It was the ones who'd stuck him with the silver dart earlier, and this time he'd actually done something, proven

himself to be a dangerous predator and not a timid victim who'd get scared when they were playing Monopoly.

Valen stumbled backwards, falling against the wall, painting it with blood as he slid down it, back into the corner. Back into being scared and helpless.

Their footsteps landed on the porch, their voices muffled through the door. "Nick!" said Bailey, sounding angry. "Stop whatever the fuck you're doing."

Valen pressed himself further into the corner. *Here it comes.*

The keys jingled, the front door swung open. Jerome entered, gun drawn. His expression went from hard to shocked when he saw Valen – and the amount of blood everywhere. "Valen!"

"I'm sorry!" Valen cried, exploding into tears and terrified tremors. It must look like crocodile tears, surely, a monster crying while still sitting in the splattered remains of his victim. But he couldn't suppress how hysterical he was. "I'm sorry! I know I shouldn't have killed him! I'm sorry! I-I-I – "

"Hey." Bailey interrupted him and knelt down, taking Valen's bloody, shaking frame in his hands. "Hey, you're okay, you're okay."

Jerome looked at Nick's corpse with some chagrin. He holstered his gun, then came and knelt on the other side of Valen. "You're okay, sweet thing, you're okay. It was self-defense. You had no choice."

It wasn't self-defense, though. I didn't have to kill him. He didn't dare say it aloud.

Valen was a monster. He'd murdered somebody and it'd made him feel good. He'd gorged himself on his victim's blood even though he didn't need it. He continued crying, huge, opened-mouthed, chest-hitching sobs, crying too hard to see. There was no coming back from this, he was a monster and he always would be.

"Breathe, baby," Bailey said. "You're okay, we've got you, you're safe."

He wasn't safe. He would never be safe, because he was a monster and a murderer and he'd never get away from that. If Bailey and Jerome had seen him

actually kill Nick, he knew they wouldn't be gentle with him like this. He'd have to keep this dark secret in his chest forever and ever.

He kept crying inconsolably even as Bailey and Jerome picked him up, one under each elbow. "You're okay," Jerome continued to soothe. "Let's get you to the bathroom and splash some water on your face."

Valen continued to drift, feeling like there was a black hole inside him, unable to stem the tide of fear and self-loathing. The humans helped him up the stairs one at a time, pausing patiently with a constant stream of reassurances every time he found himself unable to keep going.

They reached the bathroom. Bailey encouraged him to stand at the sink, and Jerome turned the faucet on.

"Here," he said, guiding Valen's hand into the stream of water. "Splash some cold water on your face, V-man."

Still gasping in sobbing breaths, Valen obediently bent over the sink and splashed a handful of water over himself. It ran red down into the sink, and that made his crying pick up again.

"Okay," Bailey said. "You're okay. Why don't you take your clothes off, and we'll get all this blood off of you, and then you can put on some clean clothes. Hm?"

Just do what they say. Just do whatever they say. He couldn't think too hard. There wasn't room in his brain for anything other than the utter devastation, the weight of what he'd done. He peeled his shirt off. It fell to the floor with a wet slap, so saturated with blood it was.

"There you go," Bailey said. He turned the shower on. "Go ahead and step in, buddy."

"I'll go get fresh clothes," Jerome said.

Valen stepped into the shower, still in his pants and socks. He hid his face in his hands, sniffling. Feeling the blood melt off of him *did* start making him feel a little better.

"I'm sorry," Valen said, voice muffled. "I'm sorry. I'm sorry. I'm sorry."

"You didn't have a choice," Bailey said. "You had to keep yourself safe." Valen burst into fresh tears.

Bailey would not be deterred. "You're okay. You're okay." As if it would become true if he just said it enough.

Jerome came in with fresh clothes. "Okay, hey, hey, sweet thing, no need to cry. You're okay. Why don't you take your pants off now?"

The command didn't even elicit the normal fearful response Valen would usually have. Valen kept his face scrunched up, face hurting from crying so hard, and unbuttoned his pants and slid them down, leaving him completely nude in the shower. The water running over him continued to wash away all the blood on him.

It did ... kind of help to get all the blood off. "There you go." Bailey handed him a bar of soap. "Go ahead and finish cleaning yourself up."

"You got a bit in your hair," Jerome added.

Valen felt completely exhausted and wrung out. He obediently moved the bar of soap over himself. He'd been here before as well, bathing in front of two hunters trying to guide him back to some semblance of normalcy. He closed his eyes and stuck his head under the water, the sound roaring in his ears.

"There you go." Bailey turned the water off, then handed him a towel. "There you go. Dry yourself off, now."

Valen complied, feeling a little better when the towel was over his head and he could no longer see the two humans looking at him. He ran it over his skin, still feeling hollow.

"There you go." Jerome unfolded his change of clothes. "Now, why don't you come out and put these on."

Still unable to make eye contact, Valen stepped out and folded the towel up, as though if he were proper and neat enough it would prove him worthy of having some kind of humanity. He was likewise meek as he dressed himself, buttoning his pants up and sliding the shirt over his head.

"There you go." Jerome rubbed the towel over his hair one more time to finish drying it. "Okay. Hey, I think I heard Lex and Ari pulling up outside. Why don't we go meet them?"

He burst into tears again. Oh God, Lex and Ari were going to come and see what he'd done. They were going to *see*. Despite the dread pounding through him, he allowed Bailey and Jerome to take his hands and lead him back downstairs.

He could already hear Lex and Ari's voices in the living room, exclaiming about the gore. His knees knocked together as he came into the dining room.

"We're in here," Bailey shouted to them, clearly not wanting to bring Valen back into the room with the evidence of his crimes.

Lex came in first, full speed, tears in her eyes. "Valen!" She clung to Valen. "Valen, oh my God, oh my God, I'm so glad you're okay."

Ari came in next, putting her arms around both Lex and Valen. "Holy shit," she whispered.

"I'm sorry," Valen sobbed. "I'm sorry I killed him. I know I shouldn't have."

"It's okay," Lex said. "You had to. You had to defend yourself."

Valen heaved and buried his face in Lex's shoulder, keening. They kept *saying* that, but it *wasn't true*.

Bailey and Jerome positioned themselves around Lex and Ari, almost but not quite making a four-person group hug around him. He was so surrounded and warm and loved, but he felt more hollow than ever.

"I'm sorry," he said, voice hoarse from crying and apologizing. "I'm sorry I killed him."

"It was self-defense," Bailey said. "I'll say it however many times you need to hear it."

He couldn't, he *couldn't* live with this in his heart for the rest of his life. He could barely live with it for the few minutes since it'd happened. "It wasn't," he whispered with terror. "It wasn't self-defense. I had him under persuasion. He couldn't hurt me. I killed him anyway."

Lex drew back slightly so she could look him in the face. He shut his eyes, squeezing more tears out, too scared to look at her. "I'm a monster. You need to execute me. I'm a murderer."

He flinched as he felt Ari's hands on his shoulders, expecting the retaliation to begin at any moment. "You are not a monster or a murderer," Ari said firmly.

"It was self-defense," Lex reiterated.

"He broke into the house to come after you," Ari continued. "That's self-defense."

Valen looked at her incredulously. "But – but I killed someone who was defenseless and I – I – I – it made me feel good."

"It made you feel good because he's a monster that tortured and abused you, and you were putting an end to it. You have the right to do that."

"But ... but I liked it," Valen said, swallowing, still not convinced. "I liked killing him. I'm a monster."

"You are not going to do that to just any random helpless person," Lex said. "You're just not. Nick doesn't count. There are circumstances."

Ari spun him around, squeezing his shoulders. "Look at me," she said, very serious. "You are not a monster. I don't fucking care. I don't care about the details about what happened here. I don't care if that spineless rat was on his knees saying sorry and begging for mercy. He broke into the house to come after you. That's self-defense."

Valen put his face in his hands, still crying. It didn't *feel* true. It didn't *feel* like it'd been self-defense. It didn't *feel* like he'd had the right to take that life.

But the four vampire hunters huddled around him, enclosing him. Supporting him. *They* thought he wasn't a monster, and wasn't that more important? They were humans. They were vampire hunters, and they were declaring him not in need of being hunted.

"Okay," he whispered. "Thank you. What do we do now?"

Ari sighed, palming her face. "Okay. So. What we do now is figure out what the fuck to do with his body. And with the pissed off teenager we have locked in the van."

25

— • —

Sebastian Kithrara was having the worst birthday ever. It was even worse than his eleventh birthday, when his parents had gotten him ten ponies instead of the full dozen he'd asked for, and it'd been a whole scene.

It was his eighteenth birthday, which was supposed to be the best one. He was a man now! He was supposed to prove he was fit and worthy of the Kithrara blood harvest web!

He was supposed to be safely at home celebrating his first catch! Not ... strung up in a human's basement.

It was humiliating. It was improper. It was ... way, way scarier than he wanted to admit.

They'd put a muzzle on him. He hadn't realized humans could really be a threat until he'd had a muzzle on, and he couldn't speak and he couldn't break the silver chains and he couldn't do *anything* –

Calm down. They're just humans. This is just a temporary setback.

He wriggled. The temporary setback continued, feeling less temporary as it went on.

He had a very bad feeling about what would happen here when that man came back. He'd been gloating over Sebastian being caught, talking about bringing vampires low. A bunch of rubbish, obviously. But he'd ... pulled Sebastian's pants down and took humiliating photos of him, and as much as it seemed like a human shouldn't be able to have this kind of domination over him, Sebastian hadn't been able to do a damn thing about it.

The photos were still over on the table, pasted into an open notebook. He could *not* let those be seen by anyone. He had to destroy them and the negatives in the dark room behind him.

Just ... just as soon as he figured out a way out of the silver chains.

He heard footsteps upstairs. He tried to stop his panicked crying. The last thing he needed was to be caught crying by the humans and be even more humiliated. He stared at the floor, trying not to let them win.

Two pairs of footsteps came down the stairs. He put off looking at them for as long as he could, but he had to eventually.

It was a man and a woman. He could *not* let them think they were intimidating to him, even though they absolutely were. He let out his meanest growl, baring his teeth, and thrashed around. It did not have quite the intended effect since all it did was draw attention to the fact that his limbs were bound, chains rattling.

"Give me a fucking break. We're here to help you, believe it or not." It was the man, but it became obvious as soon as the creature opened its mouth that its voice was too high to be a man. A female, then? Why on God's green earth did it look like that? Was it some kind of transsexual? That was ridiculous.

"Let's get you out of here," said the other one. Its voice was strained.

As badly as he wanted to *get out of here*, he couldn't stomach the thought of just letting them come over and do whatever to him, like *they* were in charge. He squirmed again, trying with all his might to break the chains. He'd never encountered silver before, never encountered chains he couldn't break with ease.

"We don't have time to piss around here," the first one shouted. "This is taking less than five minutes one way or the other, so it's up to you if we do that by just blowing your head off, got it?"

Sebastian fell into silence, finally cowed. He hated this. Why was she able to threaten him like that? She had no right. He should be able to retaliate, beat her, break her bones for talking to him like that. But as much as he hated it, her threats had weight. She *could* blow his head off and he would just be forced to deal with that.

He went red as the second one came over and pulled his pants up. She then started undoing the chains.

You fool. You ignorant creature. You're allowing for your own doom! As soon as he was no longer bound, he lunged at her, trying to restore some semblance of control over the situation. It was only then that he realized she had only detached him from the ceiling, not completely freed his limbs. He fell awkwardly, landing like a limp fish on the ground.

This was *humiliating*. Not only were they humans, but they were *females*. The only thing weaker than a human was a human *female*. And he was being overpowered by a mere pair of them.

"Hey," the more masculine one said. "Last chance, motherfucker." She tried to be scary with her words, but someone without fangs could only be so scary with their mouth. She *could* be scary with other tools, though, as Sebastian found out when she pushed the barrel of a gun against his forehead. *Don't cry. You can't cry in front of them. You're a man now.*

He continued to give half-hearted struggles as they dragged him up the stairs, knowing his best chance was to just bide his time until he spotted some opportunity, but unable to bear the humiliation of letting them manhandle him without at least token resistance.

They carted him out and into one of those vehicles that smelled so bad. He could smell the lead dripping from the engine. It was horrid. He had no idea how any vampire could stand to own such a contraption.

"I guess it's a good thing we still have the fucking coffin. Not that I'm too happy about it."

Sebastian was pro-anything that made these humans unhappy, at this point. Until the back door of the vehicle opened and he saw what appeared to be *a cage made out of silver.*

No, no, no, no, no! It was barely bigger than his own body. *You can't seriously put me in there!* He growled and thrashed as much as he could. He did succeed in getting them to drop him, but that just delayed things.

What was his plan? He had to have a plan, right? He wasn't going in that horrible-looking box, right?

One of the humans unlocked it. "You're *going* in there!" the other shouted, dragging him towards it.

He couldn't hide his fear anymore. *No, no, no, no, I can't go in there! Fuck you! Fuck you! You don't have the right to put me in there! I'm the top of the food chain, the –*

He was dumped in, and the box closed on him. He tried to keep the lid from shutting with his feet, but they just forced them back in and closed it on him.

His heart beat fast and panicked as they shut the door to the vehicle, starting the engine and driving off to who knows where.

***

He was starting to get a headache from the smell. He knew humans' noses weren't as sensitive as vampires', but could they really not *smell* it? It was making him even crankier than he already was, scared and overwhelmed and having no clue as to where they were going or what was going to happen to him. The smaller of the humans would occasionally offer him some condescending words that were probably supposed to be comforting, but he just bristled at them. *I'm a man now! You can't talk to me that way! I'm your superior! Shut the fuck up and let me out of here!*

No matter how many times he thought it, nothing changed. He was still locked in the box. He was still muzzled. *Don't cry. You can't cry in front of them. Don't cry. Don't cry. You're a man now.*

The two humans made concerned noises, and the car stopped. "Fuck, fuck fuck fuck fuck."

From his position locked into staring at the ceiling, he couldn't see it, but he heard the doors opening and their footsteps rapidly retreating.

Okay ... He turned his head as far as he could. The blinkers on the car ticked intermittently. He could hear their voices distantly, very, very faintly. Someone was crying loudly.

He rattled the cage, unsuccessful in doing anything but jingling the chains.

Surely they didn't intend to just leave him here? No, they'd left the vehicle doors open. They were coming back.

... But *when*? He let himself cry now that there was no one to see, straining to try and see out the window in the corner of his vision. He didn't even have any idea what time it was, or if he was at risk of the sun shining on him like this.

After what felt like fucking *forever*, he heard them approaching. And smelled them, even over the lead in the gasoline. They had open cuts. He hadn't really realized how hungry he was. He hadn't eaten since he'd set out. He was hungry and tired and scared and overwhelmed by bad smells and he had no idea what was going to happen and *it was his birthday, this was supposed to be a celebration*. He gave another frustrated little thrash, shaking the metal box again.

The back door to the van opened, and he immediately went still as he saw *four* humans come in this time. These two new ones were strange – effeminate. The larger one had pink hair.

The smaller one looked ... ethnic.

They started dragging his box forward. He suppressed the scared whine. *I'm a man now, you can't do this to me I'm a man now I'm a vampire I'm your superior you can't do this to me –*

A tarp was pulled over the cage, completely obscuring his view. Great, now he couldn't even see what was going on, the one thing he *could* do while locked up like this.

He felt himself being ferried up a set of stairs, then set down on the ground. In a corner, surely, forgotten and pushed to the side like a piece of furniture. The indignity of this whole thing was almost as bad as the fear and having no idea what was in store for him. But he could take it. *Do your worst!*

"Valen, get in your box," said one of the voices. "Don't get out of it till we're back. Both of you just sit tight. You hear? Sit tight. Don't move until we're back."

More sounds, shuffling around. Wood on wood, a hinge. The box? The smell of human blood was even more overwhelming here. It hung heavy in the air – surely someone was killing humans here, with that volume of blood. That was a total waste.

Wait a minute ... Valen? Valen Kithrara? Priscus's wife? He hadn't seen Valen in years. Maybe it was a different Valen. Surely it couldn't be *that* Valen, right? Why would *that* Valen be here? Evidently this second person was also being locked in a box, though, by the sound of it.

The humans continued their loud activities. More sounds of tarps rustling, things being dragged.

Keys jingling. "Sorry, kid, just hang in there for like an hour."

I'm not a kid! Fuck you! Let me out of here and you'll see what a kid I am!

The front door shut. He could hear the vehicle driving off distantly. Silence.

He tried to move, frustration growing. *Let me out! Let me the fuck out!*

He tried to call out Valen's name, but of course he couldn't. Was there anyone else here? He rattled the cage.

He had his fit until he tired himself out, falling still. He was just so tired and stressed out. He let his head loll.

He hadn't realized he'd finally fallen asleep until he jolted awake at the sound of the humans returning.

"Valen? We're back now. You can come out."

"How did it go?" It was a new voice. No, an old voice. It *was* Valen Kithrara, Priscus's wife. The one who'd made such a fuss about nothing and gone crazy and flaunted her sexual fetishes in public and ran off and embarrassed the whole family so thoroughly. And after Priscus had worked so hard to convince them it was worth it to marry a commoner! Clearly she was just of inferior breeding.

How had she ended up *here*, of all places?

"Just fine," a human said. Valen was *talking* with the humans, like a casual conversation. What was going *on*? He grunted, trying to talk, trying to get out, rattling the chains. *Come on, let me out.*

" ... Right," said one of the humans, as though remembering a pesky inconvenience. *Fuck you! I'm more important than you!* "I guess it wouldn't be right to keep that kid locked in there all day if we don't have to. There's four of us here, plus Valen, so I'm sure we can keep him under control."

Let me out and you'll see how under control I am!

"I'm trusting you to keep an eye on him, got it? We're vampire hunters, so if we let this kid go, anybody he hurts is on us. You need to make sure he gets back over the border without taking anyone, or we failed to do our job."

Fuck you!

"Yes," said Valen's voice. "I'll make sure he doesn't hurt anyone else."

Fuck you! I don't need a babysitter!

"Okay." Someone knelt nearby and the corner of the tarp lifted, showing the human's stupid face, looking right at him. "Hey, listen. We're gonna let you out. We're gonna all be civil, no fighting, no persuasion, no hurting, and then at nightfall, you're going home. You don't need to try to get away. It's daytime now, so you got nowhere to go anyway. Sound good?"

Sound good if I rip your fucking throat out? You're coming home with me. It's you, you're the one I'm taking.

"Hey," she said, like talking to a naughty dog, and that was even more fucking infuriating. "Come on, kid. I know you're tough and scary. I know, all right? I'm saying I'm going to let you out. Literally all you have to do is nothing. Just sit there and let us take you home. Easy as pie."

He hated her so, so much. He wanted to kill her so badly. But it was stupid to keep thrashing around. Even he could see that. She was going to make a stupid mistake and let him out if he just sat still for a minute.

The human stood and pulled the tarp all the way back from the cage, finally letting him see the entire room. It was a commoner's house, small and not well-furnished.

Valen was there – yes, that was definitely her, there on the outside with the humans. "Sebastian?" she gasped, eyes softening with pity.

"What, do you know him?" said the stupid human.

Valen nodded. "He's my husband's cousin. So my cousin-in-law, if that's a thing. Oh, Sebastian, I'm so sorry. I forgot he was old enough to be coming of age soon. Don't worry, Sebastian, I'm here, I'll help you."

Then let me out already! He bristled at the condescending way she was talking to him, but ... it *did* make him feel a little better. There was another vampire here, an adult – *no*, he was an adult now, he had to stop thinking like that. Well, an *older* adult, at least. Even if it was ... a mentally unstable woman.

The stupid human handed Valen the keys. "Here. Why don't you handle this?"

"Thank you." Valen slipped on a pair of gloves so she could handle the silver, then took the keys and started undoing all the various locks and chains.

Okay, this made more sense. The humans were probably servants of some kind, handing Valen the keys like that. The whole situation was very strange, but Valen must have sent her thralls to come get him. Although, Valen had originally refused to have a thrall at all, let alone four of them, so ... ? He tried to hide his relief as Valen lifted him out of the coffin. "I'm so sorry this happened to you, Sebastian ... I suppose I should say happy birthday?"

Oh come on. Sebastian glared at her.

"Sorry ... " Valen undid the muzzle, pulling it out of his mouth.

There, finally, he was more proper now. The stupid muzzle, such a horrid contraption – not fitting for even a common vampire, let alone nobility like him. The *audacity*. He licked his lips. "Valen, what on earth are *you* doing here? You ruined everything!"

Valen looked taken aback. "What? How did *I* ruin it?"

What? Look where I am! I was trapped in a cage! "I came here to catch my first human and make my family proud, and now I'm stuck here overday! Again!"

Valen looked at a loss. "And how is that my fault?"

"Erm. Well, I don't know. You're the only vampire around, so I just assumed you were running things."

Valen let out a laugh. "No, no. Here." She undid the cuffs around Sebastian's wrists and ankles, freeing him from the last of the restraints. Sebastian stood and rolled his shoulders, finally completely free. Thank fuck. "Thank you," Sebastian said brusquely. Now that the most pressing matters were out of the way ... "I need a shirt."

"Oh, uh ... " Valen went over to a wardrobe and pulled out a shirt. "Here."

Ugh, the material of the shirt was scratchy. Well, whatever. He would be able to get a nicer one soon. He slipped it on.

Second order of business. His stomach growled, and he looked over the humans. The big one looked the juiciest. "Can I drink from one of your thralls?"

"Oh, ah ... " Valen turned back to look at them. "They aren't my thralls."

"Oh. Whose thralls are they, then?"

"Nobody's."

"Oh, so they're fair game, then?"

The four humans all backed up, drawing weapons defensively. *Stupid. I can just use persuasion on you. What do you think you're going to do?* He tried not to think about the humans who had overpowered him and put him here in the first place.

Valen very quickly stepped in front of Sebastian. "No, no, you misunderstand."

Okay, well, then, explain it to me. They're just humans and they're around and they don't already belong to someone. So ... ? "Well, I'm not leaving without a thrall."

Valen grimaced. "Yes, you are, unfortunately."

Oh ... It all came back to Sebastian now, the big hubbub the whole family had been in when Valen had started kicking up a fuss. Valen hadn't just refused to

have her own thrall, she'd been against the whole family business, acting like it was morally wrong.

What a hypocrite! She *said* they weren't thralls, but obviously they were even if she didn't call them that. And she had *four*. That was wildly excessive even for Kithrara nobility. The only ones he knew of that did such a thing was the Landon family, whose members regularly went out with four or five thralls each. Everyone thought it was a gauche and tacky display, and the logistics of it were a daymare.

The big one with pink hair looked so juicy and well-fed. He had *so* much blood, and Sebastian had never gone this long without eating before. He could just take one, have a snack, and then that would be his mission on this side of the border sorted. "Come *on*, you don't need *four*, surely. Can I have one? Mother and Father aren't going to be pleased with me for coming back so late, let alone empty-handed."

"Sebastian," Valen said, exasperated. "You have no *idea* what horrible fate you narrowly escaped. You are going home unscathed and empty-handed, and you will learn to appreciate that as a victory."

Sebastian scoffed. Sure, that would go over *great. Not pleased* was a mild way of describing what his family would be. He was third in line for the Kithrara blood harvest web. If he couldn't even get his *own* human, how could he be trusted with running the network and feeding the whole country? He might even be disowned. "Why, because I was told so by my cousin's commoner-born sex-pervert wife?"

Valen's shoulders stiffened, and she went bright red. "Sebastian, you – "

"My name is Sebastian Vorigan Kithrara, son of Mordecai Asmodeus Kithrara, secondborn of Viscardi Maxwell Talon Kithrara, third in line to control the blood harvest web. My family feeds the entire nation. I'm an *apex predator*. I'm not going hungry, ever. And I'm not leaving without a human. This is my time to prove I'm worthy of my heritage, to fully step into my role as – "

"Sebastian!" Valen interrupted. "I was there when you threw a fit about not getting the right number of ponies or whatever on your eleventh birthday! You're not a fearsome predator! You're a spoiled child!"

It was Sebastian's turn to flush bright red. *How could you bring that up in front of them! That was ages ago! And besides, it was perfectly justified!* "There needed to be a dozen of them and there were only ten! Those last two missing ponies were crucial for the whole event!"

"God above, you've never been told *no* in your life, have you?"

Why was she being so *difficult?* Sebastian suddenly understood why Priscus and the rest of the family had always seemed so annoyed with her. "So, can I feed on one of them or not? I haven't eaten in two days. I'm starving."

"You do not know the meaning of the word *starving*," Valen snarled, with such ferocity that Sebastian's eyebrows shot up and he stepped back. "You impudent whelp."

What the fuck? Why was she acting this way? Valen wasn't even really part of the family. Priscus had fallen in love with her because she was supposedly intelligent and beautiful – but she was still a commoner. The audacity to talk to him, a *proper* member of the family, like this! "You can't speak to me this way. You have to show me proper respect."

"Sebastian, listen to me. You need to stop being foolish and value your life over your pride. You were caught by vampire hunters. They already proved they can beat you. Please, if – "

Don't bring that up. It doesn't count. I'm here now. And I'm hungry.

Well, if she wasn't going to do it, he'd have to take matters into his own hands. He made eye contact with the big human. "You, come over here and bare your neck."

His face went slack and he shuffled forward.

Valen *hissed* at him. He'd never seen anyone rude enough to *hiss* at him. And then, before he could even comment, she stepped forward and *slapped* him.

He reeled back, clamping a hand over his cheek to stifle the blood that came up from her claw marks. "You – you struck me!"

"I'll do much worse than that if you harm any of these humans."

Sebastian seethed. There was improper, then there was *this*. "What is *wrong* with you?"

"I could ask the same of you, but I already know the answer!"

That's it. Sebastian lunged at Valen with a growl, and Valen rolled back, head slamming into the ground. She kicked him in the stomach, sending him flying. He slammed into the ceiling, splintering wood, then fell back down on top of Valen.

He'd teach her a lesson. He grabbed her neck, choking her, baring his teeth.

Valen flailed and shredded the sleeves of his shirt. Sebastian squeezed harder, completely enraged. *Remember this next time you think of mouthing off!*

A searing pain suddenly erupted in his back. *Shit.* He'd completely forgotten that the four humans were vampire hunters – if they could even be called *hunters*. Despite his disdain for them, they were ... competent enough to pull him off Valen. His abdomen throbbed with pain as a second knife came into his stomach.

He stumbled back, now determined to just get out of here, when he was seized from behind and the muzzle went back on. Terror flooded Sebastian's system, all haughty thoughts gone. *No! No, take it off!* He couldn't stop the humiliated tears as they shackled his limbs back together. *Valen, come on!*

"Sorry, kid," said a human, a *human*. *Fuck you! Fuck you!*

He trembled in the hands of the human lifting him up, glaring at Valen as she approached. "I'm sorry, Sebastian. This is for the humans' safety. I promise it'll be okay. I'm sorry they had to hurt you. I'm sorry."

She reached forward and took out the knife in his stomach, and he screamed again into the muzzle. It *hurt*.

It ... wait a minute.

He still felt something lodged in his chest, not the knife. He hadn't even noticed.

He looked down. It was wood. It was a chunk of wood, lodged in his chest. From the ceiling; when he'd crashed into it, a piece of wood had pierced his chest.

Electric panic surged through him. Holy shit, he'd almost *died*, he could *die*. He was too scared to writhe at all, scared that it was close enough to his heart that he might accidentally push it in.

Valen, at least, looked freaked out as well, eyes wide. "You're okay. "I'll – I'll just – I'll pull this out. You're okay."

Sebastian's knees were weak. Any of these humans could walk up and kill him right now.

Valen, help!

Valen gingerly took the piece of wood and slid it out slowly. Sebastian didn't dare move or breathe until it clattered to the floor, at which point he sagged with relief, shaking.

"You're okay, lil guy," the human said, and his nerves were too shot to be upset about the condescension. "Valen is gonna take you home tonight."

He didn't even have it in him to struggle as he was locked back in the metal box. It occurred to him after he was already immobilized that he should have tried to get out, but by then it was too late.

He stared at the ceiling, trying to control his unmanly crying. He listened as the humans comforted Valen. Even though he was a man now and shouldn't need it, he rather wished someone would comfort him too.

26

— ◦ —

"Can we at least turn the television on, so he's not just alone with his thoughts all day?"

Ari looked from Valen, sitting on the couch with a look of concern on his face, to Sebastian, still locked in the coffin nearby. She sighed. "All right, fine."

Valen couldn't help flapping his hands excitedly. He hadn't watched TV in ages. Maybe there would even be a nature documentary.

Ari took the remote and flipped the TV on. It was on a news station.

"Do you have access to any nature documentaries?" he asked.

Ari handed him the remote. "Knock yourself out. Just don't buy any of the pay-per-view shit."

Ari left to go confer with the other humans. Valen flipped through the channels, laser-focused on finding something good to force Sebastian to watch.

Slowly, Sebastian's eyes drifted over to the TV.

"What would you like to watch?"

Sebastian quickly turned away again.

"Well, if you see something you like, let me know." Somehow.

Lex and Ari came back into the room. Ari plopped down on the couch, putting one arm around Valen. "How ya doing, buddy?"

"I'm doing well. Thank you, ma'am."

"Good." She gave him an awkward pat.

Valen fidgeted with the rubberized buttons on the remote. "So, Nick ... "

"We took his body back to the base," Lex said. "We made it look like Sebastian killed him."

Ari glanced at Sebastian. "You don't mind, right?"

Sebastian rolled his eyes.

"Thank you," Valen said, hugging his arms around himself. Lex scooted closer.

The phone rang. Ari groaned. "All right, here we go."

She got up and answered. Valen clung to Lex and listened tensely. His hearing was good enough that he could hear the person on the other end from across the room.

"Yo." It was a man's voice. Presumably another vampire hunter, because he continued, "What the fuck happened to Nick?"

"Huh?" Ari said. "I dunno, he finally grow some balls?"

"He's fucking dead!"

"God, I wish."

"Bitch, he's dead for real!"

"Really?"

"Yeah! What happened last night when you came to drop off the coffin?"

"Oh." Ari let out an audible grimace. "We didn't actually go out last night to return the coffin. We just told Nick we would to get him to leave. He showed up at our house, and – "

"The fuck you mean you didn't go out?"

"We didn't go out, shithead! Nick came over to harass us at our house, we told him we'd come over later to get him to leave, then we stayed home because fuck him. I didn't fucking kill him, although I kind of wish I had." This with a wink at Valen that made him flush and sink deeper into the couch. They were buying this, right? They'd believe this?

Cyril could be heard cursing on the other end. "So you didn't see what happened?"

"We were at our fucking house, dumbass. We didn't see anything that wasn't at our goddamn house. I was fucking my girlfriend last night."

"Jesus Christ. You dumb cunt."

"How'd he die? Like what happened?"

"How do you fucking think? The damn vampire he wanted to play with killed him. I guess after that old one was weak for so long, he forgot a fresh one would be, uh, dangerous."

"Right." Ari stood stone-faced for a minute. "Well, anything else?"

"Uhhhhhhh – "

"I'll take that as a no. Don't bother me again." She hung up.

Valen dashed forward into her arms, and she hugged him. He couldn't believe it. They really thought it was okay that he killed Nick, and he was going to get away with it, and then tonight he was going to get to safety, to go home.

"Put a hold on the waterworks," Ari said, and Valen wiped his eyes. "You're okay."

Valen went back to the couch and sat primly, hands on his lap. He looked over at Sebastian, feeling pleased with himself. "That man who hurt us is dead, and we don't have to worry about him anymore."

Sebastian looked relieved despite himself.

They passed some time watching a nature documentary before the phone rang again. Ari let out an even more exasperated groan.

She ripped the phone off the hook. "*What*?"

"Ariana," said a very serious voice. "This is Director Griswald."

Ari straightened up. "Ah? Hello?"

Valen clung to Lex once again, all his nerves returning. The *director*. The *boss* vampire hunter. Surely he wouldn't be able to hear Valen, right? He wouldn't be able to tell Valen was there somehow, right? Lex held him comfortingly.

"You've heard about what happened to Nick?"

"Yeah," Ari said, more nervous than she had been lying to Cyril. "Hear he got burned playing with fire."

"I've been informed you were expected to see Nick last night to drop off some restraints for the new vampire."

"Y ... yeah, we were supposed to, but we ended up not doing that."

"Why not?"

"We ... I'm sorry, Director G, we just really don't – didn't – like Nick, we didn't think it was very important."

She waited tensely for his response.

"All right," he said, finally. "It's not like Nick didn't have any restraints, and he knew how to keep the new research specimen secure. So, you didn't see anything last night? No other information to give me?"

"No, sir," she said. "We were home all night. We weren't scheduled to go on patrol. We had a night in."

The director hemmed and hmmed. "All right, Ariana. Thank you. Please call me if you think of anything or remember anything else."

He hung up. Ari replaced the phone. She let out an exhausted breath and came back over, sprawling out on the couch. "Well, I think we might have really pulled it off."

More waiting. More nature documentaries. Valen was in heaven. Every time a particularly interesting bird or fish or plant was mentioned, Valen couldn't help spilling out a monologue about other facts he knew about it that wasn't mentioned. He knew he was probably being annoying, but, well ... they wouldn't mind, right?

The phone rang again. Ari groaned, screwing up her eyes. "For the love of – " She trundled back over and picked it up. "*What*?"

Another man's voice. "Ari, dude! Director G is on the news! Flip over to channel four!"

Valen fumbled with the remote and changed the channel. There was a very serious-looking man with sandy blond hair being interviewed. The banner at the bottom of the screen read *DALTON GRISWALD, DIRECTOR, DEPT. OF NOCTURNAL SECURITY,* which then advanced to the headline *EXPERIMENT GONE WRONG?* Underneath that was the ticker tape showing which counties had the most recent V alerts.

"Thanks, Frankie," Ari said distantly. "I'll call you back." She hung up and went to stand in front of the TV.

" – save many lives," the director was saying, and Lex used the remote to turn the volume up. "The experiments were certainly controversial, but we had a strong justification."

"And why didn't you make the public aware of it?" the interviewer asked.

"There was minimal danger," the director claimed. "Except to the staff members handling the vampire, obviously."

"But how can you claim there isn't any danger when there's a vampire running around loose out there now?"

"Our guild members work tirelessly to protect the people we serve. We're spending the day checking all the places where the escaped vampire could have gone. It's no more risk than the usual presence of – "

"Mr. Griswald, how can you – "

"Please let me finish – "

"But how can you – "

"No, no, let me – "

"Director, how can you – "

"Please stop interrupting me, Nancy, I'm trying to answer your question."

The headline at the bottom changed to *GUILD SCIENTIST SLAIN*. The director took a deep breath. "The tragic loss we experienced today was the result of personal negligence, not our program with live vampires. Nick was a very close, longtime friend of mine, and our work will certainly suffer without his contributions moving forward. However, I can't deny the risk inherent in such work, and even if I believe we have a firm justification and the ability to work safely with enhanced security, I can't deny the public has all the reason to be nervous about it given what's happened. Therefore, that's why I've decided, starting today, I'm shutting down that work."

"Yes!" Lex and Ari stood, giving each other wild high-fives. "Yes!"

"*Yes!*"

"There will be no more live captures," the director continued. "No one in our organization is prepared to continue Nick's work, and the risk has proved itself to be too great."

The interviewer made a face. "There you have it, folks. We'll be right back with more after the break."

Ari flopped back onto the couch. "Fuck yeah. Fuck. *Yeah*. We did it. Those jackasses really think Sebastian got loose while Nick was alone and killed him and ran off. *And* they're not going to torture anyone else because of it. Fuck yeah."

Valen gave a few excited wiggles. "We did it! Haha!" He tried not to think about the fact that no live capture program meant Lex and Ari would have killed him when they first met.

He glanced over at Sebastian and noticed how very unhappy he looked. He didn't seem angry anymore. Valen turned back around, hands on his knees, thinking. "Um, Ari?"

"Yeah?"

"Do you think ... we could try letting Sebastian out again? He looks a lot calmer now, and he still has stab wounds. That can't be comfortable. He's just been sitting there with them the whole time."

"Oh. Uhh, yeah, sure, I guess. Long as you can keep him under control like you did before."

Valen nodded. "I'll handle it. Leave it to me." He once again unlocked Sebastian, and the younger vampire groaned and whined pathetically as Valen stood him up and helped get him out of all the restraints.

"This is so undignified," he muttered.

"You're all right," Valen said, and he propped Sebastian up to take him upstairs to the bathroom. As soon as they were alone, Sebastian started crying, letting the tears flow freely.

"Oh, it's okay," Valen said, handing him a tissue. "You're all right."

"I'm not all right," he snapped. "I'm hurt and hungry and – " He'd been about to say *scared*, but caught himself just in time.

"Let me help you," Valen cooed. "It'll be all right. We're going home at sunset."

Sebastian burst into fresh tears. "I failed. I *failed*. Mother and Father will be furious with me. Priscus doesn't have a worthy heir, and now my father doesn't either. Everyone is going to blame me for the family's predicament."

Valen took Sebastian's hands, firm and cool. "You're under a lot of pressure. It's not fair of them to expect so much from you."

Sebastian brought his hand up to his face and wiped his eye on his shredded sleeve. "B-but I'm purebred nobility. I'm better. I'm supposed to be better. Better than commoners, and especially better than humans."

Valen smiled at him and squeezed his hands. "Listen to me, Sebastian. When everyone wants you to be something that you're not, it hurts and it's okay to be sad about it. And it can be hard to see through it to decide what *you* want, but you don't have to want the same things for yourself that your parents do. There are lots of people out there who will love you even if you show up empty-handed. There are people who will love you *for* showing up empty-handed."

Sebastian scoffed. "Who? You?"

"There are more of us than you might think. We're just not very visible." It was hard to tell Sebastian that when Valen had felt so, so alone as a direct result of trying to be more true to himself. But he knew it was true. It had been the thing to give him hope and courage.

Sebastian averted his eyes, sniffling.

"Come on, let's get you cleaned up, and I'll put some bandages on you."

Valen helped Sebastian wash the blood off himself, then started wrapping him up.

Sebastian kept his eyes averted as Valen wrapped the wounds he'd inflicted on Sebastian's arms. "So ... those humans really aren't your thralls?"

"No, they're not. I'd consider them friends, if they want to call themselves that."

"Did they lie to keep us safe? Is that what they all meant about that guy on TV?"

"Yes. They saved both of us from a horrible fate."

"Okay, but why me? They're not friends with *me*."

"They didn't want to see anyone at all condemned to such a fate. They thought you could be saved. They're kind."

"Well, that's stupid."

Valen smiled at him faintly. "And yet it's why you're here."

Sebastian looked deep in thought. Then: "What do you drink if they're your ... *friends*." He said it like he still thought it was a bit ridiculous.

"They've been letting me feed on them because they didn't want me to go hungry, same as I kept you from attacking them because I didn't want them to be hurt."

"I know how *friendship* works. I'm not five years old."

"Sorry, I'm – "

"You're not my mother. You don't have to dote on me." He ripped his hands out of Valen's.

"Do I have to be your mother to be kind to you?"

Sebastian's face almost broke. He could count on one hand the number of people who'd been selflessly kind to him, with no ulterior motive, who *weren't* his mother. "Well, it's stupid."

"Come on," Valen said gently. "There's no one here to impress. You can try being nice. I won't tell anyone."

"It's weakness."

"It might feel ridiculous at first, but in the long run it makes me feel a lot better. Maybe it'll make you feel better too."

Sebastian didn't make eye contact.

A few minutes later, the pair of vampires approached Lex and Ari in the living room. "Sebastian has something he'd like to ask you," Valen announced.

Lex turned off the TV. Ari sat up straight.

"This is humiliating," Sebastian mumbled.

"Go on," Valen said.

Sebastian turned even redder, but he finally looked at Lex and Ari. "I am very hungry. May I please have some blood?"

Ari's eyebrows shot up. Lex looked delighted. "Of course! You can have some of mine!"

"Uhh ... are you sure that's a good idea?" Ari said, even as Lex slid off the couch towards Sebastian. "Considering how much we dumped on the floor?"

"It's just one time," Lex said, waving her off. "I'll be fine."

Sebastian reached out to grab Lex's hair, and Valen smacked his hand away. "Ah-ah-ah. That's not how it's done."

"That's how it's done where I'm from."

"Well, we aren't *where you're from*, are we?"

Sebastian lowered his hand, once again looking chastised.

Lex extended her arm out. "Go ahead and bite my wrist. It's okay."

That wasn't how it was *supposed* to go. Sebastian was supposed to bite her neck, as a sign of his dominance over her.

But as he lowered his head and tried to make himself gentler at Valen's direction, he found the blood quenched his thirst all the same.

***

Sebastian was still behaving himself at sunset, so they didn't shove him back in the coffin for the drive to the border.

The border. Valen could scarcely believe it. The border, the thing he'd been trying to get to non-stop for the past few months. The safety he'd only been able to dream of. It was just being handed to him. The van's tires rolled to a stop in the dirt at the expanse of trees that filled the border. Valen's boots crunched over sticks, and he hauled his backpack out behind him. Sebastian had been bundled up in a hooded jacket to hide the bandages and wounds he seemed self-conscious of.

"Well, here you are," Lex said.

"Go on, get outta here," Ari said.

Sebastian started walking towards the border. Valen hesitated.

"One more hug for the road?" Lex suggested.

Valen nodded.

Lex came over and hugged him. After a moment, Ari came up and did as well.

"You can come back, you know," Lex said softly. "I know it's been ... rough, but – you're always welcome here."

Valen patted her back.

Ari finally broke the hug. "Hah, I doubt he wants to see our sorry asses ever again. Go on, big guy."

Valen adjusted his backpack, looking unsure.

"Hey!" Sebastian shouted in the distance. "Are we going or what?"

"I'll call you to let you know I've arrived home safely," Valen says. "And I'll ... think about it, Alexis. Thank you, both."

With that, Valen turned and ran off, far faster than a human could ever hope to catch up.

27

—•—

Valen Kithrara was Priscus Kithrara's wife.

Valen had almost managed to forget. He hadn't been able to get divorced. He was still the troublesome wife who got upset over nothing. He was still *difficult*. He was still the biggest current embarrassment to the family.

Valen had gotten back to his apartment, sitting dusty and untouched but safe after months away in human territory. He'd invited Sebastian to come back too. Sebastian had obliged, sitting in Valen's apartment and putting off going back to his family, knowing they would be upset with him for coming back without a human.

When Sebastian finally went back, something happened that Valen didn't expect, although in retrospect he should have.

Sebastian's first instinct had been to blame Valen for ruining Sebastian's first hunt, without concern for how Valen could have possibly done such a thing. It turned out that was also the first instinct of the entire rest of the Kithrara family.

Mordecai and Elvira were furious. Xavier was furious. Priscus was terrifyingly furious.

Sebastian did not defend Valen. Why would he, when Valen being blamed was the reason he wasn't in more trouble?

What he *did* do was give Priscus Valen's new address. And so it happened that Valen opened the door to his furious husband on his second night back home from human territory, after six months of being brutally tortured. After a day of not being able to sleep, of being scared of being alone, of not having the mental

fortitude to just be a person again. Of needing more time to recover before he was able to function without support and do anything stressful.

Stressful like fend off his insistent husband. Like not allow himself to be carried back to the Kithrara estate. Like stand up for himself. Like not retreat back into himself and become that shell of a person he'd used to be when he'd been forced to be a woman.

Like fight to not be Priscus's wife again.

Valen pulled the fine silk sheets over his head to hide his crying. Priscus had already gotten out of bed and was dressing himself. "Come on, Valen. Get up."

"No," Valen managed.

"We're going to be late for Sebastian's first hunt party."

"I don't want to go to Sebastian's stupid first hunt party."

Priscus came over and tore the sheets off Valen, exposing him in just his night-gown. "We're *going* to Sebastian's first hunt party, because *you* ruined his *first* first hunt, and now that he finally caught a human, paying him the proper respects is the bare minimum."

Valen rolled over and put the pillow over his head.

Priscus gave an irritated breath and grabbed Valen's ankle, sliding him out from under the pillow, then grabbing him around the waist to pull him out of bed. Valen went limp and pliant, catatonic as a stress response.

Priscus's grip softened as he set Valen upright, and he sighed. "Look, I know you're going through a difficult time and you'll need more time to adjust. So you can even wear trousers instead of a dress. Okay?"

Valen figured that was probably as good as it was going to get before Priscus flipped back to being angry and started threatening violence. All vampires were an order of magnitude stronger than humans, but some vampires were stronger than others. And Valen knew from experience being slapped by Priscus hurt.

"Hey, Valen, settling back in nicely with your husband?" Sebastian said as way of greeting when they arrived, and it took every ounce of willpower Valen had to not leap on the shitty little brat and tear his throat out. Like he'd done to Nick.

Like he wanted to do to everyone who pissed him off, now that he knew he was capable of it.

"She's wearing trousers again," Mordecai said with some exasperation. "To a formal event."

"Valen is going through a difficult adjustment period right now," Priscus said generously, putting an arm around Valen. "We are working our way up to proper formality. Thank you for your patience. Just bear with the impropriety for a bit."

Valen wanted to scream. He wanted to go berserk and start ripping people's faces off like a chimpanzee. He crushed it down inside of him. *There's no bars. There's no cage or chains. You could just walk out.*

And yet he couldn't. Priscus hadn't left him alone for a single second, controlling everything happening to Valen to make it harder to run away.

And even if he ran off, where would he go? Back to his apartment, where Priscus would just come pick him up again?

To his parents, who would just call Priscus?

To any of his distant friends who'd told him he should be thrilled to be with Priscus? To human territory, where he'd been *tortured* and was even less safe?

To just find a cave somewhere and hide out in the woods and live as a hermit for the rest of his days?

He was held here not by chains or a cage but by the structure of everything happening to him. By his own lack of fortitude to help himself. By his fear of being alone. By the thought that maybe sharing a bed with Priscus wasn't *so* bad, since his arms around Valen made it easier to fall asleep because he just *couldn't* sleep out in the open anymore. By the knowledge that if he just shut up and let it happen, it would be easier for him. By the fact that there wasn't anywhere he belonged in this world.

Sebastian's human had tears on its cheeks, but it didn't seem upset or scared, and Valen knew without a doubt that was because it was under persuasion and couldn't feel much of anything right now. The Kithrara family were blood connoisseurs, so doting aunts and uncles and grandparents and excited cousins

all came up to sample Sebastian's catch, all commenting on the quality of the blood, about how it was a fine catch, could only have been improved by getting something that was AB+ instead of AB-, although a few among the group insisted that AB- was actually better and Sebastian had made the perfect choice.

"AB+ overwhelms the palate," Mordecai insisted. "AB- is much more tasteful and subtle in its flavors."

"There's a new blood bank over in Noffalk Heights," Lucille said. "Have you been? It has *the* most delightful little bar that makes custom cocktails. They made up this mixture of A+ and B- that was just – " She made a pinching hand gesture. "If you mix A and B blood together, the taste is actually much richer and vibrant than plain AB blood, I've found."

They chitchatted like this. Valen kept his eyes on the human, imagining them as Lex or Ari or Bailey or Jerome.

"I have to use the ladies' room," he announced suddenly, feeling sick.

"Oh, of course," Elvira said. She snapped her fingers at a nearby servant, who scuttled over obediently. "Show Mrs. Kithrara over to the washrooms, will you?"

Valen followed behind the servant, upset with himself. He had no idea how he'd managed to sit through so many gatherings like this for years without realizing how utterly wrong it was. How he'd managed to squash down the discomfort, when it was all he could feel right now. How intolerable this felt now that he knew something else was possible.

Should he just grab the human and run? He could drop them off at the border. It wasn't safe for him to ... go back to Lex and Ari, as much as he wanted to, so he could just run right back. And deal with everyone being extra *extra* furious with him. And then Sebastian would just go catch *another* human, not that one human even mattered when vampire society ground up humans by the thousands every day just to feed –

"Would you like me to stay and escort you back?" the servant said, and Valen blinked upon realizing they'd reached the bathrooms.

"That's quite all right, thank you," Valen said.

He locked himself in the bathroom and cried, bent over the sink in case he threw up again. When he was finally done, he came back out.

And realized he was alone.

And that there was a telephone on the end table across the hall, unguarded.

Valen walked up to it and dialed the number he'd been reciting to himself, wondering whether or not he should use it, holding his breath as it rang.

"What?" answered the irritated voice on the other end of the line. It was Ari.

"Ariana," Valen said, already back in tears again. "Please help me. I don't know what to do. I'm with my husband and I don't know what to do. Please help me."

"Valen?" said Ari's voice, tone changing dramatically. "Where are you?"

"The Kithrara estate, I – " He froze as he saw Priscus darken the doorway, staring at him.

Ah. That was why Valen hadn't used the number before this. With a shaking hand, he lowered the phone back into its cradle, silencing Ari's continued calling of his name.

Priscus was at his side in the blink of an eye. "My little turtledove," he said in a warning tone, taking Valen in his arms. "We've talked about this, remember?"

Valen swallowed.

The phone rang again. Priscus unplugged it. "Remember when you called me like that? Begging me to come save you?"

"It was diff – "

"And now you're calling *them* to come save you the same way?"

"It's not like that."

"You're not well, Valen. You need to be here where I can take care of you. You know it's dangerous for you to be on your own out there."

Part of Valen thought Priscus was right. Valen knew it was dangerous out there. Valen had been on his own out there, and he'd been caught by vampire hunters and tortured.

Valen wasn't safe on either side of the border. It'd been gradually sinking in over the past few days, and he had no idea what to do about it.

Down the hall in the drawing room, Valen could hear Sebastian starting to play his violin for the delight of the guests. Valen let Priscus lay an arm over his shoulder and lead him back to the gathering.

28

— • —

"Mistress, one of the groundskeepers found this outside. You don't know who it could belong to, do you? I don't think we've had any guests with children over recently."

Right. As the mistress of the house, it was Valen's job to oversee the affairs of the house. Like the groundskeeping. And apparently, lost and found.

He shuffled over to the servant. He'd been feeling particularly low ever since Sebastian's first hunt party a few nights ago, and being reminded of his *wifely duties* never helped.

Being in charge of the house was the least of his worries. Priscus hadn't insisted on having sex just yet, giving Valen a generous *adjustment period*, but he knew it was coming. *You can't put it off forever, you know*, Priscus had said with an annoyed smile.

Valen's train of thought completely derailed upon seeing what object the servant was holding. It was a stuffed cat. Not just *a* stuffed cat, *the* stuffed cat Lex had given him. The one he'd cuddled with in the coffin, crying into when everything got to be too much. He slowly took the cat in one hand, dumbfounded. "Where … where did you get this?"

"The groundskeeper found it on the patio."

Valen's eyes trailed up him, then over to Priscus to check if he'd noticed Valen's reaction. He was preoccupied with some business on the other side of the room, fortunately.

Valen held the cat close to himself, trying not to look too bewildered. "I don't know how it got there." It wasn't even a lie. "I'll have it washed, so it's nice and clean for whomever comes back for it."

The servant gave a polite bow and left. Valen sat down with it on his lap, very deep in thought. A very special, sentimental object from Lex and Ari's house, which he'd definitely left behind in the coffin, all the way across the border in human territory, showing up on the patio outside his door?

Right after he'd gotten a scared phone call to Ari?

The Ari who'd fearlessly charged into vampire territory to snatch Lex back from the blood farms?

There was only one explanation, and his stomach flipped with fear and exhilaration. They were *here*. That was so stupidly dangerous of them, but suddenly he was desperate to see them again.

He was so ashamed of himself. Here he was, a vampire safe in vampire territory, pathetically asking for help because he didn't know what to do, and these humans fearlessly charged in to help him at the risk of their own lives.

He couldn't let anyone else find out they were here.

But he wanted to see them so badly he could cry. Suddenly just knowing he wasn't here alone made it feel like the world had shifted. The feeling of *I want to go home* came back, but this time *home* felt like wherever Lex and Ari were to take care of him.

That was sort of what the cat represented. Comfort offered among a very hard and serious time. That was what they were trying to say to him by leaving it here. *We will still take care of you.*

He needed to get to them. He had to be strategic about it. The stuffed animal had been a calculated move to let him know they were here in a way nobody else at the estate would recognize. *Clever.*

Priscus finished talking to whatever business associate had been occupying him, dismissing him and moving back over to Valen. "Valen, you don't need to resort to toys. I got you a perfectly nice cat to suit your tastes."

The cat. The cat, Valen had to take the cat with him too. Said cat trotted into the room as if summoned, tail swishing like a feather duster. It was a white cat with luxurious, snowy fur and a pink gemstone-studded collar emblazoned with its name: *Snowball*. Priscus picked it up and set it on Valen's lap.

"Thank you, dear," Valen said. "I do appreciate the cat." He hadn't appreciated the manipulation the cat had represented, but he *did* like the cat. Priscus had gotten the cat as a "favor" to "help Valen get settled back in at home," because gift giving was the only way he knew how to placate him. Valen was familiar enough with double-edged gifts by now to see what it was really for: to make Valen less inclined to leave. Priscus could see Valen was distressed and thinking about running away again, and Priscus had made sure Valen could hear him telling the head butler to take the cat to the pound if Valen left and was no longer around to take care of it.

Well, fuck Priscus. That might have worked on the *old* Valen, who'd taken a while to notice Priscus's subtler manipulations. Valen was going to leave *and* take the cat. He sat there petting it for as long as he could without raising suspicion. Then: "Darling, I'm going to wash up before bed a bit early tonight and read in our chambers until you get there."

"It's hardly three o'clock yet."

"I'd just like to read in the quiet for a while."

"That sounds fine," Priscus sighed. He ran his finger along Valen's neck, pressing a soft kiss behind his ear. Valen's skin crawled, but he didn't pull away. "I got you some new scented soaps. Why don't you use the lilac one today?"

"All right," Valen said rigidly.

Priscus pulled away. "We'll ease into it," he said, not without disappointment. He rang a bell to summon Valen's handmaid. "Help Valen get ready to retire for the evening."

The handmaid curtsied. "Yes, Master Kithrara."

The cat leapt off Valen's lap as soon as he started moving. Priscus walked Valen to the bathrooms with a hand around his arm, then finally left him and the handmaid alone as they shut themselves in the bathroom.

The handmaid started filling the tub and putting the soap in – the lilac-scented one, so she must have been listening.

Valen stood in front of the mirror to take his fine pearl earrings off, laying them on the sink. The handmaid came over and unzipped the back of his dress.

Valen waited until Priscus's footsteps faded and he was reasonably confident no one could hear them now. He stepped out of the dress, then turned towards the handmaid.

Her name was Callidora, and she'd been one of Valen's favorites before he left Priscus. She was a simple and enthusiastic sort of girl. Most importantly, Valen trusted her. "Callidora, can I ask you to do something for me that I need you to keep absolute secret?"

"I would do anything for you, Mistress Kithrara!" Valen had always been a favorite among the staff for his kindness and down-to-earth attitude. Priscus certainly wouldn't have gotten a response like that from any of his manservants. It wasn't hard, Valen reflected, to win the adoration of servants when you were surrounded by the most stuck-up, pretentious, condescending pricks on this side of the border. It certainly helped that when he caught the servants sleeping on the job or breaking rules, he wryly declared that he didn't see anything.

"This is going to sound strange, but when I was on the other side of the border, I met a few humans that rather caught my attention. I think they might be outside the estate somewhere."

"Humans coming this far over the border? The poor things, don't they know it's dangerous!"

"Yes, that's why I was hoping you could run out there and go see if you can find them. They're probably in a beat-up old white van, you can try to smell the gasoline. They probably hid up on the hill where they could watch the estate. And do be careful not to startle them, I imagine they brought silver with them."

Callidora nodded very seriously. "I will! I'll do it on my break. There's plenty of time before sunrise."

"Do make sure you're back inside on time. I wouldn't want you to get stuck outside. If you're late back to work, just say it was because you were doing an errand for me so you don't get in trouble."

***

Valen was lying in his dressing gown on the comfy couch in the bedroom when Callidora came back. She knocked on the door as usual, and Valen bid her to come in.

When he saw who it was, he peeked his head out of the door to check for Priscus. He'd been coming in to occasionally check on Valen, to make sure he was actually reading in the bedroom like he'd said he was and not running off somewhere, and then occasionally circling in the hallway like a shark.

He wasn't anywhere nearby now, thankfully. Valen pulled Callidora in and shut the door. "I found them, mistress!" Callidora declared, beaming. "Just like you said!"

"Wonderful!" Valen said, clapping his hands together. "Thank you so, so much."

Callidora held out a folded-up sheet of paper. "They asked me to give you this."

Valen took it and opened it.

We'll be right outside the gate at sunrise. If you can wrap yourself up like you did before, come outside and meet us there.

Valen folded up the letter and threw it into the fire nearby.

Callidora watched Valen do it morosely. "You're going to leave again, aren't you, Mistress?"

Valen took her hands, rubbing gentle circles in them with his thumbs. "Yes. I know I can trust you not to mention it to anyone."

"Can I go with you?"

Callidora was obviously saddened by Valen leaving, but that did surprise him. He looked up and saw tears brimming in her eyes.

"I'm sorry," Valen said. "You are such a sweet girl. I am going somewhere dangerous, and I wouldn't risk you following me there. But I will miss you. I missed you in my first absence."

Callidora risked going in for a hug. It wasn't proper, and any other member of the nobility would have probably slapped her for attempting it. But Valen just put his hands on her back and rubbed comfortingly.

***

Valen spent the next few hours strategically rearranging things, stashing them here and there, not drawing too much attention to himself, always going back to reading like he'd said he would.

Priscus came into the room as the night wore thin, and thankfully, thankfully, thank God, Valen managed to put off restarting their efforts at producing an heir for one more critical dawn, sparing him at least that further violation.

Valen waited in Priscus's arms until Priscus had fallen asleep, then slid out of his grip. He started by walking towards the bathroom to see if Priscus would wake up, but he merely rolled over, undisturbed.

Valen changed course, padding on light footsteps downstairs. He went into the closet on the first floor, into which he'd moved things on the pretense of trying to make space in the master bedroom closet. He stuffed a duffel bag full of clothes and valuables – the ones Priscus had taken off of him upon his return, which Valen had hidden in some of the dresses in the closet. Most of his books were in the library and it pained him to leave them behind, but he could replace most of them. He just took the few most important ones, which went into the duffel bag on top of the clothes.

Still moving as quietly as he could, he set the duffel bag down next to the cat carrier, which was still in the parlor. Snowball was asleep on a couch nearby – despite the fact that she wasn't allowed on the furniture. Valen walked over and picked her up, and she gave a soft, sleepy whine of protest.

"Shh," Valen said. "Quiet, now."

Luckily Snowball was used to the carrier and let herself be shut in it without further complaint, sitting in the carrier quietly. It had a blanket inside, along with the stuffed cat plushie that had started all this.

Next, Valen changed into the only garment he had that covered almost all his skin: his wedding dress. He pulled the gloves up over the long sleeves, letting the layers billow down to cover his feet, which were clad in hiking boots. It was ... a look. He had the veil, and added more: A jacket with a hood and long sleeves, a scarf, sunglasses. He left them down for now, not stepping outside just yet.

There was one thing he had to do first, and it was something he'd been absolutely dreading.

Very, very quietly, he unlocked the deadbolt to the human quarters and came down the stairs, dress bundled in his hands. There was only one human in the quarters that wasn't braindead from repeated long-term exposure to persuasion. The only one who wasn't a hollow shell of a person.

His human.

Priscus had given him his own human, saying Valen didn't need to worry about catching his own, since *you're going through such a difficult time.* And Valen had thought about what an uphill battle it had been to convince Priscus to let him drink blood packs the first time, and how Valen didn't have the fortitude to fight Priscus on every single front. Priscus would only give on so many things, and if Valen fought about drinking straight from a human, Priscus's patience would run out and he wouldn't compromise later when he took Valen to bed.

So Valen had been selfish. He'd given up without even trying. He used persuasion on his human and bit her. And he'd used persuasion on her and bit her every

day since then. The idea of going back to being perpetually starved had just been too much to handle. He couldn't do it.

So now he had a human. She was young. Most humans on this side of the border were. They were captured that way deliberately, so they would last longer, and most didn't live to a great age.

He was tempted to leave her behind. The old him might have left her behind.

But he couldn't. He would never forgive himself. She was fresh. She still felt things. She could be saved.

His human sat bolt upright in her bed as he came down, panic on her face.

"Quiet," Valen commanded before she had the chance to say anything. "Come here."

Her face went blank and she obeyed, a helpless puppet. Her face betrayed no great emotion, though Valen could see tears brimming in her eyes.

He didn't want to look at her. Didn't want to look at the evidence of his monstrousness.

Don't look away. Lex and Ari didn't look away. Look at what you did.

She had perpetual bite marks on her neck, just like every human in the quarters. She was going to hate him, and it was going to hurt, but he would set her free and that would be the most right he could do by her now.

He also wanted to take Sebastian's human with him. That one was also still lucid. It was too late for the rest of these mind-wiped humans. And he'd promised Lex and Ari he would keep Sebastian under control, which he'd been a fool to promise to begin with.

But he was selfish. He was too scared to do anything that could jeopardize his escape. There was no way he could go get Sebastian's human from a different building. Even just this felt insanely dangerous.

"Do not make any noise," Valen commanded, voice shaking. "We have to leave as quietly as we can. Follow me." Valen's human followed as he walked back upstairs. He wrapped the scarf around his face, put on the sunglasses, then the jacket hood. The bridal veil went over the whole thing.

There, he was all wrapped up. He took his duffel bag in one hand. "Grab the cat," he whispered to the human.

She reached down and took the carrier.

Valen strode over and opened the front door. It was sunny out – of course it was, that was the point. He was fully covered, no skin showing. It wouldn't be comfortable, but he could make it as long as the van was where they'd said it was going to be.

He hadn't known what the sun felt like before. He hadn't gone out in the sun since his last failed escape attempt, which had ended with Bailey and Jerome darting him. He was scared to go out.

He took a moment to work up his nerve.

"What on earth are you doing?"

It was Priscus's voice, and that was all the push Valen needed. He immediately stepped out into the sunlight. His thrall followed, with the cat, with everything Priscus could use for leverage.

The sun prickled his skin faintly, or maybe that was just the fear. Priscus watched him with a hard gaze.

The cat meowed.

"You're mad," Priscus said. "Come back in here."

Valen took another step back, further into the sun.

"I can't keep shielding you from the consequences of your actions, Valen," Priscus said. "Stop being foolish."

Valen stood still for a moment, then slowly lifted one hand up and flipped Priscus his middle finger.

"Real mature, Valen."

Valen turned and ran. He was too scared to full-out run, and besides, he needed his human to keep up. But his heart pounded.

He came around the bend and – yes, there it was, the van at the main gate. Ari and Lex were up front. The side door opened to reveal Jerome and Bailey, hanging out, arms outstretched for him.

"Come on, baby," Bailey said, waving him on. "Get in, we're going for a ride."

Valen started crying instantly, beyond touched. He pressed the button to open the gate, and it buzzed and swung open. He ran into those arms, barely able to see for the sun and the tears blurring his vision.

He fell into their hands, letting himself be pulled up and in, and just *held*. And they just paused for one moment longer for the human following him to step in before they peeled out of the driveway, tires smoking behind them.

29

— • —

Valen just stayed in Bailey and Jerome's arms and cried for a while, everyone in the car swaying as Ari drove like hell to get them back over the border.

"We got you," Bailey said. "We got you, sweet boy. Here, here, why don't you sit over here so you're further away from the sun."

He shifted Valen into a corner further away from the window. Valen kept crying, still too scared to take all his wrappings off.

Lex had twisted around in the passenger seat to look back at him. "Are you okay? Do you – here." She clambered into the back of the van, and Ari growled with annoyance.

"Hey, hey! I'm driving!"

Jerome laughed. There was still room for joking and laughing in this life. Maybe everything was okay.

Ari held up the roadmap. "Hello? Navigation?"

"You'll be fine, right?" Lex said. "Just keep going south."

Ari muttered. Lex came over and put her arms around Valen. "There you are. Hi. It's good to see you again."

"I can't believe you came here," Valen said tearfully. "I can't believe – you – you did that for me. Risked yourselves like that."

"Yeah, well," Ari said gruffly. "You call me and I come running. Just how I am."

Lex held his hands. "You deserve the world, Valen."

"We gotta make up for what we did somehow," Bailey said. "We're your guys for life."

Valen's lip wobbled and he burst into tears again.

Ari kept driving as the four in the back dissolved into a pile of hugs around Valen as the vampire just kept sniffling and crying.

"I'm sorry," he said, finally. "If I'd just not been such a fool, I could have helped myself without you having to put yourselves in such danger."

"I don't wanna hear any of that," Ari said. "Can it." Valen's eyes drifted down.

"So ... " Lex said. She cleared her throat. "The, um. The cat is nice. And, um. So ... who's this?"

She pointed to the human, who was still under persuasion, sitting in the opposite corner watching the whole thing with the same blank expression on her face.

Valen hid his face in his hands. How could he tell them the truth? That after they'd gone through all this to rescue him, he was now no better than any other vampire noble? He was too ashamed of himself. He was too scared of what would happen once he released the persuasion.

"I'm sorry," he said quietly.

Lex patted his hand softly. "Hey. Valen. Who is this?"

"My thrall," he answered, voice scarcely above a whisper.

There was silence in the van for a moment, the vehicle rocking and creaking. "That doesn't sound like you, Valen," Jerome said. "Not at all."

"I'm sorry," he said again, still hiding his face. "I'm sorry. I didn't want this."

Lex ran her hand around the nape of his neck, stroking softly. "Okay. It's okay. We'll figure this out."

"It was either this or starving again," Valen said. "I'm sorry. It was too much for me. I couldn't. I'm sorry." Like it made any difference. Like it made him less of a monster.

"Okay," Lex said. "Okay. We'll figure this out. Don't worry."

"Can she be saved?" Jerome said, waving a hand in front of her face, to no response. "She looks braindead."

Valen hid his face in his knees. "Yes," he admitted. "Yes. She hasn't been here long. She's just under persuasion right now."

Bailey looked at Valen sharply. "Valen!"

"I'm sorry," he sobbed. "I'm sorry. I'm sorry."

"Let her go," Ari said. "We'll deal with it."

Valen curled himself up in a tight ball and released the persuasion. He half expected to be tossed out of the van as soon as she opened her mouth and told them all what he'd done.

The human gasped and shook her head, disoriented. "Please," she said, scared.

"Hey, hey, you're all right," Bailey said, holding her firmly. "You're safe. What's your name?"

She put her arms around herself. "Sarah."

"Hey, it's nice to meet you, Sarah. My name's Bailey. We're vampire hunters. We're gonna take you home."

"Why is *she* here?" Sarah demanded, tears in her eyes. "What's going on?"

Bailey followed her gaze to Valen, who had broken down into fresh sobs. "We were picking – ah – Valen is a *he*, okay?"

"I don't give a fuck!" Sarah shouted. "Fuck off! Whatever they are, they're a monster! Why haven't you killed her?"

Everyone fell silent as Ari pulled the van off to the side of the road, then put it in park.

"Um, Ari," Lex said, and Ari stepped out and opened the side door of the van, yanking Sarah by the arm.

"Don't say that shit about him in front of me," Ari hissed. "Fucking don't."

Sarah sobbed with fresh fear. "She bit me. She made me her slave. She treated me like I wasn't a person. How can you defend that?"

Valen's crying picked up.

"Fuck *off*," Sarah said, voice breaking. "Boohoo, you feel guilty about – "

"*Shut up*," Ari said, yanking Sarah forward.

"Stop!" Lex said, shoving Ari away. "Stop it, Ari."

Ari looked about to explode. "We just got Valen away from his abusive husband. That's why he treated you like that. You don't get to – "

"I don't get to – " Sarah cried. "Boohoo, Valen had an abusive husband! I had an abusive *vampire* biting me and brainwashing me!"

"It's not a competition," Lex tried.

"Apparently it is!" Sarah shouted. "Because otherwise you won't even acknowledge I'm entered!"

"I'm sorry," Valen whimpered. "I'm sorry. I'm sorry."

"Get out," Ari shouted. "Get out of my fucking car."

Sarah looked to Valen before she realized Ari was talking to *her.* "What?"

"Ari," Lex said, stepping in front of Sarah. "If we kick her out, she won't make it back on her own."

"I don't care. We're here for Valen."

"Ari," Lex hissed, and she stepped forward to the edge of the van, leaning out so she hung over Ari. Ari had to look up at her to make eye contact, and Lex reached a hand out and put one finger on Ari's chest. "Stop acting like this."

Ari broke eye contact and her face went red. She folded her arms around herself and muttered.

"I will handle Sarah and Valen. Go drive the fucking van."

Defeated, Ari got back in the driver's seat and pulled back onto the road.

Lex slid the door shut. "Everyone calm down," Lex said. "Take a breather. Everyone is safe right now. That's what's important."

"How can you say that?" Sarah sobbed. "She's *right there.*"

"Okay. Sarah." Lex took Sarah's hands. "Listen. Take a deep breath with me now. Okay. You're safe. Valen's not going to hurt you."

"She – "

"Just let me talk for a minute. Valen is someone who's very important to us, and he needed our help. So we came to help him. He's a very noble and compassionate person – "

"She didn't even ask my name!" Sarah wept.

Valen's face flushed with humiliation. He hadn't. He'd been too caught up in his own misery. He hadn't seen the point anyway – he was still going to bite her, it almost seemed insulting to converse and pretend it wasn't going to happen. "What difference would it have made!" he cried. "Would it have made the bites hurt less?"

"I don't know!" Sarah snapped. "Maybe!"

"Okay, listen," Lex said. "It's okay to be scared and it's okay to be mad at Valen. It's only natural."

Valen crumpled, crying softly.

"He isn't like that when he has a choice in the matter. What's done is done, but he's not going to do that anymore. Trust me. He's with us now. Okay?"

"No, it's not okay! I thought I was going to be there for the rest of my life!"

"He could have left you behind, you know," Ari snarled. "He didn't have to take you."

Sarah looked cowed, shying away. "Sorry, I'm sorry."

Lex glared at Ari, then hugged Sarah again. "It's okay. It's over now, that's what's important. Okay?"

Sarah looked very much not okay with it. "Okay. I guess. Can I go home?"

"Yes," Lex promised. "Yes, we'll take you home first thing, I promise."

***

In the end, Sarah wanted out of the van before getting her *home*, demanding to be let off at the first sign of civilization on the human side of the border. Lex fished around in the center console for enough change to make a phone call.

"Good luck," Jerome said, and she ignored him as she walked towards the gas station.

Valen remained curled up in the corner. He'd been clinging to Snowball for comfort for most of the ride, despite the cat starting to try and wiggle out of his

grip. He kept his face buried in her long fur. "I'm sorry. I'm so, so sorry. I didn't want to. I wouldn't have if – "

"You were asked to make an impossible choice," Jerome said. "The latest in a long line of impossible choices. We know what that's like. We're not going to hold it against you."

"I'm on your side forever," Ari said. "We owe you that."

Valen finally pulled his face out of the cat's flank. "Thank you," he said tearfully. "I-I-I don't know what I would do without you."

"Well, you got a few decades before we die and you gotta figure it out," Ari said.

It was late afternoon by the time they got back to Lex and Ari's house, and they were all ready to drop dead from exhaustion. Valen coaxed Snowball back into the cat carrier, then made sure he was all wrapped up to be escorted back into the house.

"You still have the coffin," he said, eyeing the wooden box on the living room floor.

"Yeah," Lex said. "We figured you'd need it if you ... ever visited."

Valen took her hand and squeezed it. Ari came up behind him and put a hand on his shoulder.

Bailey and Jerome came in, haggard and worn out. "We crashing here?" Bailey said hopefully.

"Sure," Ari said. "We'd appreciate the extra eyes to keep Valen safe. Last time he was here didn't go so well, after all."

Jerome nodded. "I'm gonna use the bathroom before we hit the couch, then."

The two men went upstairs. Valen let the cat out of the carrier, and it bolted behind the easy chair. "She'll adjust, I'm sure," Valen said tiredly. He eyed the coffin.

"You ready to rest?" Lex said. "Should be safe, right?"

Valen nodded. "I ... doubt my husband would follow me all the way over the border, and he doesn't know where we are anyway. I ... I think this is as safe as I

can get." It was true. Here, between Ari and Lex, was the safest he'd felt in a long, long time.

"Right." Ari motioned to the coffin. "Good night, then. Let us know if you need anything."

Valen shuffled towards the coffin, then hesitated. "Ahm, if I may ... ?"

"You may," Ari said. "What is it?"

Valen flushed. He was really about to ask this. "I ... I found that sleeping with someone's arms around me helped me sleep better than being in the box, actually." He hadn't been able to sleep at all that first day on his own, and then after that, Priscus's arms had been better than the box, somehow. Even though it had been *him*, just being held by *somebody*, to not be alone.

"Oh?" Ari said. "Oh!"

"Our bed is big enough for three, if that's what you're asking," Lex said.

Valen flushed red. That *was* what he'd been asking, but it felt *wildly* presumptive. "It would be ... inappropriate for me to share a bed with anyone who wasn't my husband."

"Your husband, huh." Ari ran a finger over Valen's shoulder, on the lacy fabric of his wedding dress. "Do you love your husband?"

"No."

"Do you want to go back to him?"

"No!"

"Do the vows this dress represents mean anything to you anymore?"

Valen gripped the fabric of the dress. Her asking the question had been the last straw, the thing to make him finally realize the answer once and for all.

He gripped the fabric of both shoulders and tore the dress off. "No!" he said wickedly, glee on his face.

He started tearing the dress apart with animalistic fervor, ripping it to ribbons. Lex and Ari stepped back to give him more space as he shredded with wild abandon.

When the expensive garment was no more than a pile of frayed white fabric at his feet, he became self-aware and flushed with embarrassment. He was standing there in just a slip now. "Er," he said, chest heaving. "S-sorry, I got a bit carried away."

Ari grinned wolfishly and swept him off his feet. "Come on, then. Let's go upstairs."

30

— • —

Ari carried him gently up the stairs bridal-style, and he spent the evening in their bed squished between them.

Despite everything, it was the best he'd ever slept. Despite everything, it was the happiest he'd ever been.

Until reality came crashing back down on him.

The phone rang the next morning at sunrise. Ari grumbled out of bed to go downstairs and answer it. Valen remained clinging to Lex, worried about who could be calling.

Ari came back up, still in her bathrobe and slippers. "We have a situation," she announced. "That was Franklyn, calling to give us a friendly heads-up. Sarah called the guild and told them what happened. That, combined with the fact that we used official guild resources to get the maps of vampire territory, tipped the higher-ups off to what we did and now the director himself is out looking for us."

Valen went rigid, holding Lex with absolute panic. The *director* knew he was here, the *boss* vampire hunter, apparently a close personal friend of Nick's to boot. He burst into tears. This was it. He wasn't safe with vampires, and he wasn't safe with humans. There was no place for him here or anywhere. He'd almost managed to forget.

"We'll run away," Lex said. "We'll keep you safe."

"Hold on," Ari said. She ground her teeth. "Let's not jump to that yet." She sat down on the bed, hand on her chin. "Franklyn called to tip us off. From the sound of it, the other hunters might be on our side too. If we gather them all up

to stand with us, the director will *have* to take us seriously. Getting permission for Valen to be here would be way better than just making him be on the run for the rest of his life."

Valen eased his death grip on the blanket, lowering it down. "A-are you sure?"

"I know not *everyone* is going to take our side," Lex said. "What about Cyril and Isaiah?"

"We can just shoot them."

"Okay, well let's not jump to *that* yet."

"Everyone already feels bad about letting Nick have Valen for so long," Ari said. "Everyone except Cyril and Isaiah ditched Nick after not too long. All we have to do is let them meet Valen and tell them all what he was doing here to win them over."

Valen wrung his hands. That sounded *extremely* stressful. He didn't have a good feeling about betting his safety on his personal likeability, because people often misinterpreted his actions and attitude. "Ari, I-I'm scared."

Ari came over and put her strong arms around him. "We will take care of you," Ari said into his hair. "I promise. No matter what. We went all the way to your husband's estate to get you. We'd do it again."

Valen melted in her arms. "Okay," he whispered. "I trust you."

Ari kissed him on top of the head. "And I'm not gonna take that for granted." She plopped him back into Lex's arms. "Lex, you and Bailey and Jerome keep an eye on him. I've got some phone calls to make and some running around to do."

***

Lex and Jerome and Bailey comforted him the whole time, but his nerves wouldn't stop twisting in his stomach.

They gathered up some things that had been left behind at his house in human territory – they'd made another trip there after he'd gone home to collect some of

them, apparently, though he couldn't imagine why. So they had some clothes for him to dress in, long-sleeved shirts and boots more to his style. They even found a mask for him to wear, putting together the same outfit he'd used to walk outside during the day in the past. He'd need it to face the vampire hunters' guild.

He was once again shrouded in black cloth, like a grim reaper walking out and about. He was perfectly protected from the sunlight and he had four vampire hunters on his side to escort him around and keep him safe.

He was *terrified*.

When Ari came back, they went as a group to the hunter's compound. Valen couldn't suppress the fearful shaking as it came into view, the same view he'd seen locked in a cage the first time.

Lex and Ari and Bailey and Jerome all got out of the van, standing in the parking lot of the hunter's base, trying to coax him to come out. Valen stayed huddled in the corner. He was grateful that the mask hid his crying. "Are you sure I can't just stay in the van?" he tried.

"It'll be okay," Lex said. "For real this time." She held her hand out for him to take. "If you trust me one more time, I promise I won't let you down again."

He'd made it this far. All he could do was try. Valen took her hand, stepped out, and let himself be steered into the hunter's compound.

His heart pounded, terror coursing through him. The last time he'd been brought in through this door, it'd been in a cage and for the purpose of months of brutal torture. He would have frozen and been unable to take himself inside if not for the four humans half-pushing him in.

They stepped into the building. All the hunters were gathered in the main room, and they all turned to face him. Valen let out a whimper and clung to Ari's side.

Ari put an arm around him, drawing him forward. "Everyone, this is Valen. You all know who he is, but let's meet him properly this time."

One of them stepped forward, rubbing his arm and looking embarrassed. "Hey. Um. My name's Franklyn. Um ... I wanted to apologize. I think we all ...

know what we let happen to you wasn't right. I'm sorry. We let you down. Ari tells us you're here to try and make things better between humans and vampires. If you're still down for that, we'd like to help."

Valen slowly uncurled himself from Ari. "Really?"

"Yeah, man."

Valen took his mask off, dangling it from one hand, feeling okay looking at them eye to eye now. Despite their declaration, a few of them shuffled nervously as he made eye contact with them.

"I've stood by and witnessed my fair share of atrocities that I didn't stop," Valen said. His voice shook, but only a little. Lex and Ari each having one hand on him helped. "What's important is that we forge a better future together."

Panic surged through Valen as the hunters crowded in on him, but it was because they were cheering and slapping him on the back. Ari started swatting them away, noting his discomfort.

"The boys have been working on something for you," Ari said, to deflect. "In the basement." The basement, the awful basement where he'd been trapped. His trembling started up again.

"It's okay," Lex soothed. "Ari took care of everything. You can trust us."

Right. He needed to trust them. It was half out of trust, half out of catatonic fear that he let himself be led back down to the basement. He kept his eyes squeezed shut until they got to the bottom of the stairs.

The basement was ... empty. Of all the things that had been in it last time he was here. The blood had been scrubbed away; there were no longer silver implements scattered about. There *were* a few lab benches with some scattered labware on top. Valen slowly uncrunched himself. "Um, I'm not sure I understand."

"We're offering to make this *your* lab," Ari said. "'Course, you went through some pretty fucked up shit here, so if you don't want that, you don't have to take it. It's your space now. If you tell us to fill it up with cement, we will. But everyone agreed that's what should happen now. We're all on your side here, and we want you to stay here with us where we can protect you."

Valen slowly turned around in the space. It felt different now that it was empty. He felt safer, here with his friends.

He couldn't believe he was actually considering this, but … maybe taking control of this space would be good for him. To have agency over what had happened to him, to have authority here. To overwrite the memories with new ones.

"We're going to pitch it to the director when he gets here," Lex said. "He's a very strategic man, so he'll be able to see that you're an asset."

Valen turned and planted his face in Ari's chest. "I'd like to try," he said tearfully. "Thank you."

His keen ears picked up the sound of a car pulling up outside. Despite his vote of confidence, he moaned in terror and hid under one of the lab benches.

"Okay, that's okay," Lex said. "It's gonna be okay, but if it makes you feel safer to hide down here for a bit, you can do that."

All four of the humans went upstairs, leaving Valen alone.

The sound of conversation from upstairs. It went on and on. Valen hyperventilated and scrambled further into the room, fumbling hand clutching the doorknob to the darkroom where Nick had always developed his photos. He fell into the room and jammed himself under the sink, pupils dilating wide in the darkness.

Footsteps on the stairs. "He's down here?" said an unfamiliar voice. A man. The director. He couldn't force his limbs to move. He stayed where he was.

The door of the darkroom creaked open. It was Lex. "Hey," she said with slight amusement. "It's okay to come out."

Valen shakily took her hand and let her pull him out.

Lex and Ari were alone in the room with a very serious-looking man with sandy hair and bite mark scars on his neck.

"Director," Ari said courteously. "This is Valen."

Valen gave into his nervous instinct to curtsey. "Hello Directly – Director Hunter – "

The director's stony face broke into a laugh. "Yes, I'd expect that reaction from anyone in your position." He extended a hand. "Better late than never on proper introductions, right?"

Valen shook his hand. This was the director, the one who'd allowed him to be tortured. Were they just going to *shake hands* like that hadn't happened?

"Firm grip!" the director exclaimed. Valen had trained himself to squeeze people's hands hard during handshakes because it was something men seemed to place inordinate value on, the firmness of the handshake. He could easily crush the director's hand right now, but that probably wouldn't endear him to anyone.

"Alexis and Ari have informed me of the proposition the hunters at this base came up with for you," the director continued. "I wasn't aware you possessed your own scientific training. I admit I was a bit hesitant about the idea at first. It's unconventional, but it would be a waste to not have you take Nick's place."

The hair on Valen's neck stood up. "You want me to – "

"Not experiment on live vampires, if that's what you're worried about. No, I think it's obvious by now that was ... a mistake. It was wrong to let that go on, and now we should move past it for the common good." That was something, at least. "Which is why, along with the job offer, I want to extend to you the offer of safety within human territory. You'd be under my personal protection. I've been informed of your experiments to try and create artificial blood, and I'd like you to continue them here with Lex and Ari."

He didn't fully trust the director after everything, but ... that was too much to pass up. That was everything he wanted. Could it really be that easy?

But no, it hadn't been *easy*. It had been hard. But maybe it had been worth it, to get here. "I'll do it."

The director smiled. "Then let's get your lab set up so we can start making a better future together."